THE BOUNTY HUNTER'S SURRENDER

OUTLAW HEARTS
BOOK TWO

KYLEE WOODLEY

PRAISE FOR KYLEE WOODLEY

The Bounty Hunter's Surrender solidifies KyLee Woodley as a veritable sharpshooter of a storyteller!

In her second Outlaw Hearts novel, Woodley skillfully corrals the tension of a showdown at high noon, complex characters, fastidious historical research, and a mystery with all the twists of a gnarled tumbleweed into a tale sure to whisk readers away on a wild ride into a hope-filled sunset.

If you're drawn to the rugged romance of the old west, consider The Bounty Hunter's Surrender your next most wanted read!"

— ANGELA BELL, AUTHOR OF A LADY'S GUIDE TO MARVELS AND MISADVENTURE

"What an absolutely gripping read! Building on her debut, KyLee Woodley brings readers another wonderfully unique romance with high stakes and incredible characters. Family secrets, complex relationships, and a house full of mystery blend with flawed characters who are yet very worthy of our respect. They both need each other's help, but there are secrets between them, loads of intrigue, and a host of surprising threats thrown in their path. I was rooting for Aubrey and Nathan despite the odds, and Woodley delivered a powerful ending that did not disappoint! Can't wait for the third book in this series!"

— *JOANNA DAVIDSON POLITANO, AUTHOR OF*
THE CURIOUS INHERITANCE OF BLAKELY
HOUSE AND OTHER HISTORICAL FICTION

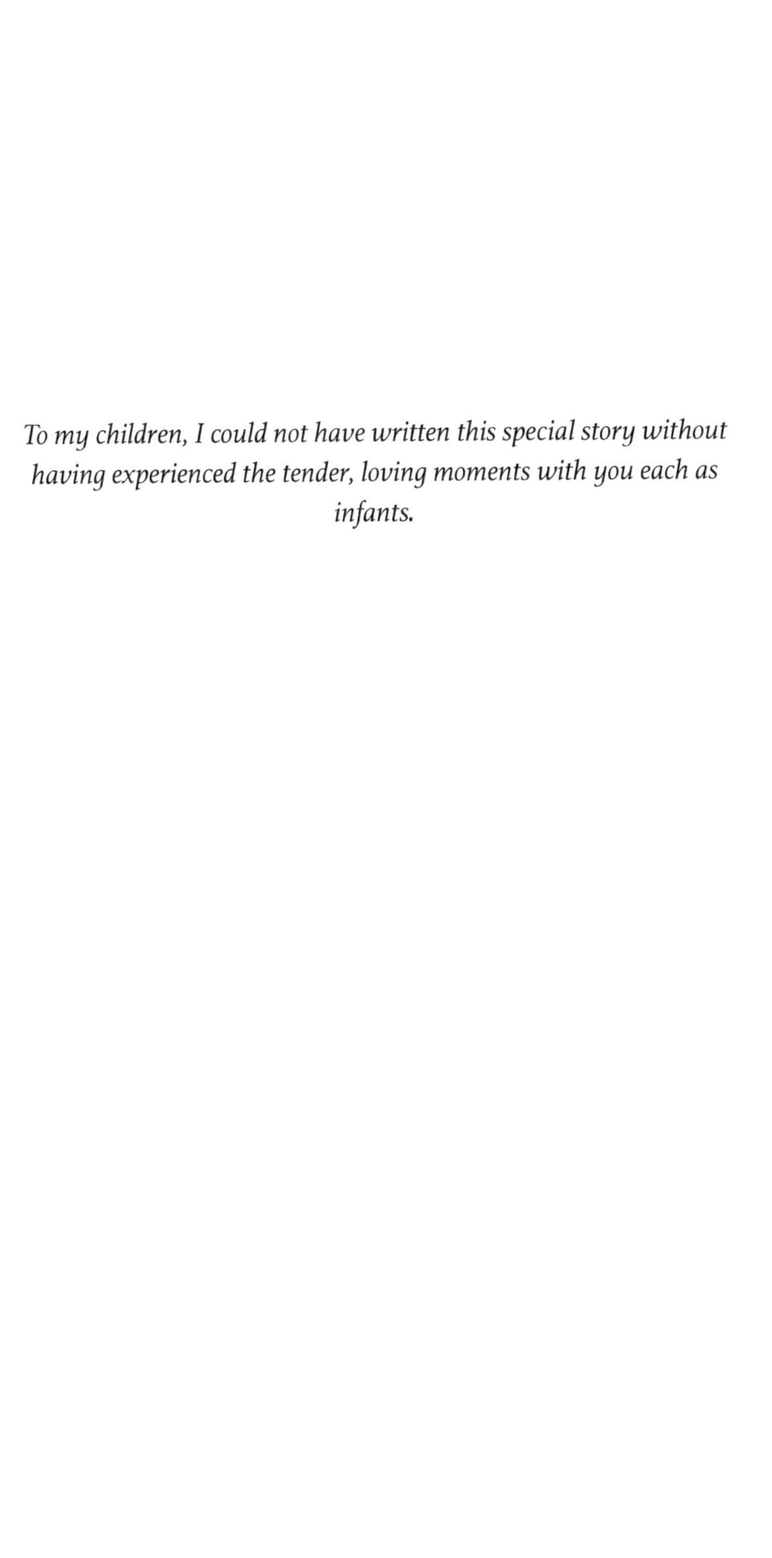

To my children, I could not have written this special story without having experienced the tender, loving moments with you each as infants.

CHAPTER 1

June 1875

A few miles outside San Francisco

He had no business being in her house, yet here he was, his snakeskin boots setting softly on the rug before the moonlit desk as he slid off the windowsill. Bounty hunter Nathan Reed navigated his way forward, the wooden surface of the desk smooth beneath his fingers.

His hand bumped something glass, and...

No!

It tumbled and hit the floor.

Nathan's heart thundered. He shifted back, one hand on the windowsill lest he needed a quick escape. All was quiet, inside the house and out where a garden sat in cool moonlit hues.

What was he doing, breaking and entering? He'd always worked within the bounds of the law, but everything was different since his sister died, leaving a baby girl with no one to care for her. He'd been unable to turn down the opportunity to work for Mr. Ellsworth—a rich banker with his hands in every kind of crime in San Francisco. Nathan had avoided men like him for years, but he was providing for more than just himself now. *Lord, have I gone too far? What else can I do?*

It was too late to back out.

Though man's laws would condemn him, he felt no conviction in his spirit, so he reached into his pocket and withdrew a match. He struck it on the tip of his thumbnail, and the end blossomed into a bright flame. The desk held only an inkwell, stacks of paper, the knocked-over glass, pencils, and quills. He pulled out the drawers, one at a time. The top right contained a gun and the one below it a folder of documents. A thrill ran through him as he glanced over papers of a legal nature. Would it really be this easy, finding them?

The light at the end of his match wavered. He needed a lamp to read over what he was looking at. If he lit the wick and turned it low, he could see well enough to search for the paperwork and likely still go undetected. The contents would save the city of San Francisco from economic ruin. Or so his employer claimed.

Pulling out another match, he surveyed his surroundings. The room was expansive yet eerily empty, considering the size. Two wingback chairs and a sofa faced the fireplace. Most of the towering bookshelves were bare, the expensively carved woodwork catching the subtle glow of the flame.

Nathan spotted a lamp on a side table near the sofa and crossed the space. The low light of a lamp should not bother any of the house's inhabitants. The staff members here were old, and the lady of the house slept in a different wing. The last thing he wanted was to come across the young widow. He removed the shade to reach the wick. Once it was lit, he set it back into place.

Faint light shone on a small revolver beside the oil font of the lamp, then onto papers scattered on the rug in front of the sofa. Nathan knelt, squinting to see. The now-deceased Louis Willot had written the letters while he was in prison, and judging by the content, they were a personal correspondence to his wife. Creases marked the pages as though Mrs. Willot had crumpled and then smoothed them out again.

If she knew Louis had fathered a child outside of marriage with Nathan's own sister, she would likely toss the letters into the fireplace.

There was a movement to his left. His gaze landed on a woman slumbering on the sofa not a foot from where he knelt. His blood chilled with the shock, freezing him in his place. Brown curls cascaded across the upholstery. He could make out her gently sloped nose and slightly pursed lips. She was beautiful.

And...

His gaze traveled down to where a white cotton nightgown hugged her very round stomach.

She—this woman who must be the Widow Willot—was pregnant? What was she doing in the study?

A faint moan escaped her, and she caressed her belly. "There, *mon tresor*." She uttered the words in a sleepy voice.

He slipped behind the sofa. The rustle of fabric stilled him.

He trapped a breath in his chest and held it like the calm before a storm.

Would the lighted lamp give him away? If she hadn't already glimpsed him, that was.

The shuffle of her gown on the upholstery signaled her movement. "Is somebody here?" Her voice rang out with a slight tremble.

Nathan pressed himself lower to the floor and closer to the couch.

"Where are you?"

Something hard scraped the wooden tabletop, and he envisioned her taking the revolver from the side table. Sure enough, her next words were, "I have a gun, and I will shoot you."

He flinched, his back prickling in expectation. Could she

see him there behind the sofa? Pressing his face to the floor, he peered beneath the furniture.

A small pair of bare feet tiptoed across a fancy floral rug, then moved toward the farthest bookcase. Vision mostly blocked, he beheld the bottom of her nightgown flutter when she stepped backward. The hinges of a door squealed. A vase, table, and white hydrangeas hit the floor with a crash, strewing glass shards, water, and flowers near her feet.

Nathan peeked around the far side of the sofa.

Mrs. Willot held a revolver before one of the bookcases—with the entire piece of furniture pulled away, revealing an opening.

A hidden door. She must have knocked the decorations over when she opened it.

"Who's in there?" She held the gun shakily, her back to Nathan. "L...Louis?"

He closed his eyes. Why had she called for her dead husband? Had she, in her weary state, forgotten he died? It was a recent death. Just four weeks. Was she used to seeing him in the secret doorway? Might the documents Nathan needed to find be stashed there?

The woman stepped forward, the dark doorway looming around her small frame. Here was his chance to run for it, but the window he'd entered through was all the way across the room. Less than four feet away, though, hung a thick floor-to-ceiling curtain. The widow had not moved, so he slipped behind it.

Moonlight flooded the yard on the other side of the beveled glass panes. Releasing a breath, he stood as still as he could. This window was locked, and the latch might click if he opened it.

A door slammed, followed by the thumping of several books falling. Nathan dared to peek between the hanging fabric. Mrs. Willot's gaze landed on the letters scattered on the rug. She thrust aside the weapon, and grasping the pages, she ripped them into tiny pieces. Then, as if weakened by the action, she sank onto the velvet settee and cupped her face.

"Lord, am I going mad?"

Nathan bowed his head, imagining God looking down past the stars and cloud-skirted moon to Nathan behind the curtains and the widow on the sofa—both in need of help. It was humbling, seeing her like this. He'd been so hurt and overwhelmed over the last two months, grieving his sister's death and worried about his infant niece... Had he forgotten other people in the world hurt too?

He had hunted Louis Willot, determined to make the man pay for his folly, but the miscreant had died in prison before Nathan found an opportunity to confront him. Still, there had to be remuneration for the loss.

"Missus?" Another woman's voice sounded in the room.

When Nathan looked, a maid with frazzled red hair, a face full of freckles, and a mean squint stalked into the room. "Missus, what is wrong?"

The mistress of the house explained in a shaky voice that a strange sound had awakened her, then she gave a nervous laugh. "Perhaps Louis was right. I've lost my mind."

"Nonsense." Her maid waved her hand as though brushing away the idea, then she took the lamp from the table. "Come to the kitchen. We will sit beside the fire and have some milk with honey and cinnamon."

"But the lamp is lit. I did not light it before falling asleep."

"Dear Mr. Dobbs must have, not wanting you to wake up and have a fright. It was pure kindness, no doubt. Now, don't let your fears make a fool of you."

The women's quiet steps retreated, then a door bumped into its frame. Nathan hooked a finger around the curtain and pulled enough to see that the room was empty of people, dark with the lamp now gone.

He hastened to the window yet paused. In the partial light from a bright moon, he could just make out the desk with the second-right drawer open. Nathan stuffed the paperwork into his shirt, lifted the window latch, climbed through, and dropped onto a boxwood hedge. After rolling with the momentum, he landed on his feet and crept along the perimeter of the house. Moonlight glanced off the massive wall, painting the blush-colored sides gray.

What a fool he'd been to break in when she was home. Despite choosing a late hour, he'd almost been caught. He should have waited for her to leave. Lord willing, he'd grabbed the right documents and would never have to see her again.

Except for the leaves whispering on birch trees nearby, the night was calm. Nathan strode down a trail into the maze-like French garden with its many square beds and a fountain in the center. All too aware of his vulnerable position when he came to the end, he hurried across a field toward the carriage house on grass still soft from spring rains. On the edge of the property, an orange grove offered welcome shelter, but Nathan did not slow his stride until he saw his horse between the dark trunks.

"Reed?" His friend Beau Fox emerged from the woods like a mystic. "Were you seen?"

"No. But nearly. I am done for tonight, so I hope this is it." He withdrew the documents, and Beau lit a match. He glanced over them, then nodded. Nathan didn't comment on him reading English. The man hadn't known how when Nathan saw him last year in Utah.

"I hope this is what Ellsworth is looking for." Beau rolled up the pages and stuffed them in his saddlebags. "I'll take them to him and bring payment to you if it is."

"Fine." Nathan untied his horse. "Did you know she was pregnant?"

Beau sighed long, then nodded. "It shouldn't matter. If it does, you might as well go back to bounty hunting."

"You know I can't."

"Then you have to get your head on straight. You can't let stuff like that bother you. I told you, you're not the man for this line of work. You think tonight was bad, wait for tomorrow. Get out, Nathan. Before it's too late."

"What should I do? Abandon Felicity?" He planted a boot in the stirrup, swung into the saddle, and flicked the reins against the horse's flanks. "I can't keep bounty hunting and be away from her." He spoke over his shoulder as Beau followed close behind on his own mount. "I have to stay in San Francisco. Ellsworth's work is the best option for me. All I've ever done is hunt bounties." And farming a lifetime ago, but he'd hated that work. Besides, everything having to do with his life in Oregon was over now. Just thinking of that place made his chest squeeze painfully. "I need this job."

When his friend remained as quiet as the surrounding trees, Nathan let the matter drop, and they headed for San Francisco. The miles were haunted by the memory of the frightened, pregnant widow.

At last, they reached the city aglow with electric street lamps. The hilly land rolled subtly, and there in the middle, towering over smaller buildings, the Masonic Hall and Occidental Hotel stood like sentinels in the night.

They parted ways, and Nathan rode down the streets until he reached Fourth. Saint Patrick's Church stood like a giant, its spire towering into the starry sky. He had been here many times, typically going around front and entering by way of the lobby, but the San Francisco Foundling Asylum and Lying in House wasn't open this late, and they only allowed visitors on Saturdays, anyways. He had to see Felicity. He steered his horse down the dark alleyway stinking of sewage.

The brick back side of the asylum was a familiar sight. It was here that his sister had taken refuge when she'd been unable to work. She'd stayed long enough to deliver the baby, only to die shortly after, at which time Felicity was moved to the infant room and Sarah to the morgue. Chilled by the memory, Nathan maneuvered his horse close to the wall. He stood on the saddle seat and reached for the second-story window frame of his choosing. He launched off the horse and pulled himself up with his upper body strength. The window slipped open easily with the nudge of his shoulder, and he settled down on the floor with the stealth he'd adapted over the years bounty hunting. If they found him sneaking in after hours, the matron would probably call the police. Luckily, Ms. Thornson, the nurse usually on duty this time of night, had listened to him the first time he broke in when he explained that he worked all day and would never get to see Felicity if he had to observe regular visiting hours. She also needed the money he paid her to keep quiet and take extra good care of Felicity.

A familiar figure in a white apron occupied a rocking chair in the corner, a baby in her arms.

"Ms. Thornson?"

She nodded, still rocking.

Good. It was still her shift. Nathan passed several beds of sleeping infants, his heart aching at the sight of such lonely creatures.

"My shift is almost over, so you'll only have a few minutes." The young nurse spoke in a hushed tone as she passed the two-month-old infant into his arms.

He thanked her yet had no excuses for being so late. What could he tell her? That he was breaking into someone's home, trying to find some papers and earn enough to hire a nurse full time so Felicity could be moved from the foundling asylum? No, that wouldn't do.

He nuzzled Felicity's feather-soft hair and walked quietly to the window. A baby needed fresh air. It was just a shame the garbage in the alley prevented it. The room was warm and stuffy, smelling like dust and old wood. Just how hot would it be once summer came?

The San Francisco Foundling Asylum was not a happy place, and certainly no place for his beloved niece. Nathan had witnessed a motionless infant being removed from one of the beds the first week after Felicity had been born. It was then he learned that over half of the babies abandoned here would not grow old enough to walk. Some had been dropped off outside and succumbed to exposure, others to unknown causes, sometimes as simple as not eating or not waking from sleep.

Nathan patted Felicity's back, her hair like silver in the faint light. In midday, it would glow as yellow as fresh butter. Barely able to breathe, he cradled her in his arms, supporting her head even though Ms. Thornson said she was strong enough to manage on her own. She yawned with her tiny pink mouth, then she continued to sleep. Sometimes he searched her face for any trace of his sister, and perhaps it was there in the slant of her eyes. But his memory of his sister was already fading—especially since he'd only seen her once in the last five years. He clutched Felicity closer. This child was all he had left of her. He had to do right by her.

He needed a steady income—something more reliable than bounty hunting—to provide a roof over her head and a nurse until she was old enough to eat normal food.

"You may sit." Ms. Thornson pointed to the chair as she went to another child.

Nathan nodded to the gracious lady and slipped her a couple bits. Though he had arranged for her to look after Felicity, which seemed terribly unfair to the other children, he didn't have money enough for all of them. Throat tight, he lowered himself into a rocking chair near a window and tipped back, setting the chair into motion. His mind turned over all he had seen at the Willot Chateau—the secret door and the pregnant widow.

Finally, Beau's warning about tomorrow. *You think tonight was bad, wait for tomorrow. Get out, Nathan. Before it's too late.* The words haunted Nathan, and his spirit stirred against his decision, but the baby in his arms kept him on his path. He had to provide for her, no matter the cost. He had to see her safely out of the asylum.

CHAPTER 2

*L*ast night, Aubrey Willot had nearly begun to believe in ghosts again. After a restless night worrying over her scare in the master study, she entered the Bank of California with the remnants of doubt following her. How strange to sense someone watching while she slept, only to wake and find nothing. She'd been drawn to the secret room, the only place in the house she'd yet to enter since returning. Odd that in her sleepy stupor, she felt sure when she opened the hidden door that her dead husband would be waiting there. If she believed in ghosts, she'd have worried that Louis haunted that space. Blessedly, she'd given up on ghost stories in her childhood. No. This was simply the imagination of a woman who had lived too long in fear. But no more.

Her heels clicked on the marble floor inside the lobby. A row of crystal chandeliers hung from the center of the ceiling and settled a tangerine glow onto the line of benches and tables beneath. Elbow-high walls set off the lobby, and on the other side of these—both the east and west—were many desks where bankers worked with clients.

People bustled past her as though they knew exactly where

they were going. She, of course, did not. Hands clasped before her large belly, she headed toward the caged cashier's desk. Light streamed through floor-to-ceiling windows, warming the sky-blue ruffles of her day dress.

A banker with a spindly mustache and a toothy smile approached her. He could help her find her business manager. Aubrey nodded in greeting, but something drew her attention beyond him. Just across the lobby stood a man of significant bearing, his gaze darting away from her. The steel-blond of his hair complemented blue-gray eyes that practically shone above a white-and-blue plaid shirt. He stood tall, arms akimbo and thumbs in the side pockets of his trousers, as though he did not need the weapon strapped to his hips.

A tall, dark-featured man approached him and shook his hand. Still, his attention shifted to her, some unforeseen draw there in his gaze.

With a twinge in her middle and her cheeks warm, Aubrey turned away. This was no mere nerves or the baby moving within. No, here was attraction—a dangerous feeling, to be sure.

The banker who'd made eye contact reached her, inclining his head. "Hello, miss. Welcome to the Bank of California. Is there anything I can help you with?"

Hardly managing to breathe, she faced the friendly banker with a height similar to her own. "Yes, thank you. Please tell Mr. Ellsworth that Mrs. Willot is here to see him. He is expecting me."

"Of course. Do make yourself comfortable in the lobby." He gestured toward a bench where other patrons waited.

She did so, hands in her lap and ankles crossed. She would prefer to meet Mr. Ellsworth at the chateau, but if she was going to manage the banking business left to her, she'd have to be braver. Coming into town was part of that, even if others did look down on her for traveling alone. Pa said she needed to learn how to run the business she'd recently inherited. Banking was all ciphers and numbers, wasn't it? And she'd always been dreadful at arithmetic. But she needed to be wise with the money and learn the business. That's why she was here, alone. She had learned that her husband died and left her his estate just four weeks before.

The news had come as a shock, followed by intense relief. She was free, able to live in a world absent the threat of his return. She'd never tell the baby that, though, and hopefully, God would forgive her for such unkindness. Now Aubrey was determined to live a full, fearless life—even though that meant moving to San Francisco while her pa and brother, Jesse, lived in Los Angeles. Pa's objections to her plan still rang in her ears from the day he, Jesse, and Jesse's fiancée left for home. *What are you going to do, Aubrey? Raise the baby on your own?*

Yes. She planned to do just that while living in the house her controlling, now-dead husband had built for her yet never let her live in. After all, she was about to have a baby, and the chateau was her dream home. It was just such a big, empty house, especially at night when her imagination got the better of her.

The man with the plaid shirt walked past, his gaze catching on her again with the same intensity. Aubrey averted her eyes, though when he slowed, warmth crawled up her back. He was even more handsome close up than she'd first thought, his hair lighter than she'd realized with a wave hanging near one eyebrow, giving a devil-may-care flare to the symmetrical lines of his face. Yet he looked at her with such intensity—nearly an urgency, as though he might actually approach her. His gaze darted around the room, hands flexed, and his chest heaved.

A door slammed. A lady screeched. Another man shouted.

The clatter of running feet swept the room like a flock of gulls taking off over water.

Aubrey spun toward the entrance.

Three masked men with saddlebags over their shoulders came from the main doors. They pointed revolvers at the patrons and bankers.

One man used what looked like an ax handle he must have brought with him to knock one of the bank guards unconscious, then he barred the double doors shut. Two others hopped the short wall and herded the bankers to the back of the room. The third masked man rushed through the lobby, disarming several of the civilians. "Drop your guns."

Aubrey tried to stand, heart slamming against her ribs, but the crowd surged away from the front doors and toward the cashier's window near where she sat. She pushed up from the bench, but a large woman knocked into her, swiping the silk ruffles of her skirt into her face. Several people stumbled into one of the marble tables, and it fell on its side with a loud crack.

Two more robbers had appeared behind the barred cashier's desk. They must have come through a back door. The crowd amassed from the left side of the lobby into a corner. The two patrons she had spied earlier—including the handsome one—removed their guns yet moved with the crowd with a sort of ease. Both watched the robbery unfold as though observing a gaggle of geese flock to a pond.

"Give me the gold, now!" a bandit shouted so near, she startled.

The last of the court cleared, so Aubrey pushed herself off the bench.

A robber with a black bandanna over his face grabbed her by the nape of the neck while two of his companions herded the people forward. "Move it, lady."

Aubrey let out a cry, powerless when he slammed her into his chest. "No one will stop us getting out of here with a pregnant lady for protection." He shoved her away from the crowd and toward the opposite side of the lobby.

With the front door barred, the robbers must plan to escape out the back. She darted away, but he snatched her closer by one arm.

Behind him, there was a swift movement. Someone was coming to help. She must maintain her captor's attention to prevent him from noticing. "Let go of me, you brute." Her voice shook when he narrowed yellowed eyes on her, but she kept on. "You...you ought to be ashamed of yourself. Accosting a pregnant woman. What...what would your mother think to see such callous behavior?"

He scoffed and jabbed the barrel of his gun against her throat.

Before he could speak, someone stepped behind him and hooked one muscular arm around his neck. It was the handsome man in the plaid shirt. The robber tried to wrestle free but lost his grip on his weapon. It clattered on the floor.

Aubrey ducked away. Remembering what Pa said about never leaving a gun cocked, she picked it up and eased the hammer down. She glanced back. Two robbers were behind the counter accosting the tellers. Two others held patrons at gunpoint on the far side of the lobby.

The shouting drowned out the wheezes of her attacker whom Mr. Plaid Shirt was in the process of strangling. If the miscreant got free, he would alert his fellow marauders.

Aubrey gripped the gun. She'd never mastered the use of a weapon, even though Pa had tried to teach her. She hated the loud noise and jarring kick of the discharge. If she fired the gun now, she'd draw the attention of the four other robbers.

Just clobber him over the head, Aubrey. Pa's exasperated voice spoke as if from memory.

Aubrey slammed the butt of the gun into the robber's temple.

Mr. Plaid Shirt jerked backward when she landed the blow so close to his face. He dropped the now-unconscious man to the floor, then pulled her behind the table that had been knocked over. "Are you all right?" He steadied her by the shoulders, glancing between her and the crowd of hostages.

Sitting on her calves, the baby pressing into her ribs, she nodded.

He withdrew a knife from one of his boots. What did he hope to do with a solitary knife? They needed help.

The guard who had been knocked unconscious was struggling to his feet at the door, but blood oozed from a gash near his temple, and he was wavering like a ship at sea.

From her vantage point, the patrons gathered to the left, and the robbers were slightly right. They stood at least six feet away from the crowd, a distance from which they could keep the guns out of reach. The tall, dark stranger who had entered the bank with Mr. Plaid Shirt stood to the side of the crowd. He said something to a man wearing riding trousers. The two were poised for action.

A lady offered a large brooch to one of the criminal gunmen. Her hand shook, and when she dropped it, the robber lowered his weapon and reached for the jewelry.

Mr. Plaid Shirt and his friend looked at one another, then went into action.

The dark stranger ran and vaulted over the short wall, heading for the robbers in the back.

The patron in riding trousers darted toward the thief who was telling his fellow to leave the dropped jewelry be and knocked his gun from his hand.

Mr. Plaid Shirt threw his knife at the bending robber. He hit his mark, and the man dropped to the floor.

Almost simultaneously, so did the other two outlaws—one downed by the patron and the other by the dark-haired man who then proceeded behind the cashier's cage to overpower the final culprit.

Just like that, all five robbers were subdued. The bank guard opened the double doors and shouted outside that the bank had been robbed.

Pandemonium broke out as people fled. Mr. Plaid Shirt rushed a few steps to the assailants, checking to ensure they were truly overcome. Aubrey tried to stand, but the crowd was moving again, this time toward the door. Rather than be trampled, she stayed behind her marble shield. The thunder of footfalls mingled with shouts from an angry banker and someone else calling for the police.

In just a few seconds, most of the occupants of the lobby had left except for a pair of roughed-up bankers, five prostrate men, and Mr. Plaid Shirt with his tall friend.

The former knelt beside a robber and withdrew a bloody knife. He'd thrown it past the crowd. Across the marble floor, he met her gaze, an unreadable expression on his face. Was that regret? Dread? Or just resignation? But why?

Knife in its sheath again, Mr. Plaid Shirt approached, reaching one open palm to her while his snakeskin boots knocked a steady rhythm.

Barely breathing, the smooth floor moist beneath her hands, Aubrey dropped her chin to her chest. All that had happened returned and rained down on her like a sudden hailstorm. The man who had pressed the barrel of his gun to her throat. His vice-like grip on her arm. Her belly slamming into him when he yanked her hard.

She'd not been so helpless since that last time Louis unleashed his frustration regarding her tardiness to a company picnic. Of course, he'd waited until it was over. Until they'd arrived home where no one save the miserable staff could know of his displeasure. Arms shaking, she pushed herself up from the floor, her panic a tide, rising ever higher, drowning out the noises, the light, even her air. *I can't breathe.*

She needed out. To run. The door was there, yet it blurred, along with all the rest of the world. Nowhere was safe. Not even a bank! She hadn't been secure since she left Papa's house in Los Angeles.

"You're safe." A man's voice spoke nearby, low and deep yet tenderly kind. "Those men can't hurt you. You're safe. Just breathe. In, with me." Then the intake of breath—not her own, but the sound made her realize she'd been holding hers. "Good, again."

Aubrey opened her eyes to find Mr. Plaid Shirt himself lightly touching one of her elbows, focused on her as his lips parted to release a subtle gust of mint-scented air. In the wake of his exhale, she smelled the freshness of orange blossoms—likely his cologne.

"You are safe." He guided her to stand and supported her with one arm around her back. "There, that's better. No one will hurt you, I promise. Look there at that photograph." His gaze shifted away from her, to the wall where a photograph hung of a steep mountainside reflected on a lake below. The details were intricate, lines scoring the mountain's face natural and imperfect. The round summit glowed against the cloudless sky. Trees skirted a sandbar rimming the placid lake, which reflected the mountain like a mirror.

Aubrey drew in a deep breath, her lungs easing at last. "It's amazing."

The lines of his stern face softened ever so slightly. "Move closer, one step at a time. One breath at a time."

She walked, her heels tapping lightly and the photograph drawing her nearer. At last, they reached a wall and stood before the piece. Feeling shaky, her skin damp, she drew in a ragged breath. "This is a Watkins photograph." She dabbed her forehead, her voice growing steady. "Did you know the photographs he took of Yosemite were shown to President Lincoln and passed around Congress?"

He raised his eyebrows, an appreciative quirk to his mouth. "I did not. For what purpose?"

She sniffed, the scent of him soothing her frazzled nerves. "To help support the Yosemite Valley Grant Act in sixty-four."

"Fascinating. You have a fondness of photography?"

"Yes. Taking photographs used to be a hobby of mine." Before *maman* died and Louis became part of her life—a lifetime ago. After escaping her abusive marriage, Aubrey had gone to Los Angeles to live with Pa and Jesse. Her brother had tried to bring her love of photography back to life when, that last spring, he had purchased her an American Optical Camera. In the end, it had been the baby within that had breathed life back into her.

Her hand rested on the bump in her middle as the hot summer sun blazed through a nearby window. Her rescuer waited, his broad shoulders so still, he likely held his breath. Had he asked her something? She raised her eyebrows.

"Have you been to Mr. Watkins's studio here in town? The Yosemite Art Gallery?"

"No, I have not."

"You should go by there sometime. See his prints. Maybe even meet him."

A thrill like a gust of fresh air into a house whose doors had long been shut up whirled inside her, clearing away the cobwebs of hopelessness. "That would be wonderful."

His arm pressed against her back, forcing warmth through her extremities.

Aubrey stepped away, touching her cheeks. "I am better now."

He watched as though checking for signs of distress.

"Truly, I am, Mr..." She extended her hand, and he gently grasped it.

"Nathan Reed."

"Aubrey Willot. I owe you a great debt." She ran her hand over her belly, the realization that he had saved her baby, not just her, hitting her with a new wave of emotions. "Thank you." Hot tears stung.

He glanced away, likely uncomfortable. "Any decent man would defend you."

"We were in a bank full of decent men, but only one came to my rescue."

Planting his hands in his pockets, he glanced back where they'd started near the table. "Actually, I think you saved me. You did knock the first robber unconscious."

"And nearly took you out in the process."

He chuckled, a rich, low sound that warmed something deep inside her. Something so deeply buried, she'd forgotten it existed. That thrill, that tender excitement, blended with a warm draw—attraction. Something she'd not felt in a long time. The man she'd believed to be her one true love had darkened her every day until all that was left was the night. That still numbness she'd retreated to when living with Louis had come to be too much.

Chilled as though it was December and not June, Aubrey stepped back. "Thank you for your assistance, Mr. Reed. I must be going now."

He opened his mouth to speak, but before he could, several policemen rushed in, nearly bumping into her. Mr. Reed stood by her side as they arrested the robbers. A sharp-nosed officer approached and spoke to Mr. Reed. He gave a quick account that did not even hint of bragging. The man in riding trousers who had subdued one of the robbers spoke with an officer, too, but where had Mr. Reed's friend gone to?

A white-haired man rushed past, reminding her of the reason she'd come to the bank. To meet with Mr. Ellsworth. Well, she was not staying now. He would have to come to the chateau. Thank goodness the man had not been present for the bank robbery. Mr. Ellsworth was aging and had seemed unwell when last she saw him, at the reading of Louis's will.

She took another step from the men, garnering Mr. Reed's attention. She plastered on a smile. "Thank you again. I'm sorry to leave so suddenly, but all of this has me feeling out of sorts, and I would like to be home." Offering her hand, she bid him good day.

"Good day, Mrs. Willot." Even through her gloves, his warmth soaked into her hand. He held on half a second longer than he needed to, then released her.

Remembering the chill, the numbness of not caring and just surviving, Aubrey turned posthaste and made it through the front doors. Outside, the midmorning warmth of summer in San Francisco hit her full in the face. A noisy streetcar passed, dinging its bell. The iron wheels creaked as it rolled down the tracks on Montgomery Street, which was often referred to as the Wall Street of the West. In the same way that Manhattan's Wall Street dead-ended at Broadway, so did Montgomery stop cold at Market.

The nearby buildings rose up around her like giants of stone and concrete, reminding her that she was here in the big city and not at her country chateau where no one bothered her. With a population of one hundred and fifty thousand, San Francisco was evolving into a booming metropolis. And she didn't belong here. While some feared wild animals and the occasional harsh weather of the country, Aubrey knew there was no evil such as that which people were capable of.

Sighting her barouche and the ancient old coachman Louis had employed, whom Aubrey hadn't the heart to replace, she made her way from the colossal bank.

No sooner had she set a hand on the barouche to steady herself than someone called her name.

"Mrs. Willot?" Mr. Reed jaunted down the bank steps, shaking his head, then he stopped before her. "I want to see you again."

She stopped breathing, the widening of her eyes so instant, she felt the sudden increase of air on them.

"To make sure you are well." He quickly finished up, as though the phrase was supposed to be included in his initial statement. "I mean, in your condition...the fright you've had..."

Warmed by the boyish blush upon his cheeks, Aubrey feigned confidence. "Rest assured, I am well, Mr. Reed."

"I dare say you are." He stepped closer, bringing his citrusy scent with him. "May I call on you?"

Wishing to say yes yet cautioned by experience to run away, Aubrey squeezed the door handle. Now she wished she'd left before he came out, and she also wished she could welcome him. Better safety than politeness. "I don't live in town and seldom have guests, being that I am a widow living alone."

"Of course. I apologize." This time, it was he who stepped backward. "I only hoped to see you fully recovered after this ordeal." The corners of her mouth tugged down.

Somehow, she'd hoped he had another reason for asking to call. Silly, since she was the size of a whale and as lithe as the ones that washed up on the beaches at San Francisco Bay.

"May I help you into the carriage, then?" He offered his hand, likely not knowing how a simple touch from him put her at risk. She could not afford to feel the tender fluttering of hope his nearness and care brought to life. Not wanting to seem rude, Aubrey slid her fingers into his grasp, which firmed around hers.

She rose, her bustle catching a little on the narrow doorway, then letting go. Settled in a nest of skirts and petticoats, Aubrey folded her hands in her lap. "The French Chateau."

Her words sounded so softly, even Mr. Reed had to incline his head when he said, "What was that?"

"The French Chateau a few miles from town. That's where I live." The slightest of smiles warmed her cheeks. "There is an orange orchard on the property."

He back-stepped, grinning as he withdrew an orange lozenge from his pocket and placed it in her gloved hand. "Sounds nice. I will give you a couple days to recuperate."

She nodded as Mr. Dobbs, her coachman, called to the horses. A warning whispered through her. *You're better off alone.*

Aubrey leaned forward in the open barouche, ready to rescind her invitation, but the carriage pulled away, and Nathan Reed faded from sight.

*N*athan had erred in thinking he could ever rob a bank, or break into a widow's house, and still think of himself as a decent man. He had compromised when he accepted the job to do something illegal and thus further damaged his soul.

I am a bad man. He settled his hands in his pockets, his shoulders so very heavy. Sick to his stomach at how far he'd fallen, he watched the Willot barouche pull into the street. The unfolded canopy hid Aubrey Willot from sight, though he imagined the stubborn tilt of her chin despite the weariness in her lovely green eyes. What were the odds that she would be in the bank today, in need of rescue? Had he been wrong to ask to call on her at her home?

Undoubtedly, but after the fright she'd had today and the one he gave her last night, her delicate condition might be compromised. It was hard to imagine that the babe she carried was Felicity's sibling. Part of him was curious to know what kind of woman she was. Mrs. Willot had surprised him, knocking that one bank robber unconscious, and again with her knowledge of Carlton Watkins and the Yosemite Valley

Land Grant. If Louis's widow was as kind, brave, and intelligent as she seemed, could Felicity someday connect with her father's family? If Nathan could not find a way to save her from the asylum, might Mrs. Willot help, or would she hate Felicity and see her as a representation of her husband's infidelity? His face heated just thinking such a thing. Felicity was the most precious person in existence. He had to protect her.

A police wagon pulled up, the black sides as haunting as the shrewd-looking man who hopped down from the driver's seat. Police officers in navy-blue uniforms emerged from the bank, pushing the group of battered robbers ahead of them.

Nathan stepped to the side, lowering his gaze. That should have been him. He was just as bad as these men, coming to the bank to take what did not belong to him. He and Beau had planned to slip into the back, to a safe which Ellsworth had left unlocked. The other robbers were to leave by horseback, but Nathan and Beau were supposed to store the gold within the bank for Ellsworth.

He could be in cuffs right now, headed for a jail cell, leaving Felicity all alone in the foundling asylum—marked as unwanted and unloved. A scourge, as so many unfortunates without parents were seen.

Head down, he crossed the street, aiming for the French cafe where Beau liked to take his meals.

God had spared him from his own folly today. Yet there would be no payoff now, likely not even for the documents he'd found. How was he supposed to take care of Felicity? Ellsworth would sooner shoot him than fire him since he intervened and bungled the robbery. And everyone would know it was him. Reporters had been at the bank, asking questions. The papers would mention his name, and while Beau had been wise enough to leave early, Nathan had spoken with the police officers. He was doomed.

He'd stepped from the cobblestone to the sidewalk beneath

a generous canopy with tassels aflutter when he caught a sudden movement around the side of the café. It was Beau, his gaze like fire. The man had taken down the other robbers, so there had been no shooting in the crowded lobby, but he clearly wasn't happy at being put in such a position.

Nathan made his way down the dark alley, the scent of garbage forcing him to breathe through his nose. He barely had time to duck before a large fist swung out from the side. Beau glared and threw another punch.

Nathan dodged, slapping away the next, then ducking two more of Beau's punches before he could manage words. "I was thoughtless, Beau."

That stilled his friend, though he remained poised to strike.

"I decided to act without considering what that meant for you, and I'm sorry for taking away your choice, but I could not let that man hurt her."

"Hurt her? You could have got us both killed." He spoke through his teeth. "You jumped a man with a weapon in a room full of people. You're lucky he didn't start shooting."

"He was hurting Mrs. Willot, about to take her as hostage. Was that part of the plan all along? To take a hostage?"

"I don't know every part of the plan, Nathan. Now get off your high horse. You said you needed money quick. Don't act like you didn't know the kind of work you were getting into."

Nathan lowered his hands. "You're right. I never should have approached you. I was desperate. Felicity..."

He could not speak further. The emotions in his throat were too tight. What if the nursery she slept in grew too hot? What if her needs were overlooked in the shifts of wet nurses who worked at the foundling asylum? What if when he arrived to see her one day, she was but a still bundle? Like the child whose bed she had been given shortly after birth?

Beau lowered his fists as well, the whites of his eyes especially bright with the tall buildings on either side, casting them in a shadow nearly the tone of dusk. He released a deep breath. "Perhaps this is best. I don't need another black mark on my record, and we could not allow women and children to be harmed."

Nathan shook his head. No way could they have left the lobby where the patrons were being held at gunpoint to venture into the back of the bank in search of the safe Ellsworth said would be unlocked. No, they could not have done that. Neither one of them, even though Beau tried to act as though he didn't care. He was different this summer, the recent loss of a friend weighing on him. Beau had refrained from sharing the details, but the man's grief had been more palpable than ever just a week ago when Nathan had found him in jail, a drunken, hopeless mess. When Beau was sober, Nathan told him about Sarah and Felicity. They'd hunted bounties as a team in the past, with Nathan filing the paperwork to turn in prisoners and receive payment. Beau liked to stay away from law enforcement.

Then, Nathan had been the one to choose the jobs and get the money to divvy up. Working for Ellsworth, Beau was in charge.

"What do we do now?" Beau slipped his thumbs into his suspenders and leaned against the brick wall behind him.

Nathan glanced back toward the street where the opening appeared as a sort of seam in the long alley. They'd stored their horses at the livery. He would need to get Sammy soon so as to avoid a larger fee. "I'm going to head to the precinct to see the wanted posters. I'll have to go back to bounty hunting after this."

"And leave the little girl?"

"I need money. That's the only thing that will help her."

"Don't you have people, though—family in Oregon?"

Just the mention of home, his past and all he left behind, made him feel smaller and the world bigger. Too big for a man like him. Pa had been right—he was nothing but trouble. Nathan sighed and slumped against the wall. "My ma and pa ain't spoken to me in years. Sarah ran away, ended up here. I didn't get to speak to her before she died, but if they were going to take her back, why would she have gone to the lying-in hospital to have her baby? She would have written them a letter. Something." If they had written back, he'd have seen the letter in her things.

"You need to get out of town, anyway. Ellsworth is going to be furious when he finds out." Beau crossed his arms and tipped his hat forward. "I gave him the documents this morning before meeting you at the bank. He may not pay you now."

Nathan groaned and bumped the back of his head on the side of the building. This was his fault for agreeing to work for a dishonest man.

A few buildings down, a porter stepped from the back door of a hotel to light a cigarette. Beau licked his lips at the sight but didn't make his own. "I heard you ask to call on Louis's widow. You think that is a smart idea?"

Nathan shrugged. "I just want to make sure she's all right."

"You sure that's all you're interested in...her health?"

"There's nothing more to it than that." Even as he spoke the words, he knew deep down that wasn't quite true. Not that it mattered. Nathan was as likely to garner the attention of that beautiful Christian lady as Beau was to join the San Francisco Police Force.

~

Aubrey pulled the lever beneath the middle shelf of the bookcase, and it clicked. Breath held, she swung the hidden doorway open to reveal a short stair that led down into darkness. When she finally inhaled, the dusty scent assailed her nose.

Her feet seemed to stick to the carpeted floor. She'd gone through every inch of the house last week, confronting violent memories of her time here with Louis and claiming it for her own with some material item. Her floral rug in the study, a figurine of a dancing couple in the sitting room, Papa's big bear painting in the lady's parlor, and so on. All things that Louis would hate but Aubrey loved, no matter how artistically out of place.

The last place she had to conquer was Louis's secret room, which she'd not dared to open except for that one terrifying night. She'd thought she'd sensed him, lurking in the shadows, watching her as he used to. Such nonsense. He was dead, thank heaven. Stilling for the gravity of such a thought, Aubrey waited for the probe of the Holy Spirit to convict her. "It's not that I hate him, Lord, but truly, he was a wretched man."

How had her heart gone from loving to despising Louis in the space of two years? Oh, she knew how. He'd changed her.

Aubrey closed the secret door with a sigh, glad to step away from it and all it represented. This was her study now, her house. She crossed to the desk, her feet brushing the soft Aubusson floral rug imported from France. It was the only feminine thing about the room. Otherwise, the study was manly with large furniture in dark colors, deep wood tones, marble lion statues, a whiskey cabinet, and a gun cabinet. A man's retreat, as Louis had called it a week before their wedding when they'd toured the house together.

She settled in the office chair with the double windows at her back. Summer sunshine lit the surface of the desk as she sorted the letters her maid, Lizzy, had left for her to find. There were also a few old newspapers. Her arrival had made the society pages. One from last week read, *Convict's Pregnant Wife Returns Home to Lick her Wounds.* Her cheeks burned, and she brushed the papers aside to glance over the latest issue, which included news of the bank robbery and the daring Mr. Reed.

Two other men had helped, but only one other was mentioned, a local businessman. Strange. At least her name was not included. The robbers would be on trial.

She opened a letter from her father and scanned the first few lines. His sweet sentiments regarding her impending maternity and how her mother had dealt with her stomach issues while expecting made Aubrey smile. Unfortunately, Pa could not come to visit and help her sort out the banking business she'd inherited. He was touring his businesses with Jesse, who had finally agreed to work for Pa.

She rested her head on her arms. What was she supposed to do with no business savvy herself?

The rays settled on a crystal inkwell and sparkled off the glass plate on her desk. She ran her finger there, the reflection reminding her of the photograph from the day before. What a thrill it would be to take pictures again. The fountain in the garden attracted birds. She might capture an image of the darling pair of finches she'd seen there recently. Aubrey just needed a camera since hers had been lost when she and her brother had been kidnapped last month.

They'd ended up in Salt Lake, where they learned the culprit behind the crime was Louis's older brother, Emil Willot. He had even used her own camera to take a photograph of her which he sent to her brother with a ransom note. In the end, they had been rescued, thanks to a female bandit whom her brother fell in love with.

Aubrey sighed. Such a romantic notion—to fall in love with a bandit who risked all to rescue you. And here she was, a twenty-three-year-old widow with an empty house, a baby on the way, and no hope of her youthful dreams. What if she could pursue photography again? Mr. Watkins's studio was just in town. She might go in and see his work. Purchase a new camera and the necessary chemicals for developing photographs.

A thrill in her chest, she sat up and withdrew a piece of

paper, where she jotted down a list of supplies—tin plates, collodion, bins to hold the silver bath, developer, clothes, and pins. All the things she would need to develop photographs.

A tap sounded on the study door.

Aubrey stilled, holding her breath. Might the handsome man from the bank have come to see her as he'd said he would? She really should not entertain any male visitors while she lived alone, but after he'd saved her, she could hardly turn him away. She rose and checked her reflection in a cabinet mirror, which required the smoothing of her hair, then carried her list of supplies to the threshold.

When she opened the door, her maid, who'd been looking away, turned quickly to face her. Though Lizzy's freckled face was a blotchy red and her eyes glistened with tears, she managed a shaky smile. "Oh, miss, you did not need to come to the door. Tell me to come in."

"A little exertion won't hurt me or the baby." She rested her hand on top of her belly. "But what is wrong? Lizzy, you've been crying?"

Lips trembling, Lizzy shook her head. "It's just that fool sister of mine. Getting herself into trouble in town." She wiped her nose on her sleeve. "But I am here because of your appointment with Mr. Ellsworth. He is here."

So it was not Mr. Reed. Well, she needed to meet with Louis's business manager and get a full review over the quarterly revenues and expenses. Dreading having to deal with something too big for her to handle, she squared her shoulders. "Please see him up and then send for these supplies." She handed the maid the list she'd just made.

Lizzy curtsied and strode away. She served as more than a maid, fulfilling some butler duties since the decrepit elderly butler also acted as coachman. Aubrey kept him on out of pity because the likelihood of him finding gainful employment elsewhere was small. He was Louis's man, though, so she would never trust him or the others of Lewis's original staff. Especially the cook, whose dislike for her was constant. It didn't help that the lady had witnessed one of Aubrey's most humiliating moments. Though a wonder in the kitchen, Cook was fierce and unpleasant. But firing her in this economy, without any legitimate cause, would be cruel. They only consulted on dinner, after all.

Aubrey should hire more staff for such a large house, but she only kept part of it open and didn't want to risk hiring the wrong person. A maid who ended up to be a thief or a butler who was a crook, for example. No, she aimed to keep her world small and risk free.

When the elderly Mr. Ellsworth entered the room, he smiled, exposing large teeth. "Good to see you, Mrs. Willot. And in such fine health." He took her hand, squeezing lightly.

"And you." She motioned toward the chairs in the corner of the room, where tall windows lit the space. "Please, sit down. Give me a moment to open the windows."

Poor Mr. Ellsworth always looked too warm, but today, his round, wrinkled face already glistened, and there were sweat stains beneath the underarms of his tan frock coat. Aubrey pushed the large lattice-paned windows open, glancing down at the hedges to make sure no one was there, as she always did. Footprints stamped the sandy soil vaguely, but she made out the shape of a boot. And there was another, as though someone had been standing there.

My goodness. Had someone been spying on her? But who would want to spy on a boring widow who did nothing important all day?

She'd grown comfortable in her own home, but that did not mean she was safe. There was obviously still a need for caution in the event an old gang member came to call. Regardless, this was her house, and she was staying.

They sat, and Mr. Ellsworth filled her in on the news about town, including the bank robbery and terrible summer heat. It was June and California was headed for another drought. Crops would be ruined, and more farmers would be forced to take out loans or be foreclosed on. Truly sad business. Next, they reviewed the quarterly financial reports on the holdings she'd inherited from Louis. The banker had been gracious to take on the management of the stocks and mining operation in Nevada when Louis was sentenced for fraud and embezzling. There had been debts and fines to pay, but Mr. Ellsworth had seen to that while Aubrey was in Los Angeles recovering at Papa's house.

"These numbers represent the profits from your shares. You see, when the bank…"

As he droned on, Aubrey peered at the numbers Mr. Ellsworth presented to her. She'd never been good at arithmetic. This is why she needed someone to oversee her assets. But for the sake of her child, Aubrey wanted to responsibly manage what God had allowed her to inherit. So far, Mr. Ellsworth's suggestions to buy stock in the Bank of California seemed to have paid off.

At last he was done, and he collected his papers with the pride of a mother hen gathering her chicks around her.

Had he noticed her general lack of knowledge when it came to Louis's business? Did he think her stupid? Pa always said that knowledge was the enemy of ignorance. How could she learn if she did not ask? "I am afraid, Mr. Ellsworth, that I still do not fully understand what my husband did, exactly."

"Well, just a few years before the two of you married, he struck it rich in Nevada, in the silver mines. Over time, he invested his capital into a number of ventures. Coastal transportation, insurance, woolen and silk mills, canal companies, hydraulic mines, Alaskan furs trade, gas works, and refineries. He was hungry, insatiably so, to gain more wealth."

"But a great deal of that financial empire was lost when he was arrested, was it not?"

"Yes, ma'am. I am afraid so. But rest assured, all that remains is more than enough to meet your needs. It is still a thriving business."

"Oh, good, because I want to invest in a new venture."

Mr. Ellsworth paused in placing the reports back in his briefcase, his mouth partly open and a wheezy breath whooshing out. "And what is that?"

"Photography. You see, photography is gaining popularity all the time. There are so many uses—family photographs, newspapers, posters and advertisements, even tourism. Why, just the other day, a lady returned from a trip to Yosemite and said that she paid a whole dollar to get her photograph taken by a waterfall. Can you imagine?"

"I see." He shifted, frowning. "What exactly would you like to invest in where photography is concerned?"

"Ah…" Her mouth remained stuck open. She'd always just dreamed of having a shop—something simple where families could come in and get photographs of babies, mothers and daughters, maybe some generational photographs. On the weekends, she could take her own shots, then sell the prints. Maybe she would set up an apartment on the second floor where she could stay with the baby. Lizzy could help with the tending, and Aubrey might hire a salesperson or staff to clean.

But that was likely on too menial of a scale for Mr. Ellsworth to consider. "I would like for you to investigate this business venture. There are factories and studios in big cities that do woell." Oh, Lord have mercy, she sounded so pathetic. Why was this so hard?

It didn't matter. This was what she wanted.

She pressed her teeth together and raised her chin.

Yesterday, when she'd been upset from the robbery, it had been Watkins's picture of the rugged hillside and peaceful lake that brought her back to herself. What if she could take a photograph like that? True, taking shots made her feel alive herself, but to help someone else feel alive—that would be a meaningful endeavor.

What if she didn't get her money back out of it, though? What if her investment failed and everyone thought she was worthless? Photography was referred to by some as the great modern art, but there could just as easily be some new invention to capture the public's fancy.

But if she didn't try, Louis would win. She needed to get back to herself, and that meant taking risks, and later teaching her baby to take risks. Aubrey ran a hand over her tight, swollen belly, her babe within rolling as though to signal affection.

"I'll make inquiries and meet with you again." Despite Mr. Ellsworth's forced smile, his reply was tense. "Of course, I cannot give you an exact date when I will be ready. You understand, seeing to the operation of the Nevada mine and trying to fill your husband's shoes on the board of the bank are very time consuming. Then I have my own properties to oversee."

"I will research as well. There is the American Optical Camera Company in New York and many others, I am sure. My brother, Jesse, and I used to be better acquainted with the camera business, but over the past few years, I have hardly thought of it." She averted her gaze, her cheeks heating just referencing her time with Louis.

"Investing in another business venture will be risky. The deals your husband made were not all honest. I have worked hard to recoup the business after the large fines and legal fees. You want to have something to pass on to your little one, don't you?"

"Yes. Of course. I am well aware that recovering from my husband's poor business choices has been a challenge.

However, according to these numbers, our profits in stocks are up, and the mine is producing at a higher rate than ever."

Mr. Ellsworth's face flushed, and Aubrey had to hide a smile. She might not comprehend all of his mathematical and economical jargon, but she'd heard Papa and Maman talk business enough to understand when she was in the red and not.

He returned the documents to his leather valise, glancing around the room. "It amuses me you choose this room to receive your guests. I seem to remember this house having a fine ladies' drawing room." He nodded to the rug. "That is a nice addition."

"This is an Aubusson rug, imported from France. My mother had one when I was a girl. I used to lie in the middle and pretend that I was in a rose garden."

He smiled, sowing creases into his puffy white skin. "If you have a daughter, perhaps she will do the same." Mr. Ellsworth set his valise aside. But rather than rise, he leaned back on the sofa and said, "I cannot say it enough, but I am very sorry for your loss."

She dared not admit the freedom she felt since Louis's death. She could pick the dress she wanted to wear without fear of smirks, criticisms, or directions to change. She had the ability to take as much jam at the breakfast table as she wanted. Her first morning after Pa and Jesse left, after the will had been read and she'd learned she was the sole heir to Louis's estate, she had smeared enough jam on toast for five people.

Then she'd cried. For the times he told her she could get fat and have her teeth rot out of her head for having too much jam. For when he noticed a droplet of strawberry sauce on her bodice before a luncheon at the park, then forced her to change and berated her like a child. That had been toward the end, when he'd worn her down and she believed she deserved such treatment. That she was as simple as a child, as stupid as an ox, and as unloved and worthless as a wife had ever been.

Aubrey shivered, trying to shake away that cold, heavy numbness that used to keep her safe through Louis's rants. She was no longer so broken, though, and he was gone. She was going to open a camera studio, even if others thought it foolish.

Mr. Ellsworth still waited on her response, so Aubrey stood to show him out. "I thank you for your kindness. Your advice and expertise in finances have been invaluable to me."

"I am glad. I only wish to help the widows and orphans, as it says to do in the Good Book."

She tried to smile, but his pity left her feeling ill. He needed to leave. She didn't want to ascribe a personal side to a business relationship. Besides, he barely knew anything about her, and all that he did know was what Louis had made her—a weak, witless woman who had lost the ability to think for herself.

Aubrey had met Louis shortly after she graduated Miss Porter's School, a private college preparatory school for girls in Farmington, Connecticut. She'd been confident—maybe even prideful—having attended the finest finishing school and college in the United States. The curriculum included chemistry, physiology, botany, geology, and astronomy in addition to the more traditional subjects taught in girls' schools. The year Aubrey graduated, the president's daughter, Nellie Grant, had attended there. Aubrey had graduated confident in her future.

When she married Louis, she'd believed she would live in the chateau and raise her children, be adored by her husband, and capture it all with a camera. Instead, she'd lost her first baby and been forced to live all the way across the country from her family. Just remembering how she'd allowed Louis to dictate what she wore, said, and eventually even thought, Aubrey hardly heard Mr. Ellsworth's comments on banking and investing as she showed him to the door.

What would she do if the photography investment didn't pan out? What if this was her last chance and she failed?

CHAPTER 4

$\mathcal{N}$athan stepped into the police station, pushing a train robber in ahead of him. After four days tracking him from random saloons and brothels, he caught up to the criminal in a mining town in Nevada. It had required another four days to arrive in San Francisco. Beau was right. Bounty Hunting was no life for a man with a baby.

The coolness of the room came as a sweet relief after being outside in the scorching sun for the past week. How had Felicity fared?

Nathan led the prisoner to a waiting area with two benches, where he handed over the criminal and filled out the paperwork to receive the reward money. A familiar voice sounded behind him, and Nathan turned as a tall lawman with graying hair and broad shoulders walked into the lobby alongside William Ralston, president of the Bank of California.

Captain Henry Hiram was one of the many police captains serving in San Francisco. Nathan had connected with him years ago when he had gone after a murderer and ended up having to fight for his life. Captain Hiram had been the officer to take custody of the prisoner when Nathan made it back to town. He insisted Nathan go to the hospital afterwards. They'd been friends since, and Nathan always made sure to stop by the captain's house when he passed through San Francisco. He preferred being in the wild and frequenting smaller towns, but there was always work to be had in the big city.

Captain Hiram stopped by the front desk, still addressing Ralston. "To be sure, the thieves will be arraigned soon."

Though Nathan had never met William Ralston, he'd not fail to recognize one of San Francisco's wealthiest socialites and entrepreneurs from the papers. Some called him the Emperor of the West because he was the wealthiest and most powerful man in California. He was of a robust frame with a receding hairline and barrel chest. "You will let me know if you learn anything more?"

"Yes, of course." Captain Hiram's gaze alighted on Nathan, and he smiled. "Well, hello, Mr. Reed. Good to see you back in San Francisco. I heard of your heroism at the bank." He thrust a hand out, and Nathan shook it. "Mr. Ralston, have you met Nathan Reed?"

"I have not had the pleasure." The businessman, too, shook Nathan's hand heartily. "I owe you a great debt, sir. Thank you for protecting the people in the bank."

The collar of his gray denim shirt suddenly too tight, Nathan swallowed. "I did what any decent man would do. I mean, with the lady in danger, I had to step in. If the other men in the bank had not intervened, someone could have gotten killed." He shrugged, feeling like a kid taking credit for his big brother's work. "I couldn't have done it alone."

"It could have gone badly, but it didn't." Mr. Ralston checked his time piece, then perused Nathan's dirt-encrusted attire. "You a bounty hunter, Mr. Reed?"

"Yes, sir." He gestured to his equally dirty canvas pants. "Just came off the trail."

"Reed here is the best bounty hunter for hundreds of miles

around." Captain Hiram crossed his arms over his blue wool uniform.

Ralston raised his eyebrows. "You ever decide to settle down, find steady work, call on me. We are always in need of guards at the bank. If not at this location, I have others. Come by the bank sometime. Allow me to repay you formally."

Did he mean a reward—money? While Nathan had not felt conviction that night he broke into the Willot Chateau, he was overwhelmed by Mr. Ralston's offer...considering Nathan had planned to rob him just last week. He was a wretched man, but he would take all the help he could get. For Felicity. To pay the nurse so she could buy better food to keep up her milk supply. And the matron who administered the infant floor, so she'd not forget Felicity and just let her die.

Nathan said, "It's generous of you, Mr. Ralston."

"Not at all. I would like to do more than this for your heroism in the bank."

When Mr. Ralston left, Captain Hiram motioned Nathan into his office. The small room was dingy with paper shades hanging in the windows, the occasional cracks letting in a few streams of light. Nathan crossed the thread-worn rug, his gut in his ribs. Why did the captain want to talk to him? He sat in a rickety chair in front of the modest desk stacked with files.

The captain plopped down and shuffled through papers on his desk. "Reed, I need new blood on the force, a man I can trust. A man who is steady, sticks with the things he starts, and has a spine made of steel." He dipped his chin. "That's you."

"You're offering me a job?"

"I am." He leaned back, more relaxed as he stroked his mustache. "We got vice, illegal imports, muggings, kidnapping, murder, riots. This is San Francisco, the zenith of pioneer glory, the Golden Gate City. And our crime rate is only growing higher with the drought and economic crisis. That bank robbery is proof of that. You know there is rumor it was an inside job?"

"Oh." The muscles up his back tensed, and he fought to keep his voice calm. Did that mean someone suspected Ellsworth was behind it? "According to whom?"

He shrugged. "Just a rumor. Nothing concrete. I'll just file the idea away and see what happens. Sometimes nothing comes of things, and other times they do. But I'm patient. Usually get my man." His gaze wandered a bit.

Was he reminiscing, or was he suspicious of Nathan? Sitting a little taller, Nathan rubbed his sweaty palms on his knees. He needed to wash up, then visit Felicity.

"Ever think of settling down, starting a family?" The question seemed to come out of nowhere and gave Nathan pause.

He had a family in Felicity. "Someday, sir. Yes."

"I got a family. Three girls and my wife. It makes a difference, you know? Having someone to come home to. A place to belong."

"I...not really." He'd been alone for so many years. Having Felicity was new, and she might not ever get to be a part of his life if he couldn't work. Here the captain was offering him a job. Why was he turning him down? "How much does police work pay?"

"One hundred and twenty-five dollars a month." Captain Hiram kept talking, going over details like shifts and duties.

Nathan's thoughts ran ahead, planning. If he brought in a few more bounties and saved enough for a down payment, he might get a home loan. He imagined approaching Mr. Ralston in his castle-like bank. Nathan didn't deserve the man's kindness, but for Felicity, he'd grovel. Once he got enough for a down payment, he could work steadily for the police.

Something like a spring breeze swept through him, quickly followed by the hard truth. Ellsworth and Beau knew he was part of the robbery. What if someone else found out? Already

Captain Hiram thought it was an inside job. Even if that truth didn't come out, it would be easy for someone to associate his name with the ambush in Oregon. Lawmen were typically a shrewd bunch. Someone would remember him as the guard who lived, and when Captain Hiram learned the truth, he'd fire Nathan and possibly arrest him. Releasing a prisoner was illegal, after all. Imagine not being able to take care of Felicity, and if he had married by then, his wife would learn what type of man he really was. Any children they had would be shamed.

A cold sweat broke over Nathan's neck, his thoughts coming faster. If he didn't get a job, Felicity would stay in the asylum. If she lived, she'd do so under the stain of being unloved and abandoned. But could he live a good life and still make ends meet? He wanted to be brave and to protect others, and to be a good father to Felicity. Did an innocent little girl even need a rough man like him? He certainly needed her. Most likely, though, he would never be good enough, even with Captain Hiram's guidance.

"What do you say, boy?" Captain Hiram had been going on the whole time Nathan's thoughts ran wild. The older man jumped to his feet and offered a hand across the desk.

Nathan rose slowly, shaking his head. "Thank you for the offer, but I got a couple things to straighten out first, before I can make such a commitment."

The police captain withdrew his hand, crestfallen, then he squared his shoulders. "Sure. It's an important decision."

Nathan headed for the door while he could, but Captain Hiram followed him.

"The wife's always saying I get ahead of myself." He chuckled, then stopped at the door with Nathan and shook his hand again. "I don't know what you're running from, son, but you can stop now. Settle down. Make a home. The good Lord's got a plan for you, and..." He grimaced, then let Nathan's hand go. "My door's always open to you. Rain or shine, you hear?"

All Nathan could do was nod, then duck out the door with the fire of conviction stinging his back.

Lord, I don't know if Captain Hiram is an angel unawares, but You sent him to the wrong man. I'm no Paul. Not even Peter. No, he was more like Thomas of the Bible, who doubted the Lord's return even though others testified to having seen Jesus alive. Honestly, Nathan having a successful police career and a loving family was as likely as someone coming back from the dead.

Another Bible verse came to mind. *Can a...leopard change its spots? Neither can you do good who are accustomed to doing evil.*

CHAPTER 5

Saturday was visiting day at the San Francisco Foundling Asylum. Nathan sat near a window in the lobby, warm light pouring behind him as he cradled sweet Felicity in his arms. Stomach curled up behind his ribs and chest aching with love for his niece, he touched his cheek to hers.

To his left, the main doors to the building held windows that gave him a glimpse of the busy street outside. Saying goodbye to the little girl hurt every time, but coming back hurt too. Felicity nuzzled her nose against his skin, letting out a moan. Smiling at her wrinkled little face, he kissed her forehead. She slept soundly, having just eaten. The attendants welcomed him to stay with her, though there was an air of expectation. When would he take the baby home?

The door opened, and the clopping of horses' hooves and rumble of wagons wheels reached him momentarily. A fancy lady in a dress with more ruffles than the river had stones entered, an ostrich feather obstructing his view of the man with her. She wrinkled her brow at him, then turned sharply with a *tsk*ing of disgust.

She must think Felicity was his and he was an irresponsible father. He held the infant closer, as though doing so could shield her from the hatred coming from the lofty lady. She demanded to see the matron, giving him a searing glare when she proclaimed she and her husband were patrons of the establishment.

Nathan stayed where he was, letting the sun move across the floor. Those people left, though he gave them no mind. He'd seen their ilk before. Unfortunately, Felicity would have to learn to live with their scorn, even if he did manage to adopt her and give her a family. He hadn't thought much of marrying since he was a kid in Oregon, trying to catch the eyes of a pretty girl at Sunday meeting.

Another woman's face came to mind, flushed and wide-eyed. After the bank robbery, Mrs. Willot had raised her chin, her gaze pointed toward the Watkins print. He'd held her firmly by the arms, wanting to stabilize her in reality so she'd not sink into fear again, and surprisingly, she'd not. He'd helped her, somehow.

Eventually, Felicity stirred, fussing with her mewling cry. A nurse came to collect her. Throat tight, he gave her over and stood there as the white-clad woman walked away, up the stairs to the warm nursery. Hands hanging loose, Nathan stared, unable to move.

"Mr. Reed?" The matron, Mrs. Miller, entered the room, her long shadow trailing behind her. Fencepost straight, she greeted him with her usual professional directness, yet her smile erased years from her face. "I'm glad you are back. Your niece is in fine health." She began to walk, so he followed her across the room.

"Yes, she is. Thank you for your care. I left some money with the secretary. I hope it helps."

Her sharp features softened as she passed the front desk and led the way to her office, which smelled faintly of licorice and coffee. "You needn't do that. We have many patrons, and you need to save your money so you can provide for Felicity."

"Yes, ma'am."

"I have something for you. A carpenter found it while repairing a floorboard in the room Sarah stayed in while here."

Nathan held his breath as Mrs. Miller unlocked a drawer to her desk, then withdrew a Key West Cigar box, of all things.

"This belonged to Sarah. She must have hidden it in the floorboards before she died." Mrs. Miller's voice grew quiet, and she extended the item. "You might find something in there to help Felicity."

He sank slowly into a ladder-back chair and placed the box on his knees, then opened the lid. Inside was a ticket to a showing of *Romeo and Juliet* at the Grand Opera House. Next were papers, letters. His stomach tightened. What might he learn about his sister and the life she led before her death? He opened the page and read. It was from Louis Willot, the cad. He must have written her from prison, judging by the date. Nathan shoved the paper back where it had been hidden.

"You should read it all." Mrs. Miller sat with her skeleton-like hands folded on the desk. "You must forgive me—I took the liberty of doing so. Felicity's father may have been a cad, but she can hope he cared something for her before he died."

Face hot, Nathan shook his head. What did it matter what Louis said or felt? He was a liar and a blackguard. Nathan would never show the letters to Felicity based solely on the indecency of the situation—a married man writing to his mistress. What if Felicity became confused and misperceived such a thing for love?

Oh, no. That was his job now. To show her what love was between man and wife—which meant he had to get married. His pulse pounded in his head as an unbidden image stirred of Mrs. Willot peering up at the Watkins photograph in the bank, her hands still clutching his.

"No." Nathan shook the memory from his mind.

The matron cleared her throat, her eyebrows raised. She must think he was speaking to her. She had no idea of the absurdities flying through his head. Nathan turned his attention back to the letter and held his breath at the last few lines, which included the promise of financial support for the child—Felicity.

"How does this help?" he asked slowly, folding the contents of the box and dreading Mrs. Miller's response.

She sighed long. "Because, Mr. Reed, Felicity has a birthright, and if the Widow Willot has an ounce of Christian charity, she will honor that. And you need her money right now." She pursed her lips, the corners of her mouth turned down. "I was recently contacted by a family wanting to adopt an infant girl, and I am afraid with Felicity's blond hair and sweet disposition..."

A vise around his heart would have hurt less. Nathan stood without speaking, found his way to the livery, then headed for the Willot Chateau.

CHAPTER 6

A book on photography in one hand, Aubrey stood in the doorway leading from the master study to the veranda. A breeze carried the scent of hydrangeas, the flowers bright white in contrast to the green boxwood hedges near the house. The bushes in their diamond-shaped beds formed an intricate maze.

She loved being in the country, away from city life, but some days, the quiet stretched as though without end, through the house and all around. The only sound was the distant singing of the men in the orange orchard farther away from the house. Day after day dragging on for so long made her dreary, and memories of the past and what could have been would do her no good.

Blessedly, the familiar tap of Lizzy's knock gave her reason to turn away from pondering. She set the book on her desk when she passed it. Perhaps the maid would tell Aubrey why she was crying the other day. The woman had been distracted and even absent some evenings. Aubrey knew she was going into town but did not know what for.

She opened the door to the hallway, and Lizzy startled

where she stood talking to a tall man. The man from the bank —Mr. Reed. Shadows lingered in his blue-gray eyes when he met her gaze. There was something sad about him despite the polite nod he gave her. No smile or warm welcome, though he had seemed eager to see her again during their last encounter.

Aubrey cocked her head toward her maid, who never brought a guest to her without first consulting her.

Lizzy's thoughts must run a similar line because she blushed. "You have a guest, ma'am. Mr. Reed, he said you were expecting him." The maid's embarrassment faded when she beamed at the handsome visitor.

My goodness, the girl was smitten, but at least she was not in tears as she had been the last time she came to the study door. "Thank you, Lizzy." Aubrey stepped back, gesturing him to enter. "Come in, Mr. Reed."

The maid hurried away, leaving Aubrey and her visitor alone.

She'd drawn the curtains to let in light, yet with the dark furnishings, the room always seemed like a den. Except for her fancy rug.

Aubrey's feet sank into the thick woolen fibers as she led him past the desk and a table with an atlas to the sitting area before a cold fireplace. "It is kind of you to call. As you can see, I am in fine health."

He did not respond, just stood with the posture of a soldier, something angular beneath one arm.

"Please sit down." She gestured toward the large wingback chair to his right.

The man was of healthy portions, to be sure, filling the chair so that it seemed smaller, though he was slightly leaner than she remembered. His skin was also tan, newly burned, as though he had spent the entire eight days since the bank robbery in the sun.

He sank into the chair as though sliding into icy water. How strange. Was he unwell? And why was he so stern? When last they spoke, he had been warm, kind, and genuine. Something must be wrong.

"I wanted to thank you again for your assistance at the bank." Though she'd expected him earlier. Somehow, his request to call when he'd helped her into the barouche the day of the robbery had carried a sense of urgency. Unlike now, when hesitancy shadowed the hard contours of his face. His frown stayed in place, though he was no less attractive for it. "Mr. Reed, forgive my forwardness, but is something wrong? You seem troubled."

"Wrong? Ah...no. That is...yes. I would have come to see you sooner, but I had an unexpected business engagement take me out of town." Mr. Reed spoke quietly before meeting her gaze. "You are feeling well, then? No signs that the baby experienced distress?"

How forward of him to notice her condition and mention the child. Her training at finishing school forbade her to engage in a conversation of such a personal nature, yet she responded. "I am well, and the baby is moving as usual. Thank you for asking."

He glanced around the room, seeming to struggle for words for he said, rather suddenly, "This is a lovely home."

He did not answer her question regarding if something was wrong, but she said, "Thank you. It is patterned after the French style."

"The mansard roof and columned windows are beautiful."

"Why, yes, they are. I chose them and the cast-iron roof crestings with the roses." As she'd chosen the bay windows, bracketed cornices, and slate shingles for the roof. The style was all the rage two years ago, and her friends had been envious and in awe. But none of them were here any longer.

"You were involved in the designing of the house?"

"Some. This room"—she motioned around them—"was designed according to my husband's taste."

"Yet you receive your guests here, not in a lady's sitting room."

"I like it here." Her sitting room had been the scene of Louis's first outburst. She'd been so foolish to think that the man who succumbed to her every whim and built this grand house in their courting days had been her soul mate. She'd dreamed of a house just like this, as she'd dreamed she would marry a Frenchman. Maman had been French and had treasured her nationality. The notion had been romantic, and somehow, Aubrey thought it might make Maman proud, though she had passed by then. Nothing had turned out as she'd hoped.

"It is a fine room." Mr. Reed drew her attention to the present.

He was so serious, with a guarded gaze and firm mouth. The curl of his hair above the left eyebrow reminded her of a boy she'd met in Baltimore when her family visited Grandmother Alexander. He, too, was quiet, though he'd been a mite sweeter when he'd asked to kiss her cheek under a sprig of mistletoe.

Aubrey tried to hold Mr. Reed's gaze but could not. What was this thrumming in her chest, the warmth in her cheeks? She had been a widow since May—a whole two months— though she'd not seen Louis for six months before that due to his incarceration.

The box beneath Mr. Reed's arm caught her eye again, the familiar labeling heightening her pulse. A Key West Cigar box —Louis's favorite brand. She'd feared men from his past might surface. Was Mr. Reed such a man? Gripping courage, she folded her hands. "Indeed, it is a fine room, but you did not come to see the house."

"I did not." He inclined his head. "I wish I had no need to

call on you, Mrs. Willot, but I have a dilemma. May I tell you a story?"

She nodded. The tension in the air seemed to thicken her intake of breath. Whatever he said, she would be calm.

"I knew a girl. She grew up on a farm, and her folks were good Christian pioneers who came west just after the War Between the States."

"Many people did come west, looking for peace after the fighting." Her father and uncle had.

"Yes, ma'am. Peace. Around the time she came of age, she fell in with a bad sort of man. The kind who says all the things ladies want to hear, offers them security and promises happiness." Mr. Reed pressed his lips together, then dropped his voice lower. "When she became with child, she was too ashamed to return home. Desperation makes fools of us all."

Not all, but certainly many. Certainly, her. Hadn't it been just after her maman passed that Louis had come into her life? The Lord had been good, providing her a way out when Jesse rescued her and Pa welcomed her home. Did this girl have someone so kind in her life? "What happened to her, the girl? And the babe?"

Face stony, he met her gaze. "She died giving birth to that man's child."

"I'm so sorry." Stomach tight and attention drawn once again to the cigar box, Aubrey toyed with the ruffled edge of her undersleeve. Clearly, this man was connected with the girl. Perhaps she had been his wife. Louis was not above pursuing other men's wives. Obviously, Mr. Reed was grieving. A verse about God being close to the brokenhearted came to mind. She'd been brokenhearted once she was finally free of Louis yet hadn't felt the least bit close to God or even wanted to think of Him. In fact, it had been that scare that night in the study when she thought someone was watching her that drove her to pray for the first time since Louis's vengeful brother had kidnapped her and Jesse.

Focusing on the man before her, Aubrey steadied her voice. "Is there any family, anyone to take care of the baby?"

"Yes, ma'am. But times are hard, and there is nothing to show for the woman's suffering. Nothing to justify what happened."

And here was the reason he—her rescuer—came. "You think money can justify what she went through?"

Mr. Reed blinked, raising his eyebrows.

Irritation sparked in her chest. "Men prey on women like her every day, Mr. Reed. It is unjustifiable. Why, even you used your charm, attractive features, and the influence afforded your gender to sway Lizzy to bring you to my door unannounced."

"Excuse me." He shifted in his seat, straightening a little. "I hardly think the comparison accurate."

"It most certainly is. That man swayed her with pretty words and preyed on her circumstances, as you preyed on Lizzy's ignorance. Both are examples of a man influencing a woman to get what he wants."

The man's brows lowered as he regarded her, and she resisted an urge to squirm.

Why had she allowed herself to be drawn into this conversation? More, why had she attacked Mr. Reed, as though he were somehow to blame? When had she come to see all the male gender in such a villainous light?

Had Louis done this to her? Her father and brother were nothing like him. There were still good men in the world. She needed to remember that.

Finally, Mr. Reed dipped his head. "I reckon life's taught you a lesson or two. I'm glad that you understand how she was preyed on. I was afraid you would judge her."

Heat rushed into her cheeks. "Why would I do that?"

"Because the man who fooled her was your husband."

Aubrey's pulse pounded in her head, his words echoing in her mind and the cigar box signaling a connection to Louis. Of course, the child was his offspring, but what was she to do? Palms sweaty where she clasped them in her lap, she forced a calm she did not feel. "I don't suppose you have any proof of this?"

"Yes, ma'am. I do." He withdrew the cigar box. Her stomach sank when he lifted the lid to expose a collection of letters. The papers rustled as he flipped through them and paused before extending one to her.

Aubrey took it and held it, the familiar handwriting like that on her own letters.

Mr. Reed spoke just across from her, yet his voice sounded far away. "Aren't you going to read it?"

The room fogged, bright edges blurry, and her head was very heavy. Still, Aubrey read her late husband's handwriting promising to take care of a woman and a baby. He said that his family would be so happy. What a wonderful blessing the child would be. It was all so reminiscent of the letters he had written her from prison when he promised not love—for she'd had enough of his brand of love by then—but financial support.

"As you can see, he signed on the bottom. And you probably recognize his handwriting as well." Mr. Reed pointed to the dreadful script.

"Yes." Aubrey handed it back, an apology on her lips, but she would not apologize for someone else's actions, especially Louis's. She had spent far too long believing she should apologize for things she did not do and that everything was her fault. No more.

Stomach churning, Aubrey pressed a hand to her lips and breathed deeply. This was all too reminiscent of Louis's presence in her life—the panic at such a moral offense. The dread of the consequences. If she exhibited signs of feeling ill, though, Mr. Reed might think her weak. She didn't need that, even if she suffered from nausea due to the pregnancy.

Mr. Reed drew in a deep breath, as though steeling himself. "Ma'am, I am sorry to bring this to you, especially while you're in such a fragile state, but it seems your husband promised to take care of that baby. I'm here, representing the family. It's wrong that the babe should suffer because of his sins or because he died before he could aid her."

Her? So the baby was a little girl? But where was she, and why was Mr. Reed here representing the family? He certainly didn't look like any kind of man to handle legal matters. "What is your profession, Mr. Reed?"

"I work with the law in bringing criminals to justice."

"Well, that is vague." She'd not thought anger could turn hot so quickly, yet when Aubrey glared at Mr. Reed and he straightened, she felt its sharp bite. "You could do any number of things, from jailer, warden, bounty hunter to…"

His eyes brightened.

"Aha. So you are a bounty hunter."

His jaw twitched. "Among other things, yes."

"Well, there is no bounty to collect here. As you can see, having likely read every word in those letters, my husband was a cad. If that poor woman had not died, he would have brought her more heartache."

His eyes opened wide. "Are you refusing to respect your husband's wishes and support the babe?"

"No. I will do the right thing, but first, I will see the child and where she is staying. To know she is well. I am no fool and will not hand money to anyone who comes to my door with love notes to my husband's mistress." She stood on shaky legs. "You can communicate my requirements to the family."

Mr. Reed rose as well, though he did not move to follow her to the door. He cleared his throat, holding the letters in one hand. "I am sorry for all you have suffered, but you aren't the only one. That baby girl didn't do anything to deserve to be orphaned, and Sarah should never have been forced to live on the street."

Aubrey raised a hand to silence him. Just hearing the name of one of the many women her husband had found outside their marriage bed made her shudder. Shaking her head, she strode to the door, muttering that she would see him out, yet not daring to look back when he followed her. All she needed was to be alone, away from Mr. Reed before she shattered into pieces. She'd known of her husband's sins, the type of man he was, for most of their relationship, yet every time she learned of something cruel he'd done, her heart ached a little more. How long would she feel the sting of his betrayal? How long must she atone for his sins?

CHAPTER 7

*N*athan followed Mrs. Willot to the foyer without speaking. What could he say? He'd not expected her to demand to see Felicity. What if she discovered Felicity was at the foundling asylum and decided that was suitable for one conceived in adultery?

As they came to the foyer, an old butler slumped on a bench near the window. He startled awake at the sight of Mrs. Willot and stood, glaring at Nathan. White-haired with a hook nose and hunched back, he looked fierce enough to roast a man, but his expression softened when the lady of the house spoke to him.

"Mr. Dobbs, Mr. Reed is leaving and will need his horse, please."

She was kicking Nathan out, and where would he go? Back to the city to find another bounty to chase, leaving Felicity behind?

Needing a moment to breathe, he stopped before a window near a potted palm. He was at an impasse and would have to tell Mrs. Willot about the asylum and his familial connection to

Sarah, admitting he had no way to care for Felicity or even move her from that sad place.

The butler reached for the tall double doors as the lady of the house came to a stop in the middle of the ornate floral rug.

"Mr. Reed?" She frowned, all disapproval and frustration, brunette wisps of hair that had escaped her bun curling around her face and giving her a frayed look. Gentleness settled in her eyes, though. Perhaps she would be charitable to Felicity in her time of need.

Nathan took a deep breath, yet before he could speak, the round maid with frizzy red hair and freckles burst into the room holding a piece of paper above her head. "It's a letter from the penitentiary in Utah."

The widow stared without moving while Lizzy offered the envelope. She did not reprimand her maid for making such a scene and announcing correspondence from a prison.

Nathan stepped nearer as the color drained from Mrs. Willot's face. "Perhaps the letter is about your late husband's effects."

Gaze locked on the envelope, she shook her head. "I received them already. It must be from my brother-in-law."

"The same who kidnapped you?"

She frowned. "How did you know he kidnapped me?"

"The papers, of course."

"Yes. Louis only had one sibling. Emil was his half brother and quite a bit older. He took his death hard. That is why he kidnapped us, my brother, Jesse, and me." She studied the paper, then opened it as hesitantly as she had accepted the letter Nathan had given her in the study. Lips pressed tightly and brows furrowed, she read quietly. "He says my mother-in-law came to America intending to visit Louis. She was devastated by news of his demise but will call on me before returning to France. She wishes to enquire after my health and Louis's child."

Lizzy gasped, the sound low but unmistakable. "What does he mean by that? Louis's child? Oh, no. They cannot mean to try and take the babe, can they? Did your father-in-law come as well?"

"I..." Her gaze darting around, Mrs. Willot spoke quietly. "I cannot say."

"When is she coming?"

"As early as June twentieth."

Lizzie's eyes grew wider. "That's today."

"Yes, I know." Mrs. Willot turned to Nathan. "You said you work with the law?"

"Yes, but I am no lawman." The admission sank something inside his chest. If he was, he could better help her. "Do you need to see an officer? I can relay a message to the police for you." He glanced at the door. His horse was in a corral a ways from the house, but he could get to him quickly.

Mrs. Willot drew in a deep breath, glancing from the door to the letter. She covered her mouth, her chest rising and falling with a deep breath.

"Mrs. Willot, do you believe your mother-in-law poses a threat to you?"

"I don't know. I only met her one time, before Louis and I were married, but I did not know about Louis's criminal activity. His parents may be law-abiding citizens." She rubbed her forehead with her palm. "But I don't know that either. She just visited Emil, and he certainly meant me harm."

The rattle of wheels on the drive accompanied the clip-clop of horses' hooves. Mrs. Willot swung around to the doors, opening the ornately carved wood that looked like it belonged in a castle. Light on either side shone around her petite frame, which appeared nearly angelic with both arms stretched wide. Her hands sank to her sides, and she straightened slender shoulders before glancing back hesitantly. "She's arrived."

"I realize you are not happy with me, after this business."

He touched the cigar box beneath his arm again. "But if you do not feel safe...well, I don't feel right leaving."

"I cannot assume she is safe." Her voice softened when she spoke again. "I would be grateful if you would remain until I know more of her business."

"Of course." Nathan accompanied her outside into the hot summer sunshine. A stately black barouche rolled down the driveway, followed by a wagon with a large crate in it. Next came three armed guards on horseback. The last guard possessed dark, all-too-familiar features.

Beau Fox met his gaze for an instant before steering his horse behind the wagon. They hadn't spoken since the bungled bank robbery. Why was he here? It did not bode well for Mrs. Willot's hope that her mother-in-law might be law abiding. Beau had been part of the Willots' illegal business.

The young widow stiffened, as though gathering her courage. Nathan moved to her side, slightly ahead. He was no hero, but if he could shield her in any way, he would. How strange that her mother-in-law retained guards. Was she expecting trouble?

A lady with graying hair and a pinned-back mourning veil emerged from the carriage. She took in her surroundings, as regal as a queen despite the black garb, until her gaze settled on Mrs. Willot. She raised her eyebrows and painted a smile onto youthful yet strained features. "*Salut*, Aubrey."

When she moved up the steps, a gangly guard with sharp features followed. A man as thick as a barrel with a wooden expression stayed in the driver's seat, gripping the reins as though ready to leave. Beau remained astride behind the wagon, his chin especially low and covered with a layer of facial hair—likely, to hide his identity.

"It is wonderful to see you. I didn't expect to find you in Louis's old house." A thick French accent laced her words as she embraced her daughter-in-law.

Mrs. Willot remained very still. "Did you not? Emil wrote to me, telling me to expect your visit, and he knew I was here. Did he not send you?"

Madame fluttered her eyelashes and tapped her chin. "I don't know what my stepson assumed. I believed you had returned to your father's house, as is customary for widows." She sliced her gaze downward, appearing to take in Mrs. Willot's simple blue day dress. Blue, not black as Madame herself wore.

The front door opened, and the butler peered around the corner, garnering Mrs. Willot's attention. "Mr. Dobbs, please see Madame Willot's horses are tended to." She nodded to the two vehicles with haltered animals, and the butler began giving the guards orders even though he had to tip his chin to see them. With his back stooped, his posture bent, and his white head situated low in front, he resembled a buzzard. Hopefully, he was only the butler and not also the coachman, because he looked as though he belonged in a rocking chair, not atop a carriage.

Nathan turned to find Madame Willot staring at him. She put her nose in the air, the edge of her veil waving with the motion. A silver streak of hair started at each temple and ran back like the stripes of a polecat into an abundance of dark curls. She narrowed her eyes as though waiting for him to melt into the porch.

Clearly, he was not welcome.

Mrs. Willot must have noticed because she moved a little closer to him as she spoke. "As you can see, I was entertaining a guest when you arrived. Mr. Nathan Reed, please meet my mother-in-law, Madame Delphine Willot. Just two weeks ago, Mr. Reed prevented the robbery at the Bank of California."

"A robbery?" Madame glanced between them, then offered her hand, which Nathan shook, not about to kiss it, no matter what was popular in French circles. He was American and not in the habit of kissing strange women anywhere, even on the hand.

"You must tell me how this occurred." Madame Willot touched her daughter-in-law's arm, their height difference making Aubrey Willot seem younger than ever.

"If you will accompany me to my sitting room, I will ring for tea. You look exhausted." They started into the tall, carpeted foyer, but another wagon rolled up the driveway. The driver was a kid Nathan had seen bounding around the train station in town. Likely, he was delivering a package. Sure enough, the side of a beechnut crate came into view when the vehicle drew nearer.

With Mr. Dobbs hobbling down the drive, trying to keep up with Madame Willot's men, he would not be available to assist with unloading—not that the decrepit old man would have been much help, anyway.

Nathan started down the steps. "I can see to the crate."

"A crate?" Madame Willot squinted. "Have you resorted to shopping from a Sears and Roebuck catalog, Aubrey?" Sarcasm laced her tone, a sneer twisting her lips for a second.

Nathan stiffened, not liking the way the woman mocked Mrs. Willot.

"Sometimes. However, I have not ordered anything since I moved here." Her daughter-in-law seemed unaffected as she shook her head. "Where is it from?"

Nathan greeted the driver and handed the paperwork to Mrs. Willot, who, glancing over it, said, "It's from Utah—Salt Lake City. From the police."

"My goodness, whatever could it be?" Madame smiled as though Father Christmas had plastered her name on the label.

Mrs. Willot frowned. "I don't know anyone in Salt Lake anymore."

"Well, let's see what it is." Madame turned to him. "Do hurry, Mr. Reed."

Upon receiving Mrs. Willot's nod of approval, Nathan assisted the young driver in prying away the boards of the three-by-three-foot box. Drawing back the wood chips used for packing, he revealed the shiny side of another wooden box. What in the world? He read the name printed on the side aloud. "'American Optical.'"

Mrs. Willot gasped and rushed forward. "My camera!" She tipped her chin up and smiled with the radiance of a sunbeam. The faintest of breezes waved her light ringlets against her cheek. The openness with which she faced him settled a calm over Nathan for an instant, then Madame spoke.

"A camera? The police sent a camera from Salt Lake City?"

"Yes. It was stolen when Emil's gang kidnapped my brother." Mrs. Willot looked pointedly at her.

Madame's eyes flashed open wide, darting to Nathan before returning to her daughter-in-law. "Aubrey," she hissed, likely trying to hush her, though Mrs. Willot observed the older woman calmly.

Judging by their reactions to one another, this was the first time they'd broached the subject together. They likely needed some privacy.

"Should I see to the camera?" Nathan offered, but as Madame turned with Mrs. Willot to go into the house, the spindly-legged guard strode up the driveway toward them.

Mrs. Willot glanced back, a pleading in her gaze. "You are my guest, Mr. Reed." She turned her attention to the delivery boy. "If you follow the men, Mr. Dobbs will see to the package."

Inside the cool house, Nathan walked alongside a guard in stiff suit. Jaw taut, the man kept his gaze ahead to where the women walked toward a parlor. How might he fair in an altercation, warding off the guards at Madame's command? Would Beau side with him? Were the men with Madame a show of force because she had come on a long journey, or would the Willots once again strike at the young widow? He brushed his forearm against the pistol on his hip, the hard wooden handle a comfort. Lord willing, this was a social visit and his services not needed. Still, when they entered a parlor, Mrs. Willot glanced back at him, ensuring he still followed. He gave her a nod, determined to not leave her until she asked him to.

~

Once they were seated in a very feminine sitting room with smaller, French-style chairs and colors of pink and lavender, Madame let out a screech. She clutched her hands over her mouth, eyes wide with horror. "What on earth is that?"

Hanging on the wall amid whimsical murals was a framed painting of a charging grizzly bear.

"My father's painting." The Widow Willot settled beside Madame, motioning for Nathan to take the velvet-covered wingback chair near her end of the couch. Her hands absent-mindedly rested on her round belly. "Papa was hunting late one fall in the Sierras when a grizzly charged him. Upon hearing his recount, an artist painted this rendering." Mrs. Willot's expression softened as she gazed at the artwork, though her mother-in-law shivered.

"How barbaric." She dabbed her nose with a handkerchief, casting uneasy glances at the portrait as though the bear might come to life and maul her. "Tell me, Aubrey dear, about this bank robbery."

Lips pursing for a moment, Mrs. Willot shook her head. "You came from visiting Emil, who is in prison for kidnapping me. Did you know he planned to steal my baby and send him or her to live with you?"

Madame's eyes went wide, reflecting true surprise, then her eyebrows flattened, and she sighed long. "I knew nothing of my stepson's fiendish activities. I was on my way to America, not aware of the happenings here. Besides, Aubrey, Emil has been estranged from his father for some time. He is a reckless, unpredictable man. Too much war and loss to rely on."

Aubrey narrowed her eyes, leaning forward a bit as though considering her words. "Yet you came from seeing him at the penitentiary in Utah and you have guards with you, men I don't know that you have brought to my home."

"I am traveling with valuables in a strange land. The guards are here for protection. It's not unreasonable, Aubrey, but if you do not trust me, I will stay in town."

"It's not that I'm accusing you, but you must admit, after what Emil did, I have reason to question the intentions of my in-laws. Is Mr. Willot here as well?"

Madame's nostrils flared. "No. Claude remained at home. We are a good French family. As for Emil, my stepson, I visited him to give him clothes and food. I also went to pay my respects to the place Louis..." Tears entered her eyes. She swallowed before pressing a handkerchief to her lips.

Aubrey raised her eyebrows to Nathan as though asking him what he thought. He had no idea if the woman was telling the truth. In fact, until he spoke with Beau, he wouldn't trust Madame or the other guards with her.

Gathering herself, Madame dabbed her nose. "I came to America to see Louis. Since he is gone, I'd hoped to connect with you, Aubrey. You carry my only grandchild, after all. Did you consult a doctor after the robbery? You know a fright can cause early labor."

"I... No, but have noticed no changes since that day, and it has been over a week."

"I wish you would consider going. Before dear Louis was born, I carried another child. A fall down the stairs put an end to her."

How could both Mrs. Willot and her mother-in-law speak so plainly about such personal, feminine matters? Had they forgotten him as though he was one of the staff? Either way, he didn't care for the talk. It had been childbirth that left his sister too weak to live. Nathan studied the rug, the floral medallion running in an arch from the tip of his boots to that of the younger Mrs. Willot. He raised his gaze and found that she, too, was looking down, the pointy tips of her shoes turning to meet. She swallowed visibly, indicating she did not care for the chastising.

Madame Willot was going on about doctors and modern medicine when the lady of the house met his gaze. He witnessed not just grief but pleading in her face.

Madame turned her attention on him, her nose lifting a bit. "And what was your part in the robbery, Mr. Reed?"

Struck by the strangeness of the question, Nathan blinked. His part had been to rob a vault, but he wasn't about to state that. Besides, in the end he'd played an opposing roll. "I..." Where to start?

"He was very courageous, inserting himself between me and one of the robbers."

Aubrey's eyes flashed with admiration that made his heart rate speed, as it had the day of the bank robbery. Yet here he sat with the cigar box beneath his arm, having fouled her day with the news that her husband's infidelity had wrought another life she was responsible for. Could he make it up to her?

Mrs. Willot adjusted on the settee. "Once the robber was incapacitated, Mr. Reed and two other men took down the remaining bad men."

"Why, you are a hero." Madame Willot shifted to face him better.

Nathan's cheeks burned. He was not a hero, not really. Seeing an opportunity and having the skills to carry out a plan did not a hero make. Yet as the conversation turned a different direction, both women seemed to look at him differently. They admired his actions. Mrs. Willot had wanted him to stay during her mother-in-law's visit because his presence made her feel safer. The thought warmed him through, a twinge similar to what Felicity made him feel. Needed. Wanted.

The afternoon ebbed, the ladies talking about social news and a little politics. France was suffering following the Franco-Prussian War. Madame had lost friends and loved ones. Travel to America had come at a price, but she wanted to make things right with Mrs. Willot. The younger of the two ladies was kind but did not seem completely convinced. She'd been slow to trust Nathan and just turn over funds, wanting to see Felicity and know she was real. Maybe even ensure she was well taken care of.

Soon Mrs. Willot was stifling a yawn. As big as her baby was, her body must quickly succumb to weariness. When Madame offered to walk him to the door, the younger woman agreed.

She stood, offering her hand to Nathan. "Thank you for your visit and all the kindness you have shown me." Her fingers were soft, clasped firmly and full of meaning. She was relinquishing him to leave, satisfied with Madame's explanation for her visit. She must feel safe because when she bid her mother-in-law good day, she invited her to stay and included the guard with a glance.

As Madame showed him to the door, her guard close behind, the French woman turned a calculating squint on him. "Monsieur Reed, we have visited for some time, but you have not yet mentioned your profession."

"By trade, I am a bounty hunter. I became acquainted with your daughter-in-law through the bank robbery."

Madame Willot's eyebrows raised. "That must be why she trusts you. Do you work with the police?"

"Sometimes."

Her heels clicked on the foyer's black-and-white tile. "I wonder if you might help me. I fear for Aubrey's safety, living here alone so near the Barbary Coast of the Pacific. Traveling around town by herself, possibly coming into any manner of trouble, as you saw at the bank."

"That was not her fault." They stopped before the door, Nathan rubbing the back of his neck, the cigar box under one arm. He still needed to tell the widow more about Felicity, which meant coming back. Once in town, he'd swing by the police station and speak with Captain Hiram about Madame and the guards. The police officer could come out and check on Widow Willot—make sure she did, in fact, feel safe.

"Aubrey should have returned to Los Angelas with her father instead of living here alone." Madame adjusted her veil, the tight line of her jaw and breath through her teeth communicating her frustration. "She needs a companion to go about with her. I wonder if you are looking for work. If, with Aubrey's knack for trouble, your skills might fit the job."

Nathan raised his eyebrows. Why would Madame ask this of him, a stranger? She should get a lady or accompany Aubrey places herself. She did say she was here to spend time with her. "Are you sure hiring me as a companion for your daughter-in-law is wise? A woman would suit better. Besides, you barely know me. And to what degree do you intend to have her guarded?"

Madame sighed wearily, her shoulders lowering a slight degree. "You are right. Aubrey needs more than a companion. She needs a guard. Louis had enemies, and I have reason to believe she is not safe. That is why I have asked you—someone I hardly know but a man of courage who has rescued her once already—to guard her."

"I'm surprised you choose a stranger over your own guards." He nodded toward the silent, fierce-looking man behind her.

She smirked, then bid the man leave her. He did so, but not without jutting his pointy chin in Nathan's direction.

"Aubrey would not allow one of them to be near her, but she seems to trust you. As for you being a stranger to me, I am a good judge of character. I have my sources, though, and if you turned out to be unreliable, well...you could just leave town." She smiled in a sickly sweet manner.

The veiled threat did not go unnoticed. On the contrary, he understood more fully why he needed to accept the job. Madame might not pay him as much as he'd make bounty hunting, but he could stay near Felicity.

"I can hardly think this will be more challenging than bounty hunting. Aubrey is reckless. I have already lost a son. I cannot lose my grandchild." She continued in her bristly way. "Will you take the job? I can offer generous compensation, and you may stay in one of the servants' rooms if you like."

"I will need to speak to Mrs. Willot before staying in her house."

"My son built this house."

"And he left it to his wife."

"She's given permission to have the men in my employment stay here. Will that satisfy your conscience, Monsieur Reed?"

He didn't like it, staying at the Willot Chateau while the business with Felicity was unsettled. But he disliked leaving Mrs. Willot here with Madame and her guards more.

"I don't want her getting some cockamamie idea in her head and leaving for town, alone, before you return to speak with her." There was a level of desperation in her tone.

Madame had said she lost a baby once. She was obviously a grieving mother, having lost her only son recently. What if she learned of Felicity? Would she try to take her? The thought rankled him. If the family wasn't so criminal, he might have welcomed the help.

Unable to avoid it any longer, Nathan agreed. He would

connect with Beau, who had worked for the Willots in the past, and find out what he was doing with Madame Willot. The woman had come from seeing Emil in prison. Was it a personal call or business? Beau could give him more information. Perhaps the job offer to guard the Widow Willot was providence. This way, he could keep her safe and earn a wage.

CHAPTER 8

*L*ater that day, Nathan leaned against the trunk of a tree in the same orange grove where Beau had stood watch the night of the break-in. Looking past the black silhouette of far-reaching branches to a radiant smattering of stars, he felt a semblance of peace. His family had traveled by wagon to Oregon when he was a teenager. They'd camped under skies that were so alive with stars, he'd felt wild and free. Occasionally, that feeling would result in a midnight swim with some other boys and, once, a surprise visit from his pa, who licked him good for leaving the safety of the camp. Those were good days, when Pa cared and Ma was happy.

Nathan smiled, though the hardening inside his chest crushed the expression. All he had left was Felicity. *Lord, help me do right by her?*

Around him, the night was alive with God's creation—an owl hooting in a tree, the soft patter of some creature's paws, and the rustling of the leaves. Maybe God had not forgotten him.

Another sound reached him—the footsteps of a man.

Nathan stood straighter, his fists clenched. Madame's

guards had avoided him that evening when he'd gone to the servants' quarters. They spoke only French, which he knew little of. If one of them followed him—the outsider—he didn't need to be caught unawares.

"Reed?" Beau emerged from shadows, heading for Nathan as though he saw him as clearly as he might in daytime.

It irked him that anyone could spot him so easily after years of training alongside Sheriff Rudy and his own practice as a bounty hunter to be unseen and unheard. But Beau had grown up in the wild in Europe, traveling country roads with his troupe, and then there was his military training.

"I didn't expect to see you here at the chateau, Beau." He offered his hand, relieved when Beau shook so firmly and clapped him once on the shoulder. In all the times they worked together, Beau was fiercely loyal. With him here, Nathan wasn't alone.

"How is the baby?" Beau asked.

"She was well when last I saw her. I may be able to move her before too long."

"That is good." Beau rolled his shoulders. "I hate these monkey suits Madame insists we all wear. I didn't expect to end up here either. It's the last place I should be, but Emil wired asking me to assist his stepmother while she was in town. After he was arrested for kidnapping and I got away, I didn't think he'd trust me."

The hairs at the back of Nathan's neck prickled. "You were part of the Alexander kidnapping?"

The night hid Beau's features, but Nathan could see well enough to decipher the nod of his head.

"Kidnapping, Beau? I never thought you would do something like that." Nathan paced before him, shaking his head. He could rant at Beau for his foolishness, but it wouldn't help anything. The question begged asking, though—could he trust

Beau? The man ran with a rough pack in Utah and had participated in robberies. But kidnapping? That was different.

Beau let out a long breath, his shoulders slightly bowed as he leaned against a tree. "It was foolish of me, but at the time, I thought it was the right thing to do. That the man who helped imprison Louis deserved to be punished. I thought I was being loyal to my countrymen, but I was wrong. Louis was an awful man who mistreated his wife. Jesse Alexander was just trying to keep his sister safe, and all Emil wanted was revenge."

"Just how active was your role in the kidnapping?"

"I physically detained both of them. Jesse Alexander fought back—often. I stopped him from escape more than once." His voice was quieter—as strong as always, yet Nathan sensed weariness in it.

"Why weren't you arrested?"

"A friend of mine, a girl I'd known all my life, was sweet on Alexander. She was poking around, going to get herself hurt if I didn't help. I led her to the hideout, then once the police came, I headed for California. She showed me kidnapping them was wrong. We weren't at war, fighting against an unjust government like back in France. Louis deserved imprisonment, and Jesse Alexander deserved to go free."

"Well, that's good. Did you see Mrs. Willot when Emil was holding her?"

Beau nodded, massaging his forehead. "When Emil had her, I told her help was coming so she'd have some hope."

Nathan sighed, shaking his head, though he refrained from scolding Beau. Nathan had his own list of sins to atone for and did not want to judge a man who was trying to live a better life. "You sure taking this job was a good idea?"

"No, but if I refused, that would prove to the Willots that I am a traitor. Madame came to America for a social visit. When she found out Louis was dead, she went to his house in Salt

Lake when it was foreclosed upon and bought some things. She just needs the valuables guarded."

Nathan crossed his arms. It was strange for Beau to reveal so much. The man was typically closed-mouthed. He and Beau had lived similar lives. Wandering. Not staying anywhere too long, although Nathan had not known until recently that Beau had a criminal past. They'd become acquainted years before in a sheriff's office when they had been on the trail of a pair of outlaws and agreed to partner together. They had each saved the other's life on that dangerous hunt and had been friends ever since, though Beau did have a way of disappearing and reappearing without notice.

Beau had a past to protect, but he had come to meet Nathan this night, openly discussing that past, so he must be willing to help. "I need to know if Mrs. Willot is in danger," Nathan said. "Emil Willot wrote her a letter from the penitentiary in Utah. The letter seemed civil, but his inquiries after her health could easily be threatening, considering their history."

"Did he say anything more?"

"Just asked that she accept her mother-in-law with the graciousness she might offer her own mother. If Madame Willot is here, is her husband as well? If so, will he be looking for revenge?"

The Frenchman's bulky frame stiffened. "I don't think Monsieur Claude Willot would come all this way. I'm shocked Madame came. The provence where they live was annexed to Germany following the war. They are suffering heavy taxation now. Why would she pay for a trip to the States?"

"Good question." He began to pace, one arm crossed and the hand of the opposite pinching his chin. "Should I be worried?"

Beau hesitated, then shrugged.

"I know you are loyal to your people, Beau, but I need to know more. Louis's widow is under my protection now."

"So I heard. The guards say you are a buck rabbit on the chase."

"Nothing could be further from the truth. I told her about Felicity and asked for money." Nathan squared his shoulders. "Did they also mention that Madame is the one who hired me?"

"It doesn't matter. This is not safe for you or Felicity. The Willots are a bad family."

That kind of generalization proved less than helpful. "And how can I keep her and myself—and even Felicity—safe if you won't tell me what is going on?"

Silence again, and Nathan let Beau have the time while he prayed. What if Madame meant Aubrey harm? What if right now, while Beau and Nathan were away from the house, she had Aubrey moved, kidnapped...or something else?

Beau scrubbed his face hard, rubbing his temples, then took a deep breath. "I can tell you what I've seen and think, but not everything makes sense. Mademoiselle Aubrey inherited everything from Louis. That is strange. He didn't care for his wife but was very close to his mére while in France. Madame is here now. I think she is looking for something. It might have to do with money or Emil—Monsieur Willot's last remaining heir."

A blow to any mother's heart. Still, his mind worked on the question—was Mrs. Willot safe? "I didn't expect you to ride up with her guards. What are you doing for her?"

"Guarding the crate and connecting her with people in the area who might help her."

"People like Ellsworth?"

Beau snickered and shook his head. "She and Ellsworth could never work together."

"You don't think Madame is here to hurt her daughter-in-law?"

"I don't know, but if she is, why would she show her face?

She would send someone to kill her and remain far away from suspicion."

Nathan stood straighter, unlocking his arms lest he needed to run to the house and to Aubrey's aide suddenly. "You think she is capable of killing Miss Aubrey?"

"I cannot say. I do not know Madame so well. Family meant everything to Emil. He didn't know Mademoiselle Aubrey was pregnant when he kidnapped her, but when he learned she was with child, he wanted to use the baby to bridge the divide between himself and his father. They had a falling out years ago. Something about French politics."

The muscles in his arms tightening, Nathan gripped his hands into fists. "Do you think there is another plan to kidnap Mrs. Willot and her baby in an attempt to reconnect with his father?"

"I do not know. If Emil were free, I would say yes, but I cannot judge his stepmother. My acquaintance with Emil was through a mutual friend in Paris when he was a soldier. He was devastated by Louis's death. The loss he suffered in France, losing his wife and son, and experiencing the atrocities of the Franco-Prussian War changed him. If he took Louis's son back to Alsace and Lorraine, he may have been accepted back into the family."

Nathan's stomach turned at the notion. Such a desire could haunt a man. Nathan's dislike for Emil had been steadily growing with Beau's explanation, yet he felt compassion for him.

Beau leaned away from the tree to stand up straighter, dusting his hands on his pants. "Listen, Nathan, I know you want answers, but I haven't any. I don't know Madame. It might be that she is a lonely lady who just lost her son and wants to be here for the birth of her grandchild."

Nathan nodded. It made sense. "Why didn't Louis's father or brother try to break him out of jail?"

"The old man was too far away. Emil might have tried, but he had little capital. He was just a regular old thief who had a pack of Frenchmen willing to follow him." Beau released a breath, the weariness that always cloaked him as palpable as the scent of oranges on the breeze.

Though Nathan knew more than he had at the beginning of the conversation, he felt no better. "Thank you for coming, Beau." He offered his hand, shaking Beau's firmly.

"I figured I owe Mademoiselle Aubrey after the scare we gave her last month."

"Sounds like out of the two of us, you shouldn't be working for Madame. If she does need help with something illegal, she'll call on you. It's expected because that's what you've done in the past."

"You want me to quit? Then you'd be all alone here when things go badly."

So Beau did believe a conflict, trouble of some kind, would occur. "True, but this just doesn't seem like a good, safe life. Like the kind of life a man can be proud of."

"It's the life I've made. You were smart to pull back when you did—stopping the robbery, I mean. Which reminds me…" Beau blew out a long breath. "The documents you got Ellsworth weren't the right ones. He needs something else."

Nathan stiffened. So even if the widow wasn't in danger from Madame, she was still in danger from Ellsworth and any accomplice he might hire to break into her house. He'd have to be extra vigilant. "Why didn't Ellsworth hire someone to search the chateau before me? Louis was arrested last year, and the house has been empty."

Beau bunched his chin. "That is a good question. I wonder if it had anything to do with Mrs. Willot moving here. We searched the Utah house but not this one. Why would Louis have important legal paperwork so far away? The other guards knew Emil in Utah. They said that the day before Louis was arrested, Jesse Alexander broke into the house in Salt Lake City and stole incriminating documents. It was the proof the law needed to arrest Louis, but before his arrest, Louis sent his valise by courier here to San Francisco."

"You think the valise contains the papers Ellsworth needs?"

"It might. He was going on the other day about the future of the city and how the papers never belonged to Louis. He's a crazy old man, though. It's hard to know if anything he says is real."

"Can you find out the names of the courier?"

Beau shrugged. "I can try."

They both stood in relative quiet, then Nathan tipped his head up. The sky was still bright, but the peace he'd felt was completely gone now. *Lord, please help me do this right—keep Miss Aubrey safe. Give me wisdom.*

"I need to be getting back." Beau started off, his head low and shoulders hunched.

"Thanks, Beau, for meeting me and telling me all this."

"Oui. Maybe it will change things. The least I can do. *Au revoir.*" He faded into the darkness like a shadow slipping away in the coming light.

Nathan followed at a slower pace, not wanting to return to the house with Beau. He'd hate to throw suspicion onto the other man. He paused at the edge of the trees. Across a meadow, the big house stood dark against the bejeweled sky. In the garden, a white figure moved as though a ghost fluttering in the wind. Miss Aubrey.

And Beau, who was halfway across the meadow, would reach the garden and give her a fright, likely alerting everyone in the house. They'd want to know what Beau was doing. Madame would want to know why Nathan, whom she'd hired to protect Aubrey, was with her own less-than-trusted guard. And Aubrey, what if she was given a terrible fright and was hurt, after all she'd been through that day?

Maybe Beau would go around to the side of the house. Nope. When he came to the garden's farthest wall, he hopped over and strode down one of the main paths directly toward the lady.

~

*A*ubrey situated her camera in the middle of the garden, on the path that led to the fountain, and breathed the fresh evening air. The drought this year would likely be as bad as the previous year. The remaining water in the fountain's basin reflected the moon as clearly as a mirror. She peered through the lenses of her camera and adjusted the bellows so her shot included the surrounding hedges. Next, she focused the camera lens. The parterre was in the center of the garden, before the fountain, and diamond-shaped beds pointed away from it like the rays of the sun.

Certain her shot was clear and level, she slid the gelatin-coated plate and holder into the camera slot, then removed the protective sheet. Next, she removed the lens cap—exposing it to the light. She held her breath for an instant before putting the lens cap back on and sliding the dark slide into the protective frame to cover the plate.

Taking a photograph at night was tricky, and she'd have to wait until the chemicals and other supplies she needed to develop the negative arrived to see how it turned out. She had asked Lizzy to order them more than a week ago. Had the maid forgotten? She had been distracted lately. Perhaps Aubrey would go into town and purchase them herself. She set the precious plate on the short stone wall beside the pistol she'd brought outside with her.

When she covered the camera, a movement to her left caught her attention. A dark shadow emerged around the garden wall, walking onto a path so the fountain hid him from view.

Was that a man striding toward her?

She stepped backward, catching her foot on one of the tripod legs. She stumbled but caught herself on the wall, flashes of memory coming to mind like photographs—the subtle light in the study as she woke from slumber, feeling someone there, the footprints in the dusty soil outside the master study.

There was an intruder on the property.

Aubrey turned and ran, hardly glimpsing a stone column before its hard side scraped her face. She staggered backward, holding her head. But she had to get away.

"Mrs. Willot!" A man's voice sounded from far away.

Dizziness and pain brought her to her knees. She propped a hand against the pillar of the porch, using it for support. Firm hands gripped her shoulders, keeping her from wavering. The sweet scent of orange blossoms swarmed her senses, and a deep, familiar voice calmed her. "I'm sorry for giving you a start. Are you all right?"

Head aching, Aubrey pressed two fingers to her temple. "Mr. Reed, why are you here?"

"Your mother-in-law hired me to guard...that is, she is worried about you and wanted me to escort you when you go out."

"She hired you?"

"Yes, ma'am. I accepted because I thought you'd prefer me to the men with her."

"Oh, you thought right." Mr. Reed had saved her once already, unlike Madame's imposing guards. Remembering the shadow at the other side of the garden, Aubrey peered that way, seeing nothing but the symmetrically arranged plots and clear paths. "I saw a man, someone walking toward me on the path. That is why I ran. Did you see him?"

Mr. Reed followed her gaze, shaking his head slightly. "I don't see anyone, but perhaps coming outside alone at night is…"

She stiffened, for surely, he did not mean to reprimand her as though she was a child.

He must have noticed because he shrugged. "Might not be safe, is all I'm saying. Never know when a great pillar might run into you head first." He slapped a hand onto the offending column, and Aubrey snickered.

She smiled as her unwarranted frustration faded, but the expression gave way to tears. When she'd sensed someone coming toward her, she'd felt that panicked sense of being prey again. If there was someone there, lurking and intending her harm, Mr. Reed would protect her. Perhaps having him present wasn't such a bad idea, though she hated to take anything Madame paid for.

"Is your head all right?" Mr. Reed tilted his own head, likely trying to see more clearly in the starlight.

She dabbed the spot where she'd hit the pillar. A wet scrape oozed just below her hairline, and her fingers came away with blood on them. "I'm bleeding."

"Let's get you inside. You ran into that column at full gallop." He took both her hands and helped her rise.

"Gallop? My goodness, Mr. Reed. I am no horse." Cheeks warm from how near he stood, and a sudden bout of dizziness throwing her balance off, she gestured for him to lead the way, but he still peered at her.

"Mrs. Willot, do you feel as though you can walk on your own?"

She grimaced. "I can. Just please don't call me that. Willot is such an ugly name. Besides, the queen has arrived. Let her have the title."

They went around the column that had caught Aubrey unaware, then down the garden path that led to the back of the chateau. As black clouds peeled back from the moon, the white arched framing atop the dormers gave the effect of eyebrows, the windows like eyes.

Inside, they made their way to the quiet, dark kitchen. Aubrey had no intention of waking Cook, who was typically as fierce as a badger on a good day. Besides, that woman knew what a fool Aubrey was where Louis was concerned, as did most of the staff. She rubbed her arms, trying to drive away the shiver of shame and embarrassment gliding through her. Sad how no one seemed surprised when Louis was arrested. Even when Mr. Reed told her of the child Louis fathered with another woman, she'd been worried but not shocked.

Mr. Reed lit a lamp, adjusting the light. Aubrey found a chair to sit on near the fire, though she longed to lower herself to the clean floor to be nearer that night's dinner coals. Though the weather in this part of California was warm, the nights cooled, and a terrible chill sank into her bones.

Aubrey held her head while Mr. Reed rummaged in a drawer for something. Aside from the sore spot, she didn't feel terribly bad. Not like the time Louis crashed the carriage and she'd suffered a concussion...and a deeper loss. She caressed her belly. "Are you all right, *mon bebe*?"

Her baby enjoyed the night hours. Thank goodness, Louis was gone and she needn't worry about his foolish antics endangering her little one. She cradled her belly and rocked, humming a lullaby Maman used to sing.

Mr. Reed wet a cloth at the water pump, glancing at her repeatedly. Storm clouds shadowed his eyes, hinting at some deep angst. Was he really so upset over her discomfort? She was a stranger. This was not the first time he'd come to her rescue if one counted him staying when Madame and her scary guards arrived. Should she apologize for her sour mood? Stating he should call her by her first name because her married name was so ugly? She'd also mocked Madame—not very respectful behavior for a daughter-in-law. If she did apologize, he'd see her as a weakling. When married to Louis, she'd learned to express regret immediately, before the screaming started, but that had made him despise her too.

Mr. Reed stepped in front of her, his broad chest so near, his warmth cloaked her front. My goodness, the man was his very own blaze, a fire that was no doubt catching onto her.

He raised a wet rag to her head, but she leaned back, taking ahold of the cloth. "I am not seriously injured."

He did not relinquish it but lowered her hand and laid it in her lap. "You hit your head hard. You might be concussed. If you are not comfortable with me helping you, I will wake up Lizzy and then fetch a doctor."

"I'd prefer you leave Lizzy be. She—" The baby kicked toward her lungs, and Aubrey caught her breath. "My goodness, be kind to your maman, *mon tresor*." She patted her tummy, though the little one gave a mighty roll, forcing her to lean back to relieve the pressure on her ribs. "Oh. Oh. The baby does flips, I think." She smiled breathlessly, groaning when her laughter made her tight insides ache all the more.

Mr. Reed stilled. Color grew in his cheeks as he gazed at her tummy.

Aubrey's throat went dry.

All she wore was her summer nightgown with a wrapper that had come untied. Aubrey closed the garment and cinched it tight. Thank heaven it was made of a good cloth and plenty long. Even so, it had been open and revealed her very prominent belly, and—saints above!—she wore no supportive underthings to keep her bosom in place. Grass and dirt marred her bedroom slippers as well. She drew them beneath her gown and cupped a hand around the opposite forearm, supporting her chest.

Mr. Reed stood quietly, then eased back a little and set the cloth aside. "You are right. The wound is not bad. May I see your eyes just to be sure? You did hit that pillar pretty hard."

Fighting embarrassment again, she forced herself to look up. His gaze flicked from one of her eyes to the other—presumably ensuring she could focus.

"Good." His impersonal manner was a comfort, his movements efficient. All concern he'd shown earlier was gone when he stood to wash his hands.

"You think I am well, then?" She tucked a bunch of unruly curls behind her ear.

He leaned against a sideboard near the pump, drying his hands. "Do you still feel ill?"

"Aside from the bump hurting, I feel as fair as could be."

The corner of his mouth tipped up. "As fair as could be, hm? I guess that's as much as anyone could ask for. Still, I will wake Lizzy to assist you."

"There is no need." Aubrey swung her legs out from beneath the chair and slipped from the seat. "She worries over much, and I don't want to wake her."

"I believe it would be wise to inform her."

Aubrey raised her chin. She'd not back down from a man. Not anymore.

The corner of his mouth tipped on the other side. Was he laughing at her?

"I suppose once you've made up your mind, that's the end of it. If you believe you are steady enough, I will not bother your maid." He opened the kitchen door and let her proceed him. "What were you doing in the garden this time of night?"

Aubrey took a lamp in hand, then led him through the house. "Did you see the moon this evening? It was beautiful. I wanted to take a photograph of it reflecting off the water in the fountain pool."

"You were outside alone, in your nightgown, Mrs. Willot,

and you have no reason to believe the guards Madame brought with her are trustworthy."

The way he said it—and the surprise, perhaps annoyance, in his voice—told exactly how he felt. "I probably shouldn't have, but I'm tired of living in fear. Staying here, in this house alone. My pa wanted me to move back to Los Angeles, especially with it being so close to the baby's birth."

"I'm surprised he didn't force you to return with him."

"He could have, but he raised my brother and me to stand by our choices." Something she almost regretted, given how foolishly she had fallen for Louis.

"I'm sorry to have startled you outside."

"That was you?" That didn't make sense. The man who had hidden behind the fountain seemed different somehow. "What were you doing on that side of the garden?"

"I get restless at night. It's hard to stay still." He glanced at her from the side as they passed into the foyer. "You never did answer my question about this companion-guard business with Madame. Will it be me or someone else, Mrs. Willot?"

Aubrey set the lamp on a table, then walked to the door with him, the silver light from outside seeping through drawn curtains on either side of the front doors.

She drew in a deep breath, remembering how insistent Louis's mother had been that she get to have a say in the picking of Aubrey's wedding gown and then the music, vows, and honeymoon. At first, she'd said she wanted to help her new daughter, especially since Maman was dead. But then Madame had pushed in very slight ways, offering to help, saying Aubrey promised something when she could not remember it, or asking questions in such a way that Aubrey had to agree for fear of being rude. Well, not anymore. Madame was not pushing or tricking her into anything she didn't want to do. But the truth was, she didn't feel safe.

Mr. Reed waited for an answer, his arms crossed. "I will

leave if you prefer, but if you don't feel safe, you need to tell someone. The police, your pa." His voice grew deeper. "No one should have to live in fear in their own home. Don't sacrifice wisdom for politeness."

What a forward thing to say, yet he was right. She was afraid of being unkind, but the baby's welfare and her own were more important.

"Mrs. Willot?" He leaned closer, as though to gage her expression better.

"If it does not cause you too much discomfort, might you call me by my given name, as you do Lizzy?"

"You wish to be referred to the same as a servant?"

"If I cannot use my father's name, I would settle for Aubrey." She straightened her shoulders. "This is the West, after all, and much less proper than back East—or perhaps simply more genuine. It is not too terribly indecent, don't you think?" Considering she was standing in her wrapper, the question was almost laughable.

Mr. Reed nodded. "If you insist, I will, but your mother-in-law may not approve."

"Always, she disapproves. At least I get to choose how I earn her ire. Although I suppose such informality might cause hardship for you now that you are her employee."

Pressing his lips together, he nodded. Would he offer for her to call him by his Christian name, welcome her friendship? Meeting his gaze was difficult, so she focused on the knot she'd tied to keep her wrapper closed. He was tall, handsome, and brave. More, she felt drawn to him in a way she'd never felt. Likely, a side effect of his rescuing her. She couldn't really know if he was a good man. A safe man. She stepped back, needing space to breathe.

Blessedly, he did not offer for her to address him informally. Her stomach sank a little. *Nathan* was such a fine name, and it suited him well. She'd been a fool for insisting he refer to her in such a casual way, yet she wearied of living among strangers. Not having friends. But forming personal connections would put her at risk. It would be better to be alone, safe.

"May I call on you in the morning to inquire after your health, Miss Aubrey?" He offered her a handshake and squeezed gently, meeting her eyes in a way that warmed her cheeks.

"I suppose so."

"Tomorrow, then." He opened the front door, allowing in a breeze that cooled her cheeks, then he was gone.

She drew in a shaky breath, still focused on the door where last she'd seen him. *Nathan.* She dared not say his name out loud, but in her heart, she hugged it close. Perhaps they could be friends. Maybe more.

Except that she'd just agreed to having him as her companion, or was he her guard? Either way, it was a professional relationship. Like her and Mr. Ellsworth. She shivered at the thought, not liking to compare the two. Had she made a mistake in agreeing? Somehow, the way he'd spoken to her made her think she needed him. She did, right?

Sometimes Louis had made her feel that way. A smile that had barely touched her lips faded. Was she being foolish? Could she even tell the difference between a good man and a bad man?

A soft knock sounded.

Aubrey pulled the great door open a crack.

Through the slanting light, concern showed on Nathan's handsome face. "I grabbed your gun when you fell. Here it is." He handed it to her, butt first. "I am going around to get your camera, so if you see me back there, don't shoot."

Aubrey tried to smile, but her cheeks wouldn't budge.

"Oh, and Miss Aubrey, don't forget to lock the door."

She pushed the door shut and turned the lock. Oh, my. She'd practically closed the door in his face.

Perhaps that was best.

CHAPTER 9

Facing her mother-in-law across the breakfast table the next morning, Aubrey worked to keep her shoulders level. The scrape on her forehead earned a flick of eyebrows from Madame, but she'd yet to comment. Nathan had moved her camera inside last night. If she purchased supplies today, she'd have her shot developed by this evening. She pressed her lips to keep from smiling. If she told Madame what she felt happy about, the woman would likely criticize Aubrey. Such was the way of the Willots.

Madame Willot pursed fine rosy lips over a china cup, a waft of steam floating up alongside her nose. "My goodness, Aubrey, just look at that scratch. I really don't know how you can be so clumsy."

And there it was, the first dig of the day. "I stepped wrong outside and bumped into a column." She poured a stream of cream into her tea, fogging the amber liquid. "It is just a scratch."

Madame set the cup down with a rattle. "Your antics will see my grandchild born dead."

Cold settled through Aubrey, and she pinched the edge of

her napkin. The breakfast room was as clear as a crystal with windows on two sides letting in the bright morning light. A sideboard lined one wall, and upon its lovely oak surface sat an array of jams, jellies, baguettes, and freshly squeezed orange juice. A healthy, refreshing breakfast except for the conversation.

Aubrey had hoped that by waking early to go to town, she might spy out Mr. Watkins's studio and avoid her mother-in-law. If she was going to convince Mr. Ellsworth photography was worth investing in, she needed to research. She could not do that sitting at home. She'd not considered that her guest would require her attention.

Lizzy entered with her shoulders hunched and face red. She must be worried about her sister again. Aubrey needed to check on her maid and offer to help, but not in front of Madame. Cook tried to avoid Aubrey after an embarrassing run in they'd had when Louis was alive. Up until now, Aubrey hadn't minded, not wanting to face judgment from anyone. But would that rift now keep her from helping Lizzy's sister, Cook's daughter? She should make things right with Cook. The Bible advised reconciliation, but where could she even start? Neither Cook nor Aubrey had sinned against one another, but there was certainly a rift. *What can I do, Lord?*

A soft clearing of a throat brought Aubrey's attention back to her guest. Madame stirred sugar crystals into tea so white with cream it hardly resembled any steeped herb. "You need a guardian—that's what you need. Someone to keep you out of trouble. First, the bank robbery, and now you run into a post. I must say, pregnancy does cause a woman poor balance, but you have always been excessively clumsy…" She switched to French and complained about cabbage-headed young women, going so far as to mention Louis's name.

The strength left Aubrey's shoulders. She knew French but didn't even try to understand what was said. How had she ever thought she might be close to this woman? Madame complained as excessively as Louis had. Never mind that she'd been saved from the robbery or quickly recovered with a simple scratch on her forehead. It was not as though the mark needed stitching.

The baby stirred. Madame was her child's only living grandmother. She needed to do her best to get along with this woman. "I will be more careful. Perhaps Pa was right about me staying here by myself."

"And so far away from civilization. I never understood why Louis built this place out here instead of a fine mansion in the city."

Aubrey loved this location, just a few miles from San Francisco with the old orange orchard nearby. Louis had bought it, claiming the act that of love. One of many lies. No doubt it made an excellent hideout for his crew of ruffians.

She pulled the ruffles that bunched at the base of her belly. This green ensemble was the only day dress she had that fit her. The soft cotton ruffles tickled her jaw, and the lace under-sleeves settled delicately on her knuckles.

Just as soon as Madame stop talking, Aubrey would leave. First, to the studio, but a visit to a doctor was also in order. She'd not seen a midwife or medical professional since leaving Pa's home. Afterwards, she'd stop by one of the department stores to purchase items for the baby and look at a dress for herself. She might not need to, though, since the baby should arrive any day. It was a shame Maman was not alive to go with her.

"And what will you do once the child is born?" Madame Willot prattled on, stirring another spoon of sugar into her tea, as though that might sweeten her bitter tongue. "You have no mother to look after you, no one but that witless maid."

"Lizzy is far from witless." Aubrey couldn't keep the ire from her voice. "I don't know what I would do without her. She has been beyond helpful. More than that, she is my friend."

"Oh, friends with the maid." She laid her spoon on the linen napkin. "Americans have no understanding of social class."

Aubrey ground her teeth and looked out a window. Where was Nathan Reed now? Couldn't he swoop in and rescue her?

"I've had an idea, Aubrey." Madame Willot set down her cup and covered one of Aubrey's hands with her own. "Once the baby is born, provided he survives, you must come to New York."

Aubrey nearly choked, then washed down a bite of baguette with some tea. "You are moving to The States?"

"Well, I think I should. Claude says that living in Germany is an option, too, but I cannot live there now that my home is no longer a part of France. If we settled in America, New York would be the best place. I could purchase Louis's old house from the current owner and raise his son there, just as he wished."

Aubrey's insides froze just thinking of the mansion that had served as her prison.

Madame kept talking, her eyes bright and voice hopeful for the first time since she arrived. "Just think of the opportunities for the child. The East Coast is far better than out here. We would be your family, and perhaps you will meet some fine young man."

Be away from Pa and Jesse again? "But my family is here."

"Where?" Madame Willot spread her arms wide.

"In California, I mean. New York is across the nation. I could not easily visit them if I lived in the East."

"Aubrey, they are too far away to help you raise this baby. I know you love this house, but how long can you live here alone? Does your child not deserve the best in education and class? You wouldn't keep your own flesh and blood from a good life for sentimental reasons, would you?" She lifted one eyebrow high.

"Of course not. I only..." Was she being selfish? Surely, the big cities in the East would offer her child more opportunities. But Maman and Papa had wanted to move west to give her and Jesse something new and unspoiled by civilization. Hadn't they?

The light tap of Lizzy's knock drew her away from sad memories. The woman had been moving in and out of the room without sound until now. Accepting the lifeline for what it was, Aubrey answered, "Come," at the exact moment Madame Willot bid the maid speak.

Lizzy stepped in wearing her new apron with her hair in a lovely braided bun.

Aubrey smiled, and the flash in her friend's eyes told her she noticed, though her face remained professional. "Mr. Reed to see you, ma'am."

Madame Willot smiled. "Show him—"

"Tell him I will greet him shortly in the foyer." Aubrey spoke over her mother-in-law, her cheeks burning at such impertinent behavior, but she had to take a stand somehow. As Lizzy bobbed a curtsy and departed, Aubrey faced the older woman. "Forgive me, Mother Willot, but I was just going out when you joined me. I will greet Mr. Reed and then be on my way."

Madame tapped her chin. "He seems like a fine, strong man. A natural protector."

Pushing back her chair, Aubrey gave her mother-in-law a patient smile. "Is that why you hired him to guard me?"

"You know?"

"Yes, ma'am. He told me. Why didn't you, though?"

Madame stood as well, her bustled black skirt nearly taking out a chair when she quickly turned to follow Aubrey. "For the very same reasons that I stated. You are not safe and do not possess the sense to see that."

"Not safe because of men like Emil. He is the only one to ever pose a threat to me." If one did not count Madame's quick-tempered son.

"Emil is a fool. He cannot hurt you from prison."

"But he wants to? You met with him on your way here. I imagine he ranted over the injustice of my going free, and my brother too."

"As I said yesterday, I visited him to aid him in his hardship." Her cheeks darkened and brow furrowed. "He is my husband's son and Claude's only surviving heir, currently." She glanced at Aubrey's belly. "If you do not take care, if something happens to our grandchild, all will be lost."

A coldness snaked down Aubrey's spine. She would take care of her baby, but what about after he or she was born? If they moved to New York, what influence might Louis's father have on her child's rearing?

"You are a wealthy woman. Beautiful too." Madame slowed her step down the hall, clasping Aubrey's arm gently and giving Lizzy time to rush ahead toward the foyer doors. "It is not uncommon for a woman of your station to be escorted by a coachman. Since yours is a fragile old man who is likely as close to the grave as he is his next meal, I insist you have a guard."

Anger ignited a spark in her breast, and Aubrey drew up short to face Madame. Regardless of the fact that Mr. Dobbs was aging and Nathan driving would give her and her foolish heart space from him, Madame's bullying chafed. "You insist?" Her voice sounded much harder than she intended.

Madame pursed her lips, her nostrils flaring. "I insist on your safety, and my grandchild is of the utmost importance."

"I appreciate—"

"I chose Mr. Reed because of his heroics in the bank and

because you seem to trust him." Her mask of anger broke, and Madame closed her eyes, a tear escaping down one cheek. "Please, Aubrey, the baby is all I have left."

Heart softening, Aubrey reached for Madame's hand.

The woman startled, then relaxed, offering her a shaky smile.

Aubrey inclined her head, then the two of them turned to the foyer to meet Nathan. She'd not meant to bring Madame to such a state of grief, only wished to set a boundary. She didn't like Madame hiring a guard for her. Somehow she'd failed to draw that line, yet pushing now, with Madame in an emotional state and the foyer and Nathan so near, was not wise. Her heart ached for the mother, regardless of how ruthless her son had been. Was connecting with her mother-in-law worth the risk of Monsieur Claude Willot's possible influence on her child's life? Was he as dangerous as his sons? Likely.

In the foyer, Aubrey nearly stopped short at the sight of Nathan. Dark rings framed his eyes, and though his shirt was pressed and his face shaved, his pallor was concerning. "Mr. Reed."

She paused at hearing the gentleness in her tone, though it was too late. His gaze locked onto her, then dropped to her belly, of all places. Likely, he was assessing the state of her health and that of the baby's.

"Good morning, sir." She curtsied a bit awkwardly, with Madame doing the same—only, regally.

Nathan inclined his head. "Good morning, ladies."

"Aubrey has agreed to accept you as her guard." Madame raised her chin, her gaze fierce. "I trust you will protect her with your life."

"Madame." Aubrey clasped her hands together. What Nathan must think of her hyperbolic statement. "I hardly think my life is in danger. I am simply running errands."

"One cannot be too careful." Madame barely spared her a glance before whisking away without so much as a good day.

So much for the French being polite. She shook her head yet stilled under Nathan's gaze. "Madame is exaggerating, of course. Rest assured, Mr. Reed, this job will be uneventful. I only agreed to this arrangement to ease her mind. She is grieving and is a worry-prone person."

He nodded, then gestured toward the door, his movements tense. "Your barouche is waiting outside."

When he opened the door, Aubrey glimpsed Lizzy slip Mr. Dobbs an envelope. He was nodding as though agreeing to something. The maid scurried away, avoiding eye contact, and Mr. Dobbs opened the carriage door. Rather than inform him that Nathan would drive her into town, since Lizzy obviously trusted the coachman and not Aubrey with her secret message, Aubrey preceded Nathan into the open-topped carriage with the canopy providing shade. The opposite seat was in the hot sun, but she sensed he would move there and bear the heat rather than take the place of honor beside her.

"The forward seat will get little shade on the ride into town." She arranged her skirts as best she could with her great walrus-belly forcing her to lean back. "Please, take the place beside me."

He flashed lovely blue eyes at her before lowering onto the bench seat. His presence, like the scent of oranges that often clung to him, clouded around her so her throat tightened and pulse raced. How silly, even juvenile, such a feeling. Here he was all beautiful masculinity and fierceness, and she could rival an elephant for size. She folded her hands in her lap, doing her best at the serene ladylike pose she'd learned at finishing school. The moment the barouche lurched into motion, her head went back with the slight force, and she resisted the urge to lean back and sleep. Oh, yes, she was very serene, like the blubbery sea lions that napped in the sun on the beaches.

How could she last the day at his side without making a complete fool of herself? What if she fell asleep and drooled on herself? The horror of the thought. Aubrey peered over the side of the coach, but dash it all, her gaze wandered back to Nathan. He stared straight ahead, his jaw set and brow firm. Why had she ever thought she'd garnered his interest? He'd been so sincere that day at the bank and last night, but that could have been genuine concern. Had she lost the ability to decipher friendship from attraction because of her experience with Louis? What a shame Mr. Dobbs had not stayed home. She was sure to make a complete fool of herself.

CHAPTER 10

As the barouche bounced along the busy cobblestone streets of San Francisco, Aubrey rested her head on the back of her seat and let the world roll by. The structures in the Golden Gate City were massive, as though made for over-sized kings. When they passed one of the many grand hotels, Aubrey turned to Mr. Reed. "Did you know that the first floor of the Occidental Hotel has thirty-foot ceilings?"

He simply nodded.

Since she wasn't comfortable seeing a doctor with him in tow and he would likely dread shopping the department stores, they simply drove. The city was beautiful, the buildings as grand as those in heaven might be. Or perhaps more like Babel of the Bible. People rushed here and there, in carts, buggies, and fancy carriages like her own. A trolley rolled by dinging its bell, a handful of boys hanging out the back and waving.

None of it seemed to faze the stoic, hard-browed Nathan Reed, who stared from the canopy of the barouche as though attending a funeral. He had only reacted when they went by St. Patrick's Church on Mission Street. Even then, he looked to be in pain, his shoulders bowed slightly. What troubled him?

When they passed The Bank of California, Aubrey, exasperated with the silence, said, "Did you know that Billy Ralston, the president of the bank, has commissioned Mr. Wilkins to collaborate with artist George H. Burgess to composite a pastiche photograph of Mr. Ralston and the board of directors?"

Nathan blinked, the vagueness in his eyes slipping away. "What is a pastiche?"

"In this instance, it refers to taking the individual portraits of the board members—over forty of them—and combining them to make one large group photograph."

"Sounds like quite a feat."

"To be sure." She could not resist a smile. After all, the photography industry was growing in leaps and bounds. What might be invented next?

Nathan calmly smiled, a breeze fluttering the hair over his brow. "I think I would prefer to see mountains and streams than people."

Like the peaceful days she'd spent at Gray's Lake with Pa, Maman, and Jesse. "I feel the same way, though I prefer when photographs have people or animals in them."

He met her eyes, though his piercing blue gaze proved difficult for her to hold. The passing shadows of the buildings alternated with sun rays across his strong physique.

"Mr. Reed?"

He raised his eyebrows. "So you want me to call you by your given name, yet you insist on calling me 'Mr. Reed.'"

It wasn't a question, so when he turned his gaze away, Aubrey let it be. She would not tell him how much she'd like that, not when he was on Madame's payroll. There was also the matter of Louis's illegitimate child hanging between them. Aubrey had forgotten that sad business when Madame came to town. Her heart was further deflated. If she could just go back to the chateau, hide away in the study, or crawl into bed and cover her head. Then she'd be safe.

She forced in a breath, that old familiar grip squeezing her chest, as it often had when Louis was alive. No. She was going to be brave. Louis couldn't win. He was gone and she was stronger. She'd planned to have a grand day, gathering supplies for her photography and seeing Mr. Watkins's studio. She turned promptly to Nathan. "I was thinking of going by 24 Montgomery Street."

"What's there?"

Warmth bubbling up inside her, she giggled.

He cocked an eyebrow, eyes narrowed slightly as the corners of his mouth quirked. A chuckle left his lips an instant before he told the driver to take them to her desired destination.

When Nathan helped her down from the barouche outside looming, four-story structures that cast shadows upon them, Aubrey's heels sounded on the boardwalk. The title sprawled across a building in bold letters—*Yosemite Art Gallery. Mr. Carleton Watkins's Photography Studio.*

Tall glass windows mirrored the busy street and the pair of them, Nathan standing so strong beside her. He moved synchronously with her to the door, and they entered together.

A clerk welcomed them with a grand smile, though his attention was on the patrons before the front desk, so Aubrey and Nathan perused the inventory in silence. Different types of cameras were on display. Photograph albums lay open on tables with chairs clustered around. More photographs lined the walls, displaying Mr. Watkins's Yosemite shots. There were various sizes, in sepia tones or black and white. Aubrey selected an orange stereoview card with dual matching photographs on it. It was about the size of a postcard. Might Jesse like to see it? She could send it to him, but her brother was probably too busy with his new girl to even care. Avoiding an inner ache,

Aubrey moved instead to the next display. She should be happy for him, and she was, but seeing them together—so obviously in love—reminded her of what she never had.

"Look at this one." Nathan spoke quietly as he perused scenic views of the California and Nevada wilderness. "'Pompompasos, Three Brothers, Yosemite.'" He read the title of the print featuring three mountaintops clustered together as a group of boys might lean on each other when posing for a picture.

She and Nathan moved down the line, picking out their favorite small cards with the photographs.

A burly man of about forty passed the clerk and other patrons, approaching them with a smile and handshake. "Good'ay, Madame and sir. I am Mr. Carleton Watkins."

He possessed a mature bearing and neatly trimmed beard. He certainly looked as though he could head into the mountains with a camera and survival pack, though his frock coat was pressed and clean.

Nathan extended his hand. "Nathan Reed, and this is Miss Aubrey Willot."

"I am pleased to make your acquaintance." As Aubrey also shook Mr. Watkins's hand, his calluses teased the soft fabric of her gloves. "Mr. Reed and I recently saw one of your photographs at the Bank of California and wished to view more."

"Well, here we are, ma'am. You may look to your heart's content." He gestured to the walls all covered with landscape scenes.

Unable to contain herself, she grinned and drifted along the side of the room with him and Nathan. The men discussed technique and how Mr. Watkins's methods had changed as the process of development did. Nathan, it seemed, knew a thing or two about the mechanics of cameras and science of developing.

The scenic photographs Aubrey passed were like windows

into new worlds. Majestic and breathtaking, even with the two-tone images. What would it be like to offer such lovely representations to the public as Mr. Watkins did? Places hidden away such as Gray's Lake. Only, no one except her family would want such a photograph. Gray's was a humble lake, after all, that just happened to be a good stopping point when they traveled in the summer with Father. And yet, when summer storms swept through, flashing lighting across the rugged hillsides, the place was otherworldly. Photographing the lightning would be an amazing feat. What a shame she and Jesse had not taken more pictures on trips while Maman was alive.

Aubrey had selected a handful of miniature stereoviews when Mr. Watkins turned a smile on her. Remembering Mr. Ellsworth's challenge to her desire to invest in photography, she said, "I am researching photography as a possible investment. What kinds of jobs do you do as a photographer?"

"Some of my latest projects include photographing the properties of rich investors. It is cheaper for them to pay me to photograph these places than to go there themselves." Mr. Watkins rubbed his chin. "The studio is doing pretty well, especially when tourists flock to the city. One might go to the beaches and offer to take photographs there."

He glanced downward so briefly, she almost missed it. Like so many others, he probably thought she should be at home. And she would be, for the baby's sake, but she'd not stay there forever. Besides, if she was going to invest, she wanted to put money into something special.

She squared her shoulders. "How did you come to open the studio?"

"Well, as with many in this area, I tried my hand at mining but found this work more to my taste. It takes capital and credit to open a studio—and of course, the inventory." He swept a hand toward the hundreds of photographs.

"Mrs. Willot is a photographer herself." Nathan crossed his

arms as he focused keenly on her. "In fact, she has a big old camera, an American Optical, I believe."

Mr. Watkins raised his eyebrows. "That is a good brand. I would love to see your work sometime, Mrs. Willot."

Aubrey smiled, her cheeks warming. "I could bring them here, if you'd like."

"Of course. You might put them on inventory in my studio if they are of high quality."

Her face grew even hotter. What if they weren't good quality and he thought her fanciful? Aubrey shrugged away those doubts. "I don't know if they are or not, but I would welcome your critique."

Mr. Watkins nodded, and Aubrey could hardly contain her smile.

Once she and Nathan had picked out a small box of twelve stereoviews, they put their coins together and purchased them.

Mr. Watkins bid them a good day, and they stepped out into the light. Nathan settled her hand in the crook of his arm. Hard lines carved his features when he trained his gaze down the street to where a man two buildings down ducked into a doorway, though he seemed to have been looking at her. Her stomach tightened. "I wonder who that is. Was he watching us?"

"Possibly." He opened the door to the carriage. "Do you recognize him?"

"No. Do you?"

"No." He stepped between her and the man as though to shield her.

She paused before the carriage door. "Perhaps he recognized me. We are close to the bank."

"Why would he?"

"My late husband worked at the bank, and people are prone to gossip." She lowered her voice despite the racket of the busy city. "I am the widow of a convict."

Nathan winced. "Forgive me. I forgot."

Aubrey resisted the urge to thank him. Too often, she felt as though she was defined solely as the spouse of a criminal. The papers had been filled with gossip when Louis was arrested, and Aubrey herself made the society pages when she moved to the chateau. Louis's illegitimate child might suffer in the same way if her mother's family did not protect him or her. Aubrey would have to warn them. Tempted to ask Nathan when she might connect with them, she sat back against the carriage seat. She would give them time to come forward to see her, and in the meantime, just take care of herself and her baby.

❧

A few days later, her backache unrelenting, Aubrey ventured deeper into the house than she'd gone since the first morning there. Going for a walk had been a mistake. The pressure was even greater. Perhaps she should do stretches as Madame suggested the evening before at dinner.

Louis had built a true mansion. Her feet skimmed across polished hardwood when she entered the dark ballroom at the very rear of the house. When she pulled back a ceiling-to-floor curtain, light speared into the space with white beams so bright, she squinted. Able to breathe a little better as the dimness fled, Aubrey leaned against the glass as she looked out.

The yard stretched away before her. The veranda off the lady's drawing room—one of her favorite spots—faced the garden to her right. Just beyond lay the master study. A shadow crept past the window. Aubrey frowned. Was someone in there? Lizzie had dusted just yesterday.

Another movement caught her eye. One of Madame's behemoth guards strode up a garden path, over the veranda, and entered the door without knocking.

Abandoning her window, Aubrey hastened across the room

and made her way to the hall. What were they thinking, going into the study? Not even Madame should be there without Aubrey.

Once she reached the door, Aubrey paused to listen. Voices sounded on the other side—male, then that of a woman. After turning the knob slowly, Aubrey pushed the door ajar. Blessedly, Lizzy was an exceptional housekeeper, and the hinges made no sound, so Aubrey could hear someone speaking in French.

"Nonsense, Camus." Madame stood before the desk, her hands on her hips as she faced two of her guards. "Louis was no fool. He would have taken diligent care of it."

Her words made little sense, but Aubrey had no time to ponder before the guard named Camus spotted her. He raised his thick black eyebrows, and Madame turned.

"Aubrey, my dear, there you are." She approached with a smile, though her voice had been strained.

What was she trying to hide?

Madame wrapped her arms around Aubrey, the embrace as clumsy as a clammy handshake.

Aubrey pulled back slightly. "What are you doing in my study?"

Madame wrinkled her nose. "Why, looking for you, of course."

Her guards stood unblinking, Camus with his straight, frail-looking features set in a distasteful frown while his shorter companion sneered. His gray mustache contrasted with his iron-black hair and eyebrows.

"No, you were not. You said that Louis had taken care of *it*. Are you looking for something?"

"I simply said that my son was diligent to take good care of this house." She turned her head to the side, touching her chest below her collarbone. "This is the last place I saw Louis, as I was merely reminiscing."

"This is my home. You may not come and go into rooms as you please." She directed her remark toward the guards as well.

Madame gasped, then huffed. "Well, I never thought... Aubrey, I was only trying to find you. I have planned an overnight trip to the beach and will leave today, and I want you to go with me. I will be staying at a hotel that overlooks the Golden Gate Strait. Wouldn't it be lovely, waking up to the Pacific in the morning?"

And while she was out, the guards would search her house. Perhaps find the secret room. It had been years since Aubrey had been down there. Hadn't Louis said there was a back door of sorts? What if someone snuck into the house through a hidden outer door she didn't know about because she was too scared to venture down those dark stairs?

Madame still waited, as did her sneering guards.

Aubrey was all alone. Not even Nathan was here, though he'd stayed with her most of yesterday evening even though she told him it was unnecessary. Where was he now?

Taking a deep breath, she folded her hands. "I don't believe traveling so far this late in the pregnancy would be wise."

Madame released a soft breath and cocked an eyebrow. "It is only to the beach. My goodness, you were gone for hours with Mr. Reed the other day. How did you feel afterward?"

She had not known how much she needed to get out of the suffocating house. Seeing the Yosemite Studio, believing for a moment there was some kind of future ahead—well, she'd felt alive.

"Aubrey?" Madame adjusted her lace collar when it fluttered on a breeze coming through the window. "Dear, I know I am not the most genteel of women, but I do care for you. An outing will bring us closer in this hard time."

Aubrey met a gaze as icy blue as Louis's had been, her insides cold and not warming at the seemingly heartfelt words. She couldn't trust herself to accurately gage Madame's sincerity, so she'd remain aloof and alone. She was safer alone.

Mouth once again pulled tight, Madame spared her guards a glance. "Camus, Grange, you may leave."

They moved at her command, showing just how much control Madame possessed.

Aubrey gripped her fists and glared at the retreating guards. "Stay out of my study. You are not welcome here, nor anywhere in my private rooms." She turned on Madame. "This is not a hotel. I live here. You may not come and go as you please."

Madame's nostrils flared. "Well, I never... Louis would be ashamed of you, treating his mother like...like a hotel patron."

The door closed behind Madame's minions, so Aubrey focused on her mother-in-law. "Louis would not permit anyone to enter this house and wander from room to room. I should not have to defend myself. Propriety dictates one does not treat a host with such little regard."

"I am his mother—"

"But this is my house."

For a moment, Madame looked as though she was ready to argue the point, then she stormed from the room in a flurry of black crepe ruffles.

Aubrey drew in a deep breath and moved to her favorite spot in the study, the sofa before the fireplace. She sank to one of the velvet-covered cushions, her hand trembling when she placed it on her chest. What was Madame thinking, moving about Aubrey's home as though it were her own? She had not come to the States to visit Louis during the duration of their marriage, yet she behaved as though she were here to take possession of his things. Turning Madame away, insisting she stay in one of the hotels in the city, would be terribly inhospitable, yet Aubrey wished she could do just that. Hopefully, Madame would spend the next couple days at the waterfront and leave Aubrey in peace.

There was a knock on the door, firm and strong. Had one of Madame's guards returned? It sounded again, then the door opened. Nathan stepped inside, taller and broader than she remembered. His gaze sliced through the room, then landed on her and softened.

"Mr. Reed." She released a breath she'd not realized she held. So great was her relief that she closed her eyes and held her hand over them.

"Miss Aubrey?" He spoke so near, he must have knelt in front of her.

The tightening in her chest warned her of tears. She drew in a deep breath and lowered her hand. "I am so glad you are here."

"What happened?" There was steeliness to his voice that steadied her nerves.

"Madame and her guards were in here. I had to make them leave." She lifted her chin, a burst of pride allowing the slightest of smiles.

"What were they doing?"

"Nothing. Talking. Madame said something about Louis."

He angled his head to one side, his eyebrows lowering. "What about him?"

"I don't know. One of the guards noticed me just after that."

"Think back, Miss Aubrey. What exactly did she say?"

My goodness, he was stern. It was not as though Madame harbored some secret regarding Louis. Then again, she couldn't accurately make that call. Emil had tried to force her to open one of Louis's safes when he'd kidnapped her, likely hoping riches were within. Was Madame here to steal from her too? "I entered quietly. Madame had stood by the desk, the guards to her right." She pointed to where they'd stood. "She said that Louis was not a fool and would have taken care of something. What do you think she meant?"

"I don't know." He went to the desk, asking to open the

drawers but finding little once Aubrey gave him permission. After studying the area around the desk and then checking the window to make sure the latch was secure, he moved to sit beside her. Elbows resting on his knees and a curl of hair slipping over his forehead, he seemed to take in all of the room. "The Willot brothers have a reputation as career criminals in these parts, but that doesn't mean Madame is." He gazed at her over one thick shoulder. "Is she?"

"I cannot say." Aubrey hardly knew Madame, having only met her when she came to the States for the wedding.

The baby gave a great stretch, and Aubrey covered the spot that felt as though her skin might break with a little limb coming through. She rubbed circles on her belly, calming the babe.

"I don't like those guards being here with you and the baby." Nathan rested his chin on the knuckles of his folded hands, not even looking at her.

What was he thinking? His nose sloped straight down, clean and neat. Such a fine face, not too stern or square but neither were his features angular. Nathan's coloring, features and temperament were level, calm...a comfort. He was strong but not fierce.

He turned blue eyes on her, not icy blue like Louis's but the calm blue of the ocean at twilight. "Miss Aubrey?" Nathan inclined his head as though he'd already spoken to her.

"Yes?"

"Would you like to speak with the police?"

She sighed, rubbing circles on her belly. "What good could that do?" She'd tried reaching out to the police in New York when she'd realized Louis would make a habit of striking her, only to be told to go home and mind her husband.

"They might know something about her guards. If any of them have criminal history, you would know and have reason to tell Madame to send them away since you are not comfortable doing so now."

"She is my mother-in-law."

"Is that a no?"

Aubrey hadn't an answer. The truth was, she didn't want Madame there at all. She too often brought Louis to mind, and she was unkind. Was that a good enough reason to throw out one's own family? She shook her head, the baby's fluttering movement reminding her she was looking out for someone else. They had to be safe. If someone got into the secret room, they could come upon her without her knowledge.

There on the bookshelf to the right of the fireplace, the third shelf up, was the hidden latch. "Mr. Reed, I need your help with something."

If anyone was going to help her, it would be him. Aubrey rose, crossed the room, and worked the latch. The door swung forward. Light from the study shone into the doorway where cobwebs clung to the corners and stairs led down into darkness. "Would you mind checking this room for me?"

He approached the door, not showing any surprise, as though it merely led to the hallway. When he took the first step, he looked back, offering her a hand. "Are you coming?" He'd barely uttered the words when those of someone else sounded from the other side of the study door.

A stream of French words came from the hall—something about the beach.

She stepped forward, Nathan moving farther down to make room for her, and then she closed them into darkness.

CHAPTER 11

No sooner had the secret door fit into place than Madame's voice filled the room. "Aubrey?"

She backed away instinctively, only to find the edge of the step. Nathan's hands slid around her ribs, steadying her, then letting go. He moved down another step yet held onto one of her arms as though to reassure her. Eyes unseeing in the darkness, a tingle crawled up her back. The stairs behind them waited like a black abyss, ready to swallow her whole. She wavered, feeling pulled in that direction, yet straightened to lean closer to the door.

"Where are you?" Madame sounded confused, almost hurt.

"I told you, missus. Miss Aubrey is not here." Lizzy replied rather defensively.

"She was just here."

"Miss Aubrey is probably resting. You have no business busting in here and bothering her, and in her fragile state too."

"How dare you!" Madame's shout sent a jolt through Aubrey, though Nathan gently squeezed her elbow, reminding her she was safe. "*I* am mistress in this house. I give the orders, not that stupid girl my son married. I told Louis she was too fanciful, but of course, he had to wed his weak, simpering American bride."

"Mrs. Willot is not—"

"That son of mine, with his notions of America." Madame continued, her voice ebbing, then flowing as though she paced or turned her head from side to side. "The new country. He only married Aubrey because she was in a family way, you know, and then the fool girl lost that babe. She will likely be the death of this babe as well, if I don't do something about her."

Aubrey stood frozen, Nathan's warmth doing nothing to thaw the betrayal gripping her heart. Why had that woman spewed such evil thoughts? Aubrey had conducted herself appropriately through her courtship with Louis. The loss she'd experienced so soon after marriage had shocked her to such a degree that she hadn't considered some people might judge her early pregnancy to be the result of promiscuity.

Nathan clasped her more firmly. She wavered, turning to him and shaking her head. "My baby..." She only managed to whisper before memories assailed her. She'd been alone in that big house back East when the pains started. All night, she'd felt them but refused to tell anyone. After all, the pains might stop, and then all would be well. When the maid woke her and found Aubrey on bloodied sheets, she'd alerted the whole house, and Aubrey had had to face the bitter truth. Her womb was soon to be as empty as her arms.

Hands covering her face, she hung her head and found Nathan's shoulder. He rubbed her back, one arm around her, steadying her as her mother-in-law threw all kinds of insults out upon her exit.

In the dark, Aubrey tried to find a way through the mire. She was sinking into numbness. Alone. Except for the gentle nudging in her middle and the man embracing her. He paused as though holding his breath. Had he felt her baby move?

"They've gone." He spoke near a whisper.

"I was nineteen when Louis came into my life. My mother had just died, and I was lonely, but I never misbehaved with him. Why would she say something so unkind?" A sob caught in her throat.

Nathan nudged her chin up with his thumb. A stream of light poured in through one of the cracks in the secret door to glow softly on his face. "You owe me no explanation, Miss Aubrey, but if it helps, I believe you."

"Thank you." She wiped away tears. "I also did not lose my first child because of some foolish escapade. That was entirely Louis's fault. He was running a phaeton far too fast and flipped it." Though her pains had not come until two days afterward, the doctor said it was a result of the accident. "I told him to slow down. He never listened to me." And she had been the fool who could not stand up for herself and demand he stop or let her off. She should have been stronger.

For a moment, it was all Aubrey could do to hold herself upright and not lean all the way into Nathan's embrace. But she resisted, not wanting to rely on someone other than herself or God to be strong.

He moved down another step, allowing her to gain her balance on her own. "You have a secret room?" A smile sounded in his voice.

Grateful that his random question put an end to the painful topic of conversation, she sniffed. "I do."

"What on earth does a woman like you do in a secret room?"

"A woman like me?"

His voice faded as though he'd glanced away. "Well, you hit that robber over the head with a gun and nearly laid me out in the process, yet you're as petite as a kitten. Now you have a lair. You're not a spy or something...?"

Snickering into the darkness, she shook her head as he took her hand. "I don't know if I should scold you for comparing me to an animal or call you childish for such fictitious imaginings as espionage."

"You have a point. I've had too much time in the wild with animals and read too many dime novels about secret agents." A *thud* correlated with Nathan's intake of breath. "Ouch."

"If my memory serves me correctly, there is a doorway at the bottom of the stairs."

"Thank you for warning me."

Smiling despite the very pitch black, Aubrey moved around him. "There should be a lamp on the wall. It's a gas lamp installed with the rest of the house."

A match fizzed to life, casting light that forced her to squint. Nathan lit the gas lamp, and Aubrey stepped into the room, the dusty scent different from what she remembered. A desk sat on one side, but other than that, the space was empty of furniture. The floor was bare, as were the walls where once hung a grand painting of ships at sea and storms. Aubrey walked forward, past the desk. On the wall were two bells in levers such as she'd seen in the kitchen and servants' quarters for when one of the family needed to summons a servant for help. Why would Louis want a signal here? Who would have signaled him? She ran her finger along the dusty rim of one. "I wonder what this goes to. Perhaps it is rigged to ring at a certain time such as when someone opens the study door."

Nathan shrugged. He stood in the corner opposite the desk where a pile of unmarked crates of a good size sat. "Makes sense he would want to know when someone was coming."

"That sounds like something he would do. He was very suspicious." She walked into the middle of the room. "Odd, that it is so empty. Louis had his favorite things arranged here before moving in. A desk from his father. Two large chairs with lion heads on the armrests. A grandfather clock that played a sweet song."

Who would have cleaned it out when Louis had been taken

to jail? She ran one finger across the desk surface, gathering dust on the tip. Had Emil overseen the transition before finding himself in jail as well? There had been a six-month gap between their arrests. If so, where were Louis's belongings? A number of things had been sold off to pay debts, as Mr. Ellsworth had reminded her. Did someone else know about this room? Someone from Louis's past? She drew in a deep breath, searching for an outer door. There wasn't one.

"There should be a door leading outside." She ventured farther in, her shadow cast long across the floor. "It's so strange. I've never seen this room so empty."

"You've been here before?" A streak of dust from the lamp marred Nathan's cheek.

"Yes. Just before we were married. Nothing mysterious. I thought it would be fun to have a secret room with tunnels that led to the other parts of the house, but he was always practical. Louis simply used it as a study. He must have had everything moved out at some point, but I have no idea when." She turned in a circle. "There used to be a safe behind the desk."

A muscle ticked in Nathan's jaw. "Does a wife typically not know such goings on in her own home?"

"I don't know. I lived in New York for most of our wedded years. Louis was gone often." And how she grew to dread his visits...his confirmation that despite all her attempts to make the house a home, to have another child, to impress his friends, she would fall short of his extremely high standards.

"We stayed in this house last August." When Louis, in an attempt to convince her of his love, had moved her to her dream house. It had only taken a few weeks to learn how loveless her marriage truly was. "We went from here to Salt Lake City. Louis was arrested in November. Soon after, my pa moved me to his house."

"In San Francisco?"

"No." She walked to the crates and ran her hand over the

smooth edges. "He lives in Los Angeles. I found out that Louis had died in June and decided to move here."

He came to her side and inspected the crates as though he avoided her gaze. "Why move here?"

"Because...this is *my* house." Her tone came out harsher than she'd expected. She heaved a sigh, her shoulders sinking. "He built this house for me when we were wed. I thought we would live here. Have children. Grow old together. He moved all my things here, but after our honeymoon, we went to New York, and that is where I stayed until last year. Sometimes he was here. Sometimes in his Utah house."

A bar and hammer lay on the floor—likely, for prying the crates open. She squatted, holding her breath when the baby pressed deep into her ribs.

No sooner had her hands closed around the tools than Nathan assisted her to stand, though she did not really need it.

She handed the heavy instruments to him. "Will you please open these crates?"

Rather than answer, he took charge of them and popped the first couple boards off, then he went to another crate. The lamp on the wall flickered. Hopefully, it would last a while longer.

She cleared away mounds of cotton to find a photograph of a fluffy kitten. Aubrey gasped and lifted it up. "Victoria."

Nathan paused to peer at her, but she had already set the likeness aside. There were more photographs of their home in Los Angeles, Maman and Papa standing near the white gazebo at Grandmother Alexander's home in Baltimore, Jesse in a library with lights streaming in, and the mare she'd had before marrying Louis. "These are my things."

Nathan lifted a stereoview of Aubrey and her friends dressed for a school dance.

"These things...I packed them when I moved from Papa's house before I married Louis. I had forgotten about them." She dug deeper into the crate, which was stacked on top of an identical one so the edge cut into her arms. Inside, she found stacks of photographs she and Jesse had developed.

Nathan, having finished with the other of the crates that was stacked on the top, set aside the tools to peer over her shoulder at a scenic shot she'd taken. "You really are good."

"I hope Mr. Watkins thinks so."

The light grew faint so quickly, Aubrey groaned. "The lamp must be in need of a cleaning. Here, will you carry some of these for me?" She handed him an armload of photographs.

"Yes. I can just get another lamp, though, and move all this into your study."

"That would be wonderful." The light flickered, and like the blinking of an eye, Aubrey remembered her husband crossing the room to a painting which he moved away to reveal a hidden door.

The painting was gone now, but in the spot where it had hung behind the desk and chair was a noticeable difference in the striped wallpaper. "What is that?" She walked to it.

Nathan set down the photographs and came to inspect the wall. He ran his fingers over the stripes, knocking before he unsheathed a knife from his belt. The light blinked, then went out.

"Mr. Reed?" Aubrey stepped forward, one hand extended.

"I'm here." There was a scraping, then the creak of hinges told her he'd found the door. "It's another secret passage."

"Lead the way."

He did, catching up her hand in a tangle of tough, strong fingers.

She followed him into the darkness.

"Should have brought a lamp from the study." He sneezed. "Sure is dusty."

A giggle caught in her throat. He could light a match, but to walk with it, he'd have to shelter the flame, which meant letting her go. They didn't really need light.

There was a loud thump, then Nathan grunted. A door jiggled and light poured in. Fresh air rushed past them along with the scent of honeysuckle and the trilling of a bird's song.

Squinting, Aubrey took in the greenery all around them.

Nathan shouldered his way through the opening, taking the claws of the branches across his arms. They emerged outside. There was the white gazebo she'd had erected for how much she loved the one in Grandmother Alexander's garden back in Baltimore. Her own garden was just around the corner of the house, its hedges barely visible.

"I guess your husband wanted a way out of the house unnoticed." Nathan released her, looking around.

Aubrey's heart sank. Out here in the daylight, she couldn't allow Nathan to take her hand and guide her. Out here, in the shadow of the towering chateau, she was simply the pitiful, pregnant Widow Willot clutching a few old photographs in hopes of doing something meaningful with them.

When Nathan glanced at her, looking for direction, she pointed to the master bedroom. Many of her things had been stored there when she moved here, though she'd refused to stay there, preferring a quaint guest room on the eastern side of the house. "Here is the veranda."

Aubrey scurried ahead of him to the ladies' drawing room. The French doors were unlocked. Inside, the elegant creams, pastel pinks, and seafoam green reminded her of the cherry blossoms in Central Park and of her youth. The heat of the room pricked her skin.

Nathan stepped through the doorway behind her, the heels of his boots knocking on the hardwood floors until he reached the rug. "Warm in here. Why are the curtains drawn?"

Aubrey joined him there, setting the armload of photographs on the table, then lowering herself to the settee.

"Last time I was here, I asked that the curtains always be open. I like the light."

He sat beside her and loosened his bandana around his neck, revealing an inch more of smooth skin. "Mr. Watkins didn't know what he was asking when he offered to consign some of your work. If the rest of your work is this good, you might set up your own studio." His voice filled with awe as he peered at the photographs.

"You think so? I mean, it's not just some fanciful hobby. Starting a real business is risky." As Mr. Ellsworth had warned her.

"Most things in life of value take risk." He held a print up and grinned. "The moon? And what is this?" He chose another and lifted it. "A cat?"

"Victoria, a kitten I rescued when I was a girl. She ran away."

"You've got a good handle on lighting and clarity. There is no way you could have photographed such a large selection if you had not." He tapped one she and Jesse had taken from a bridge. "How long have you been taking photographs?"

"I started when I still lived at home, but until the other night, I hadn't taken any in years. I need to set up a dark room."

"Your secret room would make a good dark room. It's not like the days when you have to develop right away. The gelatin-coated dry plates can be saved and developed later."

"Aha, so you are not just an admirer of photographs. You know the science of developing too."

"I do." He cleared his throat "I have an interest in photography and the methods used."

"You do?"

"I can take apart and put back a camera fast as lightening."

Her cheeks bunched in a smile. "I would like to see that." Face growing hotter and unable to hold his gaze, Aubrey went to open the doors.

She stood on the threshold, her arms crossed and resting on her belly. The breeze was subtle, carrying with it the faint scent of hydrangeas.

Nathan rose, rubbing his palms on his dark canvas pants. "I have an appointment in town in an hour or so. Will you be safe, or would you prefer to come with me?"

"Let us see if Madame has left and which of her guards she takes." She settled on a window seat for the sake of her aching back. "Perhaps while you are in town, you might stop by the police station and see if they know anything about Madame's guards. I heard her call the two in the study Camus and Grange."

"I will. You sure you will be all right here?"

"Once they leave. I don't mind being alone, usually."

He made his way toward her, handsome and tall with a calm demeanor that drew her in. Clear eyes met hers, no pretenses when he sat beside her. He still had that mark of dust on his face.

Aubrey slipped a handkerchief from her sleeve and motioned him nearer. "You have a smudge on your cheek." She dared not meet his gaze when she wiped the dirt. She leaned away, smoothing the fabric over her belly.

"So...Miss Aubrey." He folded his hands between his legs, his shoulders bent, his eyebrows furrowed. "I'd feel more comfortable if you came to town with me."

"I would prefer to stay home." Her backache would not relent. In fact, it had grown worse since their excursion underground. Hopefully, she had no dirt or cobwebs in her hair. Aubrey touched her hair, then her cheeks. "Besides, I am not in the least bit presentable." She motioned toward the loose braid over her shoulder and plain white blouse and skirt she'd donned for comfort's sake. Then there were her slipper-clad feet, marred with dirt from traipsing around secret halls.

"You present very well." Admiration filled his eyes.

Aubrey covered her throat with one hand and shrugged. After all, what could she say? She leaned her head back against the window, allowing more room for the baby under her ribs.

"Aubrey..." Nathan reached behind her as though she was falling. "That window might come open behind you."

"It is nailed shut."

"Why?"

Aubrey squirmed. "This was one of my rooms. My husband was...overprotective."

His lips tightened at the corners. "Would you like them to open?"

"I would. Why haven't I thought of that? They were always just shut." She ran a finger along the sill. "Do you have experience in carpentry work?"

"Yes, ma'am. Enough to meet your needs."

Unable to contain a smile, she stared in the opposite direction, managing a thanks that hardly sufficed.

Nathan was prying the frame free when Lizzy crept into the room, her head hanging low. Obviously, she wished for a private word. Aubrey crossed over to her, touching the younger lady on the shoulder. "What is it, Lizzy?"

The maid lifted her trembling chin. "My sister has gotten herself put away in a hospital. Ma won't go see her, and I have no way of going myself."

Warmth swirled in her heart for her crying friend. "We shall go together and take my barouche."

Lizzy pulled a crumpled bandana from her apron pocket and blew her nose loudly into it. "You sure, missus? It is terribly poor of me to ask." But not surprising, given how stern Lizzy's mother was.

Aubrey looked around the room and spied the stack of prints. "It just so happens, I was needing to take some photographs into town."

"Oh, thank you, missus. I will just put away my apron." She

hurried out of the room, working the knots behind her back as she went.

Nathan had paused his work to meet her gaze over one strong shoulder. His cheeks were high in color from the exertion and temperature in the room, yet he smiled when he pushed the first window open.

A sigh leaving her lips, Aubrey let her smile unfold with all the gratitude she felt. "Thank you, Mr. Reed." Then she went to meet Lizzy, completely forgetting to tell him she was going out. Oh, well, it didn't matter. He was going out soon, and with Madame and her guards out of the house, she didn't need to tell him where she was going.

~

How could he feel so much pain and so much love at the same time? Nathan sat in the asylum lobby, bouncing Felicity in his arms. Visits were not permitted in the rooms, so when he saw her, they sat either on one of the benches or in a chair if one was available. What would he do once she was older and started crawling? If she were to crawl across the rough wooden floor, she would get slivers in her tender little knees. Would he have her out of this place before she started walking?

Once he finished the job for Madame, he'd combine his earnings with the latest bounty. Would that be enough to take to the bank, or should he bring in more bounties? Mr. Ralston said if he ever needed help to come see him. Did said help extend to offering credit to a man with no roots?

The front door slammed, and Felicity startled. When she turned her head, the sun streamed into her eyes. She let out a cry, squishing up her little face on the first intake of ragged breath. Nathan hugged her, rocking and shushing her, but to no avail.

A nurse approached, reaching for Felicity. His chest tightened when he gave her over to the woman. He rubbed his hands on his pant legs as his baby sobbed. The woman patted her back too hard, and he winced.

"She likes to bounce softly." Gripping his hands into fists, he managed to refrain from taking Felicity back from her.

Still, the lady thumped his baby and still, she cried.

"That is too hard." He reached for Felicity and took her into his arms.

The nurse yelped at his sudden movement, then glared. "Mr. Reed, you overstep. I am completely capable of tending babies."

With Felicity's face against his neck, he kept his chin high enough so his whiskers would not scratch her head and rubbed her tiny back with his thumb. Her cries continued as frantically, but she'd stopped squirming and lifting her head.

"And that is not your child." The prickly nurse stuck her hand on her hips, her bony elbows pointing outward.

Felicity calmed, her screams turning to sobs, then moans, while the nurse fussed. He ignored her and tended to Felicity, his chest aching. How could he leave her with this woman? Would Felicity eventually learn he was not someone who could be there for her when she needed him?

"I will just tell the matron." The shrew of a nurse stormed across the lobby to the matron's office.

Nathan turned his back and tried to pray, but unless God was granting miracles today, he was wasting his time.

"Mr. Reed?" Mrs. Miller's kind voice spoke from behind him. When he faced the quiet lobby, the matron stood alone. "May I see you in my office?"

He followed her inside, taking the seat he was used to across the desk from her. Felicity lay quietly now, the wet spot beneath her mouth telling him she drooled or had spit up. He didn't care as long as he could hold her.

"Mr. Reed, there was a couple here earlier this week." Mrs. Miller sat in her usual fashion with her hands folded on the desk, her voice patient. "They are looking to adopt a baby."

His heart surged, and Nathan covered Felicity's back with one hand, holding her securely to him.

"I know this isn't what you wanted to hear, but they were quite taken with Felicity."

"I-I-I have a plan. I will give her a good home. I just need time to earn more money."

The woman looked at him with nothing short of pity, pooching out her lips slightly as though a child. "I am sure you will try, but you need to think about what is best for Felicity."

"*I* am best for Felicity. I am her only family, and I love her. If she is adopted, she will think that no one loved her." He was shaking, sweat dampening his brow as he tried to breathe. "I just need more time."

"This isn't about you. This is about what is best for your niece."

He ground his teeth together, his thoughts like frantic prayers. *God, please don't take her.* The same as he'd prayed while waiting for hours for Sarah to birth her baby, only to learn his sister had gone to heaven. Felicity fell under his protection. She was supposed to be in his care, but he had no way to even feed her.

The matron was saying something about trusting God. Nathan barely heard her until she said, "Are you any closer to having a place for Felicity?"

"I am, yes."

She smiled, sewing laugh lines in her face. "That is wonderful. And what of a nurse?"

He stared, without an answer.

"Have you considered marriage?"

He shook his head. There was no woman in his life at all. Certainly not one who would marry him—a poor bounty hunter with a babe to provide for and no house. Aubrey was the only woman he'd so much as spoken to in the last month who was of a marriageable state, and she was the last person he could propose to. No decent woman would marry him, and Felicity needed someone good to mother and love her. What if he could never provide that for her?

Mrs. Miller glanced behind Nathan to the door. Someone must have entered the lobby—a pair of women, judging by the tapping of heeled shoes and feminine voices.

They checked in at the desk, asking to see one of the recent mothers. "I am her sister," a woman said.

Mrs. Miller lowered her eyebrows, creating lines in her tall forehead. "Did you speak to Mrs. Willot?"

"Yes, I think she is willing to help. She said she would need to see Felicity." He just had not broached the subject again regarding Felicity's family. As much as he hated to admit it, he was afraid that when she met Felicity, she'd hate her for being the product of her husband's infidelity. If she knew of Nathan's connection to Sarah, her shame would deepen. Especially after the last few days. He had tried to ignore the attraction between them, but there was no denying that she felt something for him too. Aubrey was vulnerable, and if he wasn't careful, he'd hurt her.

"I am so glad to hear she is receptive to assisting you. This must be providence." Mrs. Miller stood, her long skirt catching on the armrest of her chair. "Mrs. Willot?" She called into the next room.

Nathan turned and there, framed by the office doorway, was Aubrey, all dressed for town with a wide summer hat framing her lovely face.

Mrs. Miller blocked his view when she greeted the lady. All Nathan could do was stare as a wide-eyed Aubrey entered the room and took the chair beside him. "Mr. Reed, what are you doing here?"

His throat very tight, he held Felicity closer and said, "The little girl I told you about..."

"Mr. Reed said he has apprised you of the situation of his niece, Felicity Reed, who is staying here." Mrs. Miller gestured toward his baby, her manner all business.

"His niece?" Her words, just above a whisper, intensified the pounding at his temples. "I...you mean the child my husband..." She shook her head, drawing in a deep breath. "Yes, I am aware that my husband fathered another child."

"And are you aware of the commitments he made to Felicity, to take care of her? See that she was provided for?"

"Yes, ma'am. I am aware." Aubrey shifted to the edge of her chair, wincing and blowing a soft breath between her lips. "When Mr. Reed informed me, I asked to see the child."

"Well, here she is." Mrs. Miller smiled patiently, then stood to dig through a cabinet. "I can show you her birth record to verify Sarah Reed is her mother. The letters from your husband were addressed to her."

"Yes, I...I remember." Aubrey blinked rapidly, her gaze swinging to Felicity and staying there.

What must she be thinking? Nathan resisted the inclination to turn the baby for Aubrey to see what an angel she was. Probably best not to. Felicity had blond hair, as Louis had. Besides, this had to be painful for Aubrey.

She was so still—she likely held her breath—only to jump when Mrs. Miller laid a file on the desk with a slap. "Here are all the records we have on Felicity and her mother. Her birth certificate was signed by our in-house doctor and filed with the courthouse. I took the liberty of putting down the correct name of the father, per Sarah Reed's instructions."

Aubrey slid a gloved hand across the worn desktop to the folder. She glanced through the paperwork, her only sign of emotion when she pressed a hand to her belly and winced.

A shadow rolled across Mrs. Miller's face. "Mrs. Willot, are you well?"

"Yes." Aubrey stood, suddenly touching a shaky hand to her forehead. "I did not intend to keep monetary support from Louis's child. I would never deprive a babe, any child, of Christian charity, of the support due them. I just didn't know..." Once again, she turned toward Nathan, this time meeting his gaze. "I will pay the debt due for my husband's sins, even once she is placed with a family, provided you find her a good home. Not some greedy sort of people who will only want her because of who her father was or the support I offer."

"Mrs. Willot, there is a couple who has come to see Felicity, but Mr. Reed is her only family and was hoping to adopt her himself."

Aubrey blinked as though jolted by the statement. "I did not know. He had not mentioned so." Color crept up her cheeks, and she clasped her hands. "If you can arrange everything for the babe to leave the orphanage and pass into Mr. Reed's care, I will pay for a nurse and anything else she needs. Now, if you don't mind, I would like to make it home before dark. My coachman is aging and hasn't the best sight at night." Aubrey nodded to both of them. "Good evening."

He was going to be sick. Now Aubrey knew it all. Not only that Louis had for certain broken their marriage vows and fathered a child in adultery but that Nathan couldn't take care of his own niece. Not only that—he was also to blame for her being cornered in the matron's office, like a schoolgirl brought to the head mistress for licking.

Ms. Thornson, the kindly nurse who worked the night shift, knocked on the doorpost, then crept into the room and smiled at him. "Mr. Reed, how good to see you visiting your sweet niece."

"Mr. Reed will soon be able to take custody of Felicity." Mrs.

Miller raised her chin and crossed her arms as though she'd orchestrated the changes.

Nathan stood, giving Felicity over to Ms. Thornson. Soon he could take Felicity home and not worry about losing her. It was just a shame it came at Mrs. Willot's expense. She had been embarrassed and hurt. "Mrs. Miller..." Nathan faced the matron. "I didn't tell the widow that Felicity was here. I wanted to, but I was ashamed. Regardless, just so you know, she said she'd help. Mrs. Willot is a good woman."

"You are too kind, Mr. Reed." Mrs. Miller gestured toward the door, then led him into the lobby. "There are plenty of kind people out there who still need reminding about their Christian duty."

Sick to his stomach, Nathan buried his hands in his pockets. Mrs. Miller may be right, but she didn't need to badger Aubrey to get her support.

Across the lobby, Aubrey stood before the front desk while the clerk there told her someone could stay with her sister. "We have an extra bed, and Miss Lizzy seems very helpful."

"Very well. Please tell her to let me know when she needs a ride to the house. And tell her I will pray for her sister."

Lizzy was at the asylum with her sister. Was that what brought Aubrey here? He thought back to Aubrey standing by the study door, her hand on Lizzy's shoulder as she reassured her. His focus on breaking the windows free, he'd not overheard what they spoke of. Lizzy's sister must be one of the young mothers here.

Aubrey walked toward the door, her pace slightly hitched.

Mrs. Miller frowned after her. "Who is looking after Mrs. Willot?"

"Her mother-in-law is staying with her."

"Good. If you are acquainted with the woman at all, you might see her home. She does not look well."

Nathan strode across the room, following Aubrey through

the front door and out into the muggy evening air. Mr. Dobbs was just opening the door to help her into the barouche when Nathan jaunted down the steps. "Aubrey?"

She turned flushed cheeks on him, then narrowed her eyes. "I would have helped. You didn't have to hide your relationship to the baby. I wanted to help."

"I know you would, Aubrey. I'm sorry for not telling you everything. I didn't want to hurt you."

She scoffed. "As if you could. I know the kind of man he was, and I learned early in my marriage not to hate those he consorted with because they were even bigger fools than I."

"I'm sorry. Felicity is innocent, my only family. She doesn't deserve this." He motioned toward the asylum. "It's my job to protect her, and I didn't want you to hate her."

"Hate her?" One of the feathers on her hat fluttered around the brim, but Aubrey swiped it away. "A baby. You think I could do such a thing?"

Everything he said was making this worse. Chest aching, Nathan pressed hard on his sternum. "I know now that you are a kind and heartfelt woman. I didn't the first time we spoke at your home."

"And you said you represented the family. You *are* the family. You lied."

"I wanted to be professional, to not overly alarm you." He stepped nearer, lowering his voice. "If I told you that my sister had an affair with your husband, then died, and now you have to pay for his sin...? It would have been worse."

"Pay for his sins? What else can a wife do?" She snickered, then grimaced. "Forgive me for being bitter. This is not about me. I'm sorry for all you and your family have suffered. Where your sister is concerned, well, Louis was not often physically violent. Never with anyone but me, actually." She furrowed her brow, as though just realizing or trying to remember something. Eyes glazed, she looked around the street, then found him. The glassiness ebbed, and her gaze became keen once again, wide and full of pain. "He could be quite charming, even gentle."

She was trying to reassure him that maybe Louis had not abused Sarah as he had abused her. Unable to retain the emotions ripping through him, Nathan stepped away from her, but Aubrey gripped his hand.

"I will do the right thing. And you needn't worry about anyone tarnishing her memory. I will be discreet." She let go and turned to the barouche.

He took her hand again, helping her up into the seat. "You can't go out there alone. I will get my horse."

"Madame has gone to the Bay area to see the sights."

"What about her guards?"

"They are with her." She adjusted herself on the seat, drawing in a ragged breath when she met his gaze. "I would like to be alone tonight. Today has been...taxing."

Their excursion into the secret room, finding Aubrey's beloved photographs, sharing the joy of her hobby, and seeing her dream spark to life seemed far away now. He was inclined to apologize, but he didn't know where to start.

Mr. Dobbs brushed him aside and slammed the door closed before climbing up into the driver's seat. The man moved with surprising dexterity, and when he took hold of the reins and urged the horses into the busy street, Nathan let her go.

CHAPTER 12

$\mathcal{N}$athan rode Sammy down the quiet side street, weariness from the day weighing on him. The sunset shone over the tops of the buildings, the shadows hovering close to the poorly built structures of this part of town. He had nowhere to go since Aubrey didn't want him at the chateau that night. At least she was safe. Although he hadn't done anything that warranted forgiveness, when she'd looked at him with so much hurt, he felt small.

Despite what others thought —what his Pa believed—he wasn't a betrayer. Somehow he always managed to fail, though. At least Felicity would soon be moved from the asylum. He should be thanking God, but as he headed down a darker street, all he felt was loss. Aubrey was a magnificent woman, like none he had ever met, or likely would ever meet. After witnessing her intense love for her unborn babe, he knew that Felicity needed a mother's love.

Nathan was still playing through the conversation with Aubrey and trying not to be drawn back to remembering the afternoon at her side when he entered the Broken Arrow Saloon. He'd have a hearty dinner, then find a barn to sleep in.

Barely noticing the cigarette smoke clouding the air, the loud, off-key piano being played on stage, or the toothless barkeep who slid him a plate of salmon, Nathan headed for a table in the corner. A woman pursuing a patron bumped into him, jostling his elbow so he dropped his fork. Frowning, he bent to retrieve it and caught view of Beau Fox across the room. A dark ring circled one eye, and his lip was swollen. He motioned for Nathan to follow him, so he carried his plate to one of the back tables beneath the second story that overlooked the ground floor.

The moment he lowered to a ladder-back chair, Beau pushed a shot glass of whiskey toward him. "You look like a hound just sprayed by a skunk. You all right?"

Nathan waved away the offer of alcohol. He might have lost his anchor a long time ago, but he'd abstained from liquors. If he was going to be a father to Felicity, he had to be better. "I'm fine. You're the one with the black eye."

"One of Madame's men tried to chase me off. He worked for Emil and says I betrayed them because I was not arrested when he was."

"Who won?"

"Who do you think?" Beau frowned at him.

Nathan restrained a grin. "What are you doing here? Aubrey told me all Madame's guards followed her to the Bay area."

"Not all of us. She took one with her and left one at the chateau to guard that precious box of hers. They keep it in the coach house, under guard all the time. I just got a break."

"Aubrey went back to the chateau." Nathan stood, ready to head for the door.

"I don't think she's in danger. He will stay with the box. Madame is not paternal or sentimental. Likely, she doesn't care about the baby. It is Monsieur Willot who cares so much about his line. Madame is looking for something else." Beau dropped his voice, hunching his shoulders a little.

"What?"

"I don't know. She only tells Camus and Grange."

"You know anything about them? Are they wanted?"

Beau shrugged. "I did some research into Ellsworth and the couriers like you wanted. Not sure how it will help you."

Nathan gestured for him to carry on.

"The couriers, I actually know. The Baker brothers. Worked with them just this past spring on a job—the Alexander job, actually."

Nathan paused a large chunk of red salmon on its way to his mouth.

"They didn't do much, but got themselves thrown in prison with Emil."

After finishing his bite, Nathan said, "I'll ask Captain Hiram about contacting the warden over there. See if they're willing to talk about the valise and documents."

"Must be nice, being chummy with the law." Beau pulled a deck of cards from his vest pocket and shuffled them. "I was playing cards with an old geezer who said there was an old man in town about a year ago who knew Ellsworth from the war. Knew something that could ruin him. Ellsworth was running for city council and was Ralston's right-hand man at the bank. One day, the old man left town, and Ellsworth sold a bunch of his shares at the bank to Louis at a more than fair price."

"What was the old fella's name?"

"I don't know."

Nathan scooped the rest of the salmon into his mouth, chewed, and stood. "Who's the fella who told you this?"

Scowling, Beau put away his cards and rose, looking over the heads of the other men in the room. They were a scruffy pack, to be sure, but then Nathan had come to a poor part of town where he knew he could get food cheap.

"Over there's where he usually sits." Beau pointed toward the table near the front doors.

They wove their way through the tables with patrons smoking, drinking, and playing cards. A brunette tipped her head back and laughed, her hair in a loose braid as Aubrey's had been that afternoon.

Nathan looked away and almost bumped into Beau when he stopped in front of the table. "Where's Charlie?"

The men at the table shrugged, barely taking their eyes from the card game. On the edge of the crowd, a woman in a tattered dress raised her eyebrows and tipped her head toward the door.

Beau went around the table, out the door, and stopped at the edge of the building to roll a cigarette. Nathan leaned against one of the posts supporting the awning. "I thought you stopped smoking."

"It's not for me." Beau lit the cigarette and held it between two fingers.

Nathan didn't bother asking if he wasn't smoking anymore, why he had tobacco and cigarette papers on him.

The saloon door swung open, and out slunk the lady from inside. She slipped the cigarette from Beau's fingers with ease and inhaled deeply. The smoke clouded around them. She looked up with heavily lidded eyelashes. "So you want to know about Charlie?"

"Yes, ma'am." Beau sounded respectful, yet he took the cigarette back.

"Hey, nothing is for free."

"Indeed." He flicked a coin in the air, and Nathan caught it when it flew his way.

He turned the penny in the light from the saloon window. "Say, this is almost enough to buy a shot of whiskey."

"Yeah." Beau eyed the cigarette, rolling it between his

fingers, then suddenly grinned. "How much you wanna bet Charlie's in the outhouse behind the saloon?"

"I'd bet you two bits." Nathan took a penny out of his pocket and added it to the one Beau had thrown his way.

"That's what you think. Charlie's..." The woman sealed her lips, but Beau offered her the cigarette.

She snatched it up possessively. "It's gonna take those two bits as well."

"Fine. Talk first."

She took another drag, then sighed. "You boys ain't gonna like it. Charlie's out for the night, won't be back until late. He's on a job, but I can tell you when he gets back if you let me know where you're staying."

She winked at Beau, whose genial facade fell away. He stared at the woman with a brooding expression, his black eyebrows hooding equally dark eyes.

The woman squirmed. "I'm not lying. He's got a job tonight for some rich banker Charlie said is obsessing about some papers."

Nathan stiffened. "What banker?"

"I don't know."

Beau stepped toward her, towering over her like a grizzly on its back paws.

The woman raised her arms to shield her face. "I don't know. I swear!"

"What's the job?"

"Papers. They're ransacking some rich lady's house and taking all the papers."

Beau let her go, but Nathan had already moved toward the hitching post where Sandy waited, a prayer pounding through him. *Lord, protect her! Let us reach her in time. Keep her safe, please.*

⌇

*A*ubrey pushed her way through the large double doors and into the foyer of Willot Chateau. The room was mostly dark, shadows hanging in the corners of the second story and around the edge of the stairs. She sighed, her steps heavy. Yes, she would head directly to bed to lie down. Perhaps then her backache would ease.

Mr. Dobbs followed her inside. Blessedly, the young man who helped in the stable had taken the horse and barouche to the carriage house, so Mr. Dobbs did not have to see them put away. If she had allowed Nathan to return, he would have helped with the team, but no, she'd been too upset. She'd thought only of herself.

Aubrey glanced back at his haggard face after he forced the door closed. Goodness, she would need to hire a proper coachman soon. He looked near collapse, though Mr. Dobbs would hate to be replaced.

Tempted to send him to bed, yet knowing that doing so would greatly wound his manly pride, she addressed him kindly. "Please inform Cook that Lizzy will not be returning this evening. She is visiting a relative in town. I'm sure Mrs. Jorgenson will know of whom I speak." Her daughter who had delivered a baby in a foundling asylum and laying-in house. What kind of mother was her cook if she was not there for her own daughter?

Mr. Dobbs took Aubrey's shawl from her shoulders and draped it across one arm. "Yes, ma'am. I will pray all is well. Cook said she would have dinner ready to serve upon your return."

"No, thank you." Aubrey hefted her skirts as she started up the staircase on swollen feet. "I am too tired to eat." And too upset, but she needn't share that with him.

"Cook won't like you not taking care of yourself, and neither will Madame. Already she has taken over the menu preparations and insists that we tell her…" His voice faded.

Turning back to him, Aubrey cocked an eyebrow. "Insist you what? Report my eating habits and comings and goings, as you did for my husband?"

The man had the decency to hang his head. "We didn't want to."

He seemed contrite, but a dizzy spell muddled the scene before her and forced her to hold tighter to the railing for a moment. "I would like tea and crackers in my room. That is all. Thank you."

She made it up the stairs, her entire body heavy and back aching from being in the barouche so long. Her babe had been still for some time. Though Aubrey couldn't deny that she was relieved to not feel the jabs to her insides, it scared her when there was no movement. What if she lost this baby too?

Light speared through a western-facing window in her bedroom, the panes hosting the rainbow hues of the sunset framed by pink velvet drapes. Unwilling to thwart the light, Aubrey left the lamp on her bedside table unlit and enjoyed the subtle, natural ambiance. She worked the buttons of her dress and then the special corset that provided space for her belly. Lizzy typically helped her get ready for bed, but she didn't really need assistance. Except for unlacing her shoes. Her belly was so big, reaching past it was quite out of the question—if she wanted to breathe. She managed the feat by bending each leg back so her foot was on the bed. From there, she could loose the laces and kick the shoes off. Such twisting and stretching might lead to a career as a contortionist.

She sat on the woven blue lace coverlet, rubbing her tight belly. Aubrey used the toes of one foot to push the stockings down the opposite leg. She managed one before rolling onto her side and pulling her sore feet onto the bed. Never mind the other stocking. It would eventually work its way off once she was tucked into her covers.

The carriage ride had been so bumpy, she ached in her most tender places. How much longer before this baby came? Louis had been arrested in January, so it was between that terrible fiasco in the kitchen in August and the first of the year. She'd parried his advances during that time but had grown weary of his pursuit. Cheeks heating, she shook her head, refusing vivid memories that would surely make her ill. She'd felt so empty, so dark, she'd reached out to Jesse in December. So maybe November? And this was August already, so she must be close.

She winced at the twinge in her back, similar to others she'd had for weeks now. The midwife she'd seen in Los Angeles said first-time mothers always thought they were going into labor when they weren't. That once it hit, she'd know it.

A warm flush ran down her thighs. Good heavens, she'd just relieved herself a short while ago.

She pushed off the bed to balance on the edge when her bedroom door opened. Who would dare to come into her room without knocking? Aubrey started to chastise the intruder, only to still.

A dirty man with wide eyes and grimy cheeks stared at her.

She caught her breath. Her heart slammed against her ribcage. She shielded her belly.

He placed one finger against his lips, shushing her as he stepped farther into her room.

"Get out!" she shouted, and he bolted toward her.

Aubrey ran opposite, a shriek on her lips.

He caught her arm and dragged her to the floor.

She landed hard on her hip, pain wracking her body.

He pinned her hands onto either side of her head, then straddled her, forcing the baby up into her ribs until she could hardly breathe.

She barely managed words as she pushed against him. "Let me go!"

He slapped her face, slamming her head to one side and sending a blaze of white across her vision. Her brain seemed to shudder inside her skull.

Somewhere far off, someone shouted. A man's voice.

Pain overwhelmed her and darkness clouded in, pulling her down into its depths, but she fought to see light again.

The weight lifted off of her. She rolled onto her side, belly resting on the floor. Forcing her eyes open, Aubrey raised her head.

Two men wrestled a few feet away, one shouting obscenities.

Arms shaking, she crawled away from them, bumping into her bed. Her floral quilt came into view, the ruffled edges skirting the floor. Aubrey rose to her hands and knees, but before she could climb up, her body tightened again. She froze, still gripping the coverlet. The ache in her back had evolved into a spasm.

The tightness relented, and her muscles worked again. Aubrey sagged, but someone grabbed her from behind.

"Get away from me." She shoved backward against whomever was there, but her hand slid against a muscled torso.

"Aubrey, stop fighting." Nathan turned her by the arms, his eyes wide. "You're safe."

"Oh." She nearly collapsed with relief, setting her back against the side of the bed. "Where is the man? Get him out. Now." The intruder lay on the floor, his face turned away.

"He is unconscious. I'll tie him up as soon as I know you are unharmed." Though his voice was steady and his body protected her, he scanned the room as though watching for more trouble.

Throat dry, Aubrey glanced at the bedside table, wishing for the tea she'd asked for. Instead, she swallowed and met Nathan's gaze. "Why are you here? I just left you in town."

"I heard you might be in danger, so I came."

She sat up a little straighter, but the pain was back, holding her body tighter than before. Limbs trembling, she closed her eyes until it passed. That dreadful man had pushed her, likely further hurting her aching back. What a relief she had not landed on her belly.

Above her, Nathan knelt, his steely blue eyes dark with concern. He pressed a hand to her head, so gently that her body responded, muscles softening. How kind he was, and now he had saved her again, but he'd also deceived her about the baby. Why not tell of his connection to Louis's child?

She lifted her chin to see him better, the back of her head pressing against the bed. "You may be a fine man, but I have no room in my life for someone I cannot trust."

"I don't deserve your trust. But I wouldn't..." He lowered his focus to the floor and blinked.

Aubrey followed his gaze to red droplets on her pretty pink-and-green floral rug. "Oh, no."

Another pain came, and she bent over and squeezed her eyes shut until it passed.

And then she understood. "The baby is coming. I'm not ready. I don't have a midwife here in San Francisco. I haven't any gowns or cloths for diapers." She grabbed ahold of his arm, her breaths coming fast. "Pa is away. He said he'd come if I wrote to him. I didn't write him. I didn't know."

"I'll get the doctor." He started to rise, but a loud thump in the hallway stopped him. "There must be more men in the house. Let me lock the door. We will have to wait until the authorities have cleared the house before I can fetch a doctor."

Aubrey nodded, breathing hot air through her nose, just resting and praying the next pain would not be as bad.

"I need to tie up that ruffian." Nathan nodded to the unconscious man on the floor. "You will be all right if I do that?" Fear shone in his eyes.

"I'll be fine. Go ahead."

He locked the door, then bound the intruder. Soon he was sitting beside her on the floor and placing a cool cloth from her washbasin on her forehead. "I think you should move to the bed."

Another pain came. Aubrey slammed her fist into the floor. Nathan covered it, and when she opened her fingers, he held them. Chin to her chest, she focused on relaxing her muscles. As though her body accepted her surrender, the tension strengthened to the point that her limbs quaked. She could not hold back a moan.

At last, it relented. She relaxed her hold on Nathan's hand.

Had Maman squeezed Pa's hand when she'd been in labor? Though most medical practices dictated no men be present for the birthing of children, Aubrey's papa would not leave her mother's side. Maman hadn't shared many details, just that she could not have done it without him. Aubrey had always hoped to have a similar experience, but here she was with no husband and no maman. When she'd dreamed of having a baby as a fanciful young woman, she'd expected to be taken care of, not all alone. And worse, it was her own fault for marrying a cad, then insisting on living alone.

"It wasn't supposed to be like this." Her throat tightened around the words. "Even Lizzy is gone."

"It will get better. Just as soon as we know the house is safe—"

A gunshot exploded so near that Aubrey ducked.

Nathan drew both arms around her, shielding her. One of his hands pushed against her lower back, relieving some of the pressure there.

Aubrey rested her forehead on his collarbone. "That helps. Don't move your hand. Please."

Before she could explain, the pain crashed down on her again, this time like a mighty wave of the Pacific, crushing her against a sandy beach. When she resurfaced, she clutched Nathan's shirt front as though holding to a lifeline.

He still pressed his large, warm hand to her back, where it soaked through her shift to the spot that had ached all day.

She closed her eyes and sank into the peace before the next swell. It came as she'd feared and known it would. She weathered the next few, the pain growing with each to the point it was all she could do not to scream.

"Say something," she demanded. "I will go mad in the quiet, waiting for another pain."

"I'm sorry you've been hurt because of your past with Mr. Willot. Never did I want or try to cause you pain. I didn't mean for you to look uncharitable or selfish in front of Mrs. Miller. My only concern is Felicity. She doesn't deserve to have no papa and now no mama. It's bad enough Sarah died alone, with no family." He tipped his head away, hiding his face, but not before she saw the gleam of tears in his eyes.

The poor man had lost his sister. If Jesse died, as she feared he might just a few months ago, she'd be shattered. "I'm sorry for your loss."

"I should have been there."

As he was with Aubrey now, a comforter and friend. Settling her head on his shoulder, Aubrey wrapped one arm around his neck, offering the reassurance of an embrace. She was too weary to care about propriety. Besides, soon the pain would return, and nothing else would matter. When the next contraction hit and she dug her heels into the floor, even the mess on the carpet and one stocking-less leg did not cause her embarrassment

The midwife in Los Angeles had said she would know when the time came, and she did. It was as if a black flood surrounded her and dragged her into an abyss. Occasionally, she surfaced to find Nathan still there. At times, in the depths, she heard him telling her to breathe, that she was strong.

In the distance, there was pounding and men's voices.

Nathan reassured her all was well.

The minutes came in flashes, Nathan at her side and then across the room. A tall man standing in the doorway, telling him it was safe. They'd arrested the burglars. Cook rushed through the door, instructing him to send Mr. Dobbs to town for the doctor. Then she was at Aubrey's side, her frizzy white-and-red hair aglow in the last light of day. "Of all the nights for Lizzy to be out." She swept the coverlet off the bed. "Come, Mr. Reed, move her to the bed."

Nathan cradled her in his arms and lifted her when the contraction ended. Then the mattress was beneath her, and she found a spot in the bed canopy to focus on while the world around her turned into a fog.

Her sturdy cook was there, holding her hand, giving her clear instructions. How had this woman, who she'd been at odds with since that awful night back in August, come to help with such an intimate matter? The question floated away like a piece of driftwood with the tide. A great swell was coming for her, ready to swallow her alive until she prayed for death.

CHAPTER 13

Nathan stood before one of the first-floor windows of City Hall on Kearny Street where the arrested men were held in the underground jail. Normally, he met Captain Hiram at the smaller station in another part of town, but he couldn't wait to speak to him. Across the large yard used for social gatherings, auctions, and hangings, the roofs of many buildings extended into the night sky like mountain peaks. Farther away still, in a French chateau in the California countryside, Aubrey suffered in labor.

His vision blurred until he saw not his reflection in the glass but Aubrey's body trembling in pain. Now he knew how Sarah had suffered, and though he tried not to feel guilty for being there for Aubrey and not for his own sister, it was useless.

He was a failure, after all. Just as his pa had said ten years before. Had he abandoned Aubrey while she was in labor as he'd abandoned Sarah on the farm in Oregon? What else could he have done for Aubrey, though? Laboring was a woman's business. Besides, the police who arrived at the house had needed him to help cart the robbers to the city jail.

Footfalls sounded in the lobby. A man spoke behind him—

likely, an officer coming up from the basement jail. Nathan allowed the reflection on the window to focus so it showed Captain Hiram, arms swinging in his blue regulation jacket, approaching him from behind. Nathan turned.

The older man's graying sideburns came to a point on either side of his face, setting off black eyebrows which he raised when he spoke. "Mr. Reed, it's late. I didn't think you'd wait. You could swing by the station tomorrow, you know."

"Just as soon clear up my part while I'm here so I can attend to other things."

"All right, then." He removed a pencil and notepad from his jacket pocket and scribbled something on it. "Tell me how you knew that the Willot house would be robbed tonight."

"I was in the Broken Arrow Saloon. Overheard some men talking." The lie rolled off his tongue like melting butter.

He had grown accustomed to telling falsehoods in his line of work. Anonymity was an essential part of being a bounty hunter, as was knowing when to withhold or share information. But Aubrey had said she needed people she could trust in her life. He had to change, to be better. Besides, this was Captain Hiram. Nathan might need his help.

Shoulders slumped, he opened his empty hands in front of the window. He didn't have anything to offer Felicity or Miss Aubrey.

"Actually, a girl at the saloon told me. A friend of hers, some fella named Charlie, was going out there to rob the place. I was on my way to the chateau to warn Mrs. Willot when I passed an officer on the street. I told him to get you a message right away." Perhaps if he shed more light, the half lie would not matter so much. A shame he could not tell Captain Hiram the whole mess he'd gotten himself in with Ellsworth. The man might know what to do.

"Mm-hm." The police captain paused his writing. "You know the widow?"

"Yes, sir. I'm working for her. Just protection while her mother-in-law is in town. She's transporting some valuables that might attract danger."

"You the only guard? I didn't see anyone else out there."

"There are other guards, but the mother-in-law came to town to stay at the beach. She took two with her." And the one that stayed behind likely would not leave Madame Willot's material possessions to protect Aubrey, even if he had known about the break-in.

"So maybe these men were hoping to get a chance at those valuables."

That wasn't it. Oh sure, they likely planned to take anything extra they wanted, but they'd broken in on Ellsworth's orders. They were after Louis's papers. Unless one of the arrested men talked, the old crook would go unpunished for the danger he posed to Aubrey. And here Nathan was, going along with the captain's line of questioning when he could point him to Ellsworth.

But if he told the truth, more would come out. Ellsworth would drag Nathan down with him, expose him as the same ilk that broke into the chateau this night. If Nathan was in jail for burglary and attempted bank robbery, who would protect Aubrey or care for Felicity?

Such events would also ruin his chance at police work in the future. He needed a respectable job if he was going to be Felicity's father. Bounty hunting was not a fitting career for a family man.

He released a resigned sigh. No matter what, he had to right his wrongs in his own way. Coming clean would not make Aubrey or Felicity any safer, and he needed to build a better case against Ellsworth before bringing it to the law.

Hiram turned toward the double doors in the great lobby, stifling a yawn as he walked, Nathan at his side. "Well, you've always had a keen ear for information. If you think of anything more, you can find me back at the station. I wish you luck with the Widow Willot. I sure am glad you found her in time."

"I am too." Hopefully, the Lord would see her safely through labor, as He had not seen fit to do for Sarah.

They walked side by side, the soles of their shoes clicking in the quiet, empty room.

Here was a space in the conversation for him. He just needed to ask. Taking in a deep breath, Nathan said, "Say, I need a favor."

"What is it?" The older man's gaze was sharp as a spear. He'd not commit to something without knowing what it was.

Nathan could trust the captain's grit and wisdom. He breathed easier as he voiced his request. "I need information regarding a private investigation I'm working on. There are two men, brothers by the name of Baker, imprisoned in the Utah Territorial Penitentiary who transported documents for Louis Willot in seventy-four. I need to know what was in those papers and any information about Louis—what he wanted them to do with the papers."

"I can do that. I'm acquainted with the warden down there." He paused at the exit. "If they know something, he'll find it." He gave Nathan a pat on the back, half pushing him out the door. "Now get some rest. You look ready to keel over."

Nathan shrugged one shoulder as he stepped out into the night air. He took the steps which led down into the square, mostly shadowed now. All around, the city lights were coming on, warm and golden in the twilight. Tall buildings towered above him. Somewhere out there, Ellsworth was sitting comfortable in his wealth, unaffected by what had happened. It was time to change that.

The four stories of the Occidental Hotel, one of the few luxury hotels on the West Coast, towered above the heart of San Francisco. Beau told him he was stupid, that he best not corner badgers in their holes lest he come away with teeth marks. Nathan didn't care much for metaphors and told Beau as much, then demanded he tell him where to find Ellsworth. Of course, the rich old codger chose to live here instead of in a home like a normal person. Nathan had avoided Ellsworth for too long.

Tonight he would end the threat once and for all.

Nathan hastened from the spacious lobby to the grand staircase, his boots sinking into the thick carpet. After reaching the landing, he strode down a long hallway to one of the master suites. A butler showed him in with a respectful bow.

Conversations filled the room, the occupancy mostly male. Piano music floated from a baby grand in a corner where a greasy-haired man played the keys. The scent of cigar smoke tinged the air, and businessmen in fine frock coats crowded the room, some sitting on mahogany, velvet, and gold-crested furniture. Ellsworth lived like a king yet was always grasping for more.

Drawing in a deep breath to keep his head cool, Nathan made his way past a big-bellied braggart and two spindly men who could pass for Jack Sprat's sons. There were plenty with white hair but none with the bloated face of a bulldog.

"Mr. Reed?" Mr. Ralston came from behind him, offering a handshake. "I didn't expect to see you here."

"Good day, sir. I'm actually looking for someone." Nathan greeted the bank president. A blustery laugh caught his attention, and when two annoyed-looking young men headed for the opposite side of the room, Nathan spotted Ellsworth. He appeared so genial, not at all how Nathan had expected.

"Billy." Ellsworth approached with arms stretched wide, as though greeting an old friend.

"I see you are enjoying the brandy." Ralston stuck out his hand—likely, to stop Ellsworth from embracing him. "Look who I just found. You didn't tell me you invited young Mr. Reed."

Ellsworth's fat cheeks were high in color, and a line of sweat beaded on his deeply wrinkled forehead. "Mr. Reed. Of course. The man who stopped the villains and saved the damsel at the bank. Like something out of a book. Aye, Ralston?" Although his features posed as friendly as a court jester, his eyes flared with temper when he shook Nathan's hand. Here was no friend but a cunning adversary.

"I merely did the right thing." Nathan pointed his gaze at Ralston. "Can't have innocent people harmed for such a simple commodity as money."

"Simple," Ralston murmured, then shook his head. "I've never known it to be so, whether I had too much or not enough."

"As if having too much money is even possible." Ellsworth gave a snort, throwing back a tumbler of brandy.

Nathan clenched his fists to keep from throttling the man. Was that why he'd had men descend upon the Willot Chateau without concern for Aubrey or her babe? Whatever the reason, such actions would cease after tonight. "I need a moment of your time, Mr. Ellsworth."

"Of course, you know what I mean, Billy." Mr. Ellsworth nudged Mr. Ralston's arm as though Nathan had not spoken. "With a house like Ralston Hall, you could host this get-together for a weekend."

"I refer to my estate as Belmont. The Occidental suits this gathering just fine." He smiled patiently, his gaze latching onto Nathan for an instant, then he gripped Ellsworth by the arm. "You are looking warm. Perhaps if you stepped outside, you'd feel better. And Mr. Reed did say he has something to discuss with you. Perhaps the roof?"

Raising his cloud-like eyebrows, Ellsworth nodded. "Some air might be nice." He straightened his frock coat.

Mr. Ralston cupped Nathan on the arm, slipped him a gold piece, and walked away.

Nathan tucked the coin into his vest pocket, not liking it. To refuse would be rude, though. The wealthy banker was known to hand out money in this fashion. Ralston hadn't left any opportunity for Nathan to argue. Strange that he removed himself so quickly, but then Ellsworth had imbibed too much and was somewhere between silly and intrusive.

Outside, the expanse of manmade structures sparkled across the hills to the gray mountains God had fashioned. Farther out, the bay glimmered in the moonlight. They could see everything from such a great height...including the sheer drop over the side of the building.

The instant the door to the topmost balcony closed, Ellsworth straightened and glowered. The light shining through the windows intensified his expression. Away from his wealthy friends, he straightened into the six-foot-tall, white-haired criminal Nathan knew him to be. "Reed, what is the meaning of this, your intrusion into my personal life?"

"Mrs. Willot."

Mr. Ellsworth's nostrils flared, then he rolled his eyes. "I don't need to explain myself to you, bounty hunter."

The door to the suite opened, and two burly-looking men exited.

Nathan moved so his back was facing the wall and not the balcony.

"Get him out of here." Ellsworth motioned toward Nathan —setting the ruffians into motion—and headed for the door, only to come up short when Mr. Ralston stepped through.

"Ah-ha." He crossed his arms. "I was afraid you might find yourself in trouble."

Behind him stood a tall, dark-haired man—Ralston's butler, whose demeanor reminded Nathan of one of Madame's guards. The bank president stepped farther onto the terrace and gripped the lapels of his frock coat. "You know, Captain Hiram at the police highly recommends Mr. Reed. Says he is honest, as upstanding as a man can be."

All the men remained still, even the two who would have tried to throw him off the roof.

Ellsworth rocked on his heels, his smile tight. "I hired Mr. Reed to do a job for me, one he reneged upon, losing me precious time and money. He's not as upstanding as you think. He has entangled himself with the Widow Willot and refuses to see reason on a matter of grave importance."

Face hot at the mere mention of Aubrey, Nathan stepped away from the wall. "Ellsworth has—"

"It's about the deed Louis stole!" Ellsworth cut him off.

Mr. Ralston's eyes snapped with a fierceness that reminded Nathan he was outnumbered with a four-story drop behind him. "If the widow has the deed, I need it now."

What deed? Likely, Louis had ripped these men off, and Aubrey was paying for it.

Nathan slid his thumbs into his belt, keeping his right hand near his weapon. "So that is the document you had me looking for. Perhaps if you had told me, I would have found it."

"The house had been emptied. Any remaining documents would have been significant if you had just done the job I paid you to do."

Nathan raised his eyebrows. "You never paid me for any job."

Ellsworth pressed his lips together and puffed up his chest. Likely, Ralston did not know his fellow board member had planned a bank robbery.

Ralston widened his stance, facing Nathan yet checking his time piece. "Louis brokered a silver strike in seventy-four. The earnings were to go to the bank, but the greedy man was arrested and hid all documents regarding the whereabouts of the strike. When he died, all hope of finding them disappeared."

"Until his widow moved to town." Ellsworth still stood with his arms crossed, but he seemed to have given up on hiding things from Nathan. "At that time, I learned that Louis built the chateau himself and is rumored to have hiding places, as I told you, Reed."

Nathan nodded to keep the man talking, but Ralston took over the conversation instead. "The future of the bank and this city depend on finding the deed and all documents associated with that strike, including a map showing its location."

Nathan glanced at Ellsworth. "If you legally own the deed, why all the secrecy? Why not just connect with the police to get their help and let Mrs. Willot know?"

"And let everyone know the Bank of California lost a silver mine?" Ellsworth practically shouted the words, his skin turning red again while Ralston motioned for him to quiet.

"Any amount of negative publicity in this economy might cause panic."

"And if I find the deed and location of the mine, everything Louis stole, you will leave Mrs. Willot alone?"

Mr. Ralston turned his head to the side, studying him. "Is that really all you care about, Reed? That the only payment you want?"

He nodded, not willing to accept money from either man.

"No one will harm her." Ralston narrowed his gaze on Ellsworth, his lips twisting in disgust. "And you will have the favor of the bank."

That last should have given him hope for Felicity's future, but all he felt was sick at dealing with Ellsworth again. "Aren't you worried about the men who attacked her? What's to keep them from talking to the police and admitting who paid them to break into the house last night?"

Ralston brushed his hands and backed away. "I'll have nothing to do with anyone's criminal business. If you will find the documents, Mr. Reed, I will make it worth your while."

Felicity would be taken care of because of Aubrey. He couldn't afford to be employed by a criminal ever again, even though it meant going without money he desperately needed. "I won't accept any payment. And I will go about this in my own way, speaking to Mrs. Willot as should have been done in the first place." He glanced at Ellsworth, who was flanked by the two body guards.

"Of course." His words dripped with that same agreeable friendliness that Nathan had witnessed when they were in the company of Ellsworth's friends.

When Ralston and his butler went inside, Mr. Ellsworth's mask fell away again. "You are the biggest waste of space I have ever encountered. First, the documents, then the bank."

Nathan crossed his arms. "Care to share your opinion on a robbery gone wrong with Ralston, the president of the bank?"

The vein in Ellsworth's neck bulged. "That was all fake. I told the widow to meet me there and arranged the robbery at the same time, hoping to scare her back to Los Angeles where she belongs, but then you stepped in—Mr. Hero of the Day. Now she's planted herself in that house with my deed, and you keep getting in my way." His voice grew in volume the more he spoke. "Well, don't come back here to finish the job when someone else attacks the lady."

Nathan stood frozen. "Who else?"

Ellsworth laughed, wiping spittle from his chin. "You are a small-minded man. That's probably what got you into trouble back in Oregon in 1870."

Nathan winced inwardly yet steeled himself outwardly. He

must have given away some discomfort because Ellsworth's eyes lit with a predatorial light. "That's right. I know about you, *Deputy* Reed, and your sheriff. Unless you want everyone else to know, you'll stay away from me and my business." He nodded back toward the large room full of businessmen, Ralston included.

Nathan stepped forward, ignoring the two men who tensed. "Nobody cares about what a no-account bounty hunter did half a decade ago, but you, a rich California philanthropist on the city council and the bank board...all it would take is a whisper to a newspaper reporter and any chance of you running for office would be sunk, fast as a steamer in the Pacific. You'd be ruined."

"Fine. I'll leave you alone. Both of you." He pointed his finger at Nathan, enunciating each word with the jab. "I can't hold this back. Either you get the documents, or someone else will."

He moved to return indoors but spoke over one shoulder. "You might think twice of making an enemy of me, Reed. If you or that little girl of yours ever get into trouble, don't come looking to me for help."

Blood cold at the mention of Felicity, Nathan gave a diplomatic nod, yet he doubted Ellsworth would let him get away with threatening him as he had. Hopefully, the old man was lying about another person wanting the papers. Either way, he needed to get to the bottom of this document business before another woman in his life was hurt.

CHAPTER 14

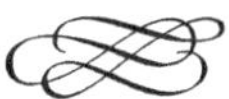

*E*xhausted yet full of hope, Aubrey held a red-faced, dark-haired babe in her arms. She was so beautiful—tiny and precious. Like a piece of Aubrey's heart swaddled snuggly, Melanie Alexis Willot fit into the crook of her arm perfectly. The feather mattress and pillows cushioned them like a nest while soft morning light peeked through the window. Aubrey sighed, leaning back despite the ache in her hips. Melanie had come early in the morning, and Aubrey had been napping since. Rousing to find her baby resting nearby and Lizzy putting away clothing had been a sweet awakening, indeed.

A soft knock sounded at the door. Lizzy stiffened.

Aubrey motioned for her to answer it.

The maid opened the door and spoke in hushed tones to whomever stood on the other side, then closed the door. She turned to Aubrey and raised her eyebrows. "It is your mother-in-law. Would you like to see her now? If not, I shall send her away."

My goodness, send Madame away? Lizzy had courage. Allowing a smile, Aubrey granted the lady entrance.

Her mother-in-law swept in, her cheeks high in color as she glowered at the maid, then shifted her gaze to Lizzy's frizzy red hair. Her shrewish expression fell away upon seeing Melanie. "The babe is lovely. An angel. A girl?" When she met Aubrey's gaze, she furrowed her brow.

Likely, she noticed the bruise on Aubrey's cheek from when she'd been struck. Not wanting to discuss the matter that Madame had already heard about, since by now the newspapers would know, Aubrey offered her the little bundle that was her baby.

Madame sank into a chair near the bed and held her hands up. "Oh, I couldn't possibly. She is so tiny. My babes were always handed straight to a wet nurse after birthing." She swept a critical gaze toward Lizzy. "Do not tell me this fuzzy kitten is your wet nurse."

Cheeks flushing with embarrassment Madame was not inclined to feel, Aubrey held Melanie a little closer. "She is not. I will nurse Melanie."

Madame gasped, her dainty hands flying to her mouth. "You nurse her? How barbaric. And you named her after your mother?"

"Yes, of course. I always wanted to have a girl named after my mother. It is fitting to honor a matriarch who has passed on."

"Of course, it is fitting. Choosing a name is not to be taken lightly. I like to think naming a child is a prediction of the life to come. Melanie means *dark*, and look how fair-skinned she is. I was thinking Louisa in honor of her father."

Aubrey's face froze, as did her insides. What kind of prediction would naming her sweet babe after that lying, scheming, and hateful man be? Composing her face and voice, she replied, "Thank you for your suggestion."

Before Madame could answer, another knock sounded.

Who could that be? She'd written Pa after giving birth, but it was too soon for him to have arrived from Los Angeles.

Lizzy answered the door, then spoke in a hushed voice and closed the door as she had with Madame. "Mr. Reed is here to see you."

"Mr. Reed?" Madame responded before Aubrey could. "Why, the audacity of the man—coming to your room. That butler needs a lesson in decorum. Imagine, bringing a single man to a bedroom. Aubrey, I must insist you allow me to take on the management of the house while you recover. These servants you have hired are truly of the lowest grade."

Aubrey raised her chin. "I did not choose them. Louis did." She made eye contact with Lizzy. "Please show my guest in."

Madame stiffened, raising a hand to stop Lizzy. "Aubrey—"

"My mother-in-law will chaperone." Aubrey raised her eyebrows in question.

The older lady's nostrils flared. "Since I have no choice. Although I know your mother raised you better than to mingle with the hired help. She did come from a distinguished French family."

Was Madame right? Was Aubrey crossing lines that ought not to be crossed? Did they matter now since Nathan had been here when her labor pains started?

The maid opened the door, and Aubrey held her breath.

In stepped Nathan, bringing with him safety and warmth. His steel-blue eyes anchored to her, an invisible connection between them like a chain holding fast. He approached, came to a stop beside her, and inclined his head in greeting. As with Madame, he focused on her bruised cheek. Thankfully, all he said was, "Hello."

"Good morning." Her soft voice gave away so much that she was forced to hide her gaze. My goodness, where had such tenderness come from? She'd only met this man four weeks prior.

"Hello, Miss Aubrey. Madame Willot." He bowed slightly, his gaze settling on the baby. "You and the baby are well?" Now it was his turn to glance away for the tenderness his tone betrayed.

Unable to hide an ounce of her joy, Aubrey smiled. "Yes. We are well. I named her Melanie after my mother. She has all her fingers and toes. A good strong heart and she does not pause when she breathes." All the signs Aubrey had been told to watch for over the years when ladies gathered at socials and mothers shared their most terrifying experiences.

Madame leaned forward, peering at Melanie with caution similar to Nathan's.

Aubrey hugged her closer, warmed by the sheer treasure of such a life.

"You will have to support her head," Nathan pointed, then promptly crossed his arms. "Babies do not have strong neck muscles."

"That's right." Aubrey beamed at him. What a sweetheart.

"Yes. Babies are fragile." Madame startled as Aubrey's little bedside clock chimed.

Something had her on edge, or was she so very uncomfortable around babies? One might expect it of a man, but Madame was a mother herself.

Checking her own time piece, Madame frowned. "My goodness, half past ten already. I'm afraid you will have to excuse me. I have a previous engagement I cannot cancel." She rose, smoothing her dress. "I just wanted to see you, Aubrey. To know you are well. Do let me know if you need anything. I will send a doctor around. We must have you monitored regularly for the next few weeks. You are still in danger." As she went to the door, she made eye contact with Lizzy and jerked her dainty chin toward Aubrey. "Do see that your mistress does not move from the bed without assistance."

"Yes, ma'am." Lizzy nodded and crossed her thick arms. She

stood like a sentinel near Aubrey's bedside, earning a nose wrinkle from Madame and a smile from Aubrey.

Upon the closing of the door, Aubrey motioned Nathan toward the chair. "Please, sit down. I will send for tea and scones."

He swallowed, looking around with uncertainty, then settling himself on the edge of the chair. Had she been too bold? The impropriety of her being abed in her nightgown might offend. If they moved outside, she could don a wrapper. "Would you like to move onto the veranda? It is a glorious day, and I don't care to be shut up in this room."

Nathan had managed a half shake of his head, yet he paused in the middle of her statement. "This is another room you dislike? But you should not be moved, should you?"

"I feel well enough, and yes, I do not like this room." She pulled a face as she scanned the immaculate furniture, massive bed, fireplace, and dressing room. "They moved me to the master once Melanie was born. I typically stay in a lady's guest bedroom."

"I see." He rubbed his palms on his knees. "Yes. I could move you to the veranda. The fresh air might do you good."

"I would like that." She shifted Melanie to one arm and reached for a blanket near the foot of the bed. Her effort was pointless since her arms seemed to have turned to gelatin.

"If you wouldn't mind assisting, Miss Lizzy?" Nathan turned to the maid, who answered as she charged across the room.

"Happy to help the missus." She grabbed the blanket Aubrey had tried to reach. "Now, you can just turn your head, Mr. Reed, I will get Mrs. Willot ready for you to carry to the veranda."

Nathan spun around as though ordered by a military commander.

Aubrey hampered a smile, which Miss Lizzy shared with her. "I forgot to ask, Lizzy, how is your sister?"

"Oh, fine. Very well, in fact, as is her son. A ruddy little tike as blonde as the morning sun." She removed the coverlets and assisted Aubrey into a modest wrapper as she spoke. "She says her husband is returning soon. Some Alaskan fishermen or something or other."

"So she is married"

"Yes, but Mam didn't know the man and didn't like her getting married without us meeting him. When he went to Alaska, Mam said her husband wouldn't come back. My sister is too stubborn to stay with us."

"You said she was in trouble."

"Yeah, she was caught stealing bread from a vendor. Blessedly, a judge took pity on 'er and sent her to the lying-in house and foundling asylum, though that is no happy place to be either. Understaffed and uncleanly." The maid straightened and smiled at Aubrey and Melanie wrapped in a blanket. "The missus is ready, Mr. Reed."

Nathan turned slowly, his shoulders tense. He hesitated a moment before slipping one arm beneath Aubrey's legs and the other behind her back. His warmth soaked through the fabric, and a sudden wave of weariness overtook her. How she wished to rest her face within the crook of his neck, but that would be terribly inappropriate. Besides, such behavior might alarm him. Her heart pattered more quickly as he stood to his full height, and she wrapped one arm around his shoulders. "My goodness, so this is what it feels like to be tall."

He grinned, gaze straight ahead on the doorway Miss Lizzy held open.

Aubrey cooed to her babe. "Pay attention, Melanie. This is likely the only time you will experience the world from such a height."

Miss Lizzy grinned unashamedly. "Unless she finds a man as tall as yours."

Nathan tensed though still held her with the tender strength that only he possessed.

Aubrey could not drag her gaze from his face. She'd been captivated by his beautiful, deep eyes from the first sight of him, yet now, held securely against his chest, the draw to this man was undeniable. Resisting the urge to press her cheek to his, Aubrey sucked in a deep breath. Gardenias scented the air as Nathan stepped onto the stone veranda.

The garden spanned away from this part of the house, the symmetrical patterns of beds of the parterre reminding her of a puzzle. To the left, a basin and fountain of granite. A pathway led from the veranda to a white gazebo Aubrey loved. French roses lined the edge of the veranda. It was clean and crisp in appearance, unlike the wildflowers that bloomed in the Idaho wilderness outside the house she'd grown up in.

"Here you are, Miss Aubrey." Nathan lowered her onto an elaborately braided and woven wicker Wakefield chase lounge. Pieces like it were considered en vogue by all her old school friends. Aubrey had once delighted in such things but now was simply grateful for the soft cushions Miss Lizzy arranged for her.

"Thank you, Lizzy."

"Not to worry, Missus. If you need anything, you just tell Lizzy." She thumped her chest. "My mama told me, 'Lizzy, don't you let anyone near her who'll hurt her. That missus has been through enough.'"

Blushing for the forwardness of the girl, Aubrey set a hand on her cheek while Nathan moved away from her. The loss of connection chilled her, though as he settled on a matching chair beside her, Aubrey focused on her talkative maid. "I appreciate that. Your mother has been a wonderful help to me." How strange to have Cook care for her although Aubrey had tried her utmost to avoid the woman since returning to the chateau.

Miss Lizzy looked around happily. "I think I'll just clip some lavender for the table in your room."

"That would be lovely. Thank you." Aubrey inclined her head.

The scent of lavender mingled with that of the roses and gardenias from where they trailed over an arbor down the walk a little way. Leaves from nearby elms fluttered in a heavenly chorus. Even nature praised God on the first day of her daughter's life. True, nature did so every day, but today was significantly more special.

Aubrey ran her finger along Melanie's cheek. "Is today not the most beautiful day, Mr. Reed?"

"Indeed." He lifted his gaze from the infant to meet Aubrey's, and this time, he did not look away. He peered at her with something akin to courage. Or was that strength? Whatever it was, it warmed her through yet sent a shiver down her spine.

Melanie let out a soft mewing and squirmed.

"Felicity slept for hours after being born. I was so scared she wouldn't wake up," Nathan whispered, his features softening.

"You were there for Felicity's birth?"

He nodded, clasped his hands together, and his hunched shoulders flexed. "By the time I found out where Sarah was, she was in labor. I went to the asylum and waited in the lobby. She died not knowing I had come."

"I'm sorry. Had it been long since you'd seen her?"

"I ran away when I was sixteen. Stole the plow horse. I went back a few years later to pay back my pa and make peace, but he was too bitter. Ma and Sarah wouldn't see me either. They just couldn't find it in their hearts to forgive me."

She nodded, though she was inclined to shake her head. How could any mother not forgive their child? Just holding Melanie, she knew she'd always love her and forgive her. The baby was so perfectly herself yet connected to Aubrey as though somewhere in the making of the baby, their souls had been linked.

"You...ah...you were right, Aubrey." He rested his elbows on his knees. "I need to be honest. I could say that secrets are necessary in my line of work, but it wouldn't be true. I used to believe that intentions to do something good justified a wrong deed. I know now that compromising, as I did when I was sixteen, comes at a cost."

"Sixteen?"

He stood and walked away, only to stop at the edge of the steps and grip one of the pillars that held up the roof. "I shouldn't burden you with my trouble. You have your baby to focus on. You must be tired. But after last night, I just didn't want you thinking I am a bad man."

"I have seen bad men. You are not that." She shook her head, holding Melanie carefully in one arm, and extended her hand to him. "Mr. Reed?"

He turned, and locking his fingers within hers, let her guide him to sit on the edge of the chase lounge. "You might not think that once you've heard everything."

A chill settled on her. She'd not liked the truth of who Louis was, and she'd had to learn that over time. Nathan offered her a glimpse of himself, and even though she could respect his transparency, she also feared it. Why did their relationship have to change, just when she'd learned to trust and care for him?

His fingers relaxed. He would pull away soon, and then what? She might lose the chance to know the real Nathan Reed. She tightened her grip and inhaled deeply. "I'm listening."

*G*rief like a festering wound paining his chest, Nathan hung his head. He had planned to tell Aubrey about the deed and his need to turn it over to the bank to keep her safe. How had they come to discuss his past?

He couldn't move, memories wrapped around him like cables. That day when he was sixteen, he'd thought he was doing the right thing, loosing Billy's chains. Nothing had been the same since then. He'd failed at every turn, and here was Aubrey—a woman who had every reason to doubt him, yet she seemed to continually accept him. He didn't deserve her.

"I know I said I'm not a bad man, but I'm not good either." A wave of numbness washed over him, and he closed his eyes to the terrible truth.

Aubrey ran her soft thumb against his skin. "You are ambitious if you hope to be a good man."

Nathan snapped his gaze up to her—a braid over one shoulder, bruise on one cheek, and eyes clear and honest.

She raised her eyebrows. "There has only ever been one genuinely good man. The rest of us just do our best."

"I haven't done my best. I gave up when I was sixteen."

Aubrey pressed her lips together, then straightened her shoulders as though mustering courage. "What happened when you were sixteen?"

He focused on her dainty hand settled over the top of his and turned his palm up so her fingers intertwined with his. She squeezed firmly, and he could breathe again. "I grew up in Oregon, farming. Eventually, I wanted to do anything but work a plow, and my pa's dearest friend—Sheriff Rudy—took me under his wing. For a while, our arrangement worked—going with him on trails, hunting criminals. The thrill, the hard work, sleeping outside—I was made for it. I even..." A smile tried to work onto his lips.

"What?" Aubrey's eyes sparkled with curiosity. "Come, Mr. Reed, do not keep me waiting to learn what brings about that mysterious smile."

"If you want to see my smile, you might consider leaving off formality and calling me Nathan."

Her gaze was like the deepest mountain lake, brightest green and clear. If only he could dive into those cool depths—leave behind his old life long enough to stop the hurt. Aubrey was an escape, a path he'd never tread, a course never taken. She was precious and too good for him.

Instead of answering his invitation to address him informally, she shrugged, looking incredibly young. She was guarded, and who could blame her? Certainly not him. Allowing her the comfort of formality was a gift, and he was honored to give it.

"You will like the answer." He traced the ridges of her knuckles with his finger. "I bought a camera in Portland, Oregon, when I collected my first bounty. I took it apart and put it back together repeatedly. Sheriff Rudy let me work in his tack shop when I was in town. I played with mirrors, lenses, and sheets until I could build a camera."

"Hm." She cocked her head to the side. "This sounds like more than an interest in photography."

"Yes, ma'am. A fascination. In fact, I had a patent for a smaller, lighter camera filed with the United States Patent Office, then I ruined it all—my chance to invent *and* my career in law enforcement." He plucked a thread from her knit blanket, focusing his attention there and not on the woman before him. "A boy I went to school with was convicted of murder. I was part of the transport when it came time to move him. Trouble was, I still don't think he did it." Even the thought hurt his chest.

Aubrey squeezed his hand. "What happened to him?"

"Billy had fallen in with some older boys, robbing stages. He was going to hang. He pleaded with me to release him. Said he didn't hurt anyone. That it was the leader of the gang, his older brother, who committed the crime he was sentenced to die for. I took the keys when Sheriff Rudy wasn't looking and let Billy out." His pulse pounded and cheeks turned hot, the memories from that day swarming in with the thunder of horse's hooves and crack of gunshots. "I didn't know, but his gang was waiting for the transport. They started shooting. Billy was always good with a rifle. He cracked me over the head with a rock, took my rifle, and picked off two guards. Knocked me out for hours. When I woke up, Sheriff Rudy was hanging from a tree."

Nathan took his hand from Aubrey's tender one and pressed his thumb and finger over his eyes, trying to block out the visuals.

"It sounds to me as though this gang would have attacked no matter what." Aubrey's voice was so hesitant, Nathan hated to disagree.

"No, Aubrey. One man survived. He said Billy shot from within the group. It caused confusion, gave him the upper hand, and the gang just swarmed in."

Aubrey stayed quiet, nothing but the wind in the trees and the distant off-key singing of Miss Lizzy.

Nathan cleared his throat, trying to push back his shoulders against the massive weight he felt. "I went back home. Worked every day as hard as I could farming, but nothing was the same. My folks fought more after that, and Sarah was never happy again. My pa hardly looked at me—as though I wasn't even his son anymore. It became so bad that one day, I took the plow horse at the end of the day and left, not returning for two years. Sheriff Rudy was my pa's best friend, and Pa couldn't forgive me. It was my fault. Pa said a man was only as good as his word. My word to the law didn't mean anything, and a man died for it.

That's when I realized…" The strength left his shoulders, and he shrugged, numb inside. "I'm a worthless man."

"That's not true." Aubrey clasped his wrist, as though trying to bring him back from the sunburned memories of Oregon. "Our worth is found in God, not the good or bad things we do."

Nathan resisted, holding himself apart from her. She was a fine, good-hearted lady who had suffered because of her own bad man. He shouldn't be anywhere near her.

He looked away, trying to block out the beautiful day he had no place in. A soft, mewing cry kept him in place. Aubrey's tiny baby turned her head, then was still. She was so innocent like Felicity. Why had God allowed him to be in their lives?

"You know the Bible says those who are forgiven much, love much?" Aubrey's voice sounded timid again.

Nathan raised his stinging eyes. "Miss Aubrey, my pa, ma, and sister—the people who should love me better than any others—could not forgive me."

Her eyes opened wide. "Why, I was speaking of God. And isn't His forgiveness, His opinion, the most important?"

Nathan sat a little taller. "Yes, ma'am."

"As for a man being worth something because of an attribute of honesty—well, honesty is a fine thing, but our true value is found in Christ."

"That's sweet of you to say, but when you're a man, folks measure your worth in how dependable you are."

She tightened her jaw, obviously not liking his comment, then her brow smoothed out. "I see. When you are on a bounty, there is no contract to uphold. If you get the man, you get the reward without the risk of failing. People see you as a strong man who brings criminals to justice. You weren't able to pursue law enforcement after that infraction, so you found another way to follow your dream. A way without the risk of letting others down."

Was she right? Was bounty hunting a way of hiding from

the expectations of others? Was he still chasing the hope of becoming a good man? He had stopped the bank robbery and saved her, then rescued her from the thief the night before. But was he good? No.

Nathan squirmed. "I wouldn't call it a dream. It's just work."

Her gaze dashed away, and she blinked.

Darn, he'd hurt her. Why had he been stupid, denying it when she was probably right? Part of him still wanted to enforce the law, be an upstanding man—someone who protected the community and fought for justice. Captain Hiram had offered him a job, and now that Aubrey had committed to take care of Felicity, he could accept it.

Well, he had to clear up this business with Ellsworth and Ralston first. Should he tell her now? Explain about his association with Ellsworth and the search for the document? Would him saving her life in the bank and then in the robbery be enough, or would she kick him out of her house? Either way, she deserved to know.

"There's something more I need to tell you, Aubrey."

"Oh?" She adjusted Melanie in her arms, peace radiating from her as she merely glanced at the child. And he would snuff that out with the truth.

"Listen to me." His stern voice caught her attention. "You're not safe. There are men your husband was associated with who are after something he stole."

Sure enough, a shadow passed across her face where there had been peace. "Does this have to do with the kidnapping in May?"

"No. Louis stole a silver mine that the Bank of California purchased. It seems he had all the information about it, even the location and deed. His business partners are after them."

"How do you know?"

He sighed long. "Because, before I met you, before the bank

robbery and before you said you'd help Felicity, I worked for them."

Her shoulders tensed, alert eyes casting about as though in search of something to ward him off with. "What exactly did you do for them?"

"I was tasked with searching for the documents related to that sale."

"Is that why you took the job from Madame, to search this house?"

"No. I took the job for Madame to keep you safe. The truth is, I never should have agreed to look for the stolen documents in the first place because to do so, I had to break the law. I was trying to move Felicity from the asylum. I couldn't leave her to go bounty hunting, so I took a local job. I was desperate, so I compromised." His gut tightened and his heart thundered. Bearing her poignant gaze was hard, but looking away would be cowardly. "I believe Louis sent the documents here from Utah at the time of his arrest. Remember, your brother broke into his house to get the evidence needed to arrest him?"

Aubrey startled. "How do you know that?"

"I have been investigating the Willots to try and gage if you are safe. If they are still after something."

"What have you found?" She glanced at the door as though expecting Madame and her guards to come through.

"So far, it seemed as though Madame is just here to visit, but I am still waiting to hear back about some leads. Until I know for sure, we cannot trust anyone."

Aubrey nodded and held her baby a little closer. "So they want something Louis stole, and you know because you used to work for them?"

"Yes. I was tasked with searching your house just a few days after you moved in."

She shook her head, likely remembering that night when

he'd lit the lamp, not knowing she was there. "I saw footprints under the study window."

"That's right—those were mine. I broke into the study through the window. When I saw how frightened you were, when you almost caught me, I knew I was wrong. Wasn't long after that, I told my boss, one of your husband's business associates, that I would not work for him any longer. I don't want to be the kind of man who breaks into homes."

Aubrey frowned. He'd expected anger, but if she cried, he'd break.

Instead, she shot a haughty scowl at him. "Should I turn you in to the police?"

He let go of her hand. "If you do, someone else will come looking for those papers, and I won't be here to help you."

"Is that what those men were doing here last night?"

"Yes. They were sent because I didn't find the documents. After we parted ways yesterday, I met with an associate and learned those men were headed out here. I passed a police officer on the way and told them of the danger. They came too."

"Oh." She raised her eyebrows. "And have you spoken to the police regarding this investigation of yours?"

"Some, yes. But if you're asking did I turn myself in for breaking and entering your house, no. If I am in jail, who will take care of Felicity? Who will investigate Madame and make sure she and Emil have not cooked up some scheme to cause you harm? If you want to press charges, fine. But I really think, at this point, that would be unwise."

She narrowed her eyes, keeping her brow hard.

There was no telling where her thoughts ran, but at last, her expression softened and she spoke. "I suppose you are right. You needn't worry that I will press charges. You came to me to make things right, so I will extend charity and forgive you."

Nathan blinked. What was he supposed to say to that? Did God want him to turn himself in? A judge wouldn't simply offer him forgiveness. He massaged the muscles in his neck. "Thank you, Aubrey. How do you feel about me searching the house for the bank's documents?"

She sighed, then shook her head slowly. "There isn't anything like that here. Louis had told his lawyers to auction this house and all the belongings off. When he died, my pa helped me stop the sale. Papa paid enough of the debts so I could retain the house, but everything had been cleaned out. Sure, the furniture is here, but it's all empty. There are no decorations, vases, ceramics, other than what my pa sent here from our home in Los Angeles. And a few things Madame has brought in without telling me."

What if she was right and the paperwork was cleared out, destroyed, before Aubrey's father had halted the auctioneers? "What about the things in the secret room?"

She nibbled her lower lip. "There is nowhere else, but those crates are my things from before I was married. It's so strange that he put them there. Do you think he believed I would find them?"

"I have no idea, but if you'll allow me, I will search everywhere. If the documents are here, I'll find them."

"Yes, that will be fine." She stared down the garden path, past box hedges and white gardenias to the patch of lavender where Lizzy knelt with enough clippings to open a flower shop. Aubrey didn't seem to notice, so listless was her gaze. She'd been so peaceful and joyful when he'd arrived, but he'd ruined that. She reclined on her settee, folded in the blanket with the babe in her arms. Perfectly maternal, feminine, and angelic, and he'd brought the stain of crime into her home.

Nathan wiped his hands on his pant legs. "I best be moving on." He'd endured her troubled gaze long enough. "Sorry, Aubrey, for everything."

"Wait." She put out her hand. "You can't mean to leave me here."

He frowned. Where else was he supposed to leave her?

"That is, I'm sorry to impose, but I had hoped you might help me back inside."

The thought of wrapping his arms around her, of being so near when his heart was raw and his shame so heavy, sent an ache right through him. But how could he deny her? "Of course, I won't leave you." His heart gave a start at the statement and how true it rang through him.

Lizzy was striding down the garden path toward them, so he knelt to reach Aubrey more easily. One hand behind her back, the other under her legs, he lifted, and as before, one of her arms rested on his shoulders. He was near enough to Melanie to smell her baby scent, and he ached to hold his own little girl.

"Mr. Reed, I..." Aubrey, too, glanced at Lizzy, who started to run when they neared the door that needed opening. Soon they would have an audience. Her voice softened even further, though he could hear her clearly with such close proximity. "I meant what I said, that I forgive you for breaking into my house and for not being completely honest with me. Your actions on the whole reflect a moral character—with the bank robbery, the break-in, and my labor. You have been ..." She shook her head, those startling green eyes like the freshest of spring buds.

"I'm not a hero, Aubrey. Any other man could have happened upon that robber last night or the thief in the bank."

"Not any man." There was a certainty to her voice. "I needed a man who was brave, strong, able, and available. I could be wrong, but perhaps God brought you here for such a time as this."

Heart thundering for the implications that only yesterday seemed impossible, Nathan held her more firmly. "Such a time as what?"

She shrugged. "My time of need when I have no one else. The thing is, it's easy to be brave when you are around. The world is just a safer place."

Shaking his head, he looked away. Lizzy reached them, pushing the door open. Nathan stepped in, hardly noticing his surroundings, only that Aubrey was in his arms and she wanted him in her life. There was no way a woman like Aubrey could think such righteous, admirable things about him. He was a swindler and a liar, yet when he set her down and she beamed up at him, he wanted to be better. Maybe he could change.

Nathan's conversation with Aubrey had drained him, but that didn't stop him from riding back into town to meet Felicity's new wet nurse. All the way, his heart floated upon a sea of uncertainty. Had he done the right thing in telling Aubrey so much, and so soon after her delivery? Was there a better way to protect her? Did she really see him as brave and good as she said?

And what about Felicity? Aubrey had told him she had instructed her business manager to arrange a monthly stipend to pay for Felicity's care. She had also sent a message to Mrs. Miller at the asylum, asking her to help Nathan find a wet nurse and all the things he would need to tend Felicity. It was another toss on his sea of confusion as he struggled against the feelings of shame. He'd been unable to take care of Felicity on his own yet wanted to be grateful to God for providing a way for her to escape the asylum. These things had just been so far outside his control or comfort.

Reining in Sammy outside the wet nurse's little apartment on Taylor Street, Nathan swung down from the saddle and tethered the horse to the hitching post. The golden summer sun was setting over the rooftops of the houses. Already, Mrs. Miller's little buggy was hitched outside, which must mean that she had brought Felicity here to meet the nurse as well.

Stomach curled up behind his ribs, he climbed the steps

and paused at the door, offering a prayer of thanksgiving and a request for mercy. He needed God to bless this meeting with the nurse who would take care of Felicity until she was weaned.

He rapped on the door. After a moment, it opened, and Nathan faced Ms. Thornson from the asylum. Though he was used to seeing her in the dark nursery, he recognized the curled bangs and high braided bun of the night nurse. The soft light from the foyer lamp showed her to be much younger than he'd realized. Indeed, she likely wasn't over twenty.

Mrs. Miller walked up behind her, Felicity in her arms. "Mr. Reed, have you met Ms. Thornson?"

"Yes. Hello again, Ms. Thornson." Nathan gripped the young woman's hand gently, Mrs. Miller looking on with an approving smile. Many of the nurses at the asylum were in their teens, unmarried yet capable of nursing an infant.

The modest foyer opened into a small parlor, but no child was there. Where was Ms. Thornson's child?

"Please, come in, Mr. Reed." She motioned toward a chair before a small stove. The furniture was sparse but clean, so that was a good sign. Mrs. Miller offered him Felicity. He slid his hands around her warm, pudgy sides, her yellow hair catching the sheen of lamp light. After he'd seen Aubrey's baby, she seemed so big. When she rested in his arms, gnawing on a fist and looking around with wide blue eyes, his heart softened.

"When I heard you were looking to hire a wet nurse, I went straight to Mrs. Miller's office to inquire about your requirements. I have nursed the babe since she was born, and I have a clean, safe home. Mrs. Miller says if you don't object, I would be a good fit for the position." Ms. Thornson looked at him with pleading eyes.

He couldn't move past two words—*the babe.* "Felicity." His voice scraped when he spoke, so he cleared his throat. "Her name is Felicity Reed."

The lady flushed and cast her gaze down as though her

lapse was unforgiveable. While Aubrey occasionally blushed an adorable dusty rose color, this was different. Ms. Thornson hung her head and gripped her hands into white-knuckled fists.

"I didn't mean to upset you." He gentled his voice. "The place is nice, and you have taken good care of Felicity in the past. I trust you will do so in the future."

"Oh, thank you, Mr. Reed. I will take care of her as though she is my own. Rest assured."

He turned up the corners of his mouth and nodded. Eventually, Felicity would need a mother. Aubrey came to mind, but could she ever really love the child Louis had fathered in adultery?

Mrs. Miller went through details about payments arranged through the bank and said no money need be passed between Nathan and the nurse. Just as well. He'd not be able to come to town much until he got to the bottom of things with Ellsworth.

Felicity began to fuss, turning her head from side to side and curling her lips into a frown.

"My, she's hungry already. Here, give her to me." Ms. Thornson took her with a tender smile as though the babe was her own.

This was good, Felicity having someone to take care of her, yet he still wanted to hold onto her. Once Ms. Thornson carried Felicity into the next room, Mrs. Miller took out some documents and organized them on the table before them. "Here are the custody papers. Felicity has your name because of Sarah, but perhaps that is for the best. If you find a wife, the whole family could have one name, and no one would be the wiser. Felicity could grow up and never know she was the product of sin."

Nathan stiffened. Felicity was a beautiful child, wonderfully made. She didn't come into the world with any more sin than the rest of mankind. Certainly, she did not carry the stain of a sin not her own—that of her parents.

Rather than starting a sermon, which he was ill equipped to do, Nathan took the pen she handed him and scrawled his name at the bottom of the paper. His head felt light, he was so relieved. Felicity was his daughter now. He had custody of her, and no one could take her away.

"I will have you know, Mr. Reed..." Mrs. Miller withdrew a pair of spectacles and perched them on her straight nose. "I recommended Ms. Thornson because she is a kind, hardworking, Christian woman in need of a husband."

That straightened his spine. He needed a nurse, not a wife. Actually, he did need a wife. Which he would get without the matron's help.

Blowing on the ink, the matron met his gaze with hawk-like keenness. "Fanny—Ms. Thornson—came to the asylum last year. She'd fallen prey to the pretty words of a philandering politician. Rather than risk his anger, she bore the child with us. Sadly, he did not survive. Having nowhere to go but the street, Fanny chose to stay as a nurse. During that time, she has worked and saved enough for this place which she shares with an elderly widow you will likely meet. Mrs. Frill is already abed." She flattened her lips. "I had hoped you would arrive earlier so you could meet her and spend more time with Fanny."

Unease simmering in his chest, Nathan took the custody papers, folded them, and placed them in his coat. "Thank you for your kindness, Mrs. Miller. I understand as the matron of the asylum, you work well in an executive role. But you may rest assured that the Lord is doing just fine managing my life, including the possibility of a future marriage."

The matron's eyes went wide, and she actually blushed. "Of course. I just knew you were looking, so..."

He had considered marrying someone just to care for Felicity, but he didn't have to rush anymore. He wasn't ready for a wife unless it was Aubrey.

The breath caught in his chest at that staggering thought. Aubrey—his wife and the girls sisters, not because they shared a father but because they were a family. Ears ringing, he shook his head. Such fanciful thoughts would get him nowhere. He was better off just thanking God for what He had provided today. As for tomorrow, that was in His capable hands.

CHAPTER 15

In the dimly lit secret room, Aubrey sat on the floor on a blanket, her belongings from long ago spread around her while Nathan stood near the desk, sorting through the camera supplies she'd purchased. She withdrew a photograph of the Pacific's long shoreline from one of the many piles needing to be sorted. Changing huts spotted the black sand, and bathers filled the beach and water, with nary a space for actual swimming. Indeed, the summer of her sixteenth year had been so hot, everyone had flocked to the seashore to cool off in the saltwater. She smiled softly, remembering the scandalous pantaloon-style bathing suit her friend had worn. Oh, to be so innocent again.

What was she thinking? She'd never want to be ignorant like that again. Had she really learned, though? Just look at Nathan. She had assumed he was a man above reproach, but he had set her straight on that. A robber who worked for men of Louis's ilk. Yet he had come to her and admitted that and more. He'd not even become angry when she questioned him and practically dared him to turn himself in to the authorities. Louis would have backhanded her for challenging him. There was a balance to men being bad or good, and somehow, she'd figure it out.

She sighed and returned to sifting through the old memories. So far, the crate she'd rummaged through contained only her things. Oddly enough, it was not the crate she'd packed as a young bride when she'd moved from Papa's home. It appeared Louis had pilfered through everything and had it repacked.

She sighed, wrinkling her nose at the dusty smell. It was best to not bring Melanie down here, even though being away from her was hard. The baby should be protected from anything potentially dangerous, and Lizzy said she would take good care of her.

"You've got everything you'll need to develop the shots you took the other night of the fountain, Aubrey." Nathan spoke with his hands on his hips, the supplies arranged neatly in front of him. "Tin plates, collodion, and ingredients for a silver bath solution. A new camera too. Why'd you get another one?"

"My American Optical is huge. I cannot take it everywhere with me, especially now that Melanie is here."

"Fair enough. Have you picked the prints you want me to take to Watkins?"

"Yes, they are over there in that pile." She rose, leaving her memories to rest for the moment and picking her way through her scattered belongings on the floor. "Do you think we could mix up a developing bath before going to see Mr. Watkins? I have some plates that need developing. I would like for him to see my most recent work."

Nathan turned wide eyes on her. "Right now? Sure."

She smiled, and he lifted his hand. For a moment, it seemed he would guide her to his side, maybe even put his arm around her, but he didn't. Why did she feel relieved yet disappointed? Nathan had trusted her with the truth, and she respected that, but what if there was more? What if a future lay before them, but she couldn't see it because she was analyzing his every word for traces of dishonesty? No one was perfect, but did that mean that any man she loved would end up hurting her?

Aubrey dug out the glass mixing cups and trays for baths. Next, she measured out the ingredients and poured them into trays, muscle memory giving a rhythm to her work.

Nathan stood back watching her, arms crossed, with the slightest of smiles in place. Aubrey finished up, and he set out soaking trays big enough to hold the plates.

"I have the slide." Nathan offered the mahogany protective slide that the plate fit into to shield it from light.

"Thank you. Will you please put the red shades on the lamps?" The room was dim already, but the darker, the better.

Nathan moved with excitement, his eyes eager once the shades were in place and he was back at her side.

Aubrey removed the dark plate she'd used the night she'd run into the column in the garden. She submerged it in the developing bath and asked over her shoulder, "Do you have a watch?"

"I do. Fifteen minutes?"

"Yes." She held her breath, trying not to smile. All too quickly, she became aware of Nathan's warmth spanning the space between them. Aubrey turned, leaning against the desk, but that only made it worse. He smiled, tipping the corners of his mouth. Warmed through, she folded her hands lest she reach out and touch him, just to feel the strong muscled arms that had carried her to safety on more than one occasion. "Did, ah..." What was she saying, thinking? *Say something, idiot.* "Did you get the money for Felicity?" Not the best topic of conversation.

"Yes, thank you."

The seconds stretched as the tension thickened. Aubrey blew through her lips, then pressed them together.

"What will you do if Watkins sells all your photographs?" Nathan spoke, some hesitancy in his voice.

She blinked, confused by the question. "Develop more."

"I know that. I mean, are you going to open a camera shop? Photography studio? If you do, what will make yours different from others?"

"That's a good question." She adjusted the cuffs of her sleeves. "I would like to photograph families. Jesse and I were able to capture so much of our lives before our mother died because of our photographs."

"So a studio that captures family life. Maybe you could go out to homesteads and photograph them with the families or couples standing out front. Then there are Christmases, birthdays..."

"Exactly. Special occasions." Her smile echoed in her voice.

"Sounds nice." A tenderness rang in his.

Aubrey bit back a smile, resisting the urge to lean into him.

What was wrong with her? She'd never struggled so much with inclinations to be near Louis or her other suitors, but with Nathan, it was like the opposite poles of two magnets drawn together. *Is this because I'm lonely, God? Alone with Melanie and wishing she could have a papa as good as mine?* Throat tight, Aubrey mentally veered away from that topic. Hopefully, Pa would arrive soon to visit her.

At last, the photograph was done, and Nathan turned the lamps up again while Aubrey held her breath and carefully lifted the tin plate. Next, she placed it in a water bath for twenty seconds, then lifted it into the red light. The photograph had finished even better than she'd imagined. The moon had been like a perfect white globe that night, and sure enough, it reflected off the water in the round fountain basin. The rest of the garden was cast in deep shadows, though some shapes took form, like the neatly manicured hedges and stone paths catching moonlight.

"That is really a piece of art." Nathan spoke near her shoulder.

"Most people don't consider photographs art."

"You captured this in a way I never could."

"What, you? The camera inventor?" She knocked her arm against his playfully.

He met her gaze over one shoulder. "I can piece together a machine. Not everyone can make photographs like this, Aubrey. In fact, I'd wager few can. You see the beauty in things that others don't."

More pleased with herself than she'd been in a long time, she propped her hands on her hips and gave a contented sigh.

Nathan's gaze lingered on her cheek, then shifted elsewhere. The bruise there from when she'd been struck had not faded all the way. Pa would be plenty cross when he saw it.

Nathan looked behind her to the piles she'd made beside the stacks of crates. "Did you see anything in that stuff that might look like the legal documents?"

"No." She sighed, contentment gone. She didn't like the idea of men possibly coming to the house, especially now that Melanie was here.

One of the bells rang near the desk. Nathan glanced in that direction, then at Aubrey. "Did you ever figure out what those bells are attached to?"

"No. I assume it's a signal, though." She tiptoed around a pile of her belongings.

"Maybe the front door." Nathan followed her. "Are you expecting a visitor?

Aubrey paused at the foot of the stairs, then she smiled. "Yes. My papa!"

~

*U*pon seeing the tall, dark-haired man waiting near the floor-to-ceiling window, Aubrey rushed across the master study and plunged into her father's embrace. His arms went around her like a great warm blanket. The door closed behind her, telling her that Nathan had remained with her.

Papa drew back, kissing both her cheeks. "The maid said she would fetch you and the baby. A daughter?" The awe in his voice confirmed that boy or not, he was pleased.

"Yes, her name is Melanie Alexis."

As if by magic, Lizzy rapped the door and peeked inside. "Ah, Missus, I thought I heard your voice." She came around the door, cradling Melanie in her arms.

Less than an hour had passed, yet still Aubrey's heart soared at the sight of her pink-faced baby. "There you are, darling."

Of course, Melanie was sleeping and heard nothing of what happened around her. Aubrey took her in her arms and handed her to her grandpa.

"She is perfect." He whispered as though he feared waking her.

As Papa supported the baby's head with his large fingertips, Melanie turned toward him, lifting her eyebrows, then resting her rumpled little chin on his chest. He was quiet, swaying slowly beside one of the large overstuffed chairs. Then he looked up, and his dark eyebrows sank low.

Nathan stood behind her, tall and resolute as usual, though he raised his eyebrows at her as though giving her leave to introduce him or send him away.

"Oh, Mr. Reed, please excuse my lack of manners." Aubrey beckoned him to approach. "Pa, this is Mr. Nathan Reed. He is a friend of mine and also...well, he's also my guard. Mr. Reed, this is my father, Mr. Titus Alexander of Los Angeles."

Pa offered his bear paw of a hand, and the men shook hands, eye to eye. "Why are you protecting my daughter?"

Aubrey stepped closer to the men. "At first, it was Madame Willot who hired him. I think she meant for Nathan to report my comings and goings, but as it happens, he has put my security before all else."

Pa looked Nathan up and down. The two men were matched in height and stature, though Pa was a little broader and Nathan lithe as cowboys tended to be. "You always work as a guard, Mr. Reed?"

"No, sir. I typically hunt bounties in California, Idaho, and Oregon."

"If that's the case, why are you here?"

Nathan's expression gave away none of the unease he must feel. "My sister had a babe here in San Francisco. When she died, the child stayed at the San Francisco Foundling Asylum where she'd been born."

Pa grimaced and adjusted Melanie in his arms, holding her a little closer. "I'm sorry to hear that. I hope you are able to remove her soon."

"I have been, only recently. She is living with her nurse in town."

"You are unmarried, then?"

Nathan nodded respectfully, his manner easy. How could he endure such a multitude of personal questions from Pa and still remain calm?

Cheeks warm, Aubrey motioned toward the sitting area, where the couch and two chairs made a square with the fireplace. "Shall we sit? I'm glad you're here, Pa. Maybe you can help us with a situation that's come up."

Pa stopped her with a hand on her arm. Likely, with the light from the window behind her, he'd just noticed the mark where she'd been struck.

Slipping her arm through his, she led him toward the fireplace. "There was a break-in a week ago, the night before Melanie was born. Mr. Reed saved me from an intruder, but not before the man struck me."

"Where is he?" Pa spoke the words through a tight jaw.

He'd always been a measure wilder than the rest of his elite family in Baltimore. Relieved to have him with her again, she lowered to the sofa with him beside her. "They were arrested."

"Have they gone before a judge?"

"I cannot answer that. I'm afraid I've yet to leave the house since Melanie was born."

Nathan sat in one of the chairs with his hands clasped before him, his muscular shoulders tense in the light-gray shirt he wore. "They were arraigned and sentenced just a few days ago. One year in prison. I fear the danger is not over, though. Madame is traveling with valuables. That may have attracted attention, or perhaps someone heard Aubrey was living here alone and thought she would be easy prey."

Why wasn't Nathan telling Pa the real reason?

"That may be." Pa looked at Aubrey, taking her hand. "Unless your mother-in-law had something to do with the break-in. Where any of them French?"

"Pa, not everyone who is French is associated with the Willots."

"I suppose you're right, *ma fille*." He used the French term for *daughter* that Mother had used in her lifetime. Warmed by the special address yet saddened because her mother was not there, Aubrey rested her head on her papa's shoulder.

Nathan stood, meeting Aubrey's gaze, then Pa's. "I have an appointment in town I have been avoiding. Now that your father is here, I will leave you in his care."

He had stayed for her sake? My goodness, how dangerous the situation must be. "Will you be back for dinner?"

"I'm afraid not." He shook Pa's hand, then promptly headed for the study door.

Why had he left her to tell Pa about the danger she faced? Shouldn't he be here to explain? Perhaps he believed Pa would keep her safe and did not need to know more. So...should she tell him?

"Aubrey?" Pa's voice sounded beside her.

"Just one moment, Papa." She patted his knee, then darted to the door and caught Nathan still in the hallway. "Mr. Reed?"

Turning, he raised his eyebrows.

Plans of the conspiracy to find a silver mine deed flown from her mind, Aubrey asked, "When will I see you again?"

He shrugged, gaze averted. What a change from when they'd developed her photographs in the study and spoken of a studio.

Clasping her hands before her, still adjusting to the difference of having a flat tummy instead of the mound that had been Melanie, Aubrey asked the question she didn't really want an answer to. "Why didn't you tell my pa about the trouble with Louis's business associates?"

"Why would I?"

"Because he might be able to help. He knows a lot of people and is a powerful man in his own right."

Nathan's jaw flexed. "You want your father to investigate this, not me?"

"Not necessarily, but he would be an asset. When Jesse and I were kidnapped, Pa connected with a number of law enforcement officers, including members of the Salt Lake City Police Department and even a U.S. Marshal."

Color bloomed in Nathan's face. He flexed his hands, his chest rising, then falling.

Why was he becoming upset?

"There's no telling who might be involved with this, Aubrey. If your pa goes poking around, he may spook the men behind this before I can collect sufficient evidence to stop them."

"Oh, I hadn't thought of that." No wonder he looked frustrated. And here she'd been jabbering on like a magpie. Aubrey touched a hand to her warm cheek, Louis's voice haunting her thoughts and driving embarrassment deeper. *Stupid woman.* He'd say it under his breath as though the thought had leaked out. Those had been the first of his words to ever slice her tender heart.

Why couldn't she be better, braver, smarter, as she'd determined to be in the bank? Yet standing in front of Nathan, she suddenly felt small. What he must think of her. No! She was intelligent. And she was right about this. "My pa would be a great asset. You can't do this on your own."

Nathan looked away, then nodded. "If you think it's best, you may do as you wish. I will be here if you need me." He headed for the front door.

"I am not stupid. Why are you walking away?"

He angled back toward her, his brow furrowed. "Is there something more you'd like to say?"

That heat in her cheeks burned hotter—not just in her face but in her chest. Why was he being so difficult? So prideful?

"If you don't want to do this, I will do it myself. I can hire investigators with Louis's money. I can hire guards as well."

Nathan's eyes widened, then narrowed as he stepped nearer —so close, she had to tip up her chin to meet his gaze. "I am not him, Aubrey."

She back-stepped, her breath releasing in a hot rush. "I know you are not. This has nothing to do with...with Louis."

"No? It seems like little you say, do, or even think doesn't have to do with him. Louis's money. Louis's study. Louis's secret room. Louis's house, locked windows and all." Nathan bent his head, eyes piercing her, and his shoulders hunched. "How long will you live in *his* world, Aubrey? You have the freedom to do what you want. Open a photography studio. Take photographs of kittens, children, and the ocean. Unlock all the windows. Burn down the house if you like."

The heat from earlier a blaze now, Aubrey glared at Nathan, gesturing to the lovely home around her. "Why would I burn down this house? I love this house."

"Do you? Why? You didn't even live here until last summer."

That quieted her. She'd not admit how weak she'd been, locked away in the house in New York. Louis had built this house for her as a wedding present, then did not allow her to live here until it was too late. Did Nathan know that as well from his criminal inquiries into her?

And yet he continued, his voice softer. "How many rooms do you avoid? You stay in Louis's study, receive your guests there. Why? To prove something...that you belong?"

"I do belong. And you are wrong. I decided to invest in photography weeks ago. I even spoke with my business manager. And the money I gave you was from me, not Louis."

"Not me. Felicity. I don't need anything from you."

She winced internally yet held her chin ever higher. "Yes, I know. Like you also don't need my pa's help. Well, that's fine. I will take care of myself, with or without your help." Emotions a fiery torrent, she forced a calming breath, yet it felt as though all the world was suddenly raining brimstone down on her. "And if more illegitimate children come forward, I will take care of them too. What an inheritance! Louis's estate is vast, indeed." She sealed her lips, hating that she'd exposed so much hurt to anyone.

Jaw twitching, Nathan held her gaze, then dropped his away. "I don't mean to cause you trouble, but Sarah and Felicity didn't deserve to be cast out into the cold."

"I did not put them there. I did not know about them!" Tears accosted her before she could stop them.

A door opened down the hall. Madame stepped from a parlor, her nose in a book. There was no way Aubrey would allow her mother-in-law to see her tears—or insert herself into a conversation Aubrey was thoroughly done with.

"Good day, Mr. Reed." Aubrey opened the door and returned to the study.

~

The moment Aubrey left Nathan in the hall, Madame looked up with a frown. Framed by the arch, she was like a painting of some regal queen come to life. She approached him like Herodias might John the Baptizer. Well, he wasn't letting her run off with his head, especially when Aubrey had just dragged his heart away with her.

The thought gave him pause. When he'd spent time with her over the past few weeks, he'd hoped for a future without realizing it. Now, such dreams seemed futile. She was too hurt, he was too broken, and what chance did Felicity have beside Melanie?

Madame clasped her book and turned her gaze toward the study. "Who is that man visiting my daughter-in-law?"

"Her father has come to see her."

She shrank away from the door. "Titus Alexander?"

"Yes, ma'am."

Considering the turn of Madame's lips, she and Mr. Alexander did not get along well. They were different in class and culture. While Mr. Alexander was wealthy, his frock coat was not extravagant, and the manner in which he'd gripped Nathan's hand set him apart as a driven, protective, but also courageous man. If Nathan had to guess, Mr. Alexander was also honest like Aubrey. Probably, Madame would not have a lot in common with him.

"Well, I suppose that clears up how much time you will be spending with Mrs. Willot." She narrowed her gaze on him. "Not that it matters. Aubrey will settle down now that the baby is born, but I still require your services to guard my things. I am sailing for France in a month, and while I do not foresee trouble, my stepson insists I keep his belongings guarded." She rolled her eyes, though Nathan's skin prickled.

So the item in need of protecting belonged to Emil? He

would have to discover what it was. "Does this mean you would like for me to serve as guard in the carriage house?"

"Yes, you may take the night watch. Under no circumstances should the item be left unattended."

He fisted his hands. Madame was obviously used to giving orders, and while he did technically work for her, he didn't like being corralled like a spring colt at the end of a whip. Best to remain as nonthreatening as possible, though. "Do you foresee trouble?"

"Trouble?" She arched her eyebrows and sniffed through her upturned nose. "Why do you think men broke into the house the other night?"

"Who would know you had valuables here?"

"Oh, I did not try to hide it when I came to town." She hugged the book to her chest and crossed her arms. "I made sure to show that I am well armed, and still, thieves came."

The balding Mr. Dobbs hobbled around a corner but froze upon seeing them.

Madame glared at him as though he had stepped in horse droppings. "Well, don't just stand there. What is your business?"

"Sorry to disturb you, ma'am, but the maid, Lizzy, is needing a ride into town. Missus Aubrey said she should take the carriage."

"The carriage?" Her mouth fell open. "A maid does not require the family's carriage and coachman."

Mr. Dobbs straightened himself as erectly as his hunched back allowed. "I'll be doing what the mistress of the house says. Thank you kindly."

Madame's nostrils flared. "If I was mistress of this house, you would be on the street. It's bad enough that Aubrey has befriended that red-headed catastrophe of a maid. Now the butler put on airs." She turned to Nathan, narrowing her eyes.

"Do see my daughter-in-law's maid makes it into town safely, and if the driver does not—well, all the better."

He hardened his jaw. "I don't think you understand what I'm willing and not willing to do, Madame."

She laughed—a high, shrill sound. "I jest, of course." She fluffed her collar, then faced the room Aubrey and her father occupied. "You will report to Monsieur Camus in the carriage house when you return in..."—she inspected a time piece—one hour. You better leave now."

～

*A*ubrey sat on the sofa, her head resting on Pa's arm. Melanie lay in his lap, cradled by his large hands. He had always had a way with babies. Though bigger than most men, he approached the tiniest and most fragile children with the gentleness of a feather.

When he kissed Aubrey's forehead, his whiskers tugged her hair. Despite his gentleness, she braced for the onslaught of advice soon to come. He'd been quiet for no less than five minutes.

At least Pa was here even if Nathan had left. Fighting another onslaught of tears at the thought of him, she closed her eyes and let the quiet sink in. How had she let that argument unfold? What were they even disagreeing about? Somehow she'd forgotten. All she could think was that he saw her as a pathetic, weak woman still living in her husband's world when she'd tried so hard to be strong—free.

Shadows of trees wavered on the curtains, and Melanie slept on, pressing her tiny feet into Pa's thumbs.

"I used to hold you like this," he whispered.

Too hurt to care about a possible conflict, Aubrey asked a question she'd long wondered. "Why didn't you stop me from marrying him?" It wasn't that she blamed Pa, but she'd been so foolish, and he was wise. He was supposed to protect her.

"I wish I had, but then we would not have little Melanie here." His voice was calm, though Pa had always been prone to a quick temper.

"You are right. I was so taken by him, so in need of love after Maman dying, I probably would not have listened to you."

"I should have tried. Forgive me?" He met her gaze.

"There is no need, Pa."

He cleared his throat, then pressed his cheek to the top of her head. "Your brother told me some of what you suffered. I, uh...don't have his gift for pretty words or describing feelings, but if you ever need to tell me of your experiences, I will listen. I'd never blame you or judge you, Aubrey. I know you've always done your best, and I am proud of the woman you've become."

Allowing the slightest of smiles, she sat upright. "I was so foolish and prideful. It's humiliating to think that he was unfaithful right under my nose. I don't know if I will ever trust myself again." She looked at the door through which Nathan had recently left. Was she right to forgive him as the Bible said, or would he be another man to make a fool of her?

"This young man, Mr. Reed...have you known him long?"

"No. But he's saved my life twice now. Once in a bank robbery and then in the break-in last week."

Pa nodded, pursing his lips for a long moment.

"Why? Do you know him?"

"No. Plenty of people I don't know, though. California's far spread."

"How do I know if he's lying?" She felt like a child coming to him with a problem, but no one fooled Pa. Maybe he could tell her his trick.

"You watch, listen for things that don't make sense. When you feel that uneasiness in your spirit, as though something doesn't match up, you don't push it away. Listen, take note. And pray for wisdom, clarity." He covered Melanie's little tummy with one of his large hands. "You let a young man close now, Aubrey, there's more to consider than just your heart. You are a mother. Would this Reed fella make a good pa?"

She rolled that question in her mind. Nathan had come to her asking for help when many men would have come with demands. His primary concern, the center of his drive, was to take care of his niece. That was a good sign, but how would he feel about another of Louis's children? Felicity was Nathan's own blood. Melanie was not.

"In a way, Louis's death gives you a second chance." Pa nodded once. "The kind of man who cheats on his wife seldom makes a good father. It's selflessness and dedication that make both good fathers and husbands."

"Then Louis wouldn't have been a good father either. I just can't believe I was such a fool. Even after he was unfaithful, he convinced me to stay in this house with him."

"You were hopeful, and I am sure you wanted to do the right thing."

"Wisdom is better than hope." She set her hand on Melanie's small arm. "I wish I could be stronger. For Melanie. I don't always know what the right thing is. I know what the Bible says is right, but then people start talking, and I just feel so confused."

"What about Reed. Has he fooled you?"

Considering the newness of their relationship, it wasn't unreasonable for Nathan to have kept his personal connection to Felicity to himself. But he'd also been a thief for hire, even breaking into her house—so yes, he had fooled her. Maybe it would be best to put some space between them.

"I am just getting to know him. I believe we strive for transparency." She released a long sigh. "I was hoping Mr. Reed might be here, since he knows more than I do. Louis has gotten me into some trouble."

That cast a shadow over her father's face, and as he listened to her recount the last month—since Nathan came into her life. He kept asking how "Reed" reacted or how he played into things. Would that Nathan was beside her, telling her father what he'd learned. He was not, though, and likely would not be for some time. So strange that he had left as he had, rejected her when she confided to him that she wanted to see him again soon. She pushed away the worry, though as the afternoon wore on, the subtle ache inside her remained. She missed him far more than she imagined possible. Far more than a passing fancy or even a genial friendship. No, this was heartache, and it wasn't going away anytime soon.

CHAPTER 16

Due to the time constraints Madame had placed on him, Nathan hadn't the time to see Felicity while in town, and that turned his stomach. The sun was high in the sky when he and Mr. Dobbs dropped Lizzy off at the asylum where her sister was recovering. Nathan grimaced at the sight of the foundling box to the side of the entrance where abandoned babies were left. The Lord had been good to him, supplying a place for Felicity even if it was through Aubrey. He needed to remember that and focus on the task at hand—protecting Aubrey and discovering what Madame and Ellsworth were up to.

The barouche rolled into cool shadows of the carriage house back at the Willot estate. After being in the sun, it took Nathan's eyes a moment to adjust. Two vehicles were stored in a large room with double doors on each side so vehicles could drive in one side and out the other. Two men slinked from a storeroom and stopped in front of Nathan.

Mr. Dobbs frowned yet didn't seem surprised at the sight of them when he moved to the heads of the horses to hold the reins. A tall and wiry man with somewhat girlish features extended a hand and spoke with a heavy accent. "Monsieur Reed, I am Eugène Camus." He pointed to his stalky friend whose gray mustache contrasted black hair and eyebrows. "This is Antoine Grange. Madame Willot tells me you are to join our ranks. Come. I will tell you the way." He turned, motioning Nathan to follow.

"I am not done here." Nathan motioned toward the haltered horses and Mr. Dobbs holding them steady so he could begin unharnessing them.

Camus's jaw twitched, and he remained unmoving. Unblinking.

Grange stepped forward, his barrel-like chest puffed out and fists clubbed at his sides.

"I can handle the team, Mr. Reed." Mr. Dobbs waved him away. "The lad who helps will be happy to assist. Arnold?" he shouted in the direction of the entrance door, still motioning Nathan to leave.

Not liking that Camus and Grange were so rude in the first place, Nathan let Mr. Dobbs have his way and followed the men into the dark storeroom. The sudden earthiness of the dirt floor and dry wood assailed his nose. Across the space, a single window spilled light into the room. The large crate Nathan had seen the day Madame Willot came to town sat in the middle of the floor. It was smaller than he remembered—about three-and-a-half feet by two-and-a-half and the same depth. Another man lingered in the shadows. Beau? Why was he skulking back?

"One man remains here at all times." Camus closed the door behind them and dropped a heavy wooden bar into place. The barricade looked new, likely installed by Madame's men. A similar unit fit the window shutters. "One man patrols the grounds. Grange and I attend Madame Willot."

Nathan knew better than to ask what *attending* meant, but he imagined they were the trusted ones in Madame's confidence. "Anything else?" Nathan asked, arms and hands loose, ready for any potential attack. Beau had gotten a black eye shortly after joining this group. Besides, Madame did not like Nathan. It would likely be as easy to have these fellas kill him and bury his body in the woods than to pay for him to be there.

"Oui." Grange stepped so near, Nathan could smell old tobacco on his breath. "Stay away from Mademoiselle Aubrey. She is …" He broke into French, and Camus interpreted, his words muffled by the sudden pounding in Nathan's ears. "She is above your station. Madame Louis Willot is not for you, American." Camus's lip curled in disgust. "Madame Willot says you are to work here, so you will, but I warn you…" He didn't step closer as Grange had, but the calm in his voice and the thumb he stroked across the butt of his gun signaled the threat. "Betray us and the coyotes will feast on your bones."

That was all. The two men left, closing the door with a hard bang. Nathan drew in a deep breath. He'd been threatened before and would not be drawn into an altercation by men marking their territory. He turned to the man in the shadows and breathed a little easier when Beau stepped into the light.

"I thought you had enough of the bad life." Beau spoke low and, turning a chair around, straddled it.

"This isn't something I can just walk away from." Nathan joined him, taking a deck of cards in the center of the table. Shuffling them calmed his nerves a bit. He had told himself he'd not fall in with a group of desperate men, but that was exactly what had happened. "I found out what he's looking for." He spoke under his breath in case Camus and Grange were still nearby.

Beau nodded.

"It's not what we thought. It's a bill of sale for a mine belonging to the Bank of California."

"Is that good or bad?"

"I don't know." The cards clattered on the table top. "I'm

looking again, though." Even though he now knew what he was looking for, what if he couldn't find the documents? Ellsworth and possibly Ralston would not stop searching. As long as Aubrey was in the chateau, she was not safe.

"You should get out, Nathan. Make that girl go home with her père. It's not safe here. Take Felicity to Oregon, to your family." Beau withdrew from his pocket a piece of wood with whittle marks to inspect it. "Fathers don't get to be selfish. What's gonna happen to the widow and Felicity if you step out of line and end up coyote scat?"

Nathan paused, his conversation with Aubrey from earlier that day crashing back. Mainly her plea that he ask her pa for help. He'd refused, wanting her to trust him, but if he was gone and no one other than Beau knew who was behind all of this, she would be in even graver danger.

~

*W*hy was facing a disapproving man so challenging—especially this one?

Aubrey sat behind Louis's desk, a frowning Mr. Ellsworth on the opposite side. He had been congenial upon entering the study and meeting her father, but when they moved to the desk and Aubrey took the place of honor, his face twitched with irritation. When last Mr. Ellsworth called, they'd sat in the sitting area—a place of civility. Here was a place of business. Did that upset the archaic old man?

He and Pa sat on the opposite side of the great mahogany desk, one looking at her with confidence and the other with confusion.

Stomach tight behind her ribs, wishing to be in her room snuggling Melanie, Aubrey folded her hands and straightened her shoulders. She wouldn't be weak or second guess herself. She didn't know everything, but having Pa here over the past week, treating her with respect and reminding her of how smart she was, had helped her come back to herself a little more.

"Thank you for coming, Mr. Ellsworth." They had exchanged pleasantries when he entered, so she waded into the business portion of the conversation. "As my note said, I wish to be apprised of the research you've done into the photography investment."

The elderly man blinked, then smiled knowingly. "I looked instead at your accounts and current investments. While Louis's business is in transition in many ways after his death, you need to hold off on such an investment. Especially if you plan to have someone step in to fill my shoes of managing your assets."

Feeling a threat in his words, Aubrey stiffened. "Where are the current investments? I do not know a lot about this business of buying and selling, but if stocks were sold, would that provide the capital for this endeavor?"

"I see you've been listening in on men's conversations." He grinned knowingly at Pa, whose expression remained unaffected. "Unfortunately, it is not as easy as that. I had to move funds at the time of Louis's arrest and then again so you could stay in this house."

She raised her eyebrows to Pa, whose expression reflected hers. "My father paid creditors so I could move into this house."

"Yes, and I had to find the staff and rehire them so you could live here. All that was remaining here was a caretaker."

"Where is he now?"

Mr. Ellsworth blinked again, then a bit of color entered his cheeks. Why did she get the impression he was skirting the issue? Distracting her? Lying to her? Was this the feeling Pa told her to notice when things did not make sense?

"When the house was opened and you returned, there was no reason to keep him on. You wanted to run things, so I let the man go." Mr. Ellsworth opened a briefcase and handed papers to her father. "Here, you can see the investment into the Bank of California is where your daughter is making a profit."

Pa slid the papers to Aubrey, who looked over the columns with a rush of anxiety. She read the words, then trailed her gaze down the lines to find differences in numbers. It did seem as though the stocks Mr. Ellsworth had bought had turned a profit. She handed one sheet of paper to Pa and proceeded to look at another.

Mr. Ellsworth rattled on about security for her and the baby and not taking risks.

Aubrey struggled to keep her eyes open. She tried to gauge Pa's thoughts, but his face was still—relaxed and unemotional.

Pa met her gaze as though her thoughts called to him, and he winked, clearly urging her to be brave. To deal with Ellsworth. Finally, Pa said, "These are good numbers, Aubrey. Perhaps I will have to speak with my business manager. The last statement we reviewed, the Bank of California stocks were not doing so well."

Mr. Ellsworth chuckled. "I fear I'm preoccupied managing my business and Louis's as well."

Aubrey stiffened. *Louis's* business. Then Nathan's voice echoed in her thoughts. *Burn down the house. Open a studio.* Such reckless statements, but his words rang true. She could do what she wanted with *her* business. "I have secured a place to sell my photographs at the Yosemite Art Gallery. Mr. Carleton Watkins's Photography Studio. Depending on how those sales go, I may be looking for a location to open my own studio. And I would like to stock products that are in demand, including cameras, equipment and accessories, and the necessary chemicals."

Mr. Ellsworth chuckled and shook his head. "My dear, when you said you would research photography businesses, I had no idea you meant to open your own. Such a fanciful notion. You have an infant son who is in need of your care."

Aubrey drew in a breath, ready to correct him, but he continued in his fatherly yet patronizing manner. "If you wish to remain home with your child, you will need employees to work the studio, and you will have to hire a professional photographer to deal with the dangerous chemicals. Not to mention securing the studio, this venture—as you so lightly call it—will require finagling of investments I have carefully managed since your husband's arrest."

Shamed by the mention of her foolish husband, Aubrey raised her chin. "Isn't this what I pay you for?"

Pa's eyes widened, then he bit his lip against a smirk.

Had she gone too far? That was rude, terribly unkind—worse still, unladylike. An apology raised in her throat, but she stamped it down, the cautionary voice in her head telling her to wait.

Mr. Ellsworth's face turned scarlet so quickly, his white hair shone on his scalp. "I took this position as a favor and have worked tirelessly to see that you are taken care of. Louis left things in a terrible shamble. It has been all I could do to keep you out of legal trouble. Without me, this business would not exist any longer."

A wave of anxiety churned in her gut...until his last statement. If Mr. Ellsworth had not stepped in when he did, Pa would have seen to it that someone he trusted was hired to oversee the business. Aubrey had arrived in San Francisco just after her escapade in Utah, met with Mr. Ellsworth at the reading of Louis's will, and consented to have the old man continue managing the business. She'd not even considered consulting her father, under whose wings she'd taken refuge since Louis's arrest. That had been a mistake. When her husband was arrested, she went to Pa. When Louis died, she should have consulted her father. Why had she mindlessly allowed Mr. Ellsworth—an associate of Louis's—to continue running the business?

"I think our time of working together has come to an end." The obvious statement rolled off her tongue, though judging by Pa's and Ellsworth's expressions, it had been unexpected. "The last time we met, you mentioned you were struggling to manage both your business and mine. Now, it appears we have come to an impasse."

"I mentioned my work load in trying to explain why I needed time to research a new investment." He spoke as though to a child, raising his eyebrows and giving her a tight smile. "Rest assured, I am capable of handling the business."

"And yet you have done no research into the new photography venture I am pursuing."

Her statement hung in the air.

Aubrey fiddled with a pen near a pad of paper, pinching the round edge. She snatched it up and jotted down a note. "We will need to meet again to go over the procedure of parting ways. I will hire someone to manage investments."

"I can help with that. You will need to hire an auditor as well," Pa said, though Aubrey merely nodded and scribbled *auditor* on the paper. "When will you be available to discuss handing over your duties to a new man, Mr. Ellsworth?"

"I will check with my secretary." He stood and pulled down his waistcoat when it lodged on his belly. "I will not be able to come to the house every time you fancy a meeting, Mrs. Willot. My office at the bank will be the place."

That would mean leaving Melanie or taking her all the way into town. So it would be difficult. Many things worthy of pursuing required sacrifice. "That will be fine." Aubrey rose and came around the desk to offer her hand. "I appreciate your time and willingness to come to the house. Rest assured, you will receive compensation for your efforts."

That painted a smile over Mr. Ellsworth's face, though it was stiff. He gave a farewell and, blessedly, Mr. Dobbs was right outside the door with a message for Pa. He handed Pa the note, then promptly saw Mr. Ellsworth out.

As soon as the study door snapped into place, Aubrey sagged back in the big chair.

Pa unfolded the note yet held her gaze. "That's my girl."

She gave him a weak smile, fighting back tears that seemed to bubble up at any moment since she'd given birth to Melanie.

Pa read the message, his brow furrowing.

"Is something wrong?"

"No." He tucked the paper in a pocket. "I will go to town tomorrow to meet with an auditor, see if we can get him started on the accounts soon."

"Do you think he will find something bad?"

He blew through his lips. "I can't say. If he does, though, I will be here to help. The audit will take time but really should have taken place as soon as Louis died. I may have to postpone my trip with Jesse."

"I'm sorry."

"Don't be. This is where I need to be. Besides, if I'm not there, Jesse can see how tough it is, managing the business without me there to guide him. Maybe that will cool his pride."

Aubrey shook her head. Her pa was a rough fellow with high expectations for his children, but one thing was for sure—he did not leave them alone to settle a problem. He always supported them. With his help, she likely would have her photography studio—a thought that blossomed a smile onto her face that held all the way to her room when she went to tend Melanie.

CHAPTER 17

$\mathcal{N}$athan sat with his sweaty hands clasped between his knees, his stomach so tight and heart so heavy that just breathing was difficult. He'd thought confessing the truth to Aubrey would be hard, but Captain Hiram and Titus Alexander did not have Aubrey's graciousness or faith. A dark shadow had scrunched the lawman's face where he sat across the dinner table. Knowing he needed to talk to the policeman and Aubrey's father, Nathan had contacted Mr. Alexander, asking to meet with him, and Captain Hiram had suggested a German café where he liked to take his lunch.

The rich aromas of sausages combined with the tangy sauerkraut made his mouth water and his nervousness all the worse. The clean café hosted a number of tables with embroidered tablecloths and curtained windows.

Mr. Alexander perched on his chair, rubbing his chin as he had for most of Nathan's explanation. His black eyebrows suddenly flew upward. "Aubrey is alone at the house."

"She's not." Nathan put out a staying hand before the man could jump up. "I have a friend at the property, and I asked him to watch out for her while I am in town. The captain here could have gone to the house to talk, but then Madame's men might become nervous. They are a suspicious bunch, but as I told you..."—he glanced around the mostly empty room and lowered his voice—"the break-in was Ellsworth's doing, not Madame's."

"You don't know how bad this is, Mr. Reed." Mr. Alexander sat on the edge of his chair, obviously ready to leave. "Your previous employer, Mr. Ellsworth, has been managing Aubrey's business since that worthless husband of hers was arrested."

Nathan's throat shrank as though a noose had been tightened around it. "He works for Aubrey?"

"Until today...when she fired him because he tried to prevent her from investing as she believes is best."

"Photography?"

Mr. Alexander nodded, his shoulders easing some. "I'm glad that old hound won't be around her anymore, but if what you say is true, the damage might already be done. I planned to meet with an auditor while I'm in town, but I'd feel better if you headed straight back to the house."

"I need to go by the Watkins's Photography Studio to drop off Aubrey's photographs while in town." Hopefully, Watkins would see their value. He had told Aubrey he would allow them in inventory *if* the quality was high enough. She seemed to have forgotten that, and who was he to dash her hopes? Besides, he'd not seen her since their last tense conversation, a fact that sent an ache in his chest.

"I will take her photographs to Watkins's studio before meeting with an auditor. That way, you may return to the house." Mr. Alexander rose, jabbing his chin at Nathan, who nodded.

"We need to make sure one of us is with her all the time until this is taken care of. Who is the man you trust so much?"

Nathan shook his head, knowing full well that Beau would not want his name mentioned. Besides, if Titus or Aubrey knew the man Nathan trusted was the same who aided in the kidnapping, they'd be even more suspicious. That was a conversation for another day, perhaps once Beau had proved himself. "I cannot disclose his identity, sir."

Mr. Alexander narrowed his eyes, his jaw flexing. Still, Nathan would not give in. Beau was a wanted man for a crime against Mr. Alexander's family. It wasn't his place, and he got the impression Beau was trying to redeem himself. It wasn't in Nathan to trip a man who was on his path to better living, even if Beau veered off track on occasion.

"I just hope Madame Willot is not a danger to Aubrey." Mr. Alexander relaxed his shoulders a bit, massaging the bridge of his nose. "This morning, she started planning some party or something or other. She wants Aubrey to settle into polite society since she's not going to move east with her."

A waiter came by, filling their mugs of lukewarm coffee. Nathan wrapped his fingers around his, not really wanting the black liquid. "Madame told me she's going back to France."

"She's probably trying to lure Aubrey into moving away with her. Aubrey says I'm wrong to judge the whole family by the behaviors of Louis and Emil, but she might do well to remember that rotten apples come from rotten trees." Mr. Alexander shrugged, then shook his head, a slow blink of his eyes and the circles around them hinting at weariness.

"Well, either way, I think keeping someone with your daughter and granddaughter to protect them is wise." Captain Hiram chimed in, pinching his mustache as he did when he was thinking. "Wiser still might be to take her away until this all blows over."

"Blows over?" Mr. Alexander drew himself up to his full height as he buttoned his frock coat. "You mean, until you make an arrest."

"Arrest him for what? Sure, Nathan here can say Ellsworth hired him to break into that big ol' house of hers, but what good does that do? It's his word against Ellsworth's, and then we're just dragging his good name through the mud. Besides, Ellsworth would say he was desperate to find the deed to the silver mine and save the city. No judge would even hear the case. We need to have more than this."

"I understand that, Captain. I fully expect to get to the bottom of this so you can make a legitimate arrest. It might take time, and we'll need this young man's continued cooperation." Mr. Alexander turned to him, his manner reminding Nathan of a mountain man, not a businessman in a fancy suit. "You are at the greatest risk. Are you willing to see this through to the end?"

"Yes, sir. I started down this road when I broke into the study last month. I have to atone for what I did."

"You are also at an advantage, since Madame has you working with her guards. Have you ever heard that what the devil meant for evil, God can use for good?"

Surprised by his show of grace, Nathan answered respectfully. "Yes, sir."

"Good." He clapped Nathan on the arm. "You're not alone. You hear?"

Nathan inclined his head, unable to react otherwise. Aubrey's father left Nathan with the police captain. Resisting a grimace now that he was alone, Nathan sipped his coffee. Would the police captain tell him a job was out of the question in light of his recent criminal activity?

"He took that better than I would have." Hiram crossed his arms over his blue coat. "I have some news for you, Reed. I don't know if it's going to help." He reached into his pocket to retrieve a telegram smudged with what looked like blackberry jam. "The warden at the Utah State Penitentiary got back to me."

"That was fast."

"It was, because there's nothing to tell. Both of them boys who you were checking into died."

Nathan scanned the telegram, confirming what Captain Hiram said. "One died in a fight, and the other fell from a wall trying to escape." Nathan handed the telegraph back to him. "Seems like it can be unrelated from this business we're dealing with. Accidents. Maybe."

Hiram stuffed the paper in his jacket pocket. "No real way to be sure. Did they have anything to do with this business with Mrs. Willot?"Nathan stood, dusting his hands on his knees. "I don't know. Say, when did they die?"

"Oh, it's been a month or so now...not long after being sentenced for kidnapping Mrs. Willot and her brother." Hiram raised his eyebrows, giving him a wide grin. "I do my research, too, sonny." His expression grew more serious. "I do hope they didn't know something that could help clear up this mess for Mrs. Willot."

"Me too."

~

*L*ord, *provide a mother for Felicity, a wife for me.* The sudden prayer of his heart sobered Nathan as he approached Ms. Thornson's apartment just before dusk two weeks later, the setting sun peeking above the tall dormer.

Nothing of note had happened since his meeting with the sheriff and Mr. Alexander. When not guarding Madame's crate, Nathan had searched the house for the deed to the silver mine but found nothing. Aubrey's search of her belongings, which her father had brought up from the secret room, had also turned up nothing. Being in the house was different now, since their quarrel. Whenever Nathan came across Aubrey, Melanie, and Mr. Alexander together, he felt as though he was intruding—an outsider looking in.

I want to stop running. To have a family. The last time he'd hoped for such, he'd ventured back to the farm in Oregon with the money he'd saved to pay Pa back. It had not been enough.

For Felicity, I'll do anything you want, God. As his prayer leapt from earth to heaven, the front door squealed open, and there stood the petite wet nurse in an apron with his blond baby on her hip. My, Felicity had become so big and pudgy.

He contained a laugh and jaunted up the remaining steps. "Hello, beautiful girl." He lifted the babe from Ms. Thornson's arms, offering her a greeting as she ushered him inside.

In the living room, dusky light peeked through half-drawn drapes, and Mrs. Frill, Ms. Thornson's roommate, sat in the chair. She wore a tight, old-fashioned bonnet that hid most of her gray hair and showed him a toothless grin. "That's a fine suit. You here a'courtin'?" She winked at Ms. Thornson.

The lady was as nosy as he remembered from their first introduction a week ago when she'd lectured him on faithless fathers and a man's duty to marry. She obviously had too much time on her hands, though she was probably just hoping to look out for Ms. Thornson. As it were, he'd wished more than once tonight that he were courting Aubrey, but since their last conversation, he'd felt less and less hopeful. "No, ma'am. Just going to a party hosted by my employer."

Mrs. Frill's smile faltered. "Oh, you still working at the Widow Willot's place?" She rolled her snake-like eyes toward Ms. Thornson, who was shaking her head.

"Yes, ma'am. Mrs. Willot and her mother-in-law have planned a summer party." And Mr. Alexander had made sure he received an invitation.

The older lady sniffed and wrinkled her nose.

Mrs. Frill had suggested, as Mrs. Miller had, that a practical solution to Felicity's need for a mother be met through marriage between Ms. Thornson and himself. He could not agree. If he'd met her before he'd known Aubrey, he might. In fact, such an arrangement would have seemed an answer to prayer, but not anymore. He'd not dishonor Ms. Thornson or himself by pretending they might have a future when Aubrey was his last thought before sleep and his first upon waking. Explaining that to his daughter's wet nurse, though, might go terribly wrong. She was always so quiet, painfully ill at ease, and embarrassed around him.

"Well, I'll get us some refreshments." Mrs. Frill pushed herself up by the arms of the chair.

"Oh, no need to rise. I will get them." Ms. Thornson rushed toward her, but the lady waved her off. "If you're sure." She turned to Nathan, shrugging, then lowered into a nearby chair.

Nathan bounced Felicity on one knee while Mrs. Frill hobbled off to the kitchen.

"Vendors are gathering tomorrow morning down at Market Street. The ferries come in with all kinds of goods. Were you aware?" Ms. Thornson asked quietly, her light-blue eyes meeting his, then skipping away.

"No. I haven't much time for shopping. Do you plan to go?"

"Oh, Mrs. Frill and Felicity and I may go. You don't mind, do you? I sometimes have to take her out on shopping trips and such. It is just impossible to do everything while she's sleeping. Mrs. Frill would watch her, but she is not always secure in her step." She leaned closer, lowering her voice. "She had a fall last week. Did you notice her limp?"

Nathan blinked, not willing to say yes when he'd just assumed the woman was whacking away at the floor with her cane in typical fashion. She moved with so much force and racket, it was a wonder how Felicity managed to take naps.

His little girl looked up with wide blue eyes and, curling her fingers in her mouth, let out a yawn. Nathan tickled her tummy until she blew spittle bubbles that had him and Ms. Thornson laughing. Mrs. Frill returned in time to suggest the three of them looked well together—like a family. There was always some comment she was making that made his neck hot. Ms. Thornson just shook her head and whispered an apology. He reassured her not to worry and enjoyed his visit with Felicity.

When the small clock on the table showed him it was six o'clock, he reluctantly handed his sweet charge over to Ms. Thornson. The babe went willingly. In reality, Ms. Thornson was a mother to Felicity. She'd been nursing and tending to her all her little life. And just look how Ms. Thornson hugged her now, dabbing drool from her chin and kissing her cheek.

She turned her attention on him, and the color of her cheeks darkened. "Mr. Reed, I wondered if I might speak to you privately before you leave."

Nathan nodded and followed the lady outside onto the porch. There she bounced the baby in her arms, glancing toward the closed door as though Mrs. Frill might have her ear pressed against the other side.

"I hate to bring this up. You know that I love Felicity like my own." Ms. Thornson failed to meet his eyes. "I didn't want to say anything too soon."

Oh, no. She was going to ask about the future, where things were going. Had Mrs. Miller and Mrs. Frill led her to believe he was a marital candidate? He certainly had never intentionally given Ms. Thornson that impression.

"You are a single man, just trying to get by. I know things have been hard for you. You were always generous when Felicity was at the foundling home. I want to be generous, too, but..." She drew in a ragged breath as though to make a bold proclamation, only to tip forward and whisper, "I've yet to receive payment for this month."

Nathan blinked, unable to reply. Aubrey had not paid for Felicity's care? But she'd never withhold kindness from a child. So why had the funds not been sent to the wet nurse?

CHAPTER 18

*L*ights glittered from chandeliers high above the large sitting room with tall windows less than an hour later. Being around such finery was strange after visiting the humble little apartment on Taylor Street where Felicity lived. Nathan had reassured Ms. Thornson that he would talk to Felicity's benefactor this very evening about the missed payment. He just had to find Aubrey and bring up the subject of money. So much for his hope of making peace with her.

People sat on velvet settees and upholstered chairs while waiters bustled about offering hors d'oeuvres. They must be recently hired and the furniture newly bought or rented. The chateau had never looked so grand. Madame had said she wanted to immerse Aubrey in polite society, and she'd certainly prepared for the upper class.

Nathan stood in a circle of well-dressed men including Aubrey's father, the photographer Carleton Watkins, and his friend John Muir. Aubrey would love to chat with them. Nathan had expected to see her, yet it had been Madame who greeted him at the front door as was customary for the hostess to do. Strangely enough, Aubrey was nowhere in sight.

Her mother-in-law approached a heavyset man with white hair and kissed his cheek. It was that snake Mr. Ellsworth. The two seemed to be acquainted, and that couldn't be good.

Nathan shifted his position to see better from near the veranda doorway. Across the room filled with couples chatting and a grand piano, Mr. Ellsworth and Aubrey's mother-in-law walked arm in arm.

"These are fine photographs." Mr. Wilkins studied images of Los Angeles and San Francisco which hung on the wall.

Nathan hadn't missed the newly framed work that had to be Aubrey's. There was the fountain in moonlight and another of a white gazebo. His chest swelled as did Mr. Alexander's when he replied to the photographer.

"Taken by my daughter. She has been talking my ears off about investing in a studio for my whole visit." Mr. Alexander chuckled. "I expect her to do so in the next year or two. I've made inquiries regarding investments."

"She did a fine job with the framing and development. It is so clear."

"It is a shame they don't have a more versatile camera for taking photographs," Aubrey's father said. "One you could easily carry and use in the field. Aubrey says someday there will be. If that's so, perhaps John could sell photography along with his written works." Mr. Alexander nudged the quiet Scotsman he had invited to the party.

The man in question glanced around the splendor of the chandelier-lit room with unease. Mr. John Muir had traveled the world and was known to prefer nature to people. His smile was congenial, though, when he turned it on Mr. Watkins. "Provided it could also handle the weather. I would have liked to have gotten a clear photograph of the last snowstorm we encountered on Mount Shasta."

"A snowstorm in July?" Mr. Alexander grinned.

"Not July. March. My goodness, what a glorious sight it was too."

"I don't know if I would say that. I've been in a snowstorm in these parts." Mr. Alexander's gaze included Nathan as though he were part of the group even though Nathan had hardly spoken. Then the older man's attention shifted beyond Nathan. "Oh, gentlemen, have you met my daughter?"

Aubrey skirted around Nathan in a wave of honeysuckle scent and another natural sweetness he could not name. Warm brown curls lay over one shoulder. Her eyes shone, and her cheeks blushed rosy pink, while a smile tugged her softly pursed lips. She wore a white ribbon about her neck with a silver pendant that dangled below the gentle curve of her collarbone. Lower still, a lace ruffle crested the beginning of cleavage.

Nathan snapped his eyes elsewhere. He couldn't breathe or move. He'd tried not to think of her over the past two weeks since they'd argued. Always, thoughts and dreams of her brought a dull ache. The pounding in his head was like that of a horse's hooves thundering down a mountainside. Had she always been so beautiful?

"And good evening to you, Mr. Reed." Aubrey's voice drew his attention back to her glowing face.

"Miss Aubrey." He took her hand and kissed it. "It's a pleasure to see you again."

She gently squeezed his hand, her eyes dancing and lips pressing together to hide a smile. So she was happy to see him.

"What is this about a snowstorm in July?" Aubrey turned her attention to Mr. Muir, who was happy to dazzle her with his tale of being trapped on the summit of a mountain in a blizzard. His thick Scottish accent curved each word into something more exotic than any tale Nathan might spin.

"That was back in March, though," he concluded. "I recently returned from an excursion to Mount Whitney. The valleys there are lovely, even with the occasional flower-crushing tourist passing through."

"Are the wildflowers in bloom so late in the summer?" Aubrey accepted a ruby crystal goblet of punch her pa offered, her glance catching Nathan's for a second.

He must be staring. In front of her father, no less.

Mr. Alexander met his gaze, his chin tipping slightly down as his eyebrows firmed. Mr. Watkins, on the other hand, barely hid a smirk. Nathan was staring like a besotted kid. He had to get a handle on himself.

Thankfully, Mr. Muir droned on. Mr. Alexander could focus on him and not Nathan. Unfortunately, Aubrey did the same thing. Nathan tugged at his collar, the tie he'd bought for this occasion feeling like a noose.

"There are the blessed Sierra heathers and primulas. All the air smells of flowers and pine." Mr. Muir smiled, a wistful glint in his eyes. "I tell you, there is nothing so wondrous as walking amid the giant sequoias."

Aubrey played with the pendant at her neck, her glass held in one gloved hand. "Do many tourists go to the mountains?"

"Oh, some. There are options for hotels and lodges—depending on your taste, of course." He glanced around the room at the finery. "There's Black's Hotel at Yosemite. I have friends who spend a fair piece of summer there."

"How lovely." She turned her attention to the quiet Mr. Watkins. "Many of your photographs are from Yosemite, are they not?"

"Yes, miss. I went about ten years ago, though not for Muir's reasons." He gave the naturalist a friendly nudge. "I had to make a living, and capturing sights that few people could see—well, it seemed the best option."

"How fine for you. I do hope there is room in San Francisco for another photographer."

Watkins smiled. "Why, of course, my dear. Your prints have

sold wonderfully at my studio. You needn't worry. I will keep your inventory as long as you need. That will help you build up a clientele, and when you are ready to open your own place of business, they will know where to find you."

Aubrey glowed with a smile, clasping her hands as she shrugged. "You are very kind."

"You needn't be so modest. You are very talented. Your work is proof of that."

Aubrey nodded, though she might not fully realize the compliment Watkins had given her. She was talented, yes, but Nathan hadn't considered what it would mean for her to open a shop with male competitors who would think her place was at home, not in commerce. It would be hard at first. Maybe always. He needed to be there to help her. To protect her from the shark-like businessmen who might resort to childish tactics.

Aubrey's gaze traveled beyond them, a crease between her brows. Madame and Mr. Ellsworth walked toward a side door. He'd forgotten about them in the light of Aubrey's splendor. The way the stars are forgotten at midday.

She met his gaze and unfolded a fan. "It's warm in here, isn't it?"

He stepped forward. "Would you care to get some fresh air?"

"I would." She slipped her gloved hand into the crook of his arm, and they excused themselves from their company.

Outside in the night air, couples in the latest fashions blocked their path, but Aubrey seemed in no hurry, so Nathan simply enjoyed her touch and the slight pursing of her lips when she sipped her punch before saying, "My mother-in-law is talking with the man who previously managed my business."

Nathan paused near an open window to avoid following too close.

Aubrey fanned her face, her gaze everywhere but on him.

"Did your inquiries into Madame unearth anything I need worry about?"

"No. I thought there would be something to learn, but nothing so far. Just this business with the Bank of California."

"It is strange. Since the day I interrupted her guards in the master study, they keep to themselves. It is as though she respected my wishes. It's hard for me to believe she is here to visit me, but then Louis was alive when she started her journey." She sighed long, the corners of her mouth pulling down.

Her excitement gone, Aubrey blinked tiredly and glanced about the splendid room as though wishing to be elsewhere. Likely, with her baby.

He should say something to distract her and make her smile again. "Have you taken any new photographs?"

"Yes. But I have not developed them. Pa said he would help me assemble the dark room, but he and Melanie keep me busy. I did sort through another crate but found nothing that resembled the papers you are looking for."

"I haven't found anything either. I will meet with Ralston this coming week to apprise him of my progress. He's not going to like it. I'm afraid the deed is gone. With parts of the estate being auctioned off, it must have been lost or destroyed. Did Emil and his gang ever live here?"

"I don't know. I fear nothing will stop the men from looking. Pa wants me to stay in Los Angeles with him." She swayed to one side, still focused on Madame and Ellsworth. "If I do, I don't know what will become of my hope to open a studio here."

Momentarily breathless at the idea of her going so far away, even though he'd pack her bags for her if it meant she and Melanie would be safe, Nathan said, "Could you open a studio in Los Angeles?"

"Yes, but I fear it would be harder without Mr. Watkins's

support. I still cannot believe he is being so generous. But Pa says I should not trust in chariots or horses."

"Horses?"

"Yes, you know that verse. 'Some trust in chariots, and some in horses: but we will remember the name of the Lord our God.'"

"He is right. I'm glad you have him to lean on." Even as he said it, disappointment struck him square in the chest. Aubrey didn't need him in her life.

"As am I. He's given me ideas for saving and investing outside of the business my late husband chose. He says that might help to provide security for Melanie and me in case there were any illegal dealings by Louis. Of course, he would take care of us if anything bad happened, but I want to be a good steward. Give Melanie something of worth once she is grown." Aubrey stopped near a pillar, intentionality in her posture despite the hesitancy in her eyes.

The few steps they'd taken allowed them to view Madame and Mr. Ellsworth conversing near a patio door. Were they heading outside? If he and Aubrey moved closer, Madame and Ellsworth might spot them, so Aubrey must plan to linger where she could observe the older couple despite the fact that Nathan's nearness obviously made her uncomfortable. Discomfort he was responsible for because he'd taken offense when she suggested her father help him. They needed to talk, to make things right. And he had to figure out why Ms. Thornson wasn't being paid.

She glanced back the way they'd come, then quickly away.

"What are you looking for?" Nathan asked.

"Worrying over things I cannot control." Her shoulders lowered slightly. "Do not be surprised if our names end up in the newspaper tomorrow."

A nearby woman smirked and held a fan before her face as

she spoke to a friend. An elderly gentleman raised his eyebrows and looked away.

They garnered the attention of many around them. He was a fool for not noticing before. Here in the upper echelon of San Francisco's elite, Aubrey would have been well known. Likely, her husband had been a business associate of many who would remember his downfall.

Madame and Ellsworth were moving again, this time to an outside doorway that led to the closed part of the house.

"There they go. Hurry." Aubrey slipped her hand into the crook of his arm, and Nathan led the way after them.

❧

The green-and-white-striped wallpaper gave the effect that the hallway was growing larger around the pair ahead. On Nathan's arm, Aubrey followed Madame and Mr. Ellsworth, her dancing slippers sinking into the fine carpet. She glanced back, but only her gown's train trailed after them.

This part of the house was mostly shadows with the gas lamps dark on the walls. Strange that Madame and Ellsworth would leave the gathering and go so deep into the chateau. They entered one of the drawing rooms, the door closing behind Madame with a flurry of her dress's purple ruffles. She had shed her mourning garb for this event, claiming Louis would prefer her to settle his wife in polite society.

Aubrey pulled Nathan to a stop just outside the doorway. He waited, so very tall and handsome in the black suit, gray waistcoat, and white cravat. She squeezed his arm, more out of nerves than anything, but when his muscle contracted beneath her fingers, she smiled. My goodness, here she was trying to focus on her conniving mother-in-law and devious business manager, and she was distracted by an attractive man.

Nathan raised his eyebrows and whispered, "Well?"

"You might peek through one of the outside windows. I can listen from the next room over."

"Aubrey, you realize they may be sneaking away for a reason other than business." Nathan spoke quietly, his voice low with meaning.

"Madame is a married woman."

Surely, she would not commit such a dalliance. Then again, she was Louis's mother. Was it fair to judge Madame by the sins of her son, though? Was it fair to judge men by Louis's actions? Aubrey had thought men typically were unfaithful in marriage, but that was not always the case.

He cocked his head to one side. "Ellsworth is married as well, but that does not always stop people from pursuing passion outside of marriage."

Aubrey's cheeks warmed at the thought of what might be behind the door. "I do not want to see any such thing."

"Well, I need answers." He leaned his ear against the wood for a moment. "I can't hear them. Does this room have an outside door?"

"Yes. They probably went outside."

"But why come all the way to this part of the house just to go outside?"

When she had no good answer, Nathan opened the door and crept inside, closing it in his wake.

My goodness. Aubrey pinched the silver heart broach at her neck. She took a step toward the door. Pressing her ear against the wood, she waited. Nothing. Well, she wasn't interested in being left behind. No, sir.

She turned the knob and peered into the dark room. Oh, no. If Madame had been intending something untoward, she would not have lit the lamps. But the sofa appeared empty, the curves of cushions barely visible in thick shadows. French doors stood on the opposite sides of the room, faint moonlight highlighting the crossing pattern of the muntins and glass panes.

The slightest of movements caught her attention. There, at the edge of the doors, stood a tall figure cloaked in shadow. Nathan? Holding her breath, she approached with an extended hand. No sooner had her fingertips connected with firm muscle than the man swept an arm around her.

"Shh." With his hand on her back, Nathan nudged her into the shadows, away from the French doors.

Skin tingling at his nearness, she faced the glass panes in the doors toward which he bent his head. His chin brushed her hair when she leaned nearer, holding onto his arm for fear of losing her balance on her high-heeled shoes. The design of the doors, with the inlaid windows, allowed them to hear what the speakers were saying.

"I told you it was a waste of time." Madame fumed, pacing the partly lit patio outside.

"Then it's Aubrey we need to look to. If Reed was going to find the documents, he would have already." Ellsworth answered in his leisurely manner.

Nathan's touch firmed, as though to reassure her. Ellsworth must be tired of waiting, but what did Madame have to do with the missing deed?

"Aubrey is just a foolish girl, not the key to this problem." Madame huffed, her voice strained. "Louis's foolish plan backfired. What am I supposed to do with Emil in prison? The mills have been heavily taxed since the Germans annexed Alsace and Lorraine." She turned her head away, her words muffled. "...the key to the entire Willot legacy."

A chill tingled down her back at the phrasing Madame used. *The key*, as Louis had dubbed her in the beginning of their marriage. She'd considered it an honor, a pet name also, but eventually, she realized how it objectified her. It was just another way he saw her as something he owned.

Ellsworth's deep voice sounded more clearly than Madame's when he asked her, "Did you learn anything from Emil?"

"Nothing—as I told you. He is as reckless as ever. There is no other option but to enact my part of the plan and set Louis's little American wife's head spinning. She will give over the documents then."

The blood in Aubrey's veins ran cold at the callousness with which Madame referred to her, as though she were a stranger whose identity was merely tied to her nationality and marital connection.

"I don't know—"

"I do," Madame hissed then her voice faded, so Aubrey peeked around the edge of the window frame.

The two approached the stairs leading to the walkway where roses gathered on either side.

Nathan cracked the door open enough for them to hear Madame's words.

"Your efforts have brought nothing, and I am running out of time. All I require is that you stay out of my way. Now, we must return to the party. Titus Alexander watches me as though he is a feral cat ready to pounce. He will notice my absence. I'm surprised you even managed an invitation."

Their voices dwindled as did their figures when shadows hid them on one side of the house. Around the corner lay the veranda, lit well for the guests' use. Following them there unnoticed would be impossible, though Nathan moved as though to do so.

Aubrey remained in place, Madame and Ellsworth's conversation soaking in her mind like a metal plate in a developing bath, images still cloudy, though once the process was done, she would have a clear picture. She knew something of what was hidden—unknown—but what was it? At the term *key*, she wanted to shrink away. Avoid all things connected to Louis, but she needed to be mindful and not fearful. *What does this mean, Lord?*

The key—it was the same thing that Emil had said when he'd kidnapped her in Salt Lake City. "Oh!" Aubrey grabbed Nathan's arm. "Salt Lake. Emil. The safe he had there. It must be it."

Nathan had one foot out the French doors but paused at her sudden exclamation. "Aubrey, what are you talking about?"

"Emil needed money. He tried to get me to open one of Louis's safes when he kidnapped me last May."

"One of the safes?"

"Yes. Yes." She spoke faster, everything becoming clear. "Louis had three safes, one for each house he owned. This house, the Salt Lake house, and the one in New York. When Emil kidnapped me, we all thought it was because of Jesse, but he had me for hours before he recaptured Jesse, and during that time, he badgered me. Tried to get me to open the safe there at the Salt Lake house. He kept saying I was the key, just as Madame said. I pretended not to know the combination." He had become angry and turned her over to a guard who, in the end, helped in their rescue.

"Slow down, Aubrey." Nathan took both her arms. "So you think the crate in the barn that supposedly contains Madame's belongings contains the safe from Salt Lake?"

"Yes. But the house there sold. Madame could have picked it up before the auction, though."

Nathan lowered his voice. "Do you know the code?"

Aubrey held her breath, then she groaned. "Possibly. Once I did, but Louis may have changed it. If you get me to the safe, I will try to open it." Her voice dwindled into a whisper. "Likely, that is what Madame meant when she said I am the key."

He swept an arm around her, hugging her to his side. "I know you hate to still be a part of Louis's schemes, but this will be over soon."

Aubrey sank against him, closing her eyes and letting her breath flow. Her heart beat steadily in time with the hand Nathan ran up and down her arm. "How can you be so sure?"

"Because even if the crate does not contain the safe, or if it does and you don't know the combination, you can safely move Melanie to your father's house. I will remain here and figure this out. Did I tell you I went to the police, as you suggested?"

"A Captain Hiram came to visit me. I told him I didn't want to press charges. You were very brave, seeking help even though doing so incriminated you."

"I'm trying to live better." Nathan rested his cheek against the top of her head as naturally as if she were his wife of many years.

Aubrey turned, her forehead on his cotton shirt, soaking in the citrus scent of his cologne. They were practically embracing, though she had no idea what kind of future they might have. One thing was certain—she didn't want to be away from him, parted by a trip to Los Angeles or conflict. "I regret snapping at you when my pa came to visit...and for pressuring you to return. If you need space, I want to respect that."

"Space?" He held her where he could meet her gaze. "I was running when I left you and your pa in the study, but I'm glad you came after me. When you suggested your father help me, honestly, it hurt my pride. I thought that meant you didn't trust me, but now I see it's safer if we work together. And I may have needed a nudge to come clean to the police. The truth is that Captain Hiram offered me a position on the force, and I didn't want to endanger that."

"Oh?" Aubrey pressed a hand against his chest. "You are pursuing a career in law enforcement again?"

"That will depend on how all this ends."

She ran her hand over soft fabric covering hard muscles, to the skin on his neck. His pulse tapped against her thumb. They needed to get to the safe, to see if she knew the combination, but first... "I missed you." *Nathan.* Why couldn't she bring herself to use his given name? It suited him so well.

His arms tightened around her back. "Aubrey, I've thought of you every day since that stupid argument."

Her fingertips grazed the silky hair at the back of his neck. "Does that mean you are sorry?"

"Yes, ma'am." The moonlit window framed his head as he looked down on her—a dark silhouette. His breath warming her face, drawing her in, she closed her eyes and lifted her lips.

Suddenly, Nathan tensed. Aubrey opened her eyes, gripping his shoulders as her knees failed her. He bent backward, craning his neck to peer out the door. "I thought I heard..."

Familiar voices sounded outside, followed by a baby's cry.

Aubrey released Nathan and hurried through the French doors in time to see a woman walking down a garden path with a baby in her arms and one of Madame's tall guards following close behind. Melanie?

CHAPTER 19

$\mathcal{A}$ubrey rushed down the steps and onto the garden path, the light from around the corner of the house silhouetting the couple's frames. Who were they? And why were they here, with her baby? Where was Lizzy, who was to be tending her for the night?

As they drew near, the infant's cries grew louder. The baby was too big to be Melanie. The woman carrying her was Mrs. Miller of the San Francisco Foundling Asylum. She glowered at Nathan, her eyebrows arched as though that tight bun of hers held them back. "Mr. Reed, something has gone terribly wrong."

Aubrey's heart slammed in her chest at the sight of the wailing infant in Mrs. Miller's arms. She didn't need to ask the identity of the child.

"Felicity?" Nathan took the baby and raised her to see, then held her against his chest and checked her face, hands, and feet. "What's happened? Why do you have her?"

"She was left in the foundling box outside the asylum, screaming at the top of her lungs." The color of Mrs. Miller's face grew redder, and she gave a huff. "I thought you wanted this baby."

"I do. I saw her at Ms. Thornson's apartment just a couple of hours ago. I have no idea—"

His explanation was drowned out by Felicity's cries. The little girl tipped her head back and screamed, her red cheeks wet with tears. Nathan bounced her, making a shushing noise.

The man with Mrs. Miller took Aubrey's elbow and urged her toward the baby. "She is hungry. You must feed her."

Why was Madame's guard guiding her to the baby? Aubrey shook him off and inhaled, ready to tell him to not touch her, but his incredible dark eyes and fierce features gave her pause. She'd seen him before. His forceful voice, massive stature, and close proximity shook loose a memory of the house in Salt Lake City. Emil raging that she was a liar and would pay for not opening the safe. He had opened a door and shoved her toward a tall, dark guard with a thick accent and angry squint. *Beau,* as Emil had called him—Lorraine's friend who was suspected of helping the police rescue Aubrey and Jesse. Why was he here?

Beau back-stepped and shifted his attention to Felicity, then to her. "She needs food." He spoke in French. Jesse had said he was forced to speak French when he was kidnapped. So Mr. Beau would suspect she spoke the language as well.

He was right, of course. She could not just let the baby go hungry, but this was not her baby.

Nathan hugged Felicity and patted her back. "There, sweet girl. It's all right. I'll…" He looked to Mrs. Miller, then Aubrey.

She stepped forward, placing her hand on Nathan's arm. "She must be nursed…now."

He shook his head, holding Felicity as though Aubrey might run away with her. What had Nathan experienced that caused his fear to counter logic? How to convince him when he clearly wanted to care for Felicity yet lacked the ability? And how much further the situation was complicated by their near-kiss moments before. Might he feel vulnerable? Desperate?

"Come, Nathan." She spoke his given name, though she should have before now. "There is nothing to fear. I must tend her. There is no one else." She extended her hands, offering to take the babe.

His blue gaze trained on Aubrey, Nathan whispered something into Felicity's ear, then gave her over.

Aubrey took Melanie's sister into her arms and started toward the sitting room from which they'd spied on Madame and Ellsworth. Carrying the babe past her guests would disturb them and attract attention.

Surprisingly, Mrs. Miller's complaints followed her. "Mr. Reed, we need to meet soon. I need to know that you have a plan to take care of your niece."

"I will see you tomorrow, Mrs. Miller. Now please..." His words faded when she entered the dark room.

Most of the house was unlit since the staff was busy with the party. By now, Felicity's cries drove Aubrey's milk into a weighty ache.

"Aubrey?" Nathan caught up to her and followed her into the room.

She settled on the sofa, Nathan's footfalls pausing behind her.

"Do you need anything? A light?"

"No light, please." Cheeks warm, Aubrey kept her back facing him and unfastened her specially made bodice. Felicity's cry muffled when she began to eat.

"There, you poor girl." Aubrey wiped tears from the babe's cheeks. "All is well."

"Is she going to be all right?" Nathan shifted away, then back.

"Yes. She is merely hungry.

"I don't understand. How did she end up in the foundling

box?" He began to pace behind the sofa. "It's a thirty-minute ride from the asylum to here, and that's at a fast clip. I wonder how long since she last ate."

Aubrey cradled Felicity to her breast. The baby clutched one of her fingers, as Melanie often did. She was larger but sweet as could be. Would there be enough milk left for Melanie once the older babe ate her fill? What if there was no other nurse to tend Felicity—or worse, what if Nathan lost custody? She could not allow that to happen.

"Nathan?" She spoke over her shoulder, only to find him nearer than she had realized. They were far enough away from the party that only moonlight came through the windows, so her modesty was intact, but Aubrey still used the cloth around Felicity to cover herself.

He stepped farther into the shadows. "You need something?"

"Yes. Please go to the kitchen and ask Cook to come. She will resist with the party in full swing, but you must tell her I need her."

Nathan left without a word, and Aubrey pulled back the cloth to see the child Nathan loved so dearly. Felicity squeezed her finger. Aubrey smiled as her heart swelled. "Rest, dear. All will be well."

❧

*N*athan sat on the edge of a chair outside the sitting room after escorting Cook, Lizzy, and Melanie to Aubrey, clutching his hands tightly together. His goal to crack open the crate and hopefully find Louis's safe there seemed of no significance in light of Felicity's appearance.

She had been placed in the drop box? His stomach tightened at the thought of that hard wooden container where unwanted children were left. If one died before being found by asylum staff, they sent word to an undertaker to pick them up. Once, he'd witnessed the morgue being three days late. Nathan covered his eyes at such a horrid idea, his heart aching for precious Felicity. Had Ms. Thornson not believed him when he said he would speak to Felicity's benefactor and make sure she got paid? Had she left Felicity there? But why? She'd worked there previously and knew Mrs. Miller, so if she had a problem, wouldn't she just talk to the matron? It made no sense, but that didn't matter. All that mattered was Felicity's wellbeing.

The door creaked open. Mrs. Jorgenson, the cook, bustled out, wiping her hands together, yet she paused when she caught his gaze. "You are Sarah Reed's brother?"

He rose slowly, his head throbbing. "You knew my sister?"

"Yes. She was a sweet girl. She would come to the kitchen early in the morning while I was preparing the bread. We became quite close." She smoothed her apron down. "Did she ever get to have that talk with you?"

"What talk? I... No."

She nodded slowly. "Sarah mentioned her folks were far away. She had no one except a brother who she'd wronged."

"She wronged me?" Nathan pointed to his chest. "You must have misunderstood. I wronged her."

"No." She placed a hand on his arm. "Sarah said she was angry over a past mistake and turned you away. She wanted to ask your forgiveness and be reconciled as a family."

Nathan lowered his head, a weight slipping from his shoulders. Sarah had wanted to be a family again. Nothing had been the same at home after his mistake and Sheriff Rudy's death. His request for forgiveness had been rejected—or so he believed for so long.

"She would be proud to see how well you take care of that baby." Cook squeezed his arm. "Lizzy and Miss Aubrey have told me how hard you worked to look after her. You know you are not alone. Just speak up if you need something. Understand?"

"Yes, ma'am." He barely uttered the words, then Cook gave him a hug—the kind some ladies at church give when you barely know them but understand their hearts are good—then she left.

Sarah forgave him. In a daze, he turned the doorknob to the sitting room and entered. Lizzy looked up from the floor where she changed a tiny baby.

On the far side of the room, Aubrey peered over the back of the sofa. "Nathan, you forgot to knock."

He blinked, unable to move. "Forgive me. I wasn't thinking."

A mew sounded from the infant Lizzy cleaned.

"Can I help?" He stepped in, drawn by the sound.

"Yes. I need those clean cloths." Lizzy inclined her head toward a pile of linen on a nearby chair.

Nathan snatched up a couple of cloths and went to her, finding that she held not his fair-haired Felicity but Aubrey's babe with her ebony tresses. The child was without clothes and punching and kicking the air with her complaints.

"She must be cold." Aubrey watched with concern in her eyes as she stood and swayed with Felicity.

As in the garden, seeing Felicity with Aubrey gave him pause. Melanie was quick to remind him that she was still in need, though. Nathan laid down a double layer of cloths and soon had the tiny girl swaddled. Supporting her head with his fingertips, he slipped her into the crook of his left arm and began to rock.

"Thank you, Mr. Reed." Lizzy stood with the soiled garment. "I am sorry, Miss Aubrey, but she was just such a mess."

"Of course. Thank you, Lizzy." Aubrey came to Nathan's side, snuggling Felicity and patting her back.

He held his breath as he cradled Melanie. He'd forgotten

how small a baby could be. Surprisingly enough, she stopped crying and studied him with large gray-blue eyes.

"There, darling." Aubrey smoothed Melanie's feathery hair back, fingers brushing against Nathan's. "I was just burping Felicity when Melanie made a mess."

Her daughter turned her head and looked at her mother.

The smile that radiated from Aubrey was like dawn on a snowy morning, bright and full of warmth.

Felicity chose that time to burp.

Chuckling, Aubrey used a cloth to clean around her mouth. "She is beautiful, Nathan. And look at this hair. Like a regular *pépite d'or*."

"What does that mean?"

"A gold nugget."

"And what does *mon tresor* mean?"

Her eyes lit. "My treasure. That is what I call Melanie. I don't remember calling her that in front of you before."

"On the veranda the day after she was born."

"Oh, that's right." There was a softness in her voice that drew him, though Nathan pressed his feet firmly into the floor. He'd nearly kissed her the last time attraction had tugged him toward her. Felicity and Melanie were here now, reminding him that whatever he did affected more than just him and Aubrey.

When Lizzy told Aubrey she needed to take the laundry to the washroom, Aubrey gave her leave, though she did not take her eyes from Nathan. They needed to talk about the near-kiss.

Once they were alone in the room, the moment seemed to stand still save the nearly imperceptible breathing of the baby in his arms.

Aubrey was the first to speak. "My cook, Mrs. Jorgenson, says I can feed both babies but that we should supplement goat's milk for Felicity. She will be able to adapt to the milk better than Melanie because she is older."

So this was the conversation they would start with. Very

well. He would follow her lead. "Has your cook done this before?"

"Yes, when she had twins."

He nodded slowly.

"I trust Cook. If I could nurse them both, I would, but...it takes...time." Her cheeks turned dark red.

Probably because he was staring at her like a simpleton. "Fine. That's fine, Aubrey. Thank you."

Her bare shoulders sank, the hair that had been arranged so perfectly in curls, ribbons, and braids earlier that evening now loose around her shoulders. The dress still pinched her slender waist like a glove, except for the bodice which was unbuttoned the first couple of buttons. He darted his gaze away, and Aubrey adjusted Felicity to cover herself.

Somehow, words tumbled from his mouth. "You're beautiful."

"I know." She cocked an eyebrow. "I don't even have to try, you know."

This was not boasting. Indeed, the flicker in her eyes hinted at anger. Likely, Louis had wed her because of such beauty without ever treasuring her sweetness, honesty, and strength. "And you are kind."

She shrugged. "Many are."

"Yes, but it comes more easily to some than others." Nathan moved a little closer. "What about honesty?"

She sighed. "That takes bravery. I don't want to hurt others' feelings or make them angry, but honesty is always worth the price."

It wasn't always possible in his line of work, but perhaps Aubrey was able to live in a black-and-white world. "Sometimes it's wise to be silent, not honest."

That brought a rumple to her brow. "Like you keeping your distance, not letting me voice my desires to be close to you two weeks ago because you believe there is no hope?"

He stopped swaying the baby, her words like a splash of icy water.

"That's why you argued with me the day my father came to visit, isn't it? Because you believed that getting close to me risks failure."

He shrugged, yet tingles in his arms and feet told him to run.

Aubrey stepped closer, likely preparing to tear down more of the internal walls he'd fortified for years. Strangely enough, it was the little girl sleeping on Aubrey's shoulder who had been the first to breach his lines of defense. Yep, Felicity had softened him up, and now Aubrey was going to finish him off.

Aubrey cocked her head, her gaze fixed on him. "You must fear that getting closer to me means others might learn of Felicity's connection to the Willot family. Or perhaps you believe that feeling attraction for me is betraying your sister's memory?"

"I had not considered all those things, but yes, they are concerns I have."

"Well, any time I have concerns, I think of practical solutions." She raised her chin and gave a practical little cock of her head. "For example, we are more alike than you think. We share a love of nature, family, and photography. We each respect God and logic. As for Sarah's memory, she and Louis are gone, in which case what we do matters little to them. Felicity is part of the Willot line, but Madame—while she loved Louis in her own way—would not publicly admit to having an illegitimate grandchild. And where our girls are concerned, well, they would have each other if we...married."

He paused his movements and held his breath. Married. Such a commitment—to be responsible to protect and love a family for the rest of his life—well, it was enough to sober any man. But she was right to mention marriage. They each had a child, and what else could a romantic relationship lead to except marriage? And hadn't he prayed for a mother for Felicity and wife for himself just that evening?

He swallowed past a tight throat. "You truly believe we could be a family? After everything between Sarah and Louis... and my wrongs?"

"Yes. You made mistakes, but you told me the truth, which I greatly respect."

The flicker of hope inside him wavered at a sudden realization. Aubrey didn't know about the bank robbery, and if they were going to consider a future, she should. "There's something else I haven't told you. More I need forgiveness for."

She raised her eyebrows, growing very still.

"I... The day we met in the bank, I was there to rob it for Ellsworth."

Aubrey blinked, and her features darkened ever so slightly. She searched his eyes, as though she could glimpse his heart by doing so. Finally, she said, "That makes sense. You were tense, agitated, and you did not remove your weapon when the robbers told everyone to. Why did you help me?"

"I could not let that man hurt you. Such a thing..."—he shook his head—"it was inconceivable. I am not a thief by trade. I never should have agreed to rob the bank, but I was desperate to move Felicity from the foundling home. Half the babies there die before they turn three."

She nodded slowly, then let out a sigh of relief. "Is there anything more, Nathan? Because I am not particularly fond of surprises."

He thought back to all the things he was ashamed of and shook his head. She knew all his failures, yet the slightest of smiles turned up her mouth. "Thank goodness." She leaned against him, resting her head gently on his chest with both babies between them.

Air trapped in his lungs, he remained still for a moment. "Does this mean you forgive me?"

She only nodded, touching Melanie's brow while her chin nuzzled Felicity's head.

"And you still think that someday we could be a family?"

Tipping her head up so the soft glow of the gas lights warmed her cheeks, she nodded. "Possibly. I feel an incredible attraction toward you, not just because you are handsome" —a smile played on her lips again—"but also because in you, I see a man I admire and respect."

"Admire and respect?" He grinned, lifting her chin with his forefinger. "I like the sound of that. As for this incredible attraction…" He dragged his thumb across the supple edge of her lip. "I feel that too." He settled his lips on Aubrey's for a few silky moments.

A knock sounded, and Aubrey drew back with a start, her eyelids fluttering. "Oh, Lizzy must have returned."

He sighed, letting go of her and earning a smile.

Aubrey told Lizzy to enter, and the ladies spoke quietly about how to settle the babies for the night. They would take them to Aubrey's room where Madame rarely visited.

When Aubrey wished Nathan goodnight, a gentle glow about her face, his doubts crowded back in. Nathan pushed them aside. If he was going to ask God for something like a family, he'd better trust His will on the matter.

CHAPTER 20

Sunlight peeled back her sleepiness, and Aubrey drew in a fresh breath of morning air. She was outside on the veranda again, her pa sitting on a chair beside her, sipping lemon water. A stone pathway led between hedges to rose bushes clustering at the base of dogwood trees. There Lizzy and Nathan walked, each with a babe in arms. At the sight of his tall stature and thick arms supporting Felicity, she smiled.

Pa frowned, the glass he held seeming small in his large tanned hand. "So Melanie has a sister?"

She had just apprised him of what she and Nathan had learned last night at the party, in addition to Felicity's true identity. "Yes, Louis had an affair with Nathan's sister. She died giving birth."

"I am sorry to hear that. It is an odd arrangement the two of you have." Pa tapped his foot in its cowboy boot.

"What's that verse that says, 'all things work together for good to them that love God, to them who are the called according to his purpose'?'"

He nodded slowly. "And you also believe you can open the safe, Aubrey? If it is, in fact, a safe."

"Yes, we will try once it's Nathan's shift."

His expression darkened. "You better tell me when. We are still outnumbered, you know." He glanced over his shoulder, likely looking to see if Madame was spying. "I'd hoped your mother-in-law would be different. That you would not have to endure more because of the illegal dealings of that family."

"Now that Felicity and Melanie are here, we have to forgive them, Pa. For everything. The girls are their flesh and blood, and we will protect them from them as well, but we can't afford bitterness to creep in."

He focused on her for a long moment. What did he hope to find? When his features relaxed, she released a soft breath.

"You are a better woman than your maman and I ever imagined." Pa squeezed her hand, and she beamed at him.

Lizzy and Nathan stopped at the fountain where little finches perched to drink at the edge. When they headed back, Pa stood to greet Nathan before he took Melanie into his arms. He peered at Felicity as though analyzing her, then softened. "I need to run into town to send a wire. We need more help here, and there are only a few people I trust." He met Nathan's gaze. "You will stay with Aubrey until I return?"

Nathan nodded, and when Pa gave Melanie over to Aubrey's care, he kissed her goodbye, then left.

"Lizzy?" Aubrey stood, tugging the layers of her ruffled skirt with her. "Will you bring Melanie to me in twenty minutes and have Cook send up some milk then?"

"Yes, ma'am." The maid adjusted Melanie in her arms, then she was on her way.

"I can take Felicity." Aubrey reached for the little girl, and Nathan gave her over with an ease that warmed her. He trusted her with his baby. "She's so heavy compared to Melanie."

Nathan grinned, rubbing the back of Felicity's head, then kissing her blond tresses.

Aubrey held her breath, her throat tight with tears. He was

so tender, a truly loving father. *Lord, could he love Melanie as much?* How she hoped God would provide them the opportunity to find out.

She turned toward the house, Felicity nuzzling into her collar in search of food. A giggle escaped when the baby began to wave her arms. "There, darling, it won't be long now."

Nathan opened the study door for her. It was easier to cut through the room to get to the nursery. They walked down a hallway and into the main part of the house in quiet, an easiness settling between them.

As they came to the front foyer, Aubrey turned toward the stairs that led to her room. "Would you like to help with Felicity when Cook sends the bottle of goat's milk, as you did this morning?"

"Yes. She seemed to eat better this morning than last night. I'd heard that babes could drink goat's milk before. I just thought it wouldn't be good enough for her."

"She's healthy as can be." The little girl in her arms pressed her elbow into Aubrey's sore chest. She adjusted her to a better position.

Nathan smiled ever so slightly, grazing a finger across Aubrey's temple. Hardly breathing for the nearness of him, she smiled, letting her eyes hold to his.

He kissed her cheek, then Felicity's, only to blink suddenly. "Milk."

"What?"

"You, at the ball last night. You smelled like honeysuckle and, uh..." He shrugged, color coming into his cheeks. "Well, milk."

Aubrey chuckled. "Yes, I suppose I do, thanks to our girls." Her chest tightened at the phrasing, and Nathan grew still.

There was no time for sentiments, though, because Felicity opened her mouth and wailed.

"Felicity!" A teary-eyed woman burst into the room with the

butler close behind. Who was this? She reached for Felicity, but Aubrey turned her shoulder, keeping the baby out of her grasp.

"Oh, Mr. Reed, I am so sorry Felicity ended up at the asylum." She wrung her hands as she spoke with a sob. "When Mrs. Miller told me she found Felicity in the box…" She choked, then covered her face with her hands and wept.

Nathan craned his head down, trying to see her. "Do you know who put her there?"

Nodding, the woman dropped her hands and stared at him with large brown eyes. "It was Mrs. Frill. She overheard me tell you that I hadn't received payment for nursing and said you were taking advantage of me. I told her it wasn't true. She took Felicity without my knowledge." She launched into another volley of tears, reaching for Felicity.

Again, Aubrey leaned away. This poor woman was obviously in no condition to see to the needs of a baby.

Nathan placed a hand on her back. "Aubrey, this is Felicity's wet nurse, Ms. Thornson." Though his voice was steady and his words made sense, a high ringing sounded in Aubrey's ears.

Ms. Thornson reached for Felicity again. Aubrey stepped backward, clutching Felicity to her chest. The baby grabbed her buttons and pressed her nose into Aubrey's collarbone.

"It's all right, Aubrey." Nathan reached for the baby too.

"But she's hungry." She back stepped, hugging Felicity to her chest. "I have to feed her."

"Excuse me, Mr. Reed, but considering I have been Felicity's nurse since she was born, and that I have been away from her for so long, it is really better if I tend her needs." The young woman tried to glare through her tears, but when she looked at Felicity again, her anger fell away. In its place were desperation and heartbreaking loss, so when Nathan reached for Felicity, Aubrey did not argue.

"Oh, darling." Ms. Thornson cradled Felicity, and the baby's cries intensified.

This woman had been Felicity's nurse all her life. Suddenly, Aubrey felt like the one who had done something wrong. A numbness settled over her as Nathan promised the nurse he would visit her later. She smiled and strode to the foyer, the baby's golden head bobbing over her shoulder.

After they left, the room fell silent. Arms empty, Aubrey stood on what felt like soft ground. "I would have taken care of her."

"I know you would, but Felicity is under Ms. Thornson's care, and you have your own baby to feed."

Though his voice was gentle, all of her felt cold.

"You are pale, and you've been sleeping all morning, Aubrey. I know that nursing both infants is hard on your body."

"I am weary, true, but healthy, and already my milk supply has increased."

Nathan glanced at her chest, then looked away. "I planned to ask you about the payments not reaching Ms. Thornson. It just didn't seem like the time has been right. And then you slept most of this morning."

She closed her eyes. "I will send a note to the bank today. Likely, with Mr. Ellsworth leaving and Pa stepping in, trying to make sure the audit takes place and business continues, the payment was missed."

Tears, unbidden, swelled in her eyes. She'd not been ready to let go of Felicity. Why had she allowed her heart to become so quickly bound to her?

"Listen, Aubrey..." Nathan took one of her hands, though she hadn't the strength to return his firm hold. "I know you are hurting. Sending Felicity with her nurse in no way changes the way I feel about you."

She blinked and shook her head. If he felt she would make a fitting mother, wouldn't he have sent away the nurse who had lost her and let Aubrey tend to Felicity's needs?

He blew out a great sigh. "I don't want to place obligations on you where Felicity is concerned—obligations that might prevent you from freely rejecting me if you find I am not the man for you."

Her jaw went slack, though Aubrey quickly pressed her lips together. "That is gracious." And brave, selfless, and caring.

"We haven't talked about how practical this is. Us possibly courting." Nathan drew her over to sit on two chairs by the fireplace. "I am not a prideful man, but I'd like to bring something to marriage when I wed."

The skin on his fingers was rough from hard work, his hands large and strong. And gentle. Just remembering how he had held each of the girls turned her heart soft. "You don't know what you bring, Nathan." She touched his chest, though confusion marred his features.

"Well, I have some pride. I won't take Louis's money and make a family with his daughters, in his house."

Aubrey pulled back, his words like a slap to the face. "Now who's living in *his* world? You've wanted to prove that Sarah's life meant something, to protect Felicity from hardship. What better way to do those things than to, yes, live in this house, with two perfect daughters?" She squeezed his hand and allowed a grin. "Or we could burn it down."

Nathan smiled sadly. "It's not so easy."

"Will you try to see that you don't have to be worthy? We have a chance to live a good life with what God has allowed for us and our girls."

He drew in a deep breath and grasped both her hands in his. "I will try to be at peace with whatever God allows. For you."

"And will you kiss me and remind me that...maybe, someday...?"

He settled his fingertips on either side of her jaw, cupping her face gently, and pressed his lips to hers with enough promise that she could hope for a someday.

~

The following afternoon, after the sun began its lazy descent toward the west, Nathan and Grange sat in the carriage house at the small table the guards used, each with their own set of cards. The bear-sized Grange hardly ever spoke. He played solitaire for hours, pausing only to walk the perimeter outside or relieve himself. Seldom did he let Nathan out of his sight, and when he did, he always managed to reappear without making a sound. He obviously did not like or trust Nathan. Getting Aubrey near the safe wouldn't be easy—not to mention, it could be dangerous. Her pa had left to gather the troops, and Nathan had told him he'd wait to do anything until he got back. Aubrey would have to tell him the combination, something he should have thought of the day before, but that kiss... He'd not been thinking clearly.

Sunlight swept through the high rafters of the carriage house as Beau pushed open the door to the tack room where the safe was stored and stepped in. He met Nathan's gaze and frowned. Grange stood, tossed down his cards, and left without saying a word.

Beau closed the door, then plopped into the chair across from Nathan. "Quick game before you leave?"

Understanding that Beau wanted to talk, not play cards, Nathan nodded and shuffled the cards, the familiar clatter a comfort. After a moment, Beau stood and peered out the window toward the house. "Looks like Grange is following his stomach to the kitchen." He sat back down across from Nathan, but instead of focusing on a card game, Beau admired the small carving of a bear he'd been working on.

"Thanks for making sure Mrs. Miller came to me with Felicity the other night."

"Madame had Grange in here guarding the crate, and since you were off with Mademoiselle Aubrey, I was patrolling the grounds. I ran into Mrs. Miller. She was ready to march into the party and confront Mademoiselle Aubrey. I was just trying to lead her away from the people. It was happenstance, really, that I found you and Mademoiselle Aubrey."

"Well, thank you, anyway." Nathan divided up the cards.

"Did you find out what happened? Why the bebe wasn't with her nurse?"

"Yes." He sighed. "Her roommate found out that Ms. Thornson hadn't been paid for her services and took matters into her own hands. Left her at the asylum. I still can't believe she put Felicity in that box." He paused with the cards, trying to breathe calmly. He'd never wanted to hurt a woman until Mrs. Frill callously shrugged over Felicity's experience when Nathan had called last night. The exchange had been short. Nathan paid Ms. Thornson and left. "I hate the idea of Felicity being there with that calculating old woman."

"There's something you should know. Madame is hiring more men. Maybe they will move the crate soon or she is expecting trouble." Beau patted his pocket, then withdrew a smaller knife and began working intricate features into the carving.

The man was obviously not going to play cards, so Nathan collected them and began sorting them. "Do you know what is in the crate?"

"No. There was a time when I would have, but the Willlots aren't so trusting since Mademoiselle Aubrey and her brother escaped. Do *you* know?"

"It's about the size of a safe. I think it's the one from Salt Lake."

Beau grew still, his head cocked up, a warning in his gaze. "Why do you think that?"

"Madame came from Salt Lake. From visiting Emil. She said the crate is his, and yesterday, I overheard Madame state that Aubrey is the key. Aubrey said Louis used to say the same thing about her. She knows the combination for Louis's safe."

"Did she tell you the combination?"

Nathan stilled his work with the cards, then slapped down a queen of hearts and said, "No."

Beau shifted his jaw to one side. He grinned. "Why don't you marry Mademoiselle Aubrey? That would solve all your problems. Your little girl would have a maman, and you could keep Ellsworth and Madame away from them."

He shook his head, his chest heavy. "Aubrey needs more time."

Beau snorted and chuckled. "More like, *you* need more time. You going to stay and try to be a steady fella? Stop your wandering and not run off on the girls?"

"You calling me a coward?"

Beau just shrugged. "Nothing so scary as caring about someone, and now you got Felicity and Mademoiselle Aubrey. Maybe even the new baby. Sometimes a family gives a man a reason to grow roots. Others run."

"I'm not running from anything ever again."

"Good, because Mademoiselle Aubrey needs you." Beau paused his whittling to meet Nathan's gaze. "If you're going to discover what's in the crate, now is the time. Mademoiselle Aubrey is going to need whatever valuables maybe in the safe because there was a run on the Bank of California where Ellsworth had all her money invested."

What? "Why didn't you say that to begin with?" Nathan leapt up and darted from the carriage house, one thought marching through his mind. He had to get to Aubrey.

～

ubrey was in her study, of course. Not on the sofa as usual but in a heap of skirts on the floor with the

contents of two crates spilled around her. She turned, looking over a lavender sleeve. Her red-rimmed eyes filled with tears at the sight of him.

"There's been a run on the bank." She tucked her chin to her chest, cupping a glass bottle of chemicals used in developing.

Nathan knelt beside her, taking one of her hands. "I heard. I'm so sorry."

"They closed at two this afternoon, vaults empty. Lizzy went into town to see her sister. Her husband finally came from Alaska, and they are getting ready to leave. He had just removed his savings from the bank this morning. Good thing, because now it's all gone."

He fished a handkerchief from his pocket for her.

Aubrey traded it for the bottle, which he placed on one of the side tables. All around her were old photographs, doilies, blankets, shawls, and newspaper clippings. He knew that Aubrey had planned to finish sorting through the crates since overhearing Madame and Ellsworth the night of the party, but judging by the condition of the room, this sorting had been done after she received the dreadful news.

"Mr. Ellsworth sank everything into the Bank of California. I was going to cash out my bonds and move my banking business next week. Now it's..." She motioned toward the crates and shrugged. "I don't know if the house is even paid off. I should have asked more questions, but I didn't feel I could handle taking over the business." She hiccupped into the cloth, tears pressing from beneath her dark eyelashes. "I am just so terrible at arithmetic, and then Melanie came. All I do is feed her and sleep. I am so tired."

Unable to refrain any longer, Nathan pulled her into his arms.

"What if I've ruined Melanie's and Felicity's futures?"

Aubrey whispered against his collarbone, her petite shoulders shuddering on an intake of breath.

Melanie *and* Felicity? He pressed his cheek to hers, loving her for her sense of devotion to both girls. How could she be so selfless in light of everything that had happened? "Melanie and Felicity will have good futures, not because of the wealth of their father but the goodness of their mother." Nathan shook his head, causing his lips to graze the corner of her mouth.

She was utterly still, then her fingers uncurled against his chest.

Eyes closed, Nathan inhaled the scent of flowers and that subtle hint of Aubrey herself. He turned his chin. Upon her intake of breath, the warmth inside him rose to a boiling. Nathan settled his lips on hers, holding her closer. Aubrey was the sweet and good woman he'd never dared to dream of. Rejecting her would be a waste he always regretted.

Her breath swept his cheek, and Aubrey pushed her arms up his chest, over his shoulders, to clasp behind his neck.

She slowed the kiss, then parted from him, though her hands still cupped his face. "Part of me feared we might not kiss again after our last conversation. You know, I am not Louis's wife, and the girls are not his. Really, if we belonged to anyone, it would be God. And wouldn't it be grand if He purposed for us to be a family?"

He shook his head at her amazing statement. "You're right. I was being prideful, wanting to be good enough to earn you. It's humbling that you care about Felicity, think of her with your own daughter..."

She brushed her fingers through the hair at the back of his neck. "I am not proposing marriage, but any man I court...well, it will be for that purpose. I want to be married again." She raised her chin, a dare in her eyes. "Even if it's not to you."

Nathan cupped the back of her neck and brought her mouth

so quickly to his that she hadn't time to say more. He kissed her, her soft moan rekindling fire in his veins. The idea of Aubrey having a sudden name change didn't seem so bad. Being near her for the rest of his life suited just fine, but she wasn't his wife yet. He tenderly pushed her a safe distance away. If she was going to be his wife, they needed to sort out this nonsense with Madame and the safe and Ellsworth and the silver mine. If Madame was hiring more guards, trouble was coming.

CHAPTER 21

*A*ubrey forced her eyes open. She'd never been taken by such passion, not even within marriage. With Louis, she'd always felt a niggling of uncertainty. As though she needed to keep part of herself buried deep inside. With Nathan, just kissing him...well, there was nothing hidden. Even now, his arms closed around her, shielding her from the world.

Nathan's dark-blue eyes narrowed. He blew out a breath, then stood, pulling her up with him. "You said you behaved admirably in previous courtships. I'd hate for you to say something different because of me."

"My goodness, I never thought..." She shook her head and rubbed her arms.

"Aubrey, we need to talk." He nodded toward the outside door.

Probably best not to stay in the study where they were alone. She hurried with him to the veranda and into the warmest part of the day. The sun neared the horizon and cast slanted rays over the nearby hills and onto the veranda, coloring the evening a pink hue.

Nathan led her to a banister that overlooked the yard and

far rolling hills. There, they sat, hands clasped. He lowered his voice, his shoulders hunched. "Beau just told me Madame went into town for more men to hire."

"Did he say why?"

"No, but he said something is about to happen. Maybe she started her part of the plan as she told Ellsworth she would. Whatever it is, we are already outnumbered."

"How do you know you can trust this Beau character? You know he worked for Emil as well?"

He blinked and drew back. "How do you know that Beau worked for Emil Willot?"

"I saw him in the Salt Lake City house when I was kidnapped. You see, my brother is marrying a lady who also worked for Emil. Her name is Lorraine. She and Mr. Fox were good friends. In the end, he helped with the rescue and to clear her name."

He opened his eyes wide, then chuckled. "You are clever. I can't believe you knew this and didn't say anything."

"I only realized it last night when he came with Mrs. Miller. He seems like a private man, and after hearing my future sister-in-law's recounting of what had happened, it sounded like Mr. Fox was mixed up in this Willot swindle like me. From what I understand, Emil was a lot like Louis. They would use the hurts and things that made you vulnerable to keep you desperate. In need. Then they could be the one to fill your need at whatever price they demanded." At that, a frown shadowed Nathan's features again, and Aubrey squeezed his hand. "Don't be cross. Neither one of them is here. They don't matter. Now, if Madame is getting more men, we need to act quickly." She leaned nearer and whispered. "I think we should look in the safe now."

"Your pa said to wait. It's not safe."

Cold tingling her skin despite the splendor of the day, she shook her head. "But Madame and Camus are still in town. The only person here not on our side is Mr. Grange."

Nathan nodded slowly, rubbing his chin. "Grange just finished a long shift, so he probably ate and went to rest." He studied her, the wind playing with his steely blond hair. "Once more men arrive, it'll be even harder to get to the crate."

"Exactly. I think it would be worth the risk. What if the missing deed is in that crate? The silver strike would be an answer to prayer with the run on the bank."

It was no wonder Mr. Ralston was so desperate to get his hands on the silver. Ellsworth was right about one thing. Getting the deed to the silver strike would save the city. Nathan ran one of his fingers in circles around her knuckles. "Aubrey, the safest option might be for you to tell me the combination."

She sighed and shrugged. "I understand that, but if I did, it might not be right, anyway. Sometimes there would be tricks that Louis would pull. He would change the order of the numbers or something. It's just better if I do it. Nathan, please? We haven't time to lose."

He studied her for a long time, then, looking around, nodded. "Fine, but at the first sign of danger, we leave. Agreed?"

Aubrey nodded, so he took her hand and started through the garden. They wove their way past hedges and around trees until they reached the carriage house at the back of the property.

Nathan rapped on the rear door. A moment later, Beau cracked the door and frowned at them. He glanced at the mansion before waving them inside.

Coolness closed in as her eyes made sense of the dim scene. The large double doors on each side let light in through a narrow set of windows at the top. Aubrey's open-topped barouche was gone, Madame having taken the best conveyance.

Nathan spoke quietly, still gripping her hand. "Miss Aubrey is here to see the item Madame is keeping."

Beau led them past the carriage and tools hanging on the wall to a smaller tack room with a single sunlit window on the far wall. Stationed in the middle of the floor was the crate she'd not seen since Madame first came. Beau helped Nathan turn it on its side, then handed him a hammer and pry bar and walked away. He stationed himself on a stool near the window and continued a whittling project—a bear.

In a matter of minutes, Nathan had one side of the crate open, the sawdust used for packing littering the floor. Since he had removed one of the sides, the safe was still in the crate with its door facing her.

"That's it." The safe from Louis's office. Thick yellow letters read, *Diebold's Special*. There was a dial and a two-spoke handle. Aubrey cranked the numbers she both feared and hoped would work, then turned the handle. The door swung open.

Nathan dropped to his knees. "It's empty." He turned, light spilling across half of his face. "Why would Madame need to guard an empty safe?"

She knelt and pressed her fingers down on the back edge of the safe floor. A panel levered up. Aubrey drew out a handful of papers and handed them to Nathan.

He raised an eyebrow. "How did you know the combination, Aubrey?"

"It was my birthday." When Nathan stilled, Aubrey shrugged. "I was like his trophy. He had my initials put on things. Used my birthday for codes."

Nathan turned away, shaking his head.

Beau leaned up in his chair. "Are those the documents you were looking for?"

"I believe so." Aubrey peered around Nathan's shoulder, reading the documents. There were letters and old shipment forms. A bill of sale with the Bank of California crest and even a map. "If this is the safe from Salt Lake City, what did Louis have the Baker Brothers transport to San Francisco?"

"I don't know." Nathan folded the pages and placed them in

his vest pocket. "We can't just stand here looking these over, though."

"I'll close the crate back up." Beau put away his whittling and strode over to them. "You should get back to the house, Mademoiselle, before your babe gets to crying."

He was right. A couple of hours had passed since she'd fed Melanie, and already her chest ached. Beau seemed to value the demands of parenthood. Of motherhood, even, which meant he must have been close to someone with a newborn.

Nathan moved toward the door, but Aubrey paused and turned back around. Beau collected the sawdust yet glanced up.

She gentled her tone. "Are you a parent, Mr. Beau?"

His gaze dropped, his broad shoulders bowing for a moment. "I was once a father."

And was not anymore? How sad. But before Aubrey could respond, a door creaked open.

A shot rent the air.

Nathan pushed her behind him. Aubrey gasped.

The man stood on the threshold was dressed like Madame's guards, but she'd never seen him before. Smoke wafted from the tip of his pistol.

Movement on her right—Nathan drawing his gun—then a second shot split the air.

The guard dropped to the floor. Nathan slid downward too. Aubrey gripped his arms, trying to keep him upright, but she sank to the dirt floor under his weight.

Someone levered a gun around the doorway, shooting blindly inside.

Aubrey ducked, her skirt caught beneath Nathan. She curled around him and squeezed her eyes shut, only to open them as footfalls sounded behind her. The guard named Grange charged through the door, raising a rifle to his shoulder.

Beau knelt to peek around the corner of the safe. He threw

a knife, as poised as Nathan had been the day he'd flung his own knife at the bandit in the bank. The projectile lodged in Grange's chest. He fell, his gun useless beneath him.

Beau ran past them to the doorway, dragging the two bodies inside, then closing and locking it. Aubrey pressed her hands into the packed dirt beneath her, her arms trembling when she tried to sit up.

"Nathan?" Beau knelt beside them.

Leaning heavily on Aubrey, Nathan gripped his chest, a dark spot forming on his gray shirt. She covered his hand to help staunch the blood.

He sucked in a breath, grimacing in pain. "Beau, close up the crate so Madame doesn't know we broke into it. Then get Aubrey to the house."

"You're not giving orders, Reed." Beau glanced over his shoulder, then at Aubrey. "Go to my saddlebags near the window and retrieve a shirt to use as a bandage." His words were a mix of English and French, but as soon as he freed her skirt from beneath Nathan, Aubrey obeyed.

Once she returned with a shirt she'd found in the bag, she pressed it to Nathan's wound. Breath hissed through his teeth, his body shaking from the pain. His gun slipped from his hand. She hadn't even seen him draw it. His must have been the second shot that took down the strange guard.

Aubrey held him tightly, her pulse pounding in her ears. Everything had happened so fast yet now seemed to slow when Nathan blinked heavily, color draining from his face.

Beau was saying something too muffled to hear as he dragged the last man out of the doorway. "Aubrey?" His faint voice barely penetrated her fog.

How were they going to transport Nathan to the house without being seen?

"Mademoiselle?" Beau gripped her arms, and his voice became clearer. "We need to move him before more guards arrive. Stay with him. I will check to see if it is clear to go to the house. Is there a place you can hide him?"

"Yes, a secret room. There is a hidden doorway in the garden Madame and her men do not know about."

"Good, if we move him before Madame returns, she may not know." Beau started to hurry away but stilled, his dark eyes hooded beneath thick black eyebrows. "Do not let him stand. His heart will have to pump harder if he moves. We will need a horse."

Her hands trembling and sweat soaking her through, she nodded. "Help me lower him here, then you can close up the safe and leave. I will lock us in."

Beau looked between the closed door and Aubrey, then nodded.

"Leave, Aubrey. Go to the house, to Melanie, and Madame will leave you alone." Nathan's voice was tight with pain, his face strained.

She reeled back. "I will do no such thing." Aubrey turned to Beau. "Are you ready?"

His gaze fixed on Nathan's bloody chest, and what color Beau possessed drained from his face while his lips moved without sound. Was the man in shock?

Aubrey nudged his shoulder. "Beau, are you ready?"

"He needs a clean cloth," Beau muttered, backing away. "He'll get gangrene." The poor man looked ready to faint, but he managed to close the crate and headed for the doors.

Aubrey locked it behind him, then rushed back to Nathan's side. His eyes were closed. She hovered her hand over his nose. Warmth brushed her skin. Thankfully, he was still alive. But for how long?

She removed the documents he'd folded and placed in his vest pocket. Along with the deed for the silver mine were personal letters and an old shipping receipt.

The crunching of the barouche wheels on the gravel drive

outside signaled that Madame had returned and, with her, more guards.

"Where did Beau put the bodies?" Nathan's fingers relaxed in her palm, and he closed his eyes. He was losing strength, and here they were about to be discovered.

Trying not to look at the corpses, Aubrey cleared her tight throat. "He moved them out of the way, but this room is the first place they will check because the crate is here. We have to move, or we will be trapped and found for sure."

"Help me up." His voice was hard now, freezing her insides.

The sensation of fear and confusion overwhelmed her, as it always did when Louis raised his voice to her. But this was Nathan, not Louis, and she had determined to live free of his influence. Besides, when one accounted for the pain Nathan was in, it was easy to understand that he might use a forceful tone.

He straightened, face creased as he tried to lever himself up and keep one hand pressed to his shoulder.

"Stop." She placed a hand upon his chest and forced him back. "Let me tie that shirt into place, then we will go."

"Beau will have a length of rope in his saddlebags. Hurry."

There in the dirt near the stool and wooden wall, the leather bags. She searched the contents, finding a piece of rope. Once she had Nathan wrapped and Beau's saddlebags thrown over one shoulder, she helped Nathan to his feet, and they started a wobbly trip toward the window.

Nathan was strong enough to swing one leg over the sill. His weight pulled hard. Aubrey held tightly as he managed the second leg, then his weight began to drag her through the window as well. A jolt might further injure him. Aubrey's grip slipped, and Nathan slid down the outside of the carriage house, his back against the wall.

Whistling came from the front of the building, likely Mr.

Dobbs, followed by low male voices. More guards must have arrived. Soon they would open the doors.

Aubrey climbed up on the stool, sat on the sill, and swung her legs over to the other side. She dropped down beside Nathan on the dried grass. A shout sounded inside the building.

The coachman would alert Madame and the staff. What might happen to Nathan if Madame learned that it was he who broke into the crate and killed a guard? Beau had said he was going to make sure everything was safe, but what if he had just run off? Should she try to move Nathan? Beau had said they would need a horse.

Nathan lay slumped against her, his head hanging low.

"Nathan?" She lifted his face and patted his cheeks. The stubbled jaw she'd cradled less than an hour ago when they'd kissed scratched her hand. What if he was really dying? She touched beneath his nose, feeling the subtle warmth of his breath. Out of the corner of her eye, she saw a large man come around the side of the building.

~

*A*ubrey hugged Melanie close, the baby's soft hair grazing her lips as she descended the secret stair. She had never considered that the secret room would be turned into a sickroom. It was certainly the last thing she wanted, but there were no better options. Earlier that day, Aubrey had led Beau to the hidden door in the garden and helped him carry Nathan's limp body down the dark passageway. No one seemed to have noticed them.

Madame had been tense at dinner, announcing that some of her guards had become drunk and fired their weapons on the property. Aubrey promptly stated they would need to leave, to which Madame informed her that she had already sent them away. She then asked if Aubrey had seen Nathan that day. Pa, who had been plenty furious when he learned Aubrey and Nathan had searched the crate without him, told Madame that *Reed* got handsy with his daughter and he ran him off. Madame had seemed to approve.

In the secret room below the study, Aubrey sank to the floor beside Nathan. A dim kerosene lamp gave the room a soft glow. Nathan lay on a pallet with a white bandage tied around his bare chest. Beau was gone, guarding Madame's precious crate, and so was Pa, who had treated Nathan's wounds. She adjusted a slumbering Melanie in her arms, then touched Nathan's brow. Sweat dampened his hair, but he was not hot. She left her hand there and prayed for God to heal him.

"Aubrey, what's wrong? Did something bad happen?" Nathan's gravelly voice cut into her prayer.

She snickered, forcing a smile. "You are shot, yet you worry about me?"

He squeezed her hand. "What happened after I was shot?"

"Beau and I moved you here by horse. Later, he told Madame someone had tried to take the crate and shot the other two guards in the process. He said he was in the house getting a bite to eat when it happened. She seemed to have believed him since he was on guard duty all day."

"What did she do?"

"Now that surprised me." She shifted to sit more comfortably. "She sent a letter to Mr. Ellsworth telling him that she would return to town tomorrow to see him. Mr. Dobbs was kind enough to bring me the letter before sending it into town."

"That makes sense." He blinked tiredly. "Ellsworth wanted the documents for the bank, so if she suspects there is a threat, she would tell him. Why go into town to see him, though? Why not just tell him in the note there was an attempt to break into the crate?"

Melanie woke, stretching her arms and peering about.

Aubrey readjusted her so she could see more clearly, and her large gray-green eyes settled on Nathan.

He turned his head more fully and smiled. "Look how bright her eyes are. She looks just like you, Aubrey." His smile faded. "Could you see if Lizzy will look in on Felicity for me?"

"I will do so myself. Did you have a chance to go over the documents?"

"Yes. I looked through them with Beau and then later your pa when he was down here. Beau is trying to stay out of sight, in case your pa wants to turn him in." Nathan reached for the bundle at his side, wincing and breathing through his teeth. "There are two sets of documents. The first is the deed to the Nevada silver mine. Your pa said he will take it into the bank tomorrow."

"I will go with him and check on Felicity. Once we've turned the deed over, all of this will be behind us. If the bank has the silver mine, then Madame will lose hope of stealing it and maybe leave. I can't imagine why she would stay." She rocked Melanie slowly but accepted a document when Nathan offered it. "This looks like personal correspondence."

"It is—at least part of it. We'll have to turn it over to the police."

Aubrey inspected several other personal and business documents. "Is this a letter to..."

"Mr. Ellsworth, yes. The old man had his own reasons for wanting the documents found. That is a receipt of shipments from the riverboat *Sarah Lee* to a Confederate officer." He pointed to a jaunty signature at the bottom of a shipping receipt. "And look—a Lieutenant Robert Ellsworth signed to have the shipment sent. Then look here." He handed her a letter written on water-damaged paper.

Aubrey finished reading through it and looked up. "Mr. Ellsworth was a traitor, and he was being blackmailed by this man, Mr. Jenkins."

"It looks that way."

Aubrey set the papers aside, frowning. "But why would Louis have these?"

"Ellsworth said Louis kept a file on people he used to control them. This must have been one on Ellsworth. I just wonder how Louis got it from Jenkins. This might be the fella Beau and I heard about when we first started investigating."

"Mr. Beau helped you investigate? My goodness." She held Melanie closer, nuzzling her little head. "Who was the fella?"

"Right after the bank robbery and Madame hiring me, I was trying to figure out what Ellsworth wanted the papers for. I learned that the year before, an old fella came through San Francisco. He was supposed to be a friend of Ellsworth's, a war buddy. One day, he disappeared."

"You don't think Louis made him disappear when he took these pages, do you?" Her chest tightened at the notion of how far her husband might have gone to control another human.

"There is no proof, and speculating might bring up different possibilities when investigating, but it's not enough, Aubrey."

The order form for military supplies lay beside her, Mr. Ellsworth's name scribbled across the bottom. "What should I do with this?"

"Get Captain Hiram at the San Francisco Police to come see me. He can keep the paperwork in his safe and turn it over to the U.S. Marshal."

"We will have to get you moved to an actual bedroom, then. It's a big house, and Madame now keeps to the living quarters." Aubrey sighed, her shoulders sinking. "Poor Mr. Ellsworth. What will happen to him?"

"He'll probably hang." He yawned, then groaned and touched his shoulder. "No wonder he has been so paranoid lately."

"There's just one thing I can't understand. Why would

Madame care so much about the silver mine? I am the one who stands to profit if the bank survives."

"Unless you die, Aubrey." Nathan raised his eyebrows, meeting her gaze.

"Oh...no." She instinctively held Melanie closer. "There has to be another reason."

"Well, maybe Ellsworth was having her look for it and offered a reward as he did with me originally. Five hundred dollars is a lot, and Beau says that the Willots' businesses are heavily taxed. He was surprised she even came to America."

Weight pressing down her middle, Aubrey shrugged. "She thought Louis was alive when she started her journey. Madame needn't have a good financial reason to travel. She adored Louis. The poor woman must be stricken with grief, and I have been a terrible hostess."

"You are too kind, Miss Aubrey. Don't ever change." He brought her hand to his lips and kissed it.

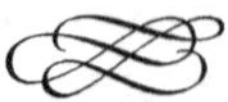

CHAPTER 22

All of San Francisco was in a hurry. The majestic buildings in this part of town gave Aubrey pause no matter how often she viewed them, but today the palace-like Bank of California drew her gaze out the barouche window.

The vehicle crawled to a stop, and Mr. Dobbs looked back to address Pa, who was sitting across from Aubrey and Lizzy. "It appears closed."

Indeed, a large sign hung across the immaculate entrance. People milled on the sidewalk and street, several police officers directing the crowd. Their shiny round helmets caught the glint of the sun. Tension hung thick in the air although the large building sat in dark stillness. As though dead.

"I don't think you will find Mr. Ellsworth here, missus." Lizzy spoke from the shadow of the large canopy, peering up at the bank with one eye squinted.

Cradling Melanie in her arms while she clutched the deed to the silver mine in one hand, Aubrey said, "He is usually at the Occidental Hotel."

Pa gave the driver directions to their new destination, and Mr. Dobbs set the barouche into motion.

As they rolled through the streets, Aubrey leaned back against the cushions, trying to calm her racing heart. Was all her money tied up in the Bank of California? Had Louis taken out a loan on the house, or was it paid off? Would she and Melanie have anything to live on?

Pa had said she should purchase stock elsewhere so her money was not all invested in one place. Her dream of opening a photography studio seemed silly in light of the current economic crisis in San Francisco.

The coachman found a place to park the carriage, and Pa strode into the building. It didn't take her long to tire of the heat, then she noticed the deed caught in the door. It must have slipped from Pa's pocket when he left the coach.

She gave her babe over to the maid, a nervous knot in her middle. Inside the hotel, Aubrey made her way across the black-and-white tile floor to the mahogany desk. A large man in a tan suit stood before the desk speaking with a clerk. She drew near, and he turned toward the door, his arms swinging. It was Mr. Ellsworth himself, but where was Pa?

She gripped the deed to the silver mine tighter. "Oh, Mr. Ellsworth?"

He glared, his eyebrows low and many deep wrinkles in his thick, sweaty forehead.

"Mr. Ellsworth, I am so sorry for the trouble at the bank. Perhaps this can help." She handed him the deed.

He unrolled it slowly, then crumpled it. "It is worthless."

"What? Isn't this what you needed to get out of debt? With the run on the bank, this might be an answer to prayer."

His mouth twisted into a sneer. "Mr. Reed told you that, did he? The mine was a setup. A fraud like the Great Diamond Hoax of Seventy-Two. Ralston fell for that too."

"Mr. Ralston? The bank president?"

"Past bank president. He resigned yesterday, after the vaults were empty and the doors closed. No thanks to Ralston who borrowed thousands and never repaid it. Oh, he begged the board for leniency, promising the silver would restore the bank. One of the chairmen told him the man who sold the silver mine was a charlatan. In prison for fraud."

"That is awful." Her stomach cramped, Aubrey drew in a deep breath. "What about my business? Was it all tied up in the bank? And the house...does the bank hold a mortgage on it?"

He startled, then glowered at her. "The house is owned by your father, stupid girl."

"What? No, it was up for auction, but I sent a message telling you to hold off. That I was moving to San Francisco."

"You can't just hold off an auction when creditors need to be paid. Your papa went to the courthouse and won the bid. He told me not to tell you."

"Papa owns the chateau?" Her papa who didn't want her to stay in San Francisco—who had railed at the preposterous idea that she would live alone, raise her child alone in the house Louis had built for her—had saved that very house and not even told her.

"Drowned. He's drowned!" Shouts came from outside, then a man ran past the window.

People rushed to the door. A nervous energy filled the place, like static electricity Aubrey had once experienced at a fair exhibit.

"Who's drowned?" A valet caught a man by the arm as he rushed inside.

"Billy Ralston. Went swimming at the Neptune Bath House like he always does and didn't come back. They just pulled his body out. Hurry—you should have time to see it."

Another patron rushed by. "Bet it's suicide since the man went broke."

Aubrey pressed a hand to her chest but was shoved from behind. The crowd pushed forward, forcing her out into the hot sunlight.

Ellsworth stepped from the doorway looking stunned, but when he caught sight of Aubrey, he seized her elbow as though he feared she might run. "You are more trouble than I could have ever believed, Mrs. Louis Willot."

"Let go!" She pulled away, stumbling into a large man who caught her by the arms.

His thick brown hair was uncombed unlike when she'd seen him at the party last week, and he needed a shave, but it was unmistakably Mr. Watkins.

"Hey, leave the lady be." The photographer guided her away from Mr. Ellsworth, who, with a glance of warning at Aubrey, turned and walked down the street, sweat stains up his back and under his arms. Mr. Watkins removed his hat. "Are you all right, Mrs. Willot?"

"Yes, sir. Thank you so much." She clasped her shaky hands.

"What goes?" Pa stepped from the bank entrance, a shadow of concern crossing his face.

"That squirrely banker Ellsworth put his hands on your girl. Best report that to the police so there is a record."

Pa fumed and glared into the passing crowd.

"I'm fine, Papa. Mr. Ellsworth was just overwhelmed. He's likely lost everything."

Mr. Watkins cocked his head to the side. "That justifies his violence toward you?"

"Well, no, of course not. That's not what I meant." Why had she excused Mr. Ellsworth's behavior as she had excused Louis's countless times? Mr. Watkins was right. No man should ever put his hands on her. "Did you hear about poor Mr. Ralston?" She rubbed her arms against a shiver despite the balmy day.

"Yes. The failure of the bank was a burden too great to bear. There isn't a business in San Francisco unaffected." Mr. Watkins gestured across the street to where the Yosemite Art Gallery stood with the *closed* sign on the door.

"Did you close your studio to avoid possible looters?"

"No, ma'am. All my business was tied up in the bank, like most everyone else's around here." A numbness settled onto his face. "My property will enter foreclosure."

"What? So quickly? The run on the bank was just yesterday. You must have some time."

He shook his head slowly. "I have nothing. All the photographs, the cameras, the..."

"Your negatives. You can reprint. The work you do is phenomenal, Mr. Watkins. Surely, you will recover all you have lost."

He winced, then shrugged, his shoulders bowed like a man defeated. "You had best go back inside. The day is hot, and the streets are dangerous with the city in an uproar."

"No, sir," Pa protested. "I am getting the ladies out of town. There's got to be another member of the board I can see later, since Ellsworth snuck out when I went up to his room." His eyes flamed, but he contained himself and offered a handshake to Mr. Watkins. "Thank you for looking after my girl."

The photographer nodded, then wandered a few steps, only to stop and stare at the Yosemite Art Gallery. The poor man.

"In you go, Aubrey." Pa opened the door for her and offered a hand.

She took the steps, the barouche levering down slightly under her weight and then more so when Pa climbed in. "There is no reason to find a member of the board. Mr. Ellsworth says the silver mine was a hoax. Like some diamond mine from a year ago."

Pa grumbled something under his breath and stared out the window, shaking his head. "It seems we've been going in circles. Nothing makes sense. It feels like Jesse should be here, even though I don't know what he might do to help."

Aubrey agreed, though she kept it to herself. As they made their way to Taylor Street, though, her dread grew. What else might go wrong? Why was Madame behaving so strangely over a silver strike which, even if it hadn't ended up being a hoax, had nothing to do with her? Aubrey was still pondering this when she arrived at Ms. Thornson's house to find the lady in hysterics yet again. Only this time, she had good cause. Someone had come to the house and taken Felicity.

CHAPTER 23

The wailing of an infant floated down the grand staircase in the chateau when Aubrey paused at the foot with Melanie in her arms. Pa and Lizzy stopped beside her, the former of whom flushed red.

"That woman has gone too far." He took the stairs two at a time, no doubt heading toward Madame's rooms.

The whole ride from town to the chateau, Pa had theorized that Madame had taken Felicity. Judging by those wails, he was correct. And to make matters worse, Melanie gnawed on her fist. She was hungry, so both babies were in need of sustenance.

Aubrey adjusted Melanie in her arms. "At least we know where she is. That she is safe. Can you take Melanie and..."

Cook stalked into the room with a bottle of goat's milk yet stilled at the sight of Aubrey. "Thank heavens you are home, Missus. That witch has done it this time—kidnapped a baby." Her round face grew in color. "Oh, forgive my language. But really. Taking poor Mr. Reed's babe, and after everything he and his sister went through..." She bit her bottom lip, large tears pooling in her eyes.

His sister? What did Cook know of Sarah Reed? Not that it mattered just now.

Aubrey handed Melanie to Lizzy, then gestured for Cook to follow her to Madame's room.

In one of the grand guest suites, Madame stood by the bed, her hands over her ears while Pa tried to console a red-faced Felicity. The babe screamed with every breath, her little legs kicking and diaper soiled.

Aubrey collected the infant and set about cleaning her up. Cook placed the bottle on a side table.

"Oh, Aubrey, do make her stop crying." Madame raised her voice to speak over the wails, her face nearly as red as Felicity's.

Had her mother-in-law lost her mind? Aubrey brought Felicity, cleaned and wrapped snuggly in a light cloth, to her shoulder and turned toward the door. "You are in serious trouble, Madame. Kidnapping a baby. What right do you even have—"

"I am her grandmother, and since Mr. Reed has abandoned her and left town, run off by your father here, I am taking her. I cannot allow Reed the chance to take the child later."

The child. Not *my granddaughter* or *grandchild*. No, Madame was not maternally inclined and was likely using Felicity as a pawn. But why?

Not having the time to question her, Aubrey exited the room, leaving Madame and Pa arguing in her wake. It took more than an hour to get both babies fed and settled, but with Lizzy's and Cook's help, the infant half sisters were sleeping soundly in their cradles when Aubrey went to find her mother-in-law again.

Madame was in the master study, of all places, pacing and fuming. "There you are." She greeted Aubrey with a strained smile.

Aubrey paused halfway across the room, folding her hands. "Let's put the pretenses away. You will not be taking Felicity.

She will stay here, with Melanie and I, to be looked after properly, and you will be leaving for New York, or wherever you're going, posthaste."

A chuckle left Madame's lips. "You know, Aubrey, I like you better now. Being married to my son was good for you."

"We only lived together six months."

"I said being his wife, not the time you spent with him. Louis was always a wild one. He could not help his wandering nature, but being married to a man like that is...challenging."

Drawing in a calming breath, Aubrey tried again. "You need to leave my home."

"Not until I get what I want." She came around the desk, past partly opened curtains which allowed in a little daylight from the hot summer sun.

"What exactly is it that you want?"

Her mother-in-law fixed a calculating stare upon her. "I don't believe that your dear Mr. Reed left town. If he had, he would have come to me for his pay. And he doesn't seem like the type to abandon a child, yet he happens to disappear the same day two of my guards are shot."

Aubrey swallowed. *Lord, help me not show the truth to this woman.* "You said you fired them for drinking. I hope you reported their deaths to the police."

"I did not. But that matters little. You've been sneaking around like a regular little spy. Where did you go this morning, Aubrey?"

"Pa and I visited Mr. Ellsworth in town—not that it is any of your business."

"As did I, and just as you were leaving the Occidental, I caught up to him. You'll never guess what he told me." She spoke in a sickly sweet voice, her expressions animated—hand sweeping the air, then touching her face in mock surprise. "You turned over one of Louis's long-lost documents that was stored in his safe. The same safe my guards are hiding in the barn."

Her voice lowered, the composure on her face slipping. "I want the rest of the documents."

Tempted to tell Madame she and Louis had been fooled because the silver mine was a hoax, she refrained and shrugged. "What I gave Mr. Ellsworth was part of the estate Louis left me. Since I inherited all of Louis's possessions, I must insist the safe be brought into the house to its rightful place."

Madame drew in a breath and folded her hands. "Aubrey, what did you think when you discovered you inherited Louis's estate?" Her voice was low and smooth, as if she were speaking to a child.

"I thought, why? I never got the impression that he trusted me with such wealth."

"You are right. Your inheriting it was a front, to keep the authorities away from Emil. My husband and I were in Europe. You were the only person Louis could entrust with his estate."

"You speak as though he knew he would die."

She closed her eyes a moment. "Because he did, Aubrey. Louis made powerful enemies. The plan was, according to my stepson, that if Louis died, you would inherit, but there was also documentation that his belongings would go to his family."

"What documentation is that? I have yet to see it. Have you? Louis left everything to me, and, true, I don't know why. Perhaps it was in some sick way to keep me chained to him, but it doesn't matter—"

"It matters!" Scarlett infused Madame's cheeks. "Louis would never forsake his family."

"He was about to be a father. Perhaps he changed his mind about leaving something to you, or perhaps Emil lied to you."

"You know. You know that is not true." Madame pressed her lips together, seeming to try and restrain herself.

A coolness settled in the room, and Aubrey shifted. "Madame, look at the facts. There was a run on the bank where all the business was tied up. There is nothing left to inherit. Taking Felicity will bring you nothing."

"There is value in the Willot legacy. I know Reed works for Mr. Ellsworth. You may tell your bounty hunter that unless he returns *all* the papers the two of you found in the safe, he will never see Felicity again." She picked up a document from the top of the desk and thrust it at Aubrey. "I am done waiting for my share."

Aubrey perused the paper and gasped. The court order she held stated Madame was the legal guardian of Felicity Reed. "I don't understand what you hope to accomplish with this. There is likely nothing left of the estate, and you don't want Louis's illegitimate child."

Scarlet infused Madame's cheeks. "I want the other documents!"

Aubrey startled, her heart racing. What on earth did she mean? Did she hope to use the papers documenting Ellsworth's treason to blackmail him as her son had?

"You stubborn girl. Don't you have any sense at all? I don't know why Louis married you."

Aubrey set the court order on the desk and turned to leave. She would not stay and be badgered, manipulated, and torn down.

"Where do you think you are going?" Madame pursued her.

Stopping before the door, Aubrey drew in a deep breath. "I am leaving. There may not be legal ramifications for what you're doing, using your granddaughter as a pawn, but I won't stay and listen to your ranting."

"I want the other documents!" Madame jerked her back by the arm.

Swinging her forearm around, Aubrey knocked Madame's grip lose. "Leave my house! Now! Today! You are not welcome here any longer."

"This is my house!" Madame reached for her again, but

Aubrey opened the door, nearly hitting Madame with it, and stormed into the hall.

Shaking with anger, she made her way to the garden. The woman was arrogant beyond belief, spoiled and entitled, just like Louis. Aubrey broke into a run, scurrying to the secret door in the garden—only to find the room inside empty.

CHAPTER 24

In one of the many guest rooms in the chateau, Nathan sat upright in bed that was as near to a cloud as he'd ever experienced. Was this what Aubrey was used to? Comfortable beds, floor-to-ceiling windows with thick drapes that kept out the heat, a fresh cup of water, and a tray of cheese and apples on the nightstand? He could not provide her with this kind of life. He'd know after his conversation with Captain Hiram if he had a future in law enforcement, though. He was done waiting.

Footsteps sounded in the hallway outside his room. He felt underneath the blankets to the papers from the safe and the hard metal revolver beneath his pillow. Beau had made sure to give him the weapon before leaving him in one of the bedrooms in a seldom-used part of the house. He'd said the guard had seemed suspicious last night. Hopefully, Cook had told Aubrey where he was. Maybe that was her coming now.

The sunlight pouring through a cracked drape told him it must be close to noon.

At a knock, Nathan called, "Come."

Lizzy poked her head in, eyebrows raised. "Captain Hiram of the San Francisco Police to see you, sir. Shall I show him in?"

Nathan inclined his head.

When Lizzy returned, she showed Captain Hiram inside, then left. "Well, I'll be…" The policeman frowned deeply, striding across the room in his dark uniform, his black boots knocking on the hardwood floor. "I should have checked on you sooner, but with all this business in town with the bank, I didn't have a moment to spare." He shook Nathan's hand. "What kind of trouble did you get yourself into, son?"

"The kind that gets you shot." Though if he had to change it, he'd do nothing differently. "I asked you here to give you these." He handed the policeman the papers from the safe.

Captain Hiram scanned the pages. "Sergeant Bartholomew Jenkins, Army of the Confederate States of America. You remember him?"

"No sir, should I?"

Hiram carefully took a seat on the end of the bed. "I suppose not. You usually only passed through town to collect a bounty and check the newly posted bills. This old codger was a beggar down at the docks. He was murdered last August."

"Louis Willot had these pages. I think he was blackmailing Ellsworth."

"I wonder if he or Ellsworth killed the old man…" Hiram bunched his chin. "Well, I would say it bears some looking into, even if there isn't much to go on. You said these pages were in the possession of Louis Willot?"

"Yes, sir."

"How did you end up with them?"

"It's my job to be discreet, sir. I don't report to the law."

Hiram grinned. "I don't suppose this has anything to do with Mrs. Willot?"

How to answer? Sure, it had everything to do with Aubrey,

but it also had to do with Felicity and Melanie and their future. "What do you think, Cap?"

He crossed his arms, smoothing one of his long sideburns. "'Bout a month ago, word in the society pages was that you and Mrs. Willot were seen in one another's company. And then, at the party the other night, you two looked mighty...attached."

Nathan rolled his eyes. "Seems you should have better things to do than read the society pages."

"I do, but my wife figured you'd been by the office and wondered if we'd ever met."

"What did you tell her?"

He crossed his ankles. "That I'd never seen you."

Nathan grinned, but the expression quickly fell. "I got a girl. 'Bout four months old." Just mentioning Felicity caused his throat to swell so much, he couldn't speak any more. All the anger that had streamed through him suddenly drained his muscles of all strength.

"What's she got to do with this?"

"It all started with her. She's..." Could he trust Hiram?

A tapping knock sounded on the door. It cracked open, and in stepped Aubrey, her green eyes wide until she met his gaze. Her smile blossomed like the sun peeking over the horizon at dawn. Nathan's pulse thundered, and the pain in his shoulder faded.

She greeted the police officer, her manners exquisite. With her hands folded serenely, she took a chair near the bed.

Hiram shifted his attention to Nathan. "Did you want to continue the discussion we were having before Mrs. Willot entered?"

Aubrey raised her eyebrows, and Nathan nodded. "You can say anything in front of her. Mrs. Willot is an intelligent woman and aware of the situation at hand. Not to mention, when all this is over, we're going to get married. Make a family for the two girls." Ears ringing for having made such a bold statement out loud, especially since he had yet to propose, Nathan reached for Aubrey's hand.

She gave it, holding tightly, though a frown marred her features. Had he misspoken, overstepped in believing they both wanted to be a family?

Captain Hiram grinned yet must have noticed Aubrey's expression because he did not comment on Nathan's statement. "Does your getting shot have anything to do with your sister?"

Nathan's breath hitched. He had not expected the lawman to turn the conversation to the topic of Sarah. "What do you know about my sister?"

"She was a sweet girl. Was friends with one of my daughters for a brief time when she first came to San Francisco, but then she fell in with a bad lot. Young woman trying to make her way. You know? It's not an easy place."

Although Hiram showed no signs of self-righteousness or condemnation, heat crept up Nathan's face, and his heart ached for Sarah. "No, sir. It ain't."

"She came by the precinct last year asking to speak with me when I wasn't there. She left a vague note saying she wanted to talk to me about Mr. Jenkins. She refused to speak to the other officers. They said she seemed scared. By the time I got her note, I couldn't locate her. Wasn't long after that, Willot left town."

Though her eyes were wide, Aubrey spoke calmly. "I wonder if she saw something, heard something, from Louis about Mr. Jenkins. Louis had the documents."

"No telling. Ellsworth was around then, too, though I don't recall Sarah being associated with him." Hiram tipped his head toward Nathan. "So you got shot obtaining these documents? Why didn't you turn them over to Ellsworth?"

Aubrey stiffened, though Nathan refrained from glancing at her. "That would be dishonest."

The captain nodded approvingly. "You know them fellas

who broke in here were bailed out, then disappeared. Two drowned out fishing, and the others left town. At least, that's what word 'round town is. I think someone hired them to loot the place and got rid of them when they were caught. One said they were looking for a document."

So one of the men had spoken to law enforcement.

"The men who broke in are dead?" Aubrey's voice sounded small and sad. She looked between Nathan and the policeman.

"Yes, ma'am. Two of them." Hiram stood, straightening his jacket and cuffs.

She sat frowning, as though trying to figure something. "What will happen to Mr. Ellsworth?"

"He will be arrested. There is no proof if it was him or your husband who killed Sargent Bartholomew Jenkins, but Ellsworth committed treason in time of war. That won't just go away."

Aubrey startled, though the lawman didn't seem to notice.

"Either way, Mr. Willot is dead, and Ellsworth will pay. God is their judge in the end. We need only be honest in our dealings with Ellsworth." He turned to Nathan. "Anything else you want to tell me, sonny?"

"No, sir."

"Hm, well, once you're all healed up, come see me about that job. You can't be out hunting bounties with a babe to tend, and if you marry the lady here and settle down." He tipped his hat and bid them a good day, and Nathan returned the goodbye.

Ellsworth would pay and Louis was dead, but what about poor Sarah? What had she known that she wanted to tell the police? Everything was coming together, yet Madame was still here, able to hurt Aubrey. There had to be more he didn't know. Something was missing.

Aubrey stared vacantly after the lawman, tapping her fingertips against her chest.

His middle tightening, Nathan cleared his throat. "Something wrong?" Was she angry he had told Hiram to speak freely and the man brought up Sarah back in August? That was when Felicity was conceived, which meant Louis had been unfaithful to Aubrey then. Or was she upset he had told Captain Hiram they would be a family? She'd frowned at that statement.

"Aubrey?" His second call brought her attention around.

Finally, she looked at him. "Nathan, I have something terrible to tell you."

CHAPTER 25

Throat tight, Aubrey inched to the edge of her chair and reached for Nathan's hand. There was no delicate way to put this, so she might as well get it over with. "Madame has a court order and took Felicity from Ms. Thornson."

He blinked, then pulled his hand from hers and tossed aside the blankets. In only a light pair of cotton underpants and a nightshirt, he swung his legs over the edge of the bed.

"Nathan, stop. You will hurt yourself." She tried to block his way, but he nudged her aside and headed toward the door. "I have taken care of her. I can bring her to see you. Get back in bed."

He stumbled near the rug and grimaced in pain. One hand on the doorframe, he steadied himself and looked over his shoulder. "Felicity was taken, and you waited until now to tell me?" The color growing in his cheeks concerned her, as did the sweat dampening his temples.

The man strode right out into the hall in his sleeping clothes, heading in the direction of the nursery. Aubrey trailed after him, gaining his side and gripping his elbow. Not that she could actually catch him if he fell.

They came to the end of the west wing where the hall turned toward the family quarters. Nathan wordlessly strode on, his face growing pale. It was amazing he'd not collapsed.

"Slow down." Aubrey caught ahold of his forearm. "She is not going anywhere."

"You don't know that." His voice was hard.

They passed the butler's closet. Odd that none of her servants were anywhere to be seen, but then Mr. Dobbs had gone to town on an errand.

"I just fed the girls a short time ago. Felicity finished with goat's milk and was fast asleep when I went to find you."

"Madame will do everything she can to keep Felicity from me."

"She does not know you are here."

He scoffed. "We know very little where this business is concerned. Ellsworth is probably a murderer. Madame might be as well."

"Do you really think she's capable of murder?"

He stopped, gaze incredulous, and practically towered over her. "Aubrey, the guard who interrupted us in the carriage house nearly shot you. If I had not been there..." He shook his head. "Ellsworth sent those hoodlums here to rob the place at the same time that Madame was out of town. She could have been in on that too."

"That was right after she arrived. Do you think she was acquainted with Ellsworth at that time?"

"We can't assume she wasn't. Ellsworth was connected to Louis and possibly Emil. Madame tried to get you to leave town the night of the robbery but left you here when you refused, remember?"

She swallowed hard and nodded.

Nathan continued forward and, jaw like granite, made his way to the nursery in silence.

Aubrey reached for the crystal doorknob and pushed the door open. Then froze.

Lizzy and Cook lay facedown on the floor, eyes wide, squirming, their hands and feet bound with rope. One of the cradles was knocked over, blankets strewn across the floor. The washstand was tipped over, the pitcher and basin shattered.

Nathan bumped into Aubrey, nudging her into the room. "Felicity? Melanie?" He checked both cradles, then yanked the blankets off the bed and dropped to his knees to peer beneath. "Where are they?" He held himself up against the post.

Lizzy and Cook both tried to speak through their gags. Tears rolled down Lizzy's cheeks. One of her eyes was swollen.

Aubrey darted to the cradles as Nathan had. The mattresses were bare, one damp with a spot where one of the girls must have spit up. Where were they?

Aubrey went to the servants, trying to pull Lizzy's gag down. It was tied too tightly. Rather than pain her further, she worked the knots free.

The maid gasped and tried to sit upright. "Men came and took the babies. We tried to stop them."

Aubrey's limbs shook. She steadied herself on the floor with a hand, then tried to loosen Lizzy's bonds. "Which way did they go? How long ago?"

"Just after you left."

And she'd been with Nathan and the policeman for at least half an hour. "Who would take the babies?"

"Your mother-in-law. She wanted them both." Nathan looked up, his sweat-damp hair hanging into his eyes. "We're too late. They will be miles away now, probably boarded the noon train."

"No." Aubrey shook her head. Melanie and Felicity were too little to be away from her. They would starve. Madame knew this. She had been sorry for taking Felicity without having a wet nurse to tend her. Someone else had taken them. "It must have been Mr. Ellsworth. He wanted his documents. He threatened me yesterday. We have to tell Captain Hiram to bring back those papers so we can get the girls back."

Nathan hung his head and shook it. "It was Madame Willot."

Aubrey stood and rushed to the door. She had to find the butler to take her into town. He wasn't in his usual spot by the door. The kitchen was empty. Room by room, she searched, Lizzy joining her. She told Aubrey to slow down and breathe.

But she couldn't breathe. In her mind's eye, she saw her babies' red, tear-streaked faces. She heard their pained cries and pressed both her hands into her temples. "My babies. Where are they?"

How had they been stolen from the house while she'd been here? She should have stayed with them instead of going to see Nathan. She'd not been there to protect them when they needed her. What if she went to town to tell the police and the men who took the girls were still hiding in the house?

Pa. Where was he?

She made her way to the study. The room was dim with light shining from beneath the heavy drapes. Aubrey strode across the rug and rent the curtains open. Light poured in, forcing her to squint stinging eyes. All was still. Even the desk was tidy, but there was a slip of paper in the middle. Aubrey lifted it into the light to read the words scrawled there.

"What does it say?" Nathan leaned against the door, supported by Lizzy.

"It's from Madame." Tears blurred her vision, and Aubrey sniffed and blinked. "She says she will treasure her visit with me, but it is time for her to leave. I have wronged her deeply, and there is only one way to put right the offense. That is to return her belongings." Her lips trembled. "What...what

belongings? What does she mean? I have nothing that..."
Madame's babbling about Louis leaving the estate to his family
returned to her. She claimed there was documentation proving
this. Madame had been so insistent. She must want Aubrey to
sign everything over to her. But there was nothing left.

Nathan came toward her, like a tall-masted ship at sea. She
was sinking into black waves, and though he reached for her,
she shook her head. No one could help her now. "Did I lose my
babies?"

Nathan wrapped his good arm around her. They sank
together into the blackness, Aubrey unleashing her tears
against his chest.

~

The babies were nowhere to be found. After Mr.
Dobbs discovered Mr. Alexander hog-tied in the
carriage house, the butler released Aubrey's father, and the
man went straight to town in search of the girls. He would also
notify the police.

There was nothing to do but wait, a notion that caused
Nathan to shake his head as he sat on the sofa with one arm
about Aubrey while the staff members gathered around them
in the master study. Cook and Miss Lizzy stood with their arms
touching and handkerchiefs ready. The poor women looked
terrible but insisted they were fine. Mr. Dobbs sat nearby, his
great white eyebrows deeply furrowed.

Someone had given Nathan a pair of pants, and his night
shirt was half buttoned. What he wore mattered little. He had
to rescue the girls but was so tired he could barely hold up his
head.

Aubrey no longer cried but was still, hardly even breathing

Had it been only last week that he'd held Felicity close, felt
her soft little fingers latch onto one of his callused ones? He'd

promised to love and protect her always. Felicity was part of his existence. He couldn't live without her.

Nathan ground his teeth. "What was Madame thinking, taking the babes with no way to tend them?"

Lizzy sniffed. "She was interviewing wet nurses last night in the front parlor. She must have been planning to take them then. I just thought she was trying to undermine Miss Aubrey since she disapproved of you nursing your baby. At least they will not go hungry."

Nearby, Cook made a sound like a growl.

Mr. Dobbs stood beside her, dabbing his nose with a handkerchief. They all waited for information from Mr. Alexander.

Footsteps sounded in the hall behind Cook. She startled and Mr. Dobbs straightened. Nathan had forgotten his handgun when he'd left his sick bed. The staff backed away from the doorway, and in strode Beau. He'd been around enough, helping Nathan since he was shot, that the staff did not react as though one of Madame's guards had entered the room. It was just a good thing that Mr. Alexander wasn't here because he would sooner shoot Beau than welcome his assistance.

Beau paused, taking in the room, then focusing on Aubrey and Nathan. "What goes?"

Aubrey covered her face, likely falling into another wave of tears, so Nathan answered. "Madame has taken both the girls."

His jaw flexed and nostrils flared. "She stole the children from you? What is your plan?"

"I'm working on that." Nathan held Aubrey's hand a little tighter. "Do you know where Madame and her guards were going?"

"No. They don't trust me. Madame sent me to town to deliver a note to Ellsworth. When I got back, they and the safe where gone."

"What did the note say?"

"That she was going to meet Monsieur Willot, and he would be disappointed to learn of Ellsworth's failure."

"She wants the documents proving Mr. Ellsworth was a traitor. That doesn't make sense." Aubrey raised her head, her bloodshot eyes heavily lidded. "If she doesn't know the silver mine is a hoax..." She shook her head. "No, it is something else. Last night when we fought, Madame said there is documentation that Louis left something to his family." She turned to Nathan, her nose bright red. "I don't know what she is talking about. I have no way to save the babies. Madame could not bring herself to hold Melanie when she was born, and when she took Felicity, she didn't even know how to soothe her. How could she take them and use them like pawns in a game? She does not love them. What if they don't have what they need? Nathan, what if..." She covered her face with both hands and gave a ragged sob.

Beau still waited, his six-shooter hanging on his hip and hat under one arm. He raised his eyebrows and turned his chin ever so slightly.

A sinking feeling settled in the pit of Nathan's stomach, then his shoulders lowered with the sensation he had lived with for years despite Aubrey easing the burden for a short time. "We missed something. The Baker brothers...I never got an answer what they brought here if the deed to the silver mine was in the Salt Lake City safe."

Aubrey's eyes brightened, and she touched Nathan's arm. "There must be a second will. Madame nearly said so. That's why she kept saying the house was hers and that she wanted all that belonged to her."

"I did some investigating into those documents," Nathan volunteered. "Louis had them sent from Utah to San Francisco when your brother broke into the Salt Lake house and collected evidence the marshals used to arrest Louis. He sent them the same day he was arrested, so he must have been in a hurry. This house must have been the only place he could have them sent to."

"But if that's the case, why didn't the Baker brothers just open the safe for Emil?"

Beau scoffed. "Those boys were dumb as rocks. They probably forgot the combination."

Aubrey frowned disapprovingly. "They weren't complete imbeciles. They managed to take that photograph of me and develop it. Besides, they would have written the combination down."

"And then lost it." Beau rolled his eyes.

Aubrey turned back to Nathan. "Your search is not done. There must be a second will, hidden somewhere in this house. I can't imagine where, though. It may have been in some of the furniture that was sold before I arrived."

"None of the furniture had anything in it." Cook crossed her arms over her buxom front. "My Willard and I cleaned everything. Why, we went through every item, hoping to present it well so Miss Aubrey would get the best price."

Aubrey snapped her attention to the servant. "Willard? Is he your husband, the caretaker Mr. Ellsworth let go?"

"Yes, he also moved the crates into the secret room so no one would sell them. We planned to send a letter to you, but then you moved in."

"Mr. Willard moved my crates into the secret room, not Louis?"

Cook nodded.

"But Louis went through everything..." Her voice died away, then she hopped up, strode across the room, and opened the secret door.

Beau, Lizzy, and Mr. Dobbs raised their eyebrows, obviously surprised. Nathan stood to follow Aubrey, but he paused when he caught his friend's eye. "Mr. Alexander went to town looking for the girls."

Beau raised his eyebrows, setting his hands on his hips. "Don't suppose we will see him again. He won't give up before he finds them. Madame could not have chosen a worse man to steal from."

"True." Beau would know better than anyone.

In truth, he was relieved that Mr. Alexander and Beau had yet to run into one another. If they did, there would be violence, and right now, they just needed to save the girls.

"Go ahead. We've work to do." Beau motioned for Nathan to proceed him down the stairs, then followed.

Just standing was painful, though nothing mattered beyond the girls being found. If what Aubrey said was true and Madame did not want her grandchildren, finding a will might satisfy her greed. Except the will was worth nothing since the run on the bank. Aubrey's father owned the house. It didn't make sense.

In the secret room, Aubrey searched everything. Every box, she checked for compartments. Papers, she held up to the light and read. The staff joined in, sorting items into piles of searched and not searched.

While Nathan sank into a nearby chair, Beau tapped on the sides of the desk. He set his ear close to the wooden edge as he went, working his way around. He found two hidden compartments, but both were empty.

Aubrey made a frustrated sound as she came to the bottom of a pile. She seized a Key West cigar box—the same kind that Sarah had stored her letters from Louis in—and tossed it so it landed on the nearby chair.

"What is this?" Nathan picked it up and popped it open.

Within were not letters but a small leather book. A diary?

He handed it to Aubrey, who shook her head. "It is just my diary from when we courted. There is nothing I want to read in there."

"Why did you keep it in a cigar box?"

She shrugged. "Louis loved the cigars. He gave this one to me full of embossed papers for writing." As she spoke, she opened the diary, fluttering the pages. Folded papers fell into her lap. She froze, then snatched them up and read quietly before she raised them over her head. "Here it is! A will signed by Louis. It is as Madame said. It leaves everything to Louis's father." She moved to Nathan's side so he could read it too. "What do we do now?"

"Go after her."

Aubrey stood up. "I am going to pack. If Pa spoke with the police, they might know where Madame is or at least which way she headed. This has to be what she was after." Leaving the will with Nathan, she bounded toward the door and called up the stairs, "Lizzy?"

Beau squatted beside him, scanning the will. "You know, this might work if..."

"If what?"

Beau tapped his teeth together, making a clicking noise.

Why wasn't he meeting Nathan's gaze? "What do you know, Beau?"

The Frenchman sighed. "Madame told Ellsworth that Monsieur Willot has come to America. He will see his oldest son. Emil is in prison, but the old man wants to get him out."

"What is the likelihood of that?"

Beau shrugged. "Not likely. He got two years for kidnapping Mademoiselle Aubrey and her brother."

Would the Willots take the baby girls as revenge? Why take two infants, which would garner more attention from law enforcement, if old man Willot hoped to get his son out of prison? "Tell me about the old man."

"He is sad but vicious." Beau sat on the chair opposite him. "I would not choose to oppose him unless I had no other way."

"Is he a soldier?"

"No. A miner. He married Madame when she was young.

Her father had no heir, and Willot was clever. He ran the business exactly how the old man wanted, then inherited everything when his father-in-law died. Alsace and Lorraine are no longer a part of France. Monsieur Willot insisted the family remain in what is now Germany rather than give up his steel and iron plants."

Nathan smirked. "I bet Madame enjoys that."

Beau gave him a knowing look. "Louis was his favorite son. He tried to get him to move back to Europe, but Louis refused. Madame came to America for her son, only to find he is dead. Even if you get her the will, she may try to keep the babies."

"That's what I am afraid of." Nathan rubbed his forehead, his heart thundering at the thought of the girls on another continent, likely lost to him and Aubrey forever.

He opened eyes he had not meant to close. The ceiling was crossed by wood beams, though he imagined the sky beyond with God in heaven looking down. *I need Your help, Lord. There is no way out of this for me unless You make it.* All the years he spent running, refusing to slow, to hurt, or to surrender to failure, yet here he was, shot in the chest with his babies gone and the woman he loved in pieces. *Lord, I can't fix this. Can't hunt Madame down and force her to give the girls back. I need You, God, to make a way.*

"I always felt bad for the old man." Beau cut into his prayer. "Emil used to stew when he got drunk."

"What kinds of things did he say?"

Beau thumbed his chin. "He said that when Louis last went to Alsace and Lorraine, their father gave him the deed to a tract of land that has valuable iron deposits."

Nathan raised his head. "Louis owned land in France?"

"Not France. Germany. We lost the war. Remember?"

"So if Louis owned valuable land in France—er, Germany, that is—and he left everything to his wife, his father cannot do anything with it."

Beau raised his eyebrows. "If it is a big tract of land, it is likely the Germans would want proof of ownership. France ceded steel and iron plants to Germany after the Franco-Prussian War. If Willot has any hope of holding onto his now that Louis is dead, he'll need the will."

Nathan sat up, though he had to steady himself by gripping the armrest. "I need you to do me a favor, Beau. A big favor. Go to Utah and find Old Man Willot. See if you can trade the will for the babies. There is money in one of the side pockets of my saddlebags. That will cover any expenses you have."

Beau was still, then he nodded. Likely, he did not want to go. After all, Beau had betrayed Emil when he helped the police find Aubrey and her brother when they were kidnapped. Madame had hired him, so she must not know that Beau had helped the police, but as Beau said, the Willots didn't trust him.

"I can do it, but there is no guarantee. Madame is not rational, and Monsieur Willot is grieving. They are both weary from loss and war."

Nathan nodded and found himself praying again. There was nothing to do but rely on God. He was the only one who could help.

CHAPTER 26

*A*ubrey was still shaking when she carried her travel bag down the stairs. No amount of sunlight pouring through the windows or glistening off the marble floors could bring light to her life. All she could think about were the girls and having them in her arms again. She should have watched Madame more carefully. She'd taken Felicity—why wouldn't she also take Melanie? As her mother, Aubrey should have known.

She paused at the bottom of the stairs, unable to move as tears once again assailed her. Ever since finding the babies gone, she had been like a pendulum swinging between hysteria and numbness. She just had to get the girls back.

The front door opened, and two men strode in, both a good size but one decidedly broader with black hair. "Papa." As he closed the door, she raced down the remaining steps and crashed into him. "Did you find the girls?" Dusty shirt pressing against her cheek, she held tightly.

Pa's arms wrapped around her, safe and secure. "No, sweetie, but we'll keep looking. Your brother is here to help too."

She peeked from her father's arms. Taller than Pa with Maman's blue eyes, Jesse stood with his arms flexed and sideways gaze filled with worry. "Sorry I couldn't come sooner." He opened his arms, and she walked into them.

"There was a second will I did not know about. Madame believed I was keeping it from her, so she took the girls."

Jesse furrowed his brows. "Girls?"

Aubrey pulled back to look at him. "Yes, Melanie has a sister. Her name is Felicity. She is only a few months older. I have been taking care of her. Madame took her away from her uncle, a good man who was raising her."

"There is another will?" Pa set his hands on his hips.

"Yes. She kept telling me I should give her what was hers. I didn't know what she meant. We didn't have the will then, but she thought we did."

"I always knew that old bird was feather brained." Jesse frowned, speaking as unkindly as he could likely manage, as mild-tempered as he normally was.

"We have the will now, but I don't know what direction she went." Salty tears burned her eyes.

"The police are checking into it. We'll figure it out." Pa inclined his head, bending nearer from his great height.

"I think she's gone to Salt Lake City." Nathan walked slowly toward them from the direction of the study. He and Beau had stayed in the secret room after Aubrey left. Was he only just leaving? He certainly didn't look well with his face pale and hair tipped with sweat. A hint of blood soaked through his white shirt.

"Nathan, good to see you are still alive. Though I reckon you should be resting." Pa shook Nathan's hand, then introduced him to Jesse. The two shared a simple exchange before Pa said, "What makes you think they are going to Salt Lake City?"

He glanced back the way he'd come, then met Aubrey's

gaze, his cheeks carpeted in blond stubble. "One of Madame's guards mentioned that Monsieur Willot is in Salt Lake City visiting his oldest son. It is likely Madame would go there."

"That's almost a two-day ride by train." Jesse wrapped an arm around her shoulders, giving her a squeeze. "We need to leave now."

Aubrey clutched her heavy skirts, ready to head for the door, when Beau strode into the foyer from the direction of the kitchen, slinging his saddlebags over one shoulder. He stopped midstride at the sight of Jesse, whose eyes went wide.

Jesse drew his gun and pointed it at Beau. The Frenchman ducked and, coming up on Jesse's right side, seized his forearm, pulling as he hooked a foot around Jesse's ankle. Her brother fell yet somehow rolled to his feet.

"Stop. He's helping us!" Nathan shouted as he ushered Aubrey toward the main stairs, pushing her away from the fray.

Jesse charged Beau, forcing him toward an outer wall near a large window. Beau shoved him off, this time punching Jesse in the mouth.

Pa bellowed and kicked Beau in the side, launching him through a glass window and into the hedges. Her brother followed, stepping on the sill with his thick leather boots and jumping into the yard. Beau raced around the side of the house with Jesse close behind.

Pa ran to the door, opened it, and then turned back toward Aubrey. "Who was that?"

"His name is Beau Fox. He has been helping Nathan investigate Madame and Ellsworth."

"Fox?" Face flushed, a vein pulsing in his forehead, Pa looked in the direction Jesse had gone. "He kidnapped you and your brother!"

Aubrey left Nathan's side to follow her pa. "Mr. Fox was part of the gang, but he had a change of heart in Salt Lake. He told me that help was coming, and you know he helped lead the police to Emil's hideout."

Nostrils flaring, Pa turned back around and stomped outside, shouting, "Jesse!"

Aubrey followed him to the door, though Nathan stopped on the porch, using the door post to steady himself. She shielded her eyes against the sunlight. A horse's hooves pounded on earth. Beau rode toward the drive on horseback, quickly leaving Jesse behind on foot.

Mr. Dobbs drove the barouche toward them from the carriage house. Madame had likely taken the closed carriage to avoid being seen.

"Call Jesse back, Pa!" Aubrey motioned for her father to return to the house. "We have to go after the babies."

Mr. Dobbs hopped down from the carriage, not seeming to notice the man racing away on horseback or how those around watched.

Lizzy rushed from inside the house, loaded down with baggage. "We are coming, too, missus."

Cook puffed up beside her, rolling her shoulders as she came to a stop. "We have everything those babies might need."

"Thank you, Cook." Aubrey hugged her, then drew back. "I would prefer if you would remain here and take care of Mr. Reed."

The older lady frowned and shook her head, but after one glance in Nathan's direction, promptly nodded. "Of course, I will." She patted Aubrey's arm, then went to help Lizzy and the coachman load the barouche.

Aubrey wasn't willing to leave Nathan's side yet. His mouth was pulled into a tight line, his face still pale. He stood on the top of the porch in the sunlight, sweat beading his brow. His gaze locked on her, then he slowly turned and disappeared into the dim house. She followed and met him at the bottom of the stairs, where he picked up the saddlebags Beau had dropped during the fight.

Nathan handed them to her. "Look inside."

A jittery sensation working up her spine, Aubrey accepted the leather pouches and worked the buckles free. There was an assortment of clothing items and five small carvings of animals. A flute of sorts, fire-starter, a rabbit's foot, a red bandana, and a necklace with a gold coin on it.

"Beau must have had the will on his person." Nathan stared away, a vagueness in his eyes.

Aubrey stood slowly and the sun slipping over the eave of the roof slid into her face. "You gave him the will?"

"Yes. He is connected with Monsieur Willot and can reach him, likely ahead of Madame. He will offer to trade the will for the babies."

"But he is a thief. A burglar for hire."

He faced her. "So was I, Aubrey. Beau is my friend. He is trying to right his wrongs where you are concerned. He helped me stop the robbery at the bank and the night you were attacked."

"That does not make him trustworthy." Pa stepped to her side, gripping her around the shoulders. "And now he has our best chance for getting the girls back."

"His actions say a lot about his character. When Emil wanted Aubrey to open the safe in Salt Lake, Beau encouraged her to hold out hope. He was kind to her when a bad man would have hurt her. And he helped despite the threat to his welfare. I believe he will come through for us "

Aubrey shook her head. "I hope you are right. The girls are gone and..."

Jesse jogged into the room through the door they'd left open, his face high in color. "If we're going to Salt Lake, we better leave now. I checked the schedule when we were in town. There's a train leaving at noon."

"What about Fox?" Pa stuck one hand on his hip.

"Pa, he already had a horse saddled and waiting. But it's probably better that way. Lorraine would be heartbroken if I actually caught him." He dusted off his hands as though not even angry while Pa rolled his eyes.

They all made their way back outside as Mr. Dobbs secured the last of the bags to the back of the carriage. Lizzy stood beside her mother, Cook lecturing her about being safe. Aubrey's feet felt staked to the gravel drive when she stood before the carriage. Nathan's gaze was glassy, his breathing labored. "Be careful when you catch up to Madame. Don't crowd her. She's not safe."

"She kidnapped my child. I could crowd her right off the back of a train."

"Beau will make it to Salt Lake. He will come through."

"What if he doesn't?" Tears filled her eyes. Everything was relying on that will. If anything happened to her babies, her life would be over. "I can't lose another child."

He wrapped his good arm around her shoulders and kissed her forehead. "Your pa and brother will keep you safe."

Aubrey clasped his hand, though he winced. "Will you stay here until we return?"

"In Madame's house?"

"Actually, my pa bought the house when it was auctioned. So you may stay. We will find Felicity and bring her back to you."

Nathan closed his eyes, his jaw taught.

Aubrey rested her head on his chest, quietly praying. The dream of being a family had been so real when both girls were between them. With them gone, darkness closed in around her, blocking out all hope. *Please, God, be with them. Let us be together again.*

"They are ready for you." Nathan spoke into her hair, and

she had the strangest sensation when she lifted her gaze to his that she was in a dream.

How was it that she was going with Pa and Jesse while Nathan, who was better suited for a potentially dangerous trip, remained here? "I wish you could come."

"So do I, but God's keeping me here. Probably because of my pride. I've been running for a lot of years, not trusting Him. Now I have no choice." He tried to smile, and though the expression faltered, certainty rang in his voice. "This will work, Aubrey. Beau is honest. Monsieur Willot needs the will so he can claim land Louis held the title to in Germany. Madame has no reason to harm the babies. Most importantly, God is watching over them, over us. We're going to be together again."

Wishing she had his faith, she pressed a kiss to his lips, then walked away from Nathan Reed, holding back a wave of fear and doubt.

CHAPTER 27

The house was terribly quiet without Aubrey. Nathan sat on a bench in the foyer after they said goodbye. Light slanted through the broken window, shining on the rug and warming the mostly dim room. The tall ceiling hovered in shadow.

All he could do was wait and ache, remembering Aubrey's promise to bring Felicity back. What if he never saw that babe again, felt her feather-soft hair, and heard her bubbling giggles between hiccups? Tears warmed his closed eyes, then ran down his cheeks. *God, please help me.*

Voices sounded in the distance. Captain Hiram must have arrived. Nathan brushed his good hand over his cheeks and sat up straighter, hurting at the slightest movement. He touched his head. Hot, so he was probably fighting a fever.

Captain Hiram strode into the foyer beside Cook, his eyebrows diving low at the sight of Nathan. "Say, sonny, you should be in bed."

"Did Cook tell you what happened?"

"Yes." He inclined his head to the older woman, who nodded and left. "She said Madame Willot took your niece and

Mrs. Willot's baby too. I sent a telegraph straightaway to the next stop on the line. The sheriff there is a good fella. He will be looking for those babies."

"Good."

He sat down beside Nathan. "You look worse for wear. Let me help you to bed."

Nathan shook his head. "Seen Ellsworth?"

"Yes, sir. I sent officers over to his house after I spoke with you. He was passed out drunk but also packed to leave town. Didn't take long to crack that crusty old buzzard. He admitted to killing Bartholomew Jenkins."

"Really? I didn't expect that."

"Well, he hasn't got much left after the run on the bank. Many a business is taking a hit, closing, or being foreclosed on. I suppose sometimes a man gets so bogged down by life, he just gives up."

That was the truth. Nathan covered his eyes with one hand. "Yeah."

"Well, I brought some folks out here to see you."

Nathan spluttered. "I'm not exactly in a condition for receiving guests." He was overdue for some pain medicine.

"Just wait here a minute." The policeman pointed a finger at him as he stood, then he strode away.

Nathan sat back, letting the spinning sensation take hold of his head. His stomach curled, and he forced his eyes open. Heaving would be too painful with the bullet hole in his chest.

"Nate?" A man's voice.

Nathan held his breath, the familiarity taking him back to his childhood. To long summer days working and evenings fishing. Ma at the hearth and Pa at her side sampling supper. No, it could not be them. He opened his eyes.

Cook and Captain Hiram flanked an older man and woman. Pa wore a bowler hat and city suit but still stood with the strength built from hard farm work. Ma clasped her hands over her mouth, her gasp more of a sob.

"Ma?" His voice sounded raspy.

She rushed to the bench and settled beside him. Holding his good hand, she kissed it. Ten years had sown wrinkles at the corners of her eyes, yet they still shone the way they always did.

Nathan's throat tightened, pain inside like a distant storm cloud pushing closer. "What are you doing here?" He placed his arm around her back to hug her, then stopped.

Pa hadn't permitted him to see Ma the last time he was at the house. He'd still hated Nathan and had said he was not a part of the family. Ma had just stood there, blank-faced with Sarah behind her.

Pa stepped forward, removing his hat. He dropped to one knee. His face had aged more than Ma's, yet it did not seem as hard as it had at their last meeting.

Nathan swallowed. "How did you get here?"

"Mrs. Jorgenson wrote us when Sarah..." He dropped his gaze, then his eyes flooded with tears.

"She told us you were hurt." Ma touched his face, her soft palm like a cooling balm on scorched flesh. "We came as soon as we could."

"The truth is, son, we—that is, I—never should have treated you as though you killed Sheriff Rudy." Pa's voice dwindled and he shook his head. "You were just a kid."

Nathan raised his voice in protest. "It is my fault. If I had said no—"

"That gang Billy was riding with would have attacked to rescue him, and you would have been hanging up there with Rudy too." Pa spoke with surety, his brow creased. "I should have been grateful you lived and helped you get through the shame of your mistake. Instead, I was selfish. Thought only of myself. Can you forgive me?"

All Nathan could do was stare. What was Pa talking about?

It was his fault. All of it. Rudy's death. The turmoil at home. "I am to blame."

"For your part, yes. Maybe you letting Billy free was a blessing in disguise. He knocked you out, so no one bothered you."

Ma cleared away her tears. "Nate, your papa and I had problems long before Rudy's passing. It just brought those things to the surface. You see..." She looked to her husband.

Luckily, Cook and the captain had already shown themselves out. Nathan glanced between his parents.

His pa nodded, and Ma drew in a ragged breath. "Don't hate me, son. Your mama did a terrible thing. Rudy had been my beau when I was young, but I married your papa. Our life was much harder than I ever imagined, with him guiding and trapping. Then the move to Oregon. Over the years, we grew apart. When Rudy took you under his wing, our friendship rekindled."

"Ma, you didn't...?"

She squeezed her eyes closed and shook her head. "Your papa caught us embracing the night before Rudy died. That was all, but it was enough. I was unfaithful in my heart. It was just a matter of time before..." Ma pressed her trembling lips together.

Pa took her hand and kissed it. "See? Your mama and I had problems of our own. Our hearts weren't right with God or with one another. We weren't ready for the temptations that came our way. When Rudy died, we focused on your mistake when we should have been working on our own."

Drawing in a ragged breath, Ma squared her shoulders. "But we are here now. You are our son. Can you forgive us?"

Nathan's eyes stung with tears. "I lost Sarah's baby." And they would not forgive him for that. Could not, just as he could not forgive himself.

Pa gripped his knee. "Sarah had a baby?"

"Yes, sir. Her paternal grandmother took her." A tremble broke through him, his body already aching and insides craving the touch of his little girl. "Her sister by the Widow Willot was taken as well. The family has promised to rescue both babies, but…"

A sob escaped Ma. Pa wrapped an arm around her, and they huddled close, bringing Nathan into the circle. And then Pa did something Nathan hadn't heard him do in a long time. Since before they came over the wagon trail to Oregon.

He prayed.

~

Jesse slipped down in the seat beside Aubrey as they rolled down the Southern Pacific Railroad track. They had crossed the Nevada border last night and should be getting into Salt Lake in the evening. She sat with open hands on the hard wooden bench, her breasts hot and aching from not having fed the children in twenty-four hours. She had hoped to sight Madame at the last train stop—and the one before that and the one before that—but at each stop, the local law enforcement said they had not seen anyone matching Madame's or the girls' descriptions. Some time yesterday, Pa had been deputized to arrest Madame for kidnapping. Aubrey wasn't sure how but assumed he must still be in contact with San Francisco.

She leaned her head on Jesse's shoulder. "What if we are going the wrong direction?"

"Mr. Reed sure seemed certain. Pa says he's an upright fellow. How'd he get shot, anyway?"

Aubrey closed her stinging eyes. "Nathan and I figured that Madame had Louis's safe, the one he had in Salt Lake City. I didn't tell you Emil tried to get me to open it when we were kidnapped."

He raised his eyebrows. "Why not?"

She leaned her head back against the seat. "I didn't think it mattered, but I also didn't want you to worry that he'd hurt me."

"What was in the safe? This will?"

"No. We found documents used as blackmail for a man in San Francisco and a deed to a silver mine that Louis stole from the Bank of California. It turned out to be a hoax, but we didn't know that."

"Why would Madame want those?"

"She didn't. She thought the will was in the safe because Emil thought that, but it wasn't. Some of her guards caught us breaking into the safe and shot Nathan."

Jesse grimaced. "Not a good sign, him getting shot. Fella might not be too smart."

Aubrey narrowed her eyes at his jesting. "Oh, he is more than smart. Nathan is skilled and quick to react. He shoved me out of the way before he drew his gun."

Jesse nodded approvingly. "So he keeps you safe. Do you fancy him?"

"Very much." She sighed. "But I can't think about him now, Jess, not when Melanie and Felicity are out there with Madame. That bitter old woman. What if she doesn't take care of them?"

"I don't think she would get on a train without a nurse. After all, the babies would cry the whole time, and that is not very discreet."

Face hot from the dusty car, Aubrey closed her eyes. Too many emotions clambered in her chest. *I need you to look after them, Lord, please?*

Aubrey had drifted off only to be jolted awake when Jesse tensed. She kept her eyes closed, listening for something significant. The iron wheels beat on the tracks, and the wooden frame of the car rattled ever so slightly. Heavy footfalls approached. They passed, then the back door slid open, allowing in the racket which the metal walls and glass windows barely muffled. The door slid shut.

Her brother held his breath for a moment. "Aubrey, the fella that just went outside has been sitting by a lady with a baby. I'm going to keep him busy. Go to the front of the car, third row, and see if you recognize the baby."

She tightened her hands. Jumping up and running down the aisle would draw attention.

Jesse stood, stretching his arms high, then he walked to the door as though he hadn't a care in the world.

Aubrey rose next, meeting Lizzy's gaze across the aisle. She, in turn, raised her eyebrows, then looked ahead.

Aubrey steadied herself on the bench in front of hers. She passed Pa, who sat beside a snoring elderly lady. Most of the passengers were men. Aubrey motioned toward the rear of the car. Pa glanced back just as Jesse passed through the door.

Near the front, a lady with an old-fashioned bonnet sat with a bundle in her arms. Aubrey's heart raced faster. She gripped the next bench. The train car rocked, knocking her off balance, so she slipped into the spot right beside the lady.

"Oh, my goodness." A woman not much older than Aubrey frowned at her and held the bundle protectively. "Miss, be careful."

Frozen, Aubrey stared at her. "Sorry. I didn't mean to..."

Wait...what was she doing, apologizing? This was a time for boldness. She moved the blanket away to reveal a blond little head. Felicity opened large blue eyes, then her face squished into a frown.

"For shame." The lady maneuvered Felicity to her shoulder and began bouncing her.

"Shame on *you*! You stole my baby!" Aubrey stood up and reached for Felicity.

Someone grabbed her left shoulder, then that hard grip

slipped. She didn't even turn. Pa's angry voice carried over the racket of the train. She sensed a tussle right behind her, but all she could focus on was the baby. Aubrey closed her hands gently around Felicity's ribs and plucked her from the woman's arms.

Scuffling sounded behind her, then a man shouted.

A little boy popped up beside the lady, who said, "Give me back my baby."

Aubrey swiveled to find Pa punching a huge man in the aisle.

The conductor burst through the door. "Stop that! No fighting in the car."

Pa punched the man again. He fell like timber, crashing into the aisle. Pa turned, his fists still raised, when the sound of a gun cocking froze Aubrey.

The conductor held the weapon aimed at Pa. "There will be no fighting on my train!"

"Yes, sir. I can respect that, but this man put his hand on my daughter." Pa motioned to the still form in the aisle. "And I've a warrant for the woman responsible for kidnapping my grand-daughter. I've been deputized to arrest anyone involved." He removed a piece of paper from his vest pocket.

The conductor eyed him but read over it, then glared at Aubrey and the woman. "Is this the kidnapped child?" He motioned to Felicity.

Aubrey's mouth hung open. What could she say? Madame had legal guardianship of Felicity, but it was wrong. Nathan had not abandoned her and never should have lost his guardianship. There was no way his rights were justly removed.

The woman who had been holding Felicity stood, gripping the bench to keep her balance while her little boy hid behind her skirts. "I didn't know the child was kidnapped. I was hired to tend this little girl by a French woman—Madame Willot."

The conductor raised his eyebrows disapprovingly. "Here is a warrant for her arrest."

Aubrey cradled Felicity, her body reacting to the nearness of the baby, her milk beginning to flow. She didn't care what the conductor said. She wasn't giving Felicity back. Aubrey turned and headed back to her seat next to Lizzy.

Felicity's soft little body curled into Aubrey. Heart aching with longing, Aubrey covered herself with a blanket, fumbled with the buttons of her bodice, adjusted her nursing corset, and began to nurse the baby.

The conductor and Pa seemed to come to an understanding, and the nurse Madame had hired sat with Pa. Jesse strode back in, wiping blood from his nose. He smiled at Aubrey until he realized what she was doing. Then he turned bright red and headed for Pa at the front of the train. Other passengers looked around curiously while Felicity's wet nurse listened to Pa and Jesse with horror-filled eyes. The poor woman obviously had no idea what she was a party to.

Pa approached and sat on a bench across the aisle from Aubrey.

"Where is Melanie?" Aubrey could hardly get the question out fast enough. Madame had likely secured a private car for them and left her nurse to travel with second-class passengers.

"She says she hasn't seen Madame or Melanie since this morning."

The part of her that had lit with hope at the sight of Felicity died. Pa kept talking. Something about Jesse taking down a guard and checking the rest of the train with the conductor. His voice seemed to echo as though in a long hallway.

Felicity's tiny fingers closed around one of Aubrey's. She shut her eyes and held on to that feeling. Even when Jesse came back and said there was no sign of Madame or Melanie, that they must have disembarked at an earlier stop, she held on.

~

The moon slipped its lonely light onto the granite sides of the Wasatch Mountains, which towered on the east of Salt Lake City. All was quiet at the depot now that the sun had set. Aubrey hugged herself as a comfortable wind blew off the hills.

Pa had gone straight to the authorities, of course, and now he and the police chief were due to meet the train. Aubrey had tried to wait at the hotel with Lizzy, but Melanie was her baby. Felicity was safe, and Aubrey simply could not remain behind when she learned that the men were going to meet the last train that night.

A noise in the street brought her attention around. A horse and carriage came to a stop near the ticket office. A finely dressed man stepped from the vehicle, accompanied by two men on horseback. They dismounted and waited beside the white-haired man. He spoke to the driver, glancing at the depot so the tangerine light shone on his face.

Aubrey's breath caught, though she should not be surprised. After all, Beau had said Madame was going to Salt Lake to meet her husband. And here he was.

"Aubrey?" Someone hissed near her ear, nearly startling her out of her skin.

She turned to find her younger brother's frowning face near hers. "You left the hotel. By yourself."

Shushing him, she forced him back around the corner. "Monsieur Willot is here."

He moved to shield her and peeked around the corner. A steam whistle sounded far away.

The door to the ticket office opened, and out stepped a man, yawning. "Last train for the night, people."

Three men in work clothes had been sitting on the ground near the office. They stood up, looking about with groggy eyes.

They did not resemble men Madame or Monsieur Willot would hire, so hopefully, it was just the two men with Monsieur Willot they would have to face.

Where was Pa?

"It is Old Man Willot." Jesse spoke low as he pushed her back. "I don't think he should see you. If he and Madame have been in contact—"

"He is here to meet the train. She must be on it. Melanie will be here too."

"Shh."

The whistle blasted closer.

Aubrey clasped her hands into fists. "What is he doing?"

"Looking in the ladies' waiting room. I wonder if he is looking for the nurse who had Felicity."

The pounding of the metal wheels sounded in the distance. Then another blast of the whistle, high and sharp in the dark night. The train came into view, a locomotive with light in front and long line of cars behind.

Several pairs of shoes knocked on the boardwalk, coming closer. Jesse's grip on her arm tensed. Aubrey focused on the tracks again, not wanting to cause a scene before Madame alighted on the platform.

"Mr. Alexander?" A man spoke with a French accent beside Jesse.

Monsieur Willot stood right there in front of them, flanked by two guards. His blue eyes, so much like Louis's, were as cold as ever. She'd not even seen him draw near. Aubrey's pulse beat hard, muffled with the pounding of the train on the tracks. Unable to move, she stared, and so did he.

Jesse answered in French, his words measured—civil yet stern. She didn't catch the exchange of greeting between them because the train rolled by, the gust of air hitting her face. Metal screeched and gears ground. A hiss filled her ears, then white steam shot onto the platform, surrounding them like a dense fog. A conductor stood at the back of the passenger car, barely visible until the steam thinned.

Monsieur Willot glanced at the train and then at Aubrey. "Daughter-in-law, I heard you have borne a child."

Jesse stiffened but did not speak, so Aubrey did. "I have two daughters." She wasn't letting go of either of them.

He raised his eyebrows. "Twins. God has blessed you."

There was calculation behind his eyes, though she could not figure his intentions. The conductor was calling for passengers to watch the step on the platform. Had Beau brought Monsieur Willot the will as Nathan believed he would? How could she ask him without giving away too much? Already she had lied about Felicity and Melanie, though it felt a truth to claim both as her daughters. If she ever made it home, they would be. And Nathan would be their father.

The passenger car windows reflected the light in such a way she could not see inside. Was Madame and Melanie there? Still, Monsieur Willot waited.

"Your wife has been to visit me." Aubrey focused on her father-in-law, who nodded. "I am afraid she did not leave on good terms."

"I heard as much."

"My intention in coming to Salt Lake is to mend the rift I unwittingly made. I hope to be at peace with my in-laws, as much as is possible."

Monsieur Willot glanced beyond her, his blond-white eyebrows arching. She sensed Pa approach at her back, from a glimpse in her peripheral and the thudding of men's boots on the platform. Monsieur Willot had always been cold around Pa. A stiffening of his sharp features deepened his wrinkles. His guards puffed out their chests, their hands too close to the firearms on their belts.

Aubrey turned as a man with a humble face and bushy beard stepped from beside Pa. She recognized him from the last time she was in Salt Lake City. He was the policeman who had helped Pa rescue her and Jesse from Emil.

"Gentlemen, I am Chief Burt of the Salt Lake City Police. If you have anything to do with the kidnapping of this woman's child, I suggest that you surrender your weapons now."

Monsieur Willot narrowed his gaze. "I am Monsieur Willot, visiting from France. I am merely here to meet my wife." He glanced to the locomotive. "Aha, and here she is now. Delphine, my dear."

Madame stood with her eyes wide, her body poised as though she had stopped walking midstride. Behind her was a woman holding a baby, and at her side, the mean-squinting Mr. Camus.

"Melanie?" Aubrey strode forward, but Madame stepped into her way. Aubrey shoved her aside and reached for Melanie. The nurse holding her darted behind Mr. Camus.

Aubrey followed. "Give her back to me!"

Madame grabbed her arm. "Stop, Aubrey. She is not yours."

"Melanie!" She pulled away and nearly fell when Madame let her go.

The guards now shielded the woman with Melanie.

Jesse reached for Aubrey. "Wait. Be smart and just let the law—"

"Let me go." She wriggled from her brother, then turned to Madame. "You wicked, wicked woman. I welcomed you into my house even though you have never said a kind word to me, and you steal my child."

Madame widened her eyes, her mouth partly open, and she shook her head. "I have done nothing but love you like a mother. As for Felicity, I did my duty as her grandmother."

"Now, you ladies need to settle down." Chief Burt stepped forward, taking a piece of paper from his uniform pocket. "I have a telegram here stating that a child, Melanie Willot, was taken from her home in San Francisco."

"Yes, that is my baby, Melanie." Aubrey could barely respond for her impatience.

"Chief Burt, I have a court order here stating that I am the guardian of Felicity Willot." Madame pointed to Melanie. "This child is my granddaughter, Felicity Willot, and I am taking her to Germany with me."

Panic wrenched Aubrey's chest. "No! You liar! That is Melanie."

Pa stepped forward. "Chief Burt, this woman stole my granddaughter, that baby right there, from her home in San Francisco. I have been deputized to take her back to California."

Monsieur Willot tensed, and Madame gasped, rushing to her husband. He wrapped an arm around her, holding tight.

The chief frowned, looking between the warrant and Madame's court order for Felicity. "Well, this is a strange turn of events. What am I supposed to do, threaten to cut the child in half as King Solomon did?"

"A wiser man would find another way." Monsieur Willot dragged his gaze away from Melanie. "I need a moment with my daughter-in-law."

"No." Pa glared at Louis's father. "Your family is a pack of lying thieves. First, your son kidnapped my two children, and now your wife does the same to my granddaughter. There will be no talking. That woman is going to prison where you all belong."

Madame gasped, then a blush crawled up her face. "How dare you? Stupid American pig." She broke into French after that, her words flying like bullets.

Still, Aubrey's father-in-law focused on her. How could he expect her to give him even a minute of her time? First, his foolish son ruined her life, then she was kidnapped by another of his sons, and now his wife stole her babe.

A mewing cry sounded from Melanie, and Aubrey's heart

quaked. She had to reach her baby. This was no time for pride. "I will speak to Monsieur Willot."

"No." Pa turned to her, his dark eyebrows pursed, yet the hard lines of his face creased in hurt. "Aubrey, honey, these people are dangerous. You said you didn't want to be fooled again. All they do is lie and cheat. You can't trust them."

"I know, Papa." More now than ever, she understood how the Willot family used cunning and words to get what they wanted. But if Beau had beat them to Salt Lake on horseback, Monsieur Willot had the will. If he wanted his wife to leave without legal ramifications for kidnapping, he needed Aubrey on his side.

She stepped away with Mr. Willot. The rest of the party waited by the ticket window, Camus and the other guards looking ready for battle. Pa and Jesse didn't look much calmer. The lawmen, too, were agitated, though Bart had his hands on his hips and was instructing Madame's men to step back and not do anything stupid.

Pa stared at Aubrey as though he feared Monsieur Willot might throw her over his shoulder and carry her away. If she chose her words wisely, she might spare them all the danger of losing completely.

They ventured a few yards away, heels knocking on the wooden platform, before Aubrey opened the conversation. "I want to find a peaceful way to solve the problem."

"I knew you would."

"I believe I have already done my part, Monsieur." She stopped and faced him, hands clutched before her. "You did receive a package from Mr. Fox, did you not?"

"Mr. Fox?" He snickered, shaking his head. "You mean Monsieur Vulpe?"

She frowned.

"Do not fret. It is the true name of your courier—a half-breed Gypsy from France. You are unwise to trust that one."

Unwilling to be distracted, Aubrey waved away the topic. "Do you truly intend to take a girl child back to Germany to raise?"

"It matters not. I will not permit my wife to be arrested, detained in your American prison."

So it was Madame for whom he came. The woman had gone too far taking Melanie, and her husband knew it. But to let her get away would be unjust. "I would always be worried that someday she would come back to take them. It is my duty to protect my daughters. Would you wish that on me, Monsieur Willot? To live in fear that at any moment my children could be stolen from me?"

"No." His face remained rigid, then he inclined his head. "You are wise. That is good. It takes a wise mother to raise good women."

"Does this mean you will convince Madame to leave the babies?"

"Yes. My wife and I will sail back to Germany now that we have what we need to survive the secession of Alsace and Lorraine." Monsieur Willot sighed, then looked back to his wife. Madame would listen to her husband. She always had, and he could keep her in Germany while their business recovered. There was no telling how much money Madame had spent on this trip.

He motioned for her to precede him back toward the crowd of people awaiting them. Pa and Jesse tensed when Aubrey went toward the guards. From her side, Monsieur Willot gestured for them to move, and when they did, Aubrey took her daughter from the pale-faced nurse. With Melanie's velvety head to her cheek, her heart quaked for how much she'd missed her baby. She fixed her gaze on her mother-in-law. "Why did you come to America?"

"We have suffered since the war. I came to take Louis back to Germany. He owned large tracks of land, including one of my father's iron foundries. We needed him home—only, by the time I arrived, he was dead." A tear spilled down her cheek, catching on a wrinkle by her nose. "I only stayed because without proof of ownership, we would lose the land in Germany. Emil said the will was in the safe and that you were the key." Madame huffed and leaned slightly into her husband.

"The will was not in the safe. Louis hid it in my things, knowing I would find it and give it back to you." She glanced at Monsieur Willot, who unlike his wife, did not look surprised. "Emil tried to get me to open the safe when he kidnapped me. I refused. He was right that I knew the combination, but nothing in the safe was of any use to you. I didn't find the will until after you stole my daughter. I never wanted anything that did not belong to me."

Madame turned a hostile, tear-laden gaze on her. "Louis was my son. He should have returned to France after completing his studies in America. That was the plan. Instead, he stayed with you, and now he is dead."

Her husband held her close. Pa and Jesse closed in behind Aubrey, supporting her the way they always did. Shaking her head, she turned away from Madame Willot, unwilling to banter with the miserable woman. God would meet her needs if she let Him, but Aubrey could not fix them. She could only look ahead. To her future with Melanie, and hopefully, Nathan and Felicity as well.

CHAPTER 28

*H*e had not intended to stay so long in her house, yet here he was, pulling himself from slumber as the sun slipped through a western-facing window. Nathan rolled over, pausing when the pain in his chest closed like a tight fist around him. Cook had insisted he stay at the chateau over the past four days. She'd kept him on a hearty diet of meat and vegetables, checked his bandages, and ensured he took medicine so he could sleep. Pa and Ma came to visit as well, but mostly, they stayed in the city where they had found work.

He closed his eyes, slumber tugging him out on a sea of rest until the memory of Aubrey's telegram resurfaced. They had the girls and were coming home. When the crunch of horses' hooves and rattle of carriage wheels rang from the driveway, he opened his eyes again.

Nathan sat up, grimacing at the pain, then working on his pants. He'd managed to slide one arm into his shirt when voices below the window struck him motionless. Cook's exclamation of joy. Unable to breathe, he rushed for the door, half dressed.

When he stopped at the landing, Aubrey, her pa and

brother, and a number of the staff clustered around the bottom of the stairs. Where the stairs spilled onto the floor below, Aubrey turned her lovely face to meet him. She held Felicity, who gnawed on her hand and made a sucking noise. There she was. Felicity. Aubrey had brought her back just as she said she would. He clutched the banister, his head suddenly very heavy.

When he sank to the top step, Aubrey darted up the stairs and met him. "Nathan. You should not be out of bed."

He wrapped his good arm around her, pulling her close. Felicity caught between them, she turned her soft cheek against his. She let out a squall of complaint, likely because he was due for a shave. Trembling overtook his body. He could not hold up his head, and no matter how hard he squeezed his eyelids, hot tears flowed from beneath them. Felicity was back. His baby, safe and sound in the arms of the best mama on the earth. God had brought them to him, even though he didn't really deserve them.

"We made it." Aubrey sniffed, touching his cheek, and when he dared to meet her gaze, she, too, cried. "I still can't believe it. Madame sent one of the nurses ahead with Felicity while she stayed behind at one of the stops. We reclaimed Felicity in Nevada but went all the way to Salt Lake City without knowing where Melanie was."

Pa brought Melanie up the stairs, handing her over to Aubrey, who held one girl in each arm. "Good to see you on the mend, Mr. Reed."

"Yes, sir." He didn't bother moving his hand from Aubrey's back to wipe the dampness from his cheeks.

"We can talk once you are recovered."

Nathan nodded again, and then Aubrey's family and staff faded away. He leaned his back against the top banister with Aubrey on the step just below him, listening to her recount all that had happened.

"In the end, Monsieur Willot wanted to return home with

Madame. She should have gone to jail, Jesse says, but honestly, Germany is farther away. I am just happy to have the girls safely home." She kissed each of their cheeks, though the younger of the two slept on.

"Beau came through as you said he would. He met with Monsieur before we did. If you hadn't sent Beau ahead to Salt Lake City, I don't know what my father-in-law would have done."

"God has worked in Beau's heart, for sure."

Aubrey held her breath for a moment. "I am afraid I have some bad news where he is concerned."

He smoothed down one of Felicity's curls, then paused. "Is he alive?"

"Yes, but he was beaten badly, then turned over to the law. Apparently, he was wanted in Utah for a bank robbery."

Which Beau likely knew when he agreed to go to Salt Lake on Nathan's behalf. Lord willing, he would recover and be blessed for being a good friend to Nathan. Hopefully, he would see Beau again someday. Make it up to him. For now, he'd hold tight to Aubrey and the girls, for as long as the Lord provided.

"Nathan." Aubrey leaned a little closer, kissing his lips for a second. "I told myself that if we made it back, I would tell you the truth. There is no better man for me. You're..." She shook her head, smiling and leaning closer. "You're exactly who I need and want. The kind of man I always hoped to meet. I think we could make a family, the four of us. If you're willing to try."

"I want nothing else but you and the girls. I never hoped or even dreamed I'd know or love a woman like you." He spoke against her lips, forgetting to draw breath. There was just Aubrey, kissing him ever so sweetly.

EPILOGUE

Five years later
Yosemite, California

In the darkroom with the glowing red lights illuminating the developing equipment, Aubrey gently blew on the sepia stereoview of a young couple in a canoe, paddling the river with the sun setting behind them over the granite monolith El Capitan. The thrumming in her chest intensified when the next photograph came to life—a young soldier saluting the sky as he stood in a precarious position on Glacier Point. Another astounding shot. Nathan and his father made an excellent team guiding tourists on hikes and taking photographs.

Aubrey occasionally accompanied them, but mostly, her days were spent at the Yosemite Falls Hotel with the children, taking family pictures and learning horticulture from John Muir—when the mysterious Scotsman was to be found.

A cry sounded from the next room just as she reached for a much-anticipated photograph. Pompompasos, also called the Three Brothers at Yosemite set against a still sky, the lake like a mirror before it, and there on the bank, three children in a line —just like the Three Brothers. Fair Felicity with her hands on Melanie's shoulders, and Melanie holding a fat little tot in a cap and overalls. It was Mr. Watkins's shot of that same sight that she and Nathan had seen in the bank years ago. Nathan would be so pleased. She could send the photograph to Mother Reed, who was minding the studio in San Francisco, and request she have a frame made. That way, it would be ready in time for the celebration marking both their fifth year of marriage and Nathan's employment with the San Francisco Police Department.

Aubrey gently moved the metal plate from the developing bath and set it aside to dry. She dashed into the adjacent, brightly lit hotel room to wash her hands, her son's cries hurrying her movement. The crying turned to screaming behind her.

"I hear you." She spoke over her shoulder. "Give your maman some patience, darling boy."

Hurriedly drying her hands, she went to the cradle near a window with the curtains fluttering in a cool breeze. She lifted her son from the mattress and hugged his round middle, rocking and shushing him. No dampness in his diaper, and he had just eaten. Perhaps his dreams had woken him. He frightened easily. She sighed, offering up prayers of blessing for him as she strode to the door.

Nathan and the girls would be coming back from their evening walk soon. Jack always calmed in his papa's arms.

Humming softly, Aubrey left the room and made her way to the main stairs. She passed other patrons on her way, greeting them with a smile and keeping the soft hum of a lullaby on her lips for Jack's sake.

Outside, the whitewashed porch stretched the length of the two-story Yosemite Falls Hotel. Guests relaxed in shaded chairs, between white columns, and on the steps. She adjusted Jack on her hip, stepping down into the soft grass. The scent of oak and heather sailed on a breeze.

Behind the whitewashed lodge, massive rock formations rose, their silhouettes dark against the tangerine sky. Water fell from the heights, glowing like liquid fire in the sunlight disappearing behind the trees to flow into the valley below. There, jogging across the yard, were Nathan and their two six-year-old girls. Aubrey let a gentle smile settle upon her lips and waved to them.

"Maman!" Felicity cried and raced to her, her freckled face smeared with red strawberries.

"Have you been in the garden again?" She hugged her with one arm.

"Papa took us there." She pointed in the direction of her father and sister, the latter of which held her pinafore out like a basket. The thing was so heavily laden, it tugged at her petite shoulders. Melanie only had one smudge of red on her cheek when she opened her apron to show Aubrey her treasures.

"We picked enough for breakfast too. But this one is for you." She lifted one hand, and still pinching one side of her pinafore, managed to offer a strawberry.

"Thank you, sweetie." Aubrey bent to kiss her head.

Jack used the opportunity to grasp for Nathan, who took him into his arms. He kissed his cheek, then lifted him into the air, turning around. The little boy burst out in laughter.

Felicity joined in, too, turning in a circle before grasping Aubrey's hands. "Spin with me, Maman."

Aubrey checked on Melanie, who moved to the porch, where she organized her bounty in a basket according to size. Always the planner in contrast with her adventurous sister. Aubrey spun with Felicity. The sky above like a spinning top, she breathed in the freshest of air and felt the grassy earth beneath her leather-soled shoes.

At last, she begged Felicity to stop, and they fell into a heap on the ground. Nathan settled near them, gripping her hand. Aubrey closed her eyes, still laughing and panting, wholly captured by the sensation that the world turned beneath her. At last, it slowed and she dared to look up. The sky above held still. She turned to find Nathan's face near hers. He smiled, his end-of-day stubble holding the slightest gleam of gold from his time in the summer sun.

She caressed his cheek. "I had forgotten how handsome you are."

He opened his arm, and Aubrey scooted into the crook. Jack kicked his feet as he lay on Nathan's chest while Felicity rested her head on Aubrey's arm.

"Mel?" Nathan lifted his head. "Come look at the clouds with us."

"Coming, Papa." Melanie picked her way down the steps, having finished organizing her strawberries, and laid down on Nathan's other side.

They stayed there, picking out the shapes of the clouds, until the first stars of night sparkled in the sky. Jack crawled over to Aubrey, then onto the grass. He headed for the hotel, his sisters chasing after him, their little black boots kicking up beneath the ruffled hems of their skirts.

Nathan rolled onto his side to see Aubrey better, holding her closer. "You are so beautiful." He spoke with the same awe from years ago.

Containing a giggle, she shrugged. "I know. It's easy—being beautiful."

He chuckled and held her gaze even when Jack's squeals filled the night air. Nathan's smile turned mischievous, and he lowered his head.

The subtle kiss warmed her through, her body responding, wife to husband, when Nathan parted her lips. One of the children's laughs broke the spell.

"For shame, Mr. Reed." She smacked his shoulder. "Out in public for everyone to see."

He blinked, then glanced around. "Oh, yeah." He chuckled and stood, pulling her up with him. "Not to worry, my love. We can finish in private where no one can see." Nuzzling her ear, he whispered, "Only me."

"If you insist." She feigned resigned duty, earning another of his laughs.

The children waited by the door, the girls fussing over who would carry Jack. Melanie settled for her basket of berries. As the door closed on the evening at the Yosemite Falls, Aubrey could not contain her smile. The good Lord had truly given her a lovely life.

THE END

~

*T*urn the page for a sneak peek of The Convict's Courtship, the next book in the Outlaw Hearts series!

Don't miss the next book in the Outlaw Hearts series!

The Convict's Courtship

Virginia City, Nevada
November 25, 1875

She had really gotten herself into trouble this time.

Clara Alexander knelt on the mine shaft floor, her head in her hands, the heat engulfing her. Throat raw from shouting, she drew in a ragged breath. The geothermal springs heated the earth until the mines felt like a midsummer day—even with snow piled waist-high outside on Mount Davidson.

This was not how she'd envisioned her first, unofficial job for the *Territorial Enterprise*. Ironically, she'd entered the mine full of determination—wearing men's clothes, her hair tucked up in a cap. Yet now, with the ore sample tucked safely in her pocket and each echo ricocheting down the tunnel, she wished to be anywhere but the Peterson Mine.

Clara pushed herself off the floor to wander on, the rough dirt sides of the tunnel hot to the touch. "Is it something I've done, Lord? I mean, I know I'm not Your favorite child, and that's fine. You have other children to dote on, and I will try to avoid trouble."

Something whispered against her leg. Clara froze, then slowly lowered to her haunches, searching the dirt beneath her. She startled as the smooth end of a tail swept across her fingers. Oh, thank heavens, it was only a rat. Soft and warm and real. Some men claimed mystic creatures called Tommy Knockers haunted the mines, alternately bringing good luck or calamity with them.

A rumble sounded from the earthen bowels.

Clara held her breath as she felt the iron tracks running along the earthen floor. One way led to a shaft and up to freedom, the other farther into darkness and heat.

The growling grew louder, like thunder still far away but drawing nearer. What if it was an earthquake or rockslide? She'd heard of miners getting trapped by rockslides. She pushed herself up and swayed to one side, her head spinning. Then she rushed forward, using the wall as a guide. A sliver of wood scraped her fingertip when she dragged it across one of the beams supporting the ceiling.

Louder, faster it came, chasing her into the deep until the backs of her eyelids seemed to glow. She stopped and thrust out a hand in front of her. "Is someone there?"

The rumbles ceased.

A scent lingered on the air, dust and something else. Not

smoke, but if there was light, there must be fire, right? She eased one eye open, but there was nothing save her own long shadow stretching in front of her. Turning, she squinted into brightness that shone past an ore car. A tall, muscular man holding a lantern stepped from behind it, the candle flame glowing upon his shirtless frame.

He was as sturdy as any miner she'd ever seen—and half naked. Likely cooler than her in her overalls and a layer of ladies' underthings. He wore a red bandana around his head, and as he ducked to peer at her, it nearly grazed the transverse beam. Some said the mines were haunted, but she didn't believe in ghosts. Did she?

"You're not a Tommy Knocker." She cocked her head. "Are you?"

"*Mademoiselle*, are you hurt?" His thick French accent curled around every word.

Mademoiselle? So he knew she was a woman. So much for her disguise. No matter. She was rescued. Knees trembling, Clara bolstered herself against the side of the tunnel and laughed. "You are real. Oh, God has not grown tired of me yet." Tears stung her eyes, and she covered her face for a moment, only to sway.

He gripped her arms with large hands, steadying her. His nearness carried a faint, earthy aroma—like clay freshly turned.

Clara tipped her chin up, panting from the heat. "Can you guide me to the shaft?"

He touched her forehead, frowning, and said something in French before switching to English. "You need water. Come." He tugged her around the ore car and down the tunnel.

Clara's view of their progression from that point was spotty, coming in flashes when she looked up from navigating the dark, dirty way. When they came upon the activity in the mine, men shouted and the cars rumbled on iron tracks. Her guide warned another miner of the car he'd left in the tunnel. Would they crash?

Clara swayed, barely holding onto consciousness. The heat was so great and her limbs so very heavy, it was all she could do to remain upright.

They were moving again, at a quick pace. He held her hand, his opposite one lifting the lantern ahead of them. She followed in his shadow, the light glowing past black curls at his neck as they wove past half-dressed miners with pickaxes and crowbars, all tapping away with methodical rhythm.

Clara held tight to her guide. He led her into a room where men gathered around a large barrel of ice water. Light reflected off its foggy, grimy surface, yet the water called to her. Wishing she could climb into the barrel, she accepted the cup handed to her and drank long gulps. It tasted awful, yet she dipped the cup in a second time.

All around her, the bare-chested, bright-eyed miners stared at her. "My goodness. I am surrounded by troglodytes."

More than a few of them scrunched their eyebrows, and several chuckles murmured from the crowd. One miner spoke, his blond mustache curled on either side of his nose. "Bringing your lady friend to work, Vulpe?"

Her rescuer—Mr. Vulpe—tensed and pulled her a little nearer. "I found the lady in one of the tunnels."

The blond man smiled, revealing block-like teeth. "My name is Mr. Dodge Peterson." He offered his hand.

Clara let the water cup fall. It clanked against the side of the barrel, hanging by a chain. It seemed her identity as a female was known, but after being lost, it mattered little. "My name is—"

"*Non.*" Mr. Vulpe shushed her, his dark eyes catching fire-light. "Do not speak."

Mr. Dodge laughed and tipped his hat to her. "I would be

honored to meet such a fine lady." He slid his gaze down her as though assessing the value of a piece of ore.

Clara's cotton chemise showed between the undone front of her shirt. She gasped and covered herself, only to have Mr. Vulpe urge her behind him with one hand as she hurried to work her buttons. No wonder the men recognized her as female. She'd also lost the miner's cap she'd donned upon descending into the mine.

"The woman must be returned to town." Mr. Vulpe spoke sternly.

Cheeks hotter by the moment, for the men in the underground room peered at her as though she'd stepped from a sporting house, Clara gripped Mr. Vulpe's arm, ready to tell him to take her to the surface.

As though knowing her intention, he turned. "Come, let us go."

"You leaving your shift before the bell rings, Vulpe?" Dodge Peterson again. Unlike the shirtless workers, this man wore long pants and a buttoned shirt. Though shorter than other men, he carried himself and spoke with the confidence of a leader. He must be the foreman of the shift. Sure enough, he stepped forward, his hands on his hips. "Get back to work. I'll see the lady out."

Mr. Vulpe stayed like a sentinel between them. Stone still, he stared at his challenger, his eyes dark as iron and square jaw firm as granite.

Mr. Dodge fumed, his shoulder heaving. "Snooty Frenchman. You're fired! I never wanted you here, anyway, and when my father hears what you've done, you'll be lucky to find a job in all of Nevada."

Rather than respond, Mr. Vulpe turned and led her away. Though he guided her with alarming possessiveness, the glare he leveled on the men they passed chased away her unease. Clara sensed safety with him. Not just because of his good size.

While the gazes of other miners roved over her like exploring hands, Mr. Vulpe's never dropped below her neck.

"Here is the way up." He stopped before the wooden frame of a shaft to hang a lantern and ring a bell. A metal cable led up into a black hole, correlating with the resounding crank of grinding gears. Mr. Vulpe let go of her and started toward a room off to one side. "How did you get down here?"

She bit her bottom lip. How could she answer without sounding ridiculous? A female reporter would be hard enough for him to accept, and she was dressed in miner's attire.

"No answer? Perhaps you have a beau who works here. He thought it would be a good idea to show you the mine?"

"No." She raised her chin. "I came down alone."

"Unlikely. Why come down at all?"

"That does not concern you."

"It does, actually, since I am responsible for you now and just lost my job protecting you." Mr. Vulpe grabbed a bundle of clothes, including a hat that he promptly placed on his head. "What is your name?"

Oh, no. She would not tell him that and have her family shamed. "I don't think, under the circumstances, that I should answer that, but I am very sorry you lost your job. I just needed to find the lift. I can make my way to the surface from here."

"I will not leave your side until I know you are safe." He knelt, his thick shoulder muscles flexing when he rolled his pant legs down around chiseled calves. "The sooner you are home, the better."

Making little impression in the darkness, the dim light of the single lantern he'd hung on a wall clung to him when he narrowed his gaze on her.

"Have you considered, mademoiselle"—he strode toward her, so large and foreboding that she had to take a step back—"that running around among men of this breed will end in your ruin?"

Unable to hold his imposing gaze, she put a couple feet between them. "When I descended the shaft, no one knew I was female."

"Doubtful. The lifts are crowded when the shifts come down." He glanced up as the lift, a large wooden platform supported by a metal cage, trundled into view.

She crossed her arms. "I was careful."

He smirked. "*Ma foi*, I doubt that."

So he thought she was a liar. "As you said, the lift was crowded. No one could see my face, and I tucked up my hair and wore a hat. No one knew I was a woman. As I prefer it."

"As you prefer?" The slightest quirk of his mouth turned his hard features nearly boyish. "A lie, I would wager, since you have been watching me as though you enjoyed the time we spent together." He slipped into a blue denim shirt, winking when he closed the front over his broad chest.

So he'd seen her interest in him. More curiosity than admiration—as she'd never seen a man shirtless before. Blushing, she turned her attention to the shaft. "A wager you'd lose."

He chuckled, low and husky, chasing a chill up her spine, and though she wished to further deny his confident claim, she kept her lips sealed. Father always said she was a terrible liar, so why further embarrass herself?

Soon they were riding up the shaft in the cage, the pulley above working to raise them. The only light came from different levels they flew past since the speed at which hey ascended would snuff out any flame. Mr. Vulpe crossed his arms with a coat thrown over one and a leg cocked out while Clara clung to the side of the cage.

She fingered the ore sample into her pocket. No one had searched her as they typically did the miners, in case one tried to steal precious metals from the mine. She just had to make it home and begin her article. Hopefully, Theo had not yet alerted her father or the authorities. If he had, search parties would be formed, pulling men from their work to search for a woman lost in the mines. Then her article would be met with outrage and no editor would ever hire her.

Beau led the lady out of the lift, which came up into the shambled building that passed for the Peterson Mine entrance just outside the small town of Gold Hill. This was a new mine, lacking the advanced equipment of wealthier setups. As Beau and the lady stepped from the cage into the dimly lit shelter, the lift operator, Mr. Perkins, eyed her and raised his eyebrows. "Your shift over, Vulpe?"

"*Oui*. We're heading to town." Beau tried not to shiver when a freezing wind whistled through the cracks in the walls.

"Best hurry, then." He glanced down as though not noticing the lady in pants. "There's a north wind blowing in." The operator nodded toward the door, which hung on rickety hinges. "Come over here so I can pat you down."

Beau, used to ore checks, raised his arms as Perkins quickly patted his pockets. "What time is it?"

The search was quick. Perkins patted his pockets, then stepped back. "A quarter to eight."

He'd lost his job within the first hour of his shift. Approaching Mr. Peterson was an option, but Dodge's petty nature made that risky.

Beau sighed, and the lady, who had been peering around the shack as though expecting to see something significant, turned at the sound. She was well-spoken and polite, moving with a gentility not even men's britches could disguise. If he was the gambling type, he'd wager that she lived on Millionaire Row in Virginia City.

When she met his gaze with eyes the deep blue of twilight, his breath thinned as it had the first moment he'd seen her.

Perhaps she was a phantom. He would find out once they neared the shops with brightly lit windows.

"It is getting late. We must be going. Here, take this." Beau offered the lady his fleece-lined jacket yet kept his knitted scarf. It would at least help to keep his neck warm.

She shook her head, blond curls fluttering around her face. "I will not take your protection from the cold."

Truly? A wealthy woman who did not believe she possessed special privileges. "My mass exceeds yours. The cold will bother me less. Besides, you have your modesty to consider."

She glanced down at her pants and snatched the coat from him, murmuring her thanks. As she slipped into the garment, the collar of her oversized shirt shifted, revealing a birthmark at the base of her neck. His breath caught, memories surfacing of a woman with the blackest hair and olive-toned skin. When he'd touched a curl at her neck, she had turned, laughing, and smacked away his hand. Behind her, the French countryside lay green and peaceful while dappled light from leafy trees above warmed her face.

His heart colder than the breeze sneaking inside, he cleared away the memory, holding tight to what was real—the stench of sulfur drifting from the water pumped up from the mine, his aching shoulders and back, his cold toes in his boots, and that hole in the right sock. He wasn't in France anymore. This was America. He wasn't a husband anymore. He was a widower.

"But what will protect you from the cold?" She peeked up from the collar of his coat, the rest of her face hidden in the deep folds, reminding him of her youth.

"Here, Vulpe, use mine," Mr. Perkins said, reaching for a spare hanging on the hook where many miners' jackets swayed.

"Merci." He accepted it. After all, it would be a two-mile trek to Virginia City—assuming she was indeed from the wealthier town.

When he pushed the rickety door open, the warm lights

from the lanterns spilled out onto the snow, aided by the lights from the nearby settlement of Gold Hill, which shone through the trees up ahead. Darkness had fallen hours ago. How long had she been in the mine? He had to get her home before every man in the area was out searching for her.

Beau offered his arm. The lady peered at the steep hills rising around them, then at him. After a moment of hesitation, she accepted.

"Do you live in Gold Hill or Virginia City?" Beau angled his head toward town.

"Virginia City." She studied the ground where wagon tracks pressed into the snow.

He hadn't bothered to look at the fresh tracks at the beginning of his shift, but he'd bet the second, narrower set was from a buggy, not the large wagon that brought groups of men to work. Was the woman looking for the rig she'd come in?

He led her away from the entrance to the mine. "Did the person who brought you tell you when he was coming back for you?"

She raised her eyebrows. "I will not respond again since you believe nothing of what I've said thus far."

"Fine." Probably better just to get to town.

The mines of the Comstock Lode were scattered across peaks of the Virginia Range, yet the primarily mass was on the eastern slope of Mount Davidson, within Virginia City limits. These mountains were his hideout. His sole focus was to work hard and save money. Keep his head low and stay out of trouble. Challenging his foreman and claiming responsibility for the woman in the mine was not laying low.

They walked through Gold Hill—a town of about eight thousand inhabitants situated in a draw. Houses with picket fences stood near enormous heaps of waste dirt, piled so high they cloaked the rooftops. Church steeples pointed like needles into the sky, including the tiled spire of St. Patrick's Catholic Church.

The road to Virginia City wound up a steep hillside. Beau tried not to think about his predicament. He'd lost his job and now had to escort a woman home and speak with her family.

"Could you slow down?" The woman beside him panted, cheeks flushed scarlet, likely because he'd all but dragged her uphill from the mine.

Not very gentlemanly, but he wasn't used to being around women. "You all right?"

"Yes, but please allow me to catch my breath." She pressed a hand to her side, glancing out at the desolate hills dotted with sagebrush and old tree stumps—remnants of the logging years. Houses dotted the hillside, one with a lantern by the front door allowing enough light on her pert nose, clear eyes, and soft lips —no miner's face, that.

"We cannot wait. Your family will be looking for you. I should have alerted the sheriff in Gold Hill to your trouble."

A breath bloomed in front of her face. "I would rather you did not. My family would be shamed if it was widely known that I dressed in this manner."

"Then we must continue on." He offered his arm this time, and she took it more easily, as though trusting him.

At last, they began the ascent up the Divide, the neighborhood between Gold Hill and Virginia City. The lady who had refused to tell him her name clung to him more securely, her lips slightly parted as she panted. He fixed his eyes ahead— best not to stare like a fool.

Virginia City was more elegant than Gold Hill. Grander churches, businesses, and homes sprawled down the flank of Mount Davidson. Clouds hid the peak and promised more snow. Below, the burned heart of the city lay under fresh layers of white—eleven blocks of blackened rubble, while newly built structures lined the principal streets that cut through the wreckage.

The fire that had ripped through the town two months earlier had taken much, but the place was on the mend, fueled by hope and the money mined from the very earth it stood on.

The thoroughfare branched into C Street—the business district—and B Street, where Millionaire Row—or what was left of it—stood. The avenues were bright with light from houses, busy shops, and tall churches—though none so high as the mine headframes that rose above them.

The lady's teeth chattered. Nose rosy red and hair so fair, she reminded him of a snow fairy—something out of a tale.

Beau pulled off his knit scarf and shoved it toward her.

She raised both hands, palms out, and shook her head. "I could not possibly take more from you, Mr. Vulpe. You should not even be here. I wish you would return to your work. I can make it on my own."

Rather than respond, he wrapped the scarf around her neck, and she quickly took over the process. When she was done, she met his gaze with a smile so sweet and youthful he could hardly breathe. What was wrong with him? Here he was about to freeze to death, and he'd lost his job, yet all he could think about was the lovely, odd lady before him.

He cleared his throat and kept his voice low. "Might you reconsider telling me your name?"

Her brows dipped, and her lips pressed together, then sprang upward in a lopsided smile. "You don't recognize me? My father is rather famous. Allow me to introduce myself." She leaned in and dropped her voice to a stage whisper. "Miss Nellie Grant, runaway debutante and mine explorer."

He frowned.

She inclined her head. "At your service."

A flicker of amusement stirred. Beau grinned despite himself. He'd read about Nellie Grant—White House weddings, travels abroad. This woman looked nothing like the real Nellie Grant, but he'd rather pretend than argue.

"Miss Nellie Grant?" he asked. "I thought you were married and living in Southampton, England."

She blinked, eyes momentarily wide, then beamed. "Ah, you've been reading the newspapers, I see. I must confess—it was all a hoax. My marriage, a clever cover for my true mission —coming west to make my fortune."

"Well, Mademoiselle Nellie..." He lowered his voice, speaking softly as if sharing a secret. "I am afraid you shall have a *triste* surprise. It is winter, you see, and a terrible time to travel. Most passes are closed, *non*? You will be stranded here until spring."

She let out a sigh and touched the back of her hand to her forehead, all mock dramatics. "Alas, I believe you are correct, Mr. Vulpe," she said with a faint smile that settled there like snow that doesn't quite melt.

He resisted a shiver and rubbed his hands together. "I am surprised to find you without your entourage."

She straightened, eyes sparkling. "I ran away, seeking adventure in the Wild West."

"What a coincidence. I am in a similar situation."

"Hmm." She gave her chin a saucy angle. "And how has your adventure been thus far?"

How, indeed? All he did was work and try not to worry about the prison he'd left behind in Utah. But such an answer would kill the fictional conversation he'd developed with this strange woman. So he hunched his shoulders against the wind and met her eyes. "Very well. I made friends with the Tommy Knockers."

Her face lit like lantern flame. "What a tall tale. Besides, Tommy Knockers are Cornish, not French."

"Maybe the Cornish miners smuggled them in."

She actually laughed. "Is that so? I suppose it is plausible.

Tell me, must they battle the rats for the Cornish meat pies miners leave them for good luck?”

“No. The rats are their partners. Why, they sniff out the food and report back to the Tommy Knockers.”

“Ah, and here I thought the rats were friends with the miners. Don’t they warn them in the event of a cave-in?”

“Yes. When the Tommy Knockers are angry or hungry, they cause the ground to shake. The rats run for safety, and in doing so, warn the miners.”

Her rosy cheeks bunched with a smile, round and youthful —not like Amalie’s high cheekbones, so tanned and warm. Why was he thinking of Amalie? He’d avoided thoughts of her for years, and mostly succeeded. Why did the memory of her waver near just now when he was with a lady who looked and conducted herself so differently?

She looked up the dim snowy street with lights on both sides. “I suppose we should be going.”

He agreed and they started off again. Snow crunched beneath their feet. Were they heading toward the mansions still standing after the fire, or had the lady lost her home and been forced to dress as a man to find work?

“Miss Grant” slipped on the icy street and gripped his arm for an instant, warming him through. She quickly let go. After all, men did not walk arm in arm, and she still needed to conceal her identity. He let her take the lead, and sure enough, she headed for Millionaire Row.

“My name is Clara.” The lady gave him an apologetic glance as they passed the first charred remains of a mansion.

“Clara Grant, I suppose?”

She giggled yet ducked into the shelter of his scarf when a painfully cold wind swept down the street. “Of course.”

“Beau Vulpe.” He gave her the name he’d begun using after leaving the penitentiary—his legal name in France but not

America, and always one he'd been unworthy of. If only he had a better one to give.

She slipped again, and this time, he wove her arm through his and covered her hand as he would when walking with any proper lady. It was dark, so no one should see them. He avoided her gaze, but her touch—despite the fabrics between them—was like the familiar embrace of a friend.

The sooner he got her home, the better. This woman warmed in him feelings he'd not felt since before the war. Her beautiful figure, her quick wit... He best keep his distance. He wasn't staying in Virginia City, and if he had a choice, he'd leave the States altogether.

Did you enjoy this book? We hope so!
Would you take a quick minute to leave a review where you purchased the book?
It doesn't have to be long. Just a sentence or two telling what you liked about the story!

Love Christian Historical Romance?
Looking for your next favorite book?
Become a Wild Heart Books insider and receive a FREE ebook and get exclusive updates on new releases before anyone else.
Sign up for our newsletter now.
https://wildheartbooks.org/newsletter

ACKNOWLEDGMENTS

Firstly, and always, I thank God for guiding my life and gifting me with the call to write. For a woman who was practically illiterate at the age of fifteen, this is a testimony to His miracle-working greatness. You said to write stories for You, and I am doing my best. As long as You provide, I will continue. Secondly, thank you to my children and husband who have believed in me and supported me over the years. I do not deserve such confident cheerleaders. To my youngest child, Lilly, who two years before this book was printed sat down with me to look at historical photographs and came up with the idea of Aubrey. (Jesse in book one needed a sister who also loved photography. It was something he could give her to bring her back to herself. This was Lilly's idea. Way to go, Lil!)

Many writers from American Christian Fiction Writers have supported me and my work for years, thanks to Kelly Borjas, Christie Kern, Karissa Riffel Fisher, Stephanie Goddard, and Darcy Fornier for your priceless critiques. Karissa and Christie, you sacrificed time from you busy lives to read the entire book. Thank you! Darcy, brainstorming with you is helpful but also fun. Thank you!

To the team at Wild Heart Books, thank you for your dedication to excellence, especially my editor, Denise Weimer. Your kind guidance and exceptional editorial skills helped to get me through this one.

AUTHOR'S NOTE

Dear Reader,

I hope you enjoyed Nathan and Aubrey's love story. Their situation was a unique one I had many concerns about, but I do believe in the end, their happily ever after was perfect. Thank you for joining me!

Finally, I would be ever so grateful if you would post a review of *The Bounty Hunter's Surrender* at Amazon.

Praying for blessings and inspiration in your reading-life.

~ KyLee

HISTORICAL NOTES

Here are some fun historical tidbits for you history lovers.

The Bank of California was a real bank San Francisco, CA, in the 1800s. Mr. William (Billy) Ralston was considered one of San Francisco's wealthiest socialites and entrepreneurs. Some called him the Emperor of the West because he was the wealthiest and most powerful man in California. There was a run on the Bank of California on Thursday, August 26, 1875. Ralston resigned as the bank president due to embezzlement. The next day, he went to the Neptune Bath House and swam out into the ocean. Shortly after, he drowned. There was a lot of speculation regarding suicide, but the coroner said the cause of death was a stroke.

John Muir was a naturalist and today is known as the Father of the National Parks. He explored and mapped, and cataloged the wildlife of what is now Yosemite National Park. His appearance in the book came about because of another famous historical figure, photographer Carleton Watkins. Watkins and Muir's connection is tenuous at best. However, they were both in San Francisco in 1875, and Muir was known to study Watkins's photos of Yosemite, so I took creative license with that connection. Muir's descriptions of what it was like to be in the mountains of Yosemite were taken from his personal correspondence, in which he described the "blessed Sierra heathers, primulas, pines, and giant sequoias."

Another historical feature in this book is the prolific and tragic figure of Carleton E. Watkins. He was considered one of the greatest photographers of the American West. As Aubrey states in the book, Watkins's photographs of Yosemite helped influence Congress to establish Yosemite as a National Park in 1864. Sadly, as in the story, Watkins lost his studio in San Francisco in 1875 due to the Bank of California. In fact, his creditors took all his creative works, including negatives, which they developed and continued to sell. Attempts to reestablish his photography career ultimately failed with the destruction of his studio and its contents in the 1906 San Francisco earthquake and fire. Watkins died in a mental hospital in 1916 and was buried on the grounds. Despite his misfortune, Watkins's contributions to recording the history of the West before the onset of development remain significant.

If you've made it this far into the historical note, you're probably wondering about the San Francisco Foundling Asylum. Yes, it's real. The asylum was located on Mission Street near Fourth in San Francisco, to the right of St. Patrick's Church (circa 1875). The San Francisco Lying-in Hospital and Foundling Asylum was incorporated in 1868 as a childbirth center, home for unwed mothers, and a refuge for abandoned children. According to historical data, including testimony from nurses and Dr. W.F. Cheney, the mortality rate for infants hovered around sixty percent throughout its existence. Dr. Cheney reportedly bragged about this statistic, noting that other city orphanages had near-100% mortality rates. It wasn't until 1916, with the implementation of better medical oversight and modern health strategies, that significant changes occurred. By

1934, the mortality rate had decreased to 1.6%. However, as the need for foundling homes diminished, the asylum closed in 1948 due to lack of funding.

For new releases and special promotions, subscribe to KyLee Woodley's mailing list: https://KyLeeWoodley.com

ABOUT THE AUTHOR

KyLee Woodley is a cheery romantic who loves to write about bygone days and heartwarming romance with a pinch of adventure. She teaches preschool at a lab school in Texas, where she lives with her husband of nineteen years and their three children. On weekends, KyLee cohosts and produces the **Historical Bookworm Show**—a steadily growing author interview podcast for history lovers and readers of historical fiction.

Keep up to date with KyLee's news on book releases, signings, and other events at https://kyleewoodley.com

Murmur in the Mud Caves by Kathleen Denly

He came to cook for ranch hands, not three single women.

Gideon Swift, a visually impaired Civil War Veteran, responds to an ad for a ranch cook in the Southern California desert mountains. He wants nothing more than to forget his past and stay in the kitchen where he can do no harm. But when he arrives to find his employer murdered, the ranch turned to ashes, and three young women struggling to survive in the unforgiving Borrego Desert, he must decide whether his presence protects them or places them in greater danger.

Bridget "Biddie" Davidson finally receives word from her older sister who disappeared with their brother and pa eighteen years prior, but the news is not good. Determined to help her family, Biddie sets out for a remote desert ranch with her adopted father and best friend. Nothing she finds there is as she expected, including the man who came to cook for the shambles of a ranch.

When tragedy strikes, the danger threatens not only her plans to help her sister, but her own dreams for the future—with the man who's stolen her heart.

~

Tides of Healing by Sandra Merville Hart

A Southern belle fights to reclaim her home, but will her spying destroy the Union officer she never meant to love?

Savannah Adair has endured the unimaginable, hiding in a cave while her beloved Vicksburg was under siege. With the city now occupied by Union soldiers, Savannah cannot stand by and do nothing. So when one of the gaunt, half-starved Confederate prisoners asks her to spy for the South, she can't refuse the chance to take back her home.

First Lieutenant Travis Lawson takes pride in the Union army's hard-fought victory, but he quickly realizes that the challenges of rebuilding and reconciliation are just beginning . . . and not everyone is appreciative of changes he's making. Namely, the fiery and alluring Savannah Adair. Despite their differing loyalties and the societal divide between them, Travis cannot deny the growing feelings he has for her. When he is tasked with finding Southern spies in Vicksburg and he captures a female spy, Travis is forced to consider that the woman he's beginning to love may be the enemy.